VALOUR

THE CHRONICLES OF THE BLACK LION, BOOK THREE

RICHARD CULLEN

First published in Great Britain in 2025 by Boldwood Books Ltd.

Copyright © Richard Cullen, 2025

Cover Design by Colin Thomas

Cover Images: Colin Thomas

The moral right of Richard Cullen to be identified as the author of this work has been asserted in accordance with the Copyright, Designs and Patents Act 1988.

All rights reserved. No part of this book may be reproduced in any form or by any electronic or mechanical means, including information storage and retrieval systems, without written permission from the author, except for the use of brief quotations in a book review. This book is a work of fiction and, except in the case of historical fact, any resemblance to actual persons, living or dead, is purely coincidental.

Every effort has been made to obtain the necessary permissions with reference to copyright material, both illustrative and quoted. We apologise for any omissions in this respect and will be pleased to make the appropriate acknowledgements in any future edition.

A CIP catalogue record for this book is available from the British Library.

Paperback ISBN 978-1-83603-376-9

Large Print ISBN 978-1-83603-375-2

Hardback ISBN 978-1-83603-374-5

Ebook ISBN 978-1-83603-377-6

Kindle ISBN 978-1-83603-378-3

Audio CD ISBN 978-1-83603-369-1

MP3 CD ISBN 978-1-83603-370-7

Digital audio download ISBN 978-1-83603-373-8

This book is printed on certified sustainable paper. Boldwood Books is dedicated to putting sustainability at the heart of our business. For more information please visit https://www.boldwoodbooks.com/about-us/sustainability/

Boldwood Books Ltd, 23 Bowerdean Street, London, SW6 3TN

www.boldwoodbooks.com

PREFACE

In 1211, King András II of Hungary, seeking to secure his eastern borderlands, extended an invitation to the Order of Saint Mary, commonly known as the Teutonic Knights, to settle in the frontier region called the Burzenland. This strategic move aimed to establish a military presence along the vulnerable Carpathian Mountain passes, which had long served as invasion routes for the Kipchak Turks, known to medieval Europeans as Cumans.

Hermann von Salza, Grand Master of the Order of Saint Mary, recognising both the opportunity and challenge presented by this wilderness territory, acted swiftly upon receiving the royal charter. Within a short period, five stone fortresses had been positioned strategically along the mountain range. These imposing structures served as both defensive bastions and symbols of Christian authority extending into formerly contested lands. To solidify their presence and develop the region economically, the Order also initiated a settlement programme, inviting German colonists from their homeland to establish communities throughout the Burzenland.

By the early 1220s, the threat of Cuman attacks, which had

previously terrorised the region, diminished significantly under the vigilant watch of the Order. This military success extended beyond merely repelling raids and reached into Cuman society itself, with several clans abandoning their traditional nomadic lifestyle and ancestral religious practices to accept Christianity.

However, not all Cuman clans embraced these changes. By 1223, some clans remained steadfastly committed to their pagan beliefs and nomadic way of life, but as a result their position became more precarious. Not only were their traditional raiding routes into Hungary now blocked by Christian fortresses, but their ancestral territories in Cumania faced mounting pressure from a formidable new threat emerging from the east...

PROLOGUE
CUMANIA – 1223AD

The wind growled across the plain like a wounded beast, whipping sparks from the campfires. Shoruk watched those fires dance, each ember a dying light that heralded only ill fortune for the Clan of the White Wolf.

Yurts dotted the flattened grass, their felt walls straining against the gale that swept down from the distant Carpathians. The horses shifted restlessly in their pickets, huddled together against the chill, long manes flowing in the bitter wind. Once there would have been hundreds of mounts, enough to shake the earth with their thunder when the clan rode to war. Now barely fifty remained, their ribs showing beneath winter-thick coats.

Shoruk pulled his fur-lined cloak closer. The wind carried the familiar scent of horse, roast game and charred wood, but something was missing. The laughter and songs that had once filled their camps had grown quiet in recent years, replaced by the fear of what lay beyond every horizon.

To the north-west, beyond the distant peaks of the Carpathian Mountains, Christian armies had stolen their hunting grounds.

Year after year they pushed further east, building their stone fortresses, clearing forests for their farms, erecting their crosses of wood and iron. Those warriors brought their armoured horses and their accursed god, driving the clan ever eastward like wolves before a forest fire. Their white cloaks were stained with Cuman blood, their swords had drunk deep of so many warriors Shoruk had called brothers that his hatred for them knew no bounds.

He spat into the dirt. Ten years ago, they would have fought. Ten years ago, Chief Tarkhan would have led them in a glorious charge, arrows blackening the sky as they fell upon their enemies like a storm. Shoruk's grandfather had told of such victories – how the clan had made its enemies flee in terror, how they had burned their wooden dwellings and scattered their flocks. But their chief had grown old, cautious. Weak. Now they fled at the first sight of those steel-clad devils who guarded the way to the west.

Shoruk's gaze shifted across the fire to where Tarkhan was seated, his weathered face lined with shadows cast by those dancing flames, his hands trembling slightly as he warmed them. The chief's once-proud shoulders had begun to stoop, though he still carried himself with the dignity of his station. His coat was richly decorated with patterns of wolves and eagles, but the embroidery was faded, the fabric worn thin in places. Like the clan itself, it was nought but a shadow of former glory.

'Remember when we would share tales of victory on nights like this?' Shoruk asked, unable to keep his peace any longer. 'How we would boast of the warriors we had killed, the villages we had raided? Now we speak only of where to run next.'

Tarkhan's eyes remained fixed on the fire, their dark depths reflecting the dancing flames. 'Better to run and live than die needlessly, my bold friend. Stories of dead heroes warm no one.'

Valour 3

'Is that what we've become? Rabbits, darting from burrow to burrow?' Shoruk gestured at the scant yurts. 'Look at us. Once we were the terror of the plains. Now we can barely feed ourselves through winter.'

'We do what we must to survive.' Tarkhan's voice carried the weight of too many hard decisions, too many retreats, too many dead friends. 'But fear not. The world changes, whether we wish it or no. Even the great river must bend around the mountain. And perhaps I have found a way for us all to survive—'

A horse's whinny cut through the night, followed by shouts of greeting from the sentries posted at the camp's edge. Shoruk rose in one fluid motion, hand instinctively moving to his sword hilt as hoofbeats thundered closer, and the guards' torches illuminated the approach of a lone rider.

The horse was lathered with sweat despite the cold, sides heaving as the warrior reined to a halt. Both beast and man bore the marks of hard travel – the man's face was wind-burned and gaunt, his eyes wide and so haunted they made Shoruk's hand tighten on his weapon until he recognised it was Boril, a scout they had sent east for news.

Tarkhan stood, suddenly looking every bit the chieftain he had once been, despite his age. His back straightened, his chin lifted, and for a moment Shoruk saw the warrior who had led them through many hard years.

'Speak,' Tarkhan commanded, his voice carrying the authority of a chief.

Boril slid from his saddle, his legs nearly buckling as he dropped to one knee. His horse stood trembling, steam rising from its flanks. More of the clan gathered around the fire, drawn by the commotion.

'Great Chief,' Boril gasped, 'I bring word from the east. The

Kalka River runs red with the blood of our people. The plains are black with corpses – Cuman and Rus alike.'

'Stand, my brother Boril,' Tarkhan said. 'Tell us your tale.'

'The followers of the Khan Chingis have pushed westward. They faced the kingdoms of the Rus at the river. The princes united to face this horde but were defeated. Slaughtered and routed. The great Chief Koten of the Terteroba Clan fled for his life, his warriors cut down like wheat before the scythe. So many dead. Thousands. The eastern khan's horsemen... They are like nothing we have ever faced. They gave no quarter, showed no mercy. The heads of so many of those princes now adorn their banner poles, their eyes pecked out by crows.'

Shoruk's fists clenched until his knuckles whitened. 'How many survived?' he demanded, though he dreaded the answer.

'Too few.' Boril's eyes were haunted, seeing again the horrors he had witnessed. 'Those princes of the Rus who were captured were buried alive and suffocated as the Khan's generals feasted atop their dying bodies.'

'But Chief Koten lives?'

'He does,' Boril replied.

'Then we must ride east,' Shoruk declared, turning to Tarkhan. 'Join with him and the surviving clans, face this threat together as we always have. United, we can—'

'No.' Tarkhan's voice was quiet but firm.

'No?' Shoruk struggled to contain his anger, aware of the many eyes watching their exchange. 'Our brothers cry out for aid, and you would abandon them? Have you forgotten all the times they stood with us against our enemies?'

'Our future lies to the west.' Tarkhan spoke with the finality of one who had already made his decision.

'The west? Where the Christians block every pass? Where

Valour

they build their stone nests and cut down any of our people who dare to cross their borders?'

'Yes.' Tarkhan met his gaze, unflinching. 'The very same.'

Shoruk leaned in close so the others might not hear. 'Have you lost your mind, great chief? They would sooner put us to the sword than—'

'Not if we embrace their god.'

Shoruk stared at Tarkhan, certain he had misheard. The wind seemed to die away, leaving only the crackling of the fire and the laboured breathing of the exhausted Boril.

'What did you say?' Shoruk replied, barely believing what he had heard.

Tarkhan let out a great sigh, his face looking resigned. 'It seems it is time. Gather the clan. All of them. They must hear this now.'

One of the warriors – Darman – took out his horn and blew, its deep note carrying on the bitter wind. The sound was both familiar and ominous – the call that had summoned them to war and to mourn their fallen. Shoruk watched as they emerged from their yurts – men, women and children – drawn by the summons. The firelight caught on faces that showed varying degrees of concern and curiosity as they gathered in a rough circle, with Tarkhan at its heart. Even now, with the prospect of dire news, there was something in his bearing that commanded attention.

'People of the White Wolf Clan,' Tarkhan began. 'For generations, we have followed the way of our fathers. We have worshipped Tengri in the endless blue sky above, and Eje in the earth beneath our feet. Our ancestors watch us from the stars, their spirits ride with us in battle, their wisdom guides our steps. But the world changes, and we must change with it... or perish.'

Mutters rippled through the gathering, warriors shifting uneasily, as if sensing an unseen threat. Shoruk felt his jaw tighten as he prepared for Tarkhan to deliver the gravest of tidings.

'We have heard news from the distant Kalka River. Our eastern brothers lie dead or scattered, their blood feeding the grass, their bones picked clean by wolves. The horse-lords of the Khan who defeated them will not stop there – they will push west, as surely as winter follows autumn.' Tarkhan's gaze swept the crowd, meeting eyes both young and old. 'We cannot defeat them alone. We need allies. Strong allies, with stone walls and steel armour.'

'The Christians?' someone called out – Artak, one of Shoruk's most trusted warriors. 'But they are our enemies. They have killed our brothers, stolen our lands, profaned our sacred places.'

'It is the only way,' Tarkhan replied with the patience of a father explaining harsh truths to a child. 'I have already sent word to their priests. And they have replied to that word with hope. A holy woman is coming to show us the way of their god. She will teach us their customs, their prayers, their—'

'Their chains.' Shoruk's voice sounded harsh, even to himself. 'You would have us abandon our gods? The gods who have protected us since our forefathers tamed the first horse? You would have us kneel to these foreign priests who call us savages, who claim their god is the only true one?'

'I would have us live.' Tarkhan's tone had hardened, taking on the edge that had once commanded men in battle. 'The Christian warriors are strong. Their fortresses stand against any attack. Their armies grow larger each year. If we join them, accept their faith, we can keep our lands, our horses, our way of life.'

'What life?' Shoruk spat, taking a step forward. 'As their dogs? Dancing to their tune while they strip everything that makes us who we are? Better to die with—'

'Enough,' Tarkhan bellowed, silencing Shoruk, the crowd.

Valour

Even the wind seemed to quell at his thunder. 'The decision has been made. As chief of the Clan of the White Wolf it is mine to make. Would you defy me, Shoruk?'

All eyes were on him now. But could he? Would he stand against the man who had been as a father to him for all his life? A father to them all?

Shoruk lowered his gaze, offering an almost imperceptible shake of his head.

'What I do, I do for the good of us all,' Tarkhan said, his voice softening once again. 'I do it for our survival. Now go, sleep. Tomorrow we travel west toward the mountains where we will join a new road. One where we might at least find hope.'

The crowd dispersed, breaking into small groups that buzzed with conversation. Some cast fearful glances at the sky, as if expecting Tengri himself to strike them down for even considering such blasphemy. Others huddled close to the fires, speaking in low voices of practical concerns – of survival, of change, of the future that seemed to grow darker with each passing day.

For his part, Shoruk stormed away from the firelight, his shadow stretching long and dark before him across the cold ground, each step carrying him further from the man he had once called father in all but blood. The fury in his chest burned hotter than any fire, threatening to consume him from within.

'Your anger burns bright tonight, warrior. Like a flaming star fallen to the earth.'

The voice froze him in place, sending ice through his veins despite his rage. Moldir emerged from the shadows, her black robes making her seem part of the night itself. Even after years of knowing the old woman, Shoruk had to fight the urge to retreat from her like a spooked horse.

The high priestess's eyes gleamed with an unnatural light. The cold burn of the void between stars, the chill of the tomb.

She was a servant of the old ways – the Kam Katun of the Clan of the White Wolf, who spoke with spirits that were best left unnamed.

'You heard?' he asked.

'I hear everything.' Her lips curved in what might have been a smile, showing teeth that seemed too sharp in the darkness. But of course, she had heard. The birds were her spies, the winds carried whispers to her ears. 'Tengri will not forgive this betrayal easily. The sky god's wrath will shake the mountains themselves.'

'Then we must stop this madness. But Tarkhan...' Shoruk trailed off, unable to voice the thought that had been growing in his mind since his chief's announcement.

'The old wolf has lost his teeth.' Moldir stepped closer. 'Perhaps it is time for new blood. Someone strong. Someone who still hears the voices of the true gods.'

The implication hung in the air between them, and Shoruk felt a chill that had nothing to do with the wind. 'What you suggest is—'

'Necessary.' Her hand touched his arm, cold even through the leather. 'But do not fear, warrior. The gods themselves will guide your hand. The spirits hunger for sacrifice, and they are ready to reward those with enough courage to deliver it.'

She melted back into the darkness like a nightmare fading at dawn, leaving him alone with his thoughts. Or almost alone. Movement caught his eye, and he turned to see Talshyn, Moldir's young priestess, watching from the shadows. Her expression was unreadable in the darkness, but he felt the weight of her gaze. Did she realise the import of what had just transpired? What had been decided in the dark?

Shoruk turned back toward the camp, where Tarkhan stood by the fire, outlined against the flames like a statue. The old chief's shoulders were bowed, as if already bearing the weight of

Valour

his decision. Once, Shoruk would have died to protect him. Now he wondered if his blade would be sharp enough to sever the bonds of loyalty forged over so many years of battle and brotherhood.

But in his heart, he knew the choice had already been made.

Their gods had to be honoured, even if the price was betrayal.

PART ONE: INTO THE WILD

BURZENLAND – 1223AD

1

The scent of roasting pork carried on the autumn air along with the sound of revelry. Estienne stood at the edge of the village square, watching the settlers in their festival attire mingle with visiting traders. The women wore their finest kirtles in autumn colours – russet, gold and forest green – while the men had donned clean tunics and freshly polished boots. Towering above, Rosenau fortress rose from its rocky perch watching over them all like a sentinel, its grey walls catching the last light of the fading sun.

Those walls were the only reason such festivities were possible in this place. Beyond them lay the wild passes of the Carpathians, where danger lurked at every turn. But here, in the shadow of that fortress, the villagers could forget, for a time, that they lived on the very edge of Christendom's grace. Estienne had stood guard on those walls enough times to know every crenel and merlon, every arrow slit and murder hole. From the highest tower, you could see for leagues in every direction – west across the Burzenland toward the settled lands of Hungary, and east over the mountain peaks toward the wilderness of Cumania. The sight always reminded him of how precarious their position was, this tiny outpost of civilisation clinging to the edge of the Christian world.

A cheer went up as two farmers faced off in a makeshift arena, each gripping one end of a long saw. Their muscles strained as they worked the blade through a thick oak log, sawdust falling like snow. The blade's teeth sang against the wood with each push and pull, adding its voice to the general din of the festival, as nearby two teams of men dug their heels into the earth for a tug of war, the hemp rope creaking under the tension as they strained against each other.

Children darted between the legs of the crowd, playing some game that involved much shrieking and laughter. Their high voices carried over the general hubbub of merchants hawking their wares, women gossiping by wine barrels, men arguing good-naturedly over the contests.

A small boy crashed into Estienne's legs, then looked up at his towering height with wide eyes, before scampering away. No time to offer a reassuring smile or ruffle the lad's hair before he fled. It reminded Estienne of how much he was changed from the youth he'd been in England.

He adjusted the white surcoat he wore, conscious of how it marked him as different, even here among his fellow knights. Where his brothers in the Order of Saint Mary wore the black cross on white, his surcoat bore a black lion instead. He was a *halb-brüder*, in the language of the Order – half-brother. Not quite one of them, but still a valued friend. The distinction felt especially sharp on days like this, when the knights of Saint Mary mingled so easily with the common folk they protected.

'You look like you're ready for battle, Wace.' Amalric appeared at his side, offering a clay mug of beer and his usual easy smile. 'Maybe try enjoying yourself for once.'

Valour

'Old habits.' Estienne accepted the drink, letting the bitter ale wash down his dry throat. The local brew was dark and strong, with a hint of honey, and he almost gasped at how good it tasted. 'Someone has to keep watch while everyone else makes merry.'

'That's what those walls are for.' Amalric gestured toward Rosenau with his mug. 'And the men walking them. Even God rested on the seventh day.'

'God didn't have the pagans for neighbours,' Estienne replied dryly.

Amalric laughed, the sound genuine despite the grim truth of the words. 'You're right there.' He took a long pull from his mug. 'But the horse nomads have been quiet lately. Too quiet, some would say.'

'That's what worries me.' Estienne watched a pair of merchants haggling over the price of wool, their animated gestures drawing laughs from onlookers. 'They're always quietest before the storm.'

A chorus of cheers drew their attention toward the arena, where a group of villagers was now attempting to lift increasingly heavy stones. Each success was marked with shouts and raised drinks, each failure with good-natured jeering. The largest stone – a rounded boulder that must have weighed as much as a small pony – stood unconquered at the end of the row.

'Berthold the miller's son has been boasting he can lift the heaviest one,' said Amalric, nodding toward a stocky young man warming up at the edge of the crowd. The youth was built like the millstones he helped his father turn, all solid muscle earned through honest labour. 'Five copper pennies says he can't get it past his knees.'

'I don't take bets I know I'll lose.' Estienne watched as another competitor failed to budge the stone. The man's face had turned

16   RICHARD CULLEN

red as a beet with effort, veins standing out on his neck, but the boulder didn't shift an inch.

'Knights of Saint Mary!' A voice called out from the crowd. 'Surely you'll show us how it's done?'

Estienne suddenly realised all eyes were turning toward them. More voices joined in, calling for the knights to demonstrate their strength, and Estienne felt sudden discomfort in the light of such attention – they were meant to be the protectors of these people, not entertainment for them. But when he glanced at the eager faces in the crowd, he saw no mockery there. Only admiration, and perhaps a desire to see their defenders as men of flesh and blood rather than distant watchmen on the walls.

'Come on,' Amalric said quietly. 'What harm a little friendly competition? Besides, I've been wanting to prove I can best you at something.'

'Well, there's a first time for everything,' Estienne replied with a grin.

The pair made their way forward into the makeshift arena. Estienne shrugged off his surcoat and tunic, the autumn air raising gooseflesh on his bare arms. A murmur ran through the crowd at the sight of the scars that crossed his body – old wounds that told their own tales. Those stones waited in the centre of the arena, four of them, each successively larger and heavier than the last.

The first one came up to Estienne's shins, and he bent his legs, got his arms around it, and lifted. Though heavy, it came up smoothly to his chest. He held it there a moment before setting it down with a thud.

Amalric matched him easily to the delight of the crowd, then turned with his usual bright smile. 'That wasn't so difficult.'

Estienne didn't reply, saving his breath for the task at hand. The second stone was half again as large as the first. This time

Amalric went first, wrapping his arms around it carefully. His face reddened with effort as he raised it, muscles trembling slightly before he managed to get it to chest height. Estienne followed, hoisting the stone upward. The weight tried to pull him forward, threatening his balance, but he held it steady.

'Still think this is easy?' he asked through gritted teeth.

This time it was Amalric's turn to save his breath.

The third stone drew worried murmurs from the crowd. Nearly knee-high, it squatted in the dirt like a sleeping beast. Neither man spoke now – the challenge had grown beyond friendly competition.

Estienne attacked it first, legs spread wide for balance. The stone resisted, then slowly began to rise. Every muscle burned as he fought to control the weight. With a final surge of strength, he managed to get it to his chest, holding it just long enough to stir the crowd into a flurry of applause before letting it drop.

'Ready to yield yet?' he asked, trying to hide how much the effort had cost him.

Amalric didn't reply immediately, studying the stone like a general planning a siege. When he finally moved, it was with precision, his back straight, knees bent, chin raised. His technique served him well – the stone came up smoothly, though sweat streamed down his face and his arms shook with the strain. Then he dropped the stone with a gasp, and stepped back, chest heaving.

The two knights faced each other, both breathing hard, neither willing to concede defeat. The final stone waited – a monster that looked like it had been torn from the mountains themselves.

'I'm starting to wonder if this was such a good idea,' Amalric murmured under his breath.

'No turning back now, my friend,' Estienne replied, advancing on the monstrous boulder.

He knelt, grasping it, straining until the veins stood out on his neck like cords, but the stone refused to budge even an inch off the ground. The attempt left him gasping, his arms trembling with exhaustion. In his turn, Amalric fared no better, his well-practised technique useless against such an immovable mass.

Just as the crowd began to voice their disappointment, a shadow fell across the arena, and a deep laugh rolled out like distant thunder. Rotger Havenblast stood watching them fail, his massive frame blocking the setting sun. The newest knight of the Order was built like a bear, with hands like hammers and shoulders that seemed wide enough to carry the world. His surcoat strained across his chest, the black cross distorted by the sheer bulk of muscle beneath.

'May I?' he asked, still chuckling.

Without waiting for an answer, he stepped up to the stone. His laugh faded to a grunt of effort as he wrapped his arms around it and tested its weight. Then the impossible happened – the stone began to rise.

Rotger's face turned red, his teeth bared in a grimace that could have been a smile, as the stone came up past his knees, then his waist, then finally to his chest. The muscles in his neck stood out like guy ropes, and his breath came in short, sharp gasps. He held the vast stone there for a heartbeat before letting it crash back to earth, the impact sending tremors through the ground that Estienne felt in his feet.

The crowd's cheers were deafening. Someone started a chant of 'Rotger! Rotger!' that quickly spread through the gathering, and the big knight accepted their praise with a bashful grin.

'God's blood,' Amalric breathed, shaking his head in amazement. 'That man's a beast.'

Valour 19

'Aye. Just count your blessings he's on our side,' Estienne added.

As the cheers rose to a crescendo, the thunder of hooves cut through the celebration, and the crowd parted as Carsten Schado rode into the square. The man's perpetual scowl seemed deeper than usual, his balding head flushed with what might have been anger or exertion.

'Enough of this foolishness!' he spat, eyes fixed on Estienne and Amalric's bare chests with obvious disapproval. 'Have you forgotten your duties? Or perhaps you think the defence of Christendom can wait while you cavort like common farmhands?'

The festive atmosphere deflated. Children who had been playing nearby scurried away from Carsten's harsh voice, and the villagers began to drift from the arena. Even the pig on its spit seemed to turn more slowly, as though trying not to draw attention to itself.

'Come now, Brother Carsten,' said old Steffen the carpenter, stepping forward with a mug of beer extended in offering. 'Surely even the men of your Order can spare an afternoon for the harvest celebrations? The day is a fine one, the beer is flowing—'

'The day is wasting,' Carsten cut him off, ignoring the offered drink. 'And we have more important matters to attend to than childish games.'

Estienne stiffened at the insult in Carsten's tone. The man had never fought a real battle, never stood shoulder to shoulder with common men against a common enemy, yet he spoke to them as though he were their lord. He was the son of a rich merchant, given his position in return for a generous donation to the Order's coffers – so generous it had seen Carsten gifted the rank of Komtur. A senior office he didn't deserve, and Estienne would have told him as much, but Amalric's hand on his arm kept him silent.

'Marschall Dieter has sent word ahead of his imminent arrival,' Carsten continued, his voice carrying across the now-quiet square. 'He is bringing important missionaries from France who intend to spread the light of God to one of the pagan clans. A holy woman of the church, accompanied by Dominican friars no less. She will be received with all due ceremony and respect, by order of the Hochmeister himself.'

His gaze swept across the gathered knights, as though challenging any of them to question his authority. Rotger's good humour had faded, replaced by a hangdog expression that ill-suited his massive frame. Likewise, Amalric's smile had reduced to a set jaw. Together, they retrieved their tunics and surcoats and followed Carsten's strutting steed back toward Rosenau.

Estienne cast one last look at the square. The villagers were already starting to pack away their stalls, the joy of the day soured by Carsten's interference. But perhaps for the best. The jollity of a festival day could not last forever. Especially not with the threat of what lurked just beyond those mountains. Whoever these approaching missionaries were, they must have possessed a staunch faith indeed to try and to shed the light of Christianity beyond the Carpathians.

2

Estienne shifted his weight and adjusted the white surcoat bearing his black lion. The wind cut through the fabric, but he still stood unmoving. Around him, the other knights of the Order were like statues, their black crosses stark against their white mantles. Only their breath, rising in pale clouds, betrayed any sign of life.

'Here they come,' Carsten barked across the courtyard.

Estienne glanced through the open gates, seeing distant riders appear against the frost-covered landscape. Marschall Dieter von Goslar led the party, his massive destrier's hooves kicking up clods of earth. Behind him rode a woman on a white palfrey, flanked by two brown-robed friars who looked as comfortable on horseback as fish in a tree.

As the group rode within the confines of the castle walls, he could see the woman sitting straight-backed in her saddle despite what must have been an exhausting journey, her travelling clothes simple but well-made. Though her face bore the lines of middle age, there was a keenness in her blue eyes as she surveyed the fortress. A wooden rosary was wrapped around one gloved fist, and unlike her nervous companions, she carried herself with a quiet confidence.

Carsten stepped forward. 'Welcome to Rosenau, honoured guests. I am Komtur Carsten Schado.'

'Thank you for your welcome, Komtur,' the woman replied, her voice carrying clearly across the courtyard. She dismounted with surprising grace, the two friars scrambling to follow her example. 'I am Fabrisse of Avallon, duly appointed as Christian envoy by the Bishop of Acre. These are Brothers Galien and Rabel.'

The shorter of the two friars – Galien, Estienne presumed – offered a jerky bow, his tonsured head shining with sweat despite the cold. His companion simply stared at the fortress walls as though he had never seen anything so imposing.

Carsten offered a bow of his own. 'We are honoured to—'

'Show the lady to her quarters,' the Marschall ordered, cutting across whatever Carsten had been about to say. 'She and her companions will need rest after their journey. And see that fires are lit in their rooms – the road has been a bitterly cold one.'

Carsten's face reddened, but he gestured for a pair of serving brothers to lead the visitors away. As they disappeared into the keep, Amalric leaned in closer to Estienne.

'She must have powerful friends in Rome,' his friend whispered. 'The Order doesn't usually extend such courtesies to wandering missionaries.'

'Powerful friends won't help her beyond those walls.' Estienne watched as stable boys led the horses away. 'The pagans don't care how many bishops you know when they're peeling the skin from your bones.'

'Perhaps she'll reconsider once she's heard the night wolves howling,' Rotger offered hopefully. 'Nothing sends missionaries

Valour 23

running back to civilisation faster than a night at the edge of the frontier.'

'Let's hope that she does,' Estienne replied. 'Though I doubt it. There's something in her eyes... the look of someone who won't be turned aside easily.'

'Dismissed,' Carsten bellowed, before they could talk further.

As the other knights of the Order filed away, Estienne could only gaze toward the keep where Fabrisse had disappeared, wondering what kind of conviction would make a woman willingly throw herself into the wilds for a chance to bring the light of God to those who would only do you harm.

* * *

The great hall of Rosenau was hardly worthy of its name – just a long room with rough-hewn beams and arrow-slit windows that let in fingers of cold air. But the servants had done their best to make it welcoming, hanging tapestries to cover the bare stone walls and setting out the Order's best pewter plates. The scent of roasted venison and sweet spices filled the air, mixing with the smoke from the hearth.

Estienne sat between Amalric and Rotger, watching Carsten make another attempt to dominate the conversation. The Komtur had been holding forth about the challenges of maintaining order on the frontier for the better part of an hour, his voice growing louder with each cup of wine. His face had taken on the ruddy sheen that promised belligerence before the night was through. Estienne had been hoping the Marschall would cut him down to size at some point, but Dieter had remained silent, most likely still fatigued after his recent travels.

'Of course, one must be firm with the locals,' Carsten said, gesturing with a half-empty cup. 'They're little better than peasants, truth be told. Why, just last month I had to have three of them reprimanded for failing to deliver their seasonal tithe of grain. You have to maintain discipline, you see. Show strength.'

'An interesting perspective,' Fabrisse replied, delicately picking at her venison. 'Though I've often found that understanding breeds better results than a scolding.'

'Understanding?' Carsten laughed, a harsh sound that echoed off the stone walls. 'My lady, you don't know these people. They're—'

'I know them perfectly well. They are children of the Lord, as are we all. Even those beyond the bounds of this fortress. Those pagans who wish to be embraced by Christendom.'

'Those pagans are a different breed altogether. You'd have more luck trying to convert a wild beast.'

'And yet, convert them I will,' Fabrisse replied, so firmly it silenced the table.

Carsten was dumbstruck for a moment, reminding Estienne of how unused he was to being contradicted. 'But... how will you even accomplish such a thing? They speak no language we know.'

'But thankfully I am well-versed in all the Kipchak dialects, Komtur. Indeed, I have read much about them, but I would be interested in knowing what *you* have learned from the clans of the Cumans during your time here. What can you tell me of their ways?'

Her sudden question silenced Carsten, along with the rest of the table. Marschall Dieter shifted uncomfortably in his seat, though he had nothing to reply.

'Anyone?' she asked. 'What about you?' Her eyes settled on Estienne.

He was surprised at being drawn into the conversation, but there was something about her that made him want to offer as best an answer as he could.

'I've learned they're excellent shots with a bow,' he replied drily. 'And that they prefer to attack when you least expect it. Usually just before dawn, when men are at their most tired.'

'Which is why this mission of yours is folly,' Amalric said, then quickly added, 'Begging your pardon, my lady.'

'You think bringing God's word to the heathens is foolish?' There was no anger in her voice, only genuine curiosity.

'I think getting yourself killed serves no one,' Amalric replied, pushing his plate away. 'The Cumans are not like the peasants you're used to converting. They're warriors, raiders. They respect strength, not sermons.'

'Then it's fortunate that the word of our Lord is compelling indeed.' Fabrisse set down her cup, the metal making a soft ring against the wood. 'And that I have already arranged to meet with one of their clan chiefs. He and his people are most eager to be welcomed into the arms of Christ.'

'It sounds like you have thought of everything,' Amalric offered.

Fabrisse smiled. 'Perhaps not everything, but enough. The rest is in the hands of God.'

'And the hands of the Cumans,' Estienne added, unable to hold his tongue on the matter. 'Let's hope they're as open to the word of God as they claim. For your sake.'

'Indeed. I have prayed for it every day since I received word from their chieftain. In fact, I would pray for it now, before I retire for the evening. Would there be somewhere appropriate?'

Carsten shoved his chair back. 'Indeed there is. I can show you the way, and perhaps we can further discuss—'

'The Lady of Avallon has heard enough of your blether, Schado,' the Marschall said. 'Wace, you will escort her to the chapel.'

Expectant eyes turned once more to Estienne. With no other choice, he rose and made his way toward the archway from the great hall with Fabrisse close behind. They proceeded through the castle in silence, but for the howl of the wind outside. Despite the Lady of Avallon holding no official rank within the church other than the blessing of a bishop, Estienne felt as though he were escorting some important dignitary, and kept a respectful silence as a consequence.

The chapel of Rosenau was small. A crude wooden cross dominated the far wall, unadorned save for a crown of thorns someone had woven from local briars. The air was thick with the smell of tallow candles and old incense, underlaid with the musty scent of damp.

'It's not much,' Estienne said, suddenly conscious that even the smallest village church would have put this place to shame. 'But it serves its purpose.'

'God's house needs no ornament.' Fabrisse moved to stand before the cross, her fingers teasing her rosary beads. 'Though I imagine it's quite different from the great cathedrals of England. York Minster, perhaps? Or Canterbury?'

'It's that obvious I'm from England?'

'Your accent is hard to disguise. English with a hint of Anjou, though I can't tell which is the stronger.' She turned to face him, amusement dancing in her eyes. 'But your Deutsch is excellent.'

'You have a good ear,' he conceded grudgingly.

'I have good eyes, too.' She studied him in the flickering light, her gaze uncomfortably penetrating. 'When I look at you, I sense a man running from something. The question is, what has driven you so far from home?'

A long tale indeed. One he had no intention of sharing with anyone. Not least a holy woman he barely knew.

'We all have our reasons for being here.'

'Indeed.' She returned her attention to the cross, reaching out to touch one of the thorns. 'Though some reasons are worthier than others. Tell me, Estienne, what do you believe in?'

More questions, provoking more memories. This time of righteous fury and endless sands. Of faith. Of loss.

'I believe in brotherhood,' he replied shortly. 'And I believe in steel.'

'And in God?'

'He's somewhere on the list, I suppose.'

She looked away, as though disappointed. 'You have not put God above all things. I find that a little sad. How empty your world must be.'

'Better empty than filled with false hope that you can mould the world in God's image.' The words came out harsher than he'd intended. 'Forgive me, my lady, but you don't know what evil those pagans are capable of. The things they do...' He trailed off, remembering what he had seen in the short time he'd manned this frontier garrison.

'I know exactly what they're capable of,' Fabrisse replied quietly. 'I've studied their ways, their beliefs. They worship Tengri in the sky above, and Eje in the earth below. They believe a man's worth is measured by his strength, his courage in battle. But they're not devils, Estienne. They're men, like any other. And men can change.'

'Not all men. I've seen too much evil to believe that.'

'Have you?' She stepped closer, and he fought the urge to step back. 'Tell me, what did you witness in the Holy Land that made you so certain of men's nature? What broke your faith so completely?'

'How did you know—?'

'I told you.' She smiled again. 'I have good eyes.'

Her insight made him feel suddenly ill at ease. That she

should be able to read him so deftly made Estienne wonder what else she might have seen lurking within his soul.

'My faith was not broken. Just cracked a little. I was raised to follow a code. To do the right thing no matter the cost. But in the Holy Land I saw men's principles clouded by greed. Saw pious men abandon their faith for fortune. Saw young men die in the name of God, only for it all to be for nothing.'

'And for that you have abandoned that code in favour of this holy order?'

In truth, Estienne barely knew. Had he forgotten the code taught to him by Goffrey, instilled in him by the Marshal? Or did he still cling to it?

'I have made no vows to the Order of Saint Mary. But neither have I forgotten the lessons taught me by my master.'

Fabrisse looked on with some sympathy. 'It seems you are all at sea, Estienne Wace. A lost sailor in search of the shore.'

'I should leave you to your prayers,' he said stiffly, suddenly feeling as though he were being put to the question. 'It's getting late.'

'Of course.' Her voice was gentle, almost maternal. 'Though I think perhaps you could use some prayer yourself, Estienne. These lands are too dangerous for a man without faith.'

'And those beyond the mountains are more dangerous still.'

'What better reason than for us both to pray, then?'

'Perhaps... another time,' he replied, simply bowing before striding from the chapel.

The night air hit him as he stepped out onto the walls of the castle, and he sucked in great lungfuls of it, trying to clear his head of unwanted memories. When he eventually made his way back to the great hall it had emptied save for a handful of knights gathered around the feast table. Guttering candles cast uncertain light over the scraps of meat and bread, the spilled wine looking black as old blood on the tablecloth. Outside, the wind had picked up, making the arrow-slit windows whistle like distant battle horns.

Carsten sat slouching, his face flushed with wine, while the Marschall maintained his usual stone-faced dignity. Amalric and Rotger occupied the bench opposite, the latter still picking at a half-stripped capon with remarkable dedication.

'Well?' Carsten demanded as Estienne approached, his words slightly slurred. 'Is our holy woman settled in to pray for the night?'

'She's at her devotions,' Estienne replied, dropping onto the bench beside Amalric. 'For all the good it will do her beyond the mountain pass.'

'We shouldn't discourage these missionaries too strongly about the dangers,' Carsten said, swirling the wine in his cup. 'After all, bringing God's light to the heathens is a noble calling. Perhaps this is the moment He has chosen to turn the rest of the Cumans from their savage ways. To bring them all into the fold of Holy Mother Church.'

'And perhaps your horse will sprout wings and fly you to the moon,' Amalric muttered. 'We have a duty to warn them of what they're riding into. To discourage them from this foolish crusade.'

'Our duty is to the Order,' Carsten snapped, slamming his cup down. 'And if the Order has decided to support this mission—'

'The Order has decided to offer them hospitality,' the Marschall interrupted, his quiet voice brooking no argument. 'Nothing more. What they choose to do beyond our walls is their own affair. Though God knows, they'll need more than prayers where they're going.'

'But surely we can't just let them ride to their deaths?' Amalric protested. 'They have no idea what's waiting out there.'

'She seems to think God will protect them,' Estienne said, the memory of her penetrating gaze clear in his mind. 'Though I've yet to see faith stop an arrow or turn aside a blade. I'm with Amalric on this, we should—'

The Marschall pushed back from the table, his chair scraping against the stone floor. 'Enough. The decision isn't ours to make. The Lady of Avallon has insisted they travel alone. A military escort will only send the wrong message to the clan they intend to convert. Hers is a mission of peace, and we are to take no part in it, other than guiding them along the mountain pass to meet with the pagans.'

An uncomfortable silence fell over the table. Even Rotger stopped chewing. In the distance, a wolf howled, the sound carrying clearly through the arrow slits. It was answered by another, closer, and then a third.

The Marschall rose, his shadow stretching across the table like a giant's. 'Get some rest, all of you. Tomorrow may bring its own troubles.'

As he strode from the hall, Estienne couldn't shake the feeling that tomorrow's troubles might arrive sooner than any of them expected. He reached for the wine jug again but found it empty. Perhaps for the best. At least now he could face tomorrow's troubles with a clear head.

3

Dawn crept over the Carpathians, and Estienne watched those distant peaks emerge from darkness as he tightened his destrier's girth strap. The warhorse shifted restlessly, steam rising from its flanks in the morning air. Around him, the fortress courtyard buzzed with activity – stable hands rushing back and forth, horses stamping and shying, weapons being given one final check before departure.

'I still think this is a damn fool thing to be doing,' Amalric muttered from where he was securing his own mount's bridle. 'We are leading these people to their doom.'

'It is not our place to make that judgement, brother,' Estienne replied, stepping back from his mount. 'These orders come from the Hochmeister himself. Besides, the Lady of Avallon seems to know what she's doing. I get the sense God's watching over her, if he's watching over any of us.'

Rotger approached leading his own horse, the massive destrier making even his bear-like frame seem modest in comparison.

'Good morning for a ride,' he said cheerfully, apparently

immune to both the cold and the general mood of tension. 'The mist should burn off by midday. View along the pass will be a beautiful one.'

Amalric grinned at the big knight's optimism. Estienne merely gazed up at the fortress walls, where tendrils of fog still clung. The moisture had left a sheen of frost on the stone that would melt and refreeze until spring, making the steps treacherous. Everything about this morning felt treacherous.

The creak of the keep doors drew his attention. Fabrisse emerged, flanked by her holy companions. She had traded her travelling clothes for a simple grey robe and white wimple, a wooden cross hanging at her throat. Friars Galien and Rabel followed in their brown habits, looking decidedly less comfortable with the prospect of the journey ahead.

'My lady,' Estienne said with a slight bow as she approached. 'I trust you slept well?'

'Well enough,' she replied. 'Though the wind howls through these walls like nothing I've ever known.'

Before he could respond, Amalric appeared at his shoulder. 'The horses are ready, and we have loaded supplies for two days.'

'We won't need supplies for two days,' Brother Galien interjected, his voice pitched slightly too high. 'The Cuman camp is less than a day's ride.'

'Best to be prepared,' Estienne replied. 'There's no guarantee these Cumans will even show when they say. They're not known for their reliability. We might have to wait a while and the weather in these mountains can change in an instant. You never know when you might get caught out.'

Fabrisse regarded the peaks with serene confidence. 'God will guide us through whatever weather He chooses to send.'

'I'd still rather have extra food,' Rotger muttered.

The sound of hooves brought Estienne's attention to the gate,

Valour 33

where squires stood waiting with three stout steeds for Fabrisse and the monks. The gate itself was already open, showing the long pass through the Carpathians beyond.

'Time to mount up,' Estienne announced.

He helped Fabrisse onto her palfrey, noting how she sat the saddle with practised ease. No stranger to riding, then, despite her religious calling. With the rest of them ready, Estienne mounted his own destrier and led the way through the gate. The wind teased his face as he crossed the threshold, as though reminding him he was now beyond the frontier. Beyond the protection Rosenau afforded. Nevertheless, Fabrisse seemed undaunted, riding along with her chin raised, an almost eager look to her.

The trail wound between towering walls of grey stone, so high that Estienne had to crane his neck to see their peaks. Their horses' hooves struck a steady rhythm against the hard ground, the sound echoing off the cliff faces. The Carpathians had ways of making a man feel small, reminding him how insignificant he was in such an ancient place.

A raven's harsh cry made Brother Galien start in his saddle, and even Rotger's usual cheerful expression had given way to grim concentration. Fabrisse alone seemed unaffected by the oppressive atmosphere, her back straight, her gaze fixed ahead. More than once, Estienne's hand strayed to his sword hilt, only to find he was reacting to nothing more threatening than a wind-bent sapling quivering in the wind, or a tumbling rock. But in these mountains, he knew, it was better to be too cautious than too complacent. The difference might be fatal.

They reached the far end of the pass just as the sun cleared the mountaintops, the rolling hills and wild plains of Cumania spreading out before them beneath the vast sky.

The Cumans were already waiting.

Six riders sat atop their small, shaggy horses with the easy grace of men born to the saddle. Their fur-trimmed coats were dyed in deep blues and reds, the colours stark against the winter-pale landscape. Curved bows rode in leather cases at their saddles, the weapons looking deceptively delicate compared to the thick yew bows of western armies, but Estienne knew better – he'd seen arrows fired from those bows pierce mail and gambeson at a hundred paces.

'Stay alert,' he murmured to Amalric as they drew closer. 'But keep your hands away from your weapons.'

The lead Cuman urged his mount forward. His face was weathered as old leather, black hair bound in a single long braid that hung down his back. Gold rings gleamed in his ears, and he looked on impassively from a grim face.

Fabrisse guided her palfrey forward to meet him. What followed was a rapid exchange in their tongue, the harsh sounds at odds with her usual measured tone. Estienne fought to keep his expression neutral as he studied the men who had come to greet them. Each warrior bore the scars of combat; these were not mere herders or hunters, but veteran raiders. Most likely they had burned villages. Slaughtered innocents. But he was not here for retribution. One caught his gaze and held it, dark eyes glittering with barely concealed hostility. Estienne would gladly have offered him challenge, but he managed to hold himself in check as Fabrisse continued her conversation.

'The Cuman says they will take good care of us,' Brother Rabel translated quietly, though his trembling voice suggested he didn't entirely believe it. 'That their chieftain, Tarkhan, looks forward to our arrival.'

The lead Cuman was speaking again, gesturing eastward toward a pass between two hills. His manner seemed respectful enough, but Estienne noticed his men had subtly positioned themselves to flank the three knights if things turned sour. Old habits died hard, it seemed.

'I am afraid this is where we part ways,' Fabrisse said, turning in her saddle. 'I thank you for your escort. The Cumans can guide us from here.'

'My lady—' Estienne began, but she cut him off with a raised hand.

'I know what you would say, Estienne. But these men are our brothers in waiting, not our enemies. Faith will deliver us.'

He wanted to argue – to point out how many men he'd seen die thinking faith would protect them – but he knew it would do no good. Instead, he bowed slightly in his saddle.

'God go with you then, my lady.'

'And with you.' She smiled, and for a moment he saw something in her eyes that might have been uncertainty, but then it was gone.

The Cumans wheeled their horses, forming a loose circle around Fabrisse and the friars. As they rode east, Estienne couldn't shake the feeling that he was watching them ride to their deaths. The last thing he saw before they disappeared into the pass was Brother Galien looking back over his shoulder, his face pale with fear.

'God will protect them,' Rotger said, breaking the silence. The big knight crossed himself, his usual cheerful expression replaced by something more solemn.

'I keep hearing that,' Estienne replied grimly, unable to keep the edge from his voice.

He wheeled his own horse around, and led his companions back along the pass.

'The Lady of Avallon knows what she's doing,' Rotger insisted. 'And the Cuman chief has requested this conversion. Why would he do that if he only meant her harm?'

'Chiefs can change their minds,' Amalric said quietly. 'Especially when their warriors grow restless. If there's any dissent among this Tarkhan's clan he may just as easily sacrifice all three of them to his sky god.'

They rode in silence for a while, each lost in their own thoughts. Estienne couldn't shake the memory of those Cuman warriors – their hard faces, their predatory grace. As much as he admired Rotger's optimism, he couldn't help but think things would not be so straightforward for Fabrisse.

They rode through Rosenau's gates as the sun was beginning to dip behind the mountains, to find Carsten waiting in the courtyard. He stood with his arms folded, as though desperate to disapprove of something.

'Well?' he demanded before they'd even dismounted. 'I trust our guests are safely delivered?'

'As safely as one can be delivered to a pack of wolves,' Amalric replied, swinging down from his saddle.

Estienne and Rotger did likewise as stable hands came forward to take their reins. The gates through which they had ridden were slammed shut against the wind, and a hush fell across the courtyard.

A sudden rumble in Estienne's gut reminded him he hadn't eaten since the morning. Before he could think of filling his belly, the broad figure of Marschall Dieter appeared from the keep.

'Well done, brothers,' he announced. 'I know that cannot have been easy.'

'God will protect,' Rotger answered, repeating his previous confidence in Fabrisse and her cause.

Estienne might have argued, but Amalric tapped him on the shoulder, gesturing across the courtyard. He turned to see a trio of men had entered the western gate, each clasping a cap in their hands, heads bowed.

Valour 37

'What's this?' Carsten demanded, but Estienne was already moving toward the men.

'Pardon our intrusion, my lords,' one of them said in clipped Deutsch. 'We have come from a settlement to the south. And we...'

He stopped, as though too afraid to continue.

'Speak, man,' Carsten insisted, and none too gently.

'We need help,' said one of the others, this one a little younger than the first, though no less craggy about the face. 'A bear has strayed into woods near our farmland. Three sheep killed already. And a boy is badly mauled. Bear came down from the high country, bold as brass. Took the sheep in broad daylight, and when young Klaus tried to drive it off...' He trailed off, shaking his head.

'How bad?' Estienne asked.

'Bad enough. The healer's with him now, but she says he might lose an arm.'

'That's bad news,' Carsten replied dismissively. 'But I'm not sure what—'

'These people put bread on your table, Komtur,' Estienne said. 'And pay their tithes to the Order.'

'Then it is our duty to do something about it.' Marschall Dieter descended the keep steps. 'Komtur Carsten, you will take Wace and the others and deal with this matter.'

'But Marschall,' Carsten protested, 'surely there are more important duties—'

'More important than defending the very people we invited here to start a new life?' Dieter's voice carried the weight of command.

'But... I am just Komtur. This is a military matter.'

'The experience will do you good. It's past time you rode out to help those under our protection.'

Estienne caught Amalric trying to hide a smile. Even the amiable Rotger showed a hint of satisfaction at Carsten's discomfort.

'As you command, Marschall,' Carsten said stiffly, before turning to the others. 'Well? What are you waiting for? Get fresh horses and supplies. We leave within the hour.'

As they moved to comply, Amalric fell in beside Estienne.

'From missionary escort to bear hunt,' he muttered. 'Never a dull moment on the frontier.'

'Better a bear than the pagans,' Estienne replied quietly. 'At least with a bear you know where you stand.'

'True enough.' Amalric glanced at Carsten, who was already shouting at a stable boy to prepare his horse. 'Though I'm not sure the Komtur will be so easy to convince.'

Estienne allowed himself a grim smile. 'Whatever else happens, watching Carsten try to maintain his dignity during a hunt promises some entertainment.'

Amalric offered a wicked smile of his own. 'Assuming the bear doesn't eat the bastard first.'

4

The sun was falling beyond the eastern sky as their small party crested the final rise. Fabrisse pulled her palfrey to a halt, taking in the sprawl of the Cuman camp below. Dozens of round felt-covered yurts dotted the windswept plateau, arranged in a circle around a larger central tent. Horses stamped and shifted at their pickets, their braided manes adorned with strips of dyed leather and polished beads that caught the dying light.

Their escorts had maintained a grim silence throughout the journey east, their stony faces revealing nothing. Now they sat upon their mounts with ease, waiting – as though they were proud to display their clan before an honoured guest.

'*Ave Maria, gratia plena...*' Brother Galien's whispered prayer barely carried on the wind. His hands trembled where they gripped his reins, knuckles white with tension.

'Be at peace,' Fabrisse said quietly. 'We are here by invitation, and under God's watchful eye. He will protect, brother.'

Rabel made a sound that might have been agreement, though none too convincing. Both friars had grown increasingly agitated as they'd left the relative safety of the mountain pass behind. She could hardly blame them – they'd grown up in the bosom of Christendom. Now they found themselves in the heart of a pagan camp, surrounded by heathen warriors.

Fabrisse urged her horse closer to the camp, and one of the riders galloped ahead to warn of their approach. She gripped her rosary tighter in her fist, mouthing a silent prayer. For all her words of reassurance to the brothers, it still wouldn't hurt to remind God that His servants might require a little extra attention.

When they reached the boundary, a woman paused in her work to watch them pass, a basket of mushrooms and herbs balanced on one hip. Her face was lined with sun and wind, her dark eyes evaluating. More faces turned toward them – children peeking from behind their mothers' skirts, warriors tucking thumbs in belts with deliberate casualness.

'Remember why we're here,' Fabrisse said, as much to herself as to her companions. 'These are not our enemies, but souls waiting to be brought to Christ's light.'

Brother Galien nodded, though his complexion remained pale beneath his hood. 'Yes, my lady. Though perhaps... perhaps we should have brought men who might protect us?'

'That would only demonstrate a lack of trust,' she replied. 'We must rely on God's protection, and in Chief Tarkhan's honour.'

Their escorts led them deeper into the camp, past cooking fires where women stirred iron pots, and children who looked up in wonder at the blue-eyed woman riding through their midst. The entire clan looked to be following them in a procession, though none of them seemed particularly welcoming. The centre of the camp drew closer, and with it the largest yurt, which she could only assume was Chief Tarkhan's by its size and the elaborate designs worked into its felt walls.

Its heavy hide entrance flap swung aside, and Tarkhan

emerged into the last light of day. Despite his grey hair and the lines etched deep in his face, he moved with the confident air of a born horseman. His coat was richly decorated with intricate embroidery, the wolf-fur trim marking his status as surely as any crown. But when he smiled, the years seemed to fall away from his features.

Their escorts dismounted, touching their fists to their hearts, their task done. Tarkhan strode forward, and to Fabrisse's surprise, offered his own hands to help her from the saddle.

'Welcome, holy one,' he said, as a murmur ran through the gathering crowd at the honour shown to this foreign woman. 'My home is yours.'

'You are most gracious, Great Chief Tarkhan,' she replied. 'I am Fabrisse of Avallon. Appointed by the Bishop of Acre to assist in your conversion.'

She took his rough hand and allowed him to help her down. Tarkhan gestured toward the entrance of his yurt.

'I thought we might first speak in my dwelling. Your companions will be taken care of while we do.'

Fabrisse turned, seeing the look of fear on Galien's face, while Rabel looked merely exhausted.

'Brothers, I will see you soon.'

Rabel opened his mouth as though he might argue but then thought better of it. What would he do anyway to defend her should things go wrong? He was no warrior, and even if he were it was doubtful he would last long, surrounded as he was by these seasoned fighters.

Fabrisse followed Tarkhan inside, the air heavy with the scent of burning herbs and smoke. A small fire burned in a metal brazier at the centre, casting dancing shadows on the felt walls. Elaborately woven rugs covered the packed earth floor, and Tarkhan gestured by the fire.

'Please, sit.'

As Fabrisse settled herself, women entered bearing cups of fermented mare's milk, and she accepted without hesitation even though the sour smell made her stomach turn.

'You have travelled far,' Tarkhan said, watching her over the rim of his own cup. 'I trust the journey was not too difficult?'

'It was swift, thanks to your warriors.' Fabrisse took a careful sip of the milk, managing not to grimace at the sharp taste. 'They were most expert guides.'

Tarkhan nodded. 'Good. Though I confess, I did not expect...' He paused, choosing his words with obvious care. 'When I first sent word seeking guidance in the ways of Christ, I did not think they would send a woman.'

'Does it trouble you?' Fabrisse asked quietly.

'No. Perhaps it is even fitting. The word of my gods is spoken by a priestess. But I thought your Christian priests were all men. I suppose change comes in many forms, does it not?'

She studied him in the flickering firelight, noting the intelligence in his dark eyes, the way he held himself – proud but not arrogant, confident but not overbearing. Here was a leader who understood the delicate balance required in such moments as this.

'You speak of change,' she said. 'Tell me what you hope to achieve by accepting the word of God.'

Tarkhan absently turned one of his many rings, the gold catching the firelight. 'My people face threats from all sides. The Christians push from the west with their stone fortresses. And now word comes from the east of great armies that devour everything in their path. The Clan of the White Wolf cannot stand alone against such enemies.'

'And so you turn to Christ.'

'I turn to survival.' Tarkhan's voice sounded heavy with regret.

Valour 43

'The Christian kingdoms are strong. If we join them, accept their faith, then perhaps we can keep our lands, our horses, our way of life.'

'You are a plain speaker, Tarkhan,' she said, choosing her next words carefully. 'So I will speak plainly in return. You wish to preserve your people. The Church wishes to save their souls. Both are possible, if you are willing to accept the light of God into your heart.'

Tarkhan leaned back, satisfaction warming his hard features. 'Your word pleases me, holy one. Perhaps this is why they sent a woman – to cut through the pride of warriors and strike at the heart of things.' He touched his chest. 'My heart tells me this is the right path. The only path. We will accept your Christian god, and pray he proves as strong as you claim.'

'He is stronger,' Fabrisse said softly. 'And his love knows no bounds.'

The chief rose, gesturing for her to follow. 'Come. My people should meet the one who will guide them to this new light.'

Outside, the night had come alive. A great fire blazed in the centre of the camp, sending sparks spiralling up toward the star-strewn sky. The clan gathered around it, passing cups of milk and skewers of roasted meat. The flames painted their faces in shades of gold and shadow as they danced, their movements fluid and wild as the fire itself.

Fabrisse's heart lightened to see Brothers Galien and Rabel among them, both looking more at ease than she'd seen since leaving Rosenau. Someone had pressed cups into their hands and Galien was eating his fill of the meat. Rabel was even attempting a clumsy dance with one of the clan's children, a little girl who giggled as she tried to teach him the proper steps.

For a moment, watching them all, Fabrisse allowed herself to hope that such carefree joy was just the start. Then movement in the shadows drew her attention.

Two women stood watching nearby, their stillness striking against the busy activity around them. The taller wore dark robes, her face proud, almost regal, with high cheekbones and eyes dark as pits. The younger woman beside her kept her hood pulled forward, though Fabrisse could still see her narrow eyes watching.

'Who are they?' she asked Tarkhan.

The chief followed her gaze. 'Ah. The tall one is Moldir, our Kam Katun – what you might call a high priestess. The other is Talshyn, who studies our old ways under her guidance.'

A young warrior paused as he passed the priestesses, touching his forehead in a gesture of respect. Others regarded them with respect as they passed, one even with fear. These were not mere religious figures, Fabrisse realised, but representative of the pagan gods themselves. The living embodiment of everything she hoped to replace.

'Perhaps they would join us?' she suggested, careful to keep her tone light. 'I am intrigued to learn more about their ways.'

'Another time,' Tarkhan said quickly – too quickly. 'Tonight we feast. But first, you should meet Shoruk, my best warrior. The one who will lead when I am gone.'

He led her through the revelry, closer to the dancing fire. No sooner could she feel the intensity of it begin to warm her, than a warrior approached – tall and broad-shouldered, his face bearing the scars of many battles. His eyes were hard as he evaluated Fabrisse, and she noted how his hand never strayed far from his sword hilt.

'Shoruk,' Tarkhan said. 'Our honoured guest.'

'Welcome to our lands, holy one.' The warrior offered a slight bow, his words and the gesture somehow managing to convey more threat than respect.

Before Fabrisse could respond, another warrior appeared from the gathering darkness. 'Great Chief. There is a matter that requires your attention.'

'Very well.' Tarkhan replied. 'You must excuse us. Shoruk and I have duties to attend. Please, help yourself to meat and milk. You are most welcome.'

As they walked away, Fabrisse stood alone, watching the activity of the camp. There seemed a kind of wildness to proceedings, the dancing much less rigid than in the west. The laughter louder and more raucous. For a moment, Fabrisse began to envy these people their freedom – to ride the plains without border or shackle. To live without boundary, taking what they wanted with no care but to survive...

'They say you come from a land far to the west.'

Fabrisse turned to find Talshyn, the priestess in waiting, standing nearby, her hood pushed back to reveal her face fully for the first time. She was younger than Fabrisse had first thought, perhaps twenty summers at most.

'Yes,' Fabrisse replied. 'From a place called Avallon, in the kingdom of France.'

'A journey of many miles?'

'Hundreds.'

The girl looked impressed. 'And why would you come so far to try and deny our gods?'

Fabrisse was suddenly taken aback. She had not really considered the consequences of what conversion might mean to those who had followed their pagan gods for so long. Not least a woman who had been raised up to preach their word.

'That is not my intention. I merely wish to bring the word of the Lord. The word of the one true God.'

'That sounds a lot like you're denying my gods to me.'

'That's not how it is,' Fabrisse replied, though the more she thought on it, the more she realised just how much it was. 'I'm sure Tarkhan has—'

'Has explained to us the only way we will survive is to embrace the Christians and their beliefs. That if we do not, we will all die.'

'I suppose... the truth of it is, that your gods can no longer protect you. But God's love is great. His protection stronger than any other power.'

'And all I have to do is accept this God? To speak his word?'

'No one can force you. It is something you must do freely.'

'And then I will be saved?'

Fabrisse felt for a moment as though she was getting somewhere. If she could persuade this girl, this priestess, then surely the rest of the clan would follow.

'You will. You *will* be saved.'

The girl's face clouded with uncertainty. She opened her mouth to respond, then stopped, her eyes fixing on something over Fabrisse's shoulder. Without another word, she hurried away into the darkness.

Fabrisse turned but saw nothing other than people dancing around the flames. Whatever had spooked Talshyn was gone now, though Fabrisse was sure she knew what it might be.

At some point she was sure she would be able to bring Talshyn into the light of God's grace. The high priestess Moldir might be an altogether more challenging prospect.

5

Estienne's destrier snorted, its breath joining the fog as they followed the three farmers along the narrow trail. They had stopped as soon as night fell, resting for a short time only to rise with the first rays of sunlight and continue their journey through the mist that had descended overnight. Carsten was positioned at the front of their small party, making a show of his authority. The farmers leading them cast nervous looks over their shoulders every few paces, their anxiety growing more pronounced the further they ventured from Rosenau's walls.

'Ever hunted bear before?' Amalric asked quietly.

'No. Boar, deer, but never bear.' Estienne replied. 'You?'

'Once. Though I was only a boy then, hardly more than a spectator.' Amalric grinned. 'The bear got away, and part of me was glad of it.'

Behind them, Rotger's massive frame filled the rear of their column, his giant warhorse easily carrying his considerable bulk. The big knight hummed tunelessly to himself, apparently unbothered by the prospect of facing such a dangerous beast.

'I've killed one,' Carsten announced from the front, clearly having overheard their conversation. 'The trick is to make sure it's surrounded. Offer it no means of escape. The beast will become almost timid when it realises it's beaten. Just a matter of striking the killing blow then.'

Estienne and Amalric exchanged a knowing look. It was obvious Carsten had never faced anything more threatening than an angry peasant. Still, Estienne kept his peace. No point antagonising the man before they'd even reached their destination.

The trail wound deeper into the forest, their horses' hooves making little sound on the damp earth. One of the farmers – the youngest of the three – stumbled on a root and caught himself with a curse. The sound echoed unnaturally in the fog.

'Quiet,' Carsten snapped, though his own voice carried far more than the farmer's. 'Do you want to warn every creature in the forest that we're coming?'

Estienne ground his teeth at Carsten's overreaction, but again said nothing. Most likely he had snapped at the young lad because of his own fear. Nothing to be ashamed of in the circumstances, but Estienne could only hope that fear wouldn't dull Carsten's judgement. If the man was even capable of making a good decision.

The village appeared through the thinning forest: thatched roofs first, then timber walls, then the people moving between them like spectres in the mist. Thin streams of woodsmoke rose from morning fires, carrying the scent of burning pine and cooking oats. The settlement was larger than Estienne had expected – perhaps thirty houses arranged in a rough circle around a central well, with livestock pens scattered between.

As they reached the edge of the village, figures emerged from doorways to watch their arrival. Estienne saw fear in their faces and did his best to stop it from unsettling him. If these hardy frontier folk were stricken with terror at this beast, it must be a formidable creature indeed.

A white-haired man hurried to meet them – the Aldermanus, Estienne guessed, noting the iron chain that marked his office. Carsten made a show of dismounting first, his spurs jingling as he landed.

'Welcome,' the old man said, bowing as deeply as his aged spine would allow. 'God bless you for coming so swiftly to our aid.'

'All is well now, old man,' Carsten replied, drinking in the gratitude. 'The Order of Saint Mary will see this beast slain. But first tell us all you know of these attacks.'

The Aldermanus straightened slowly, his wrinkled face grave. 'Three sheep taken in two days. The first was dragged away in the night – we found only blood in the morning. The second was taken at dusk, before we could get the flocks in. The third...' He paused, swallowing hard. 'The third was during the day... when young Klaus tried to drive the beast away.'

'He lives?' Estienne asked.

'He does,' the Aldermanus replied. 'Though whether he will recover the healer cannot say.'

More villagers had gathered now, forming a loose circle around the knights and their mounts and Estienne noticed how their eyes kept darting toward one particular cottage – larger than most, with bundles of dried herbs hanging from its eaves.

'The healer's house?' Estienne asked, gesturing toward the cottage.

The Aldermanus nodded. 'Yes. The boy is there still.'

'We should speak with him,' Estienne said, swinging down from his saddle. 'He will be able to tell us most about this beast.'

'No,' Carsten cut in. 'We should begin the hunt at once, before the trail grows cold.'

'With respect, Komtur, we should find out as much as we can before rushing headlong after this monster.'

The Aldermanus seized on this suggestion. 'Yes, yes – perhaps if you spoke with Klaus. He has been fevered, but his mind is clear this morning. And he saw the beast closer than any of us.'

Carsten's eye twitched as he visibly struggled with the challenge to his authority. Finally, he gave a curt nod. 'Very well. But be quick about it. We waste daylight with every moment we delay.'

The Aldermanus led Estienne across the settlement toward the large cottage. He didn't stop to knock before pushing the door open and entering. Inside, the room was dark and close, thick with the sharp scents of drying herbs and burning feverfew. Bundles of plants hung from the rafters: chamomile, yarrow, rue, thyme. In the dim light filtering through the shuttered windows, Estienne saw the boy lying on a narrow bed against the far wall, his skin waxy and pale. A woman who must have been his mother hovered nearby, wringing her hands in her apron. But it was the bandaged stump where his right arm should have been that drew Estienne's eye, the white linen spotted with dried blood.

'Klaus?' Estienne kept his voice gentle as he approached the bed. The boy's eyes fluttered open, fever-bright but alert. 'Klaus, I need to ask you about what happened. About what you saw.'

The boy licked his cracked lips. His mother hurried to bring him water, supporting his head as he drank.

'It came for the sheep again,' he began. 'I thought... I thought I could drive it off with a pitchfork. Father always said bears fear men if you make yourself big enough, if you shout... but it didn't run. It turned and... it was so fast. Faster than anything that size should be.'

Valour

'You were brave,' Estienne said. 'Many grown men would have fled facing—'

'And there were arrows,' Klaus continued, 'old arrows stuck in its hide. Like someone else had tried to kill it and failed.'

That detail made Estienne's scalp prickle. A bear that had survived previous attacks would be far more dangerous than a normal one. It would be cunning. Would have learned to be cautious of men and their weapons.

'Enough of this,' Carsten said from behind him. 'We waste time with children's tales while the beast roams free. We should—'

'These *children's tales* might save our lives.' Estienne rounded on him. 'This isn't just any beast; it's one that's survived combat with men. That makes it far more dangerous than you seem to realise. It will be wary of us. Perhaps even know how to stalk us. We are as much the hunted as the hunters, Carsten. You would do well to remember that.'

The two knights glared at each other in the dim cottage. Finally, Carsten turned on his heel and stormed out, ducking to avoid the herbs hanging from the rafters. With a final look at the dozing Klaus, and with a nod of thanks to the boy's mother, Estienne followed.

Outside, the sky had grown brighter, though a chill wind still cut through Estienne's gambeson. The four knights gathered in a loose circle, while curious villagers watched from a respectful distance.

'We should begin the hunt at once,' Carsten declared. 'The beast clearly favours this area so it can't have gone far.'

'We need a proper tracker,' Estienne countered. 'Someone who knows these forests, who can read sign and spoor. Otherwise, we're just stumbling blind. And as we've established, this is no docile beast we hunt.'

'You put too much store by that boy's tale.' Carsten bit back. 'I've tracked game since I was a young—'

'This isn't game,' Amalric cut in, absent of his usual good humour. 'This is a wounded predator. We need every advantage we can get.'

The Aldermanus suddenly cleared his throat. 'There is a man who might help. Jurgen, a trapper. He knows these lands better than any of us. Lives in a hut on the village outskirts.'

'We are knights of the Order of Saint Mary,' Carsten sneered. 'We don't need some—'

'Yes,' Estienne said firmly. 'We would be grateful for his aid. Take us to him.'

Carsten cast him what he would have intended as a withering glance, but Estienne ignored him as the Aldermanus shuffled away from the centre of the settlement. Jurgen's hut squatted at the forest's edge like a toad on a riverbank, its stone walls darkened with age and weather. Smoke rose from a clay chimney, and stakes outside held stretched pelts: fox, wolf, and what might have been lynx. The deep bark of a hunting dog heralded their approach before they'd even drawn close. A black and tan hound approached them from the doorway of the hut, and the five of them stopped in their tracks.

'Clovis! Pipe down, you damn noisy fool.'

The hound fell silent at his master's command but continued watching the knights with intelligent eyes. Its muscled shoulders and broad chest marked it as a trained hunter, not some farmer's cur.

A man emerged from the hut's low doorway, straightening to reveal impressive height. His leather jerkin and boots showed signs of hard use, and his grey-streaked beard was neatly trimmed. This was no wild man of the woods, but a trapper who took pride in his craft.

'What brings four knights of the Order to my door?' Jurgen asked in a gruff voice.

'We hunt a bear,' Estienne said simply. 'One that's already killed sheep and maimed a boy. We need someone who knows these forests.'

'Ah.' Jurgen scratched his beard thoughtfully. 'The big one that's been causing all the trouble. Would've hunted the thing myself, but I've seen its tracks – bigger than any I've found in ten years of working these forests. You'd be a damned fool to hunt it alone.'

'But you'll help us?' Estienne asked.

Jurgen regarded him for a moment, as though he was assessing the value in it. 'Aye, I suppose. I'll do the tracking, but you can do the killing. And you'll want spears, not swords. Bear's hide is too thick for a blade to do much good, and you'd not get close enough to swing one anyway.'

'We know how to kill our quarry,' Carsten interrupted, his tone suggesting he found the very conversation beneath his dignity. 'We don't need—'

'Bear that size, wounded and angry,' Jurgen continued as if the Komtur hadn't spoken, 'it'll take at least three men working as one to bring it down. And even then...'

'All you need do is track it,' Estienne assured him. 'We can do the rest.'

Jurgen studied him for another long moment, then nodded toward Clovis. 'He'll do the tracking. Best nose in the Burzenland. Just follow his lead and don't get in the way.'

'How soon can you be ready?' Estienne asked.

'Give me time to find you a spear apiece and put proper boots on. Then we'll see what Clovis can find for us.' He paused in the doorway, looking back at them with sudden severity. 'But understand this – out there, I'm in charge.'

Carsten opened his mouth as if to argue, but Estienne cut him off. 'We understand. We'll do as you say.'

The trapper disappeared into his hut, and they could hear him moving around inside, gathering equipment. Clovis remained outside on guard, still staring at them intently.

'This is intolerable,' Carsten muttered. 'To be ordered about by some common—'

'Would you rather take the lead, Komtur?' Estienne asked. 'Be the first to face this animal?'

Carsten's silence was answer enough.

Despite the dread of what they were about to face, Estienne still managed to enjoy the sudden quiet.

6

The light of early morning filtered through the smoke hole of the yurt, reflecting off the silver of the chalice Fabrisse was polishing, though it needed no more attention. Her hands wanted to keep moving, to stay busy with these final preparations rather than dwelling on the magnitude of what lay ahead.

The vessel of holy water caught those morning rays, as though reminding her that God's grace could shed light in even the humblest of settings. The beaten copper bowl that would serve to baptise an entire clan sat on a cloth of undyed wool, while around it she had arranged the other sacred implements with careful precision: the crucifix with its delicate silver corpus, the cloth for anointing, the small vessel of sacred chrism she had carried all the way from France.

'The vestments, Brother Galien,' she said softly.

The monk's hands trembled as he brought forth the folded garments. The white surplice was worn but clean. The humeral veil offered the only splash of colour she would don. Fabrisse noted how Galien's fingers shook as he laid them out, how the sweat beaded on his tonsured brow despite the morning chill.

'Be at peace,' she told him, though her own heart beat faster than she would have liked. 'We do God's work this day and He is watching.'

'Yes, my lady of Avallon.' His voice sounded so small in the confines of the yurt. 'But I cannot help but think of all that could go wrong if...' He trailed off, unable to find the right words.

Fabrisse understood his fears. She had heard the dire fates of many missionaries who ventured beyond the borders of Christendom. But fear would not serve them now.

'Light the incense, Brother Rabel,' she instructed, turning to where the other monk hovered uncertainly near the yurt's entrance. 'And join me in prayer, brothers. Let us ask for God's blessing on this holy work.'

Rabel nodded before doing as he was bid. As the rich scent of frankincense began to fill the space, Fabrisse knelt in the centre of the yurt. The brothers knelt beside her, and as their voices joined in prayer, Fabrisse felt some of her unease begin to fade.

With a renewed feeling of faith, she stood and allowed Rabel and Galien to dress her in the surplice. Reverently, Rabel placed the humeral veil over her shoulders, and together the brothers took up the bowl and holy water.

Her rosary still wrapped about her fingers, Fabrisse grasped the Bible she had brought, and clutched it to her chest. 'Are we ready, brothers?'

Galien and Rabel nodded, though they both looked anything but. Still, it was no reason for them to delay. God's work had to be done.

When Fabrisse emerged from the yurt, she found the clan already gathered in a great circle, their breath rising in pale clouds in the sharp morning air. Dozens of faces turned toward her – some eager, some uncertain, but it was only to be expected.

Tarkhan stood at the circle's centre, resplendent in his long leather coat, the fur trim at his collar and cuffs riffling in the breeze. Yet something about his bearing struck her as forced, as though he were acting in a play whose ending he could not quite be certain of.

'Greetings, Tarkhan of the White Wolf Clan,' Fabrisse said as she came to stand before him.

'And to you, Fabrisse of Avallon.'

It was then she noticed that Moldir and her young protégée were not present among the gathering. The high priestess's absence felt wrong – even if she opposed this conversion, surely she would want to bear witness?

'I trust your people are ready to be brought into the light of God's grace?' Fabrisse asked, as though to reassure herself.

'The Clan of the White Wolf is ready,' Tarkhan replied.

'Very well. Then we should begin.'

A horn sounded in reply – deep and resonant, its note carrying across the plateau. The crowd shifted, creating a path through which the first converts would approach. Fabrisse raised the crucifix, preparing to speak the words that would begin the ceremony, but movement at the circle's edge caught her eye.

Shoruk stepped forward, his face a grim mask. Several warriors moved with him, as though it were he, and not Tarkhan, who was their leader.

'Will you truly do this?' The young warrior's voice carried clearly in the morning air. 'Will you truly turn your back on Tengri, who has watched over us since our ancestors first walked these plains? Will you spurn Eje, the earth mother who has nurtured us for thousands of years?'

'The decision is made,' Tarkhan replied in frustration. 'This has been forced upon us, whether we wish it or no. We have no choice in this.'

'Do we not?' Shoruk took another step forward. More

warriors emerged from the crowd to stand with him, hands close to their weapons. 'Must we kneel to these foreign priests who call us savages? Must we abandon the gods who have protected us since—'

'Enough!' Tarkhan's voice was a wolf's snarl. 'I am still chief of this clan. The decision is mine to make.'

'No longer.'

Shoruk moved with the speed of a born warrior, his blade clearing its scabbard and catching the morning light as it swept up and across. Tarkhan's eyes went wide as the steel bit deep into his throat. His hands rose, clutching uselessly at the wound as blood sprayed forth in a crimson arc, spattering the pure white of Fabrisse's surplice. He tried to speak, but only managed a wet gurgle before collapsing to his knees.

The world seemed to stop for a heartbeat.

Then chaos took hold.

Screams started all at once, a wail of terror that seemed to tear the air apart. Fabrisse grabbed Brother Galien's arm, yanking him backward as warriors surged forward, steel flashing in the morning light. Brother Rabel stumbled after them, his face chalk-white with horror.

'This way,' she urged, pulling them back through the crowd as it surged around them.

Steel rang against steel nearby, as men shouted and died mere feet away. Warriors loyal to Tarkhan and Shoruk fought one another, where just a day earlier they had stood side by side as brothers. As Fabrisse ran, the Bible slipped from her fingers, falling forgotten in the frozen grass as they fled.

A woman ran past them, clutching a crying child to her breast. Two warriors followed, their blades already darkened with blood.

Still grasping Brother Galien's arm, Fabrisse looked vainly for

Valour 59

shelter, and they eventually hunkered behind a yurt, as the camp raged around them.

'Oh God, oh God, oh God...' Brother Rabel's voice rose in pitch with each repetition. His eyes were wide and unseeing, like a spooked horse about to bolt.

'Be still,' Fabrisse commanded, but the words came too late.

Rabel turned and ran, his brown robes flapping as he fled blindly toward the edge of the camp. A warrior spotted him, shouting something harsh she couldn't quite understand. An arrow buzzed through the air, taking the fleeing monk in the back. He stumbled but kept running, another arrow joining the first before he disappeared into the morning gloom.

'We have to—' Brother Galien started to rise, but Fabrisse pulled him back down.

'We can do nothing for him now,' she said, though the words tasted bitter. 'God guides his soul.'

More screams echoed across the camp as Shoruk's warriors hacked down those loyal to Tarkhan. Smoke began to rise as someone set fire to one of the larger yurts, flames catching quickly, and the acrid smell made Fabrisse's gorge rise.

Before she could think what to do next, a shadow fell across them. She looked up to see a warrior looming, his blade raised high, face painted with crimson streaks. His lips pulled back in a savage grin as he prepared to bring the weapon down—

'Stop!'

Talshyn materialised from the smoke, her dark robes billowing about her slight frame. The warrior hesitated, his blade still raised.

'These godless bastards are—'

'These two are not to be harmed,' the young priestess said. 'Moldir wants them alive.'

The bloodlust waned in the warrior's eyes at mention of the high priestess, before he lowered his weapon.

'Thank you,' Fabrisse whispered, but Talshyn's expression remained cold.

'Do not thank me yet, Christian,' she replied. 'There are worse fates than death by the sword.'

As if to emphasise her words, a great cheer went up from the centre of the camp. The sounds of fighting had begun to die away, replaced by the victorious howls of Shoruk's warriors.

'Come,' snarled the warrior, still gripping his bloody sword. 'Time to offer your respects to our new chief.'

He grabbed Fabrisse's arm and dragged her from her hiding place, through the smoke-filled air toward the centre of the camp. Brother Galien stumbled along beside her, Talshyn following behind.

The morning sun had risen fully now, illuminating the aftermath of the slaughter with bleak clarity. Bodies lay scattered across the frost-whitened grass, their blood already congealing in dark pools. The great circle where she had hoped to perform her baptisms had become an execution ground.

Shoruk stood beside Tarkhan's corpse, his blade still wet with his chief's blood. Other warriors were systematically stripping the dead of anything valuable – rings, weapons, even boots. The methodical nature of their looting seemed more heartless than the killing itself.

'Kneel,' the warrior growled, shoving Fabrisse forward. When she remained standing, he kicked the back of her knee, forcing her down. Brother Galien dropped down beside her with a whimper.

Shoruk approached, his blood-spattered face terrible in its triumph. Without warning, he reached down and tore the veil from her head. Fabrisse's blonde hair tumbled free, and a murmur ran through the watching warriors.

'So,' Shoruk said, his voice thick with contempt. 'This is what Tarkhan would have had us become. Weak. Tame. On our knees.' He raised his blade, looking out over his followers. 'I think it's time we showed these Christians what becomes of those who try to chain the wolf.'

There was a howl of approval, but Fabrisse raised her chin, meeting his gaze. 'I do not fear death. God's love is stronger than your hate.'

Shoruk's blade touched her throat, its edge ice-cold against her skin. 'You must think your god powerful indeed. Let's see if he can save you now.'

'Stay your hand, my son.'

The voice was chill as a shard of ice. Moldir appeared from the gathering smoke, her face bearing an expression of such terrible purpose that even Shoruk took a step back.

'These Christians are mine,' she continued. 'Their deaths must serve a greater purpose than mere vengeance.'

'What purpose?' Shoruk demanded, though he lowered his blade.

Moldir's lips curved into a contemptuous smile. 'Our gods demand redress for this insult, warrior. And here are worthy sacrifices.'

'Then let it be done,' Shoruk demanded, brandishing his blade with eagerness.

'Patience, Shorukhan. Patience.' Moldir's dark eyes fixed on Fabrisse with horrible intensity.

'Please,' Brother Galien whispered, but whether he was begging God or their captors, Fabrisse couldn't tell. Either way his pleading went unheard.

'Bind them well,' Moldir commanded. 'And have them watched. They must come to no harm until the time is right.'

As eager hands seized her arms, Fabrisse saw that the camp had become a vision of hell. Burning yurts sent columns of black smoke into the sky, while warriors moved among the dead like carrion birds, taking what they wished.

She had come to cleanse these people. To save them.

Now it seemed they would all be damned together.

7

The forest pressed in close, branches clawing at them as they followed Jurgen's lead through the undergrowth. The mist still clung between the trees, so they could only see a few yards ahead, though shafts of wan sunlight occasionally pierced the canopy above, lighting the trail.

Jurgen moved nimbly, despite his years, eyes constantly scanning the surrounding vegetation. His hound, Clovis, padded silently beside him, nose working the ground.

The four knights followed close behind, gripping their spears tightly. Rotger brought up the rear, moving with surprising agility for a man of his size. Estienne and Amalric crept side by side, while Carsten walked ahead. His eyes darted from side to side, as though he expected them to come under attack at any second. Estienne couldn't shake the feeling his caution was well-placed.

'We must be getting close by now,' Carsten announced, breaking the silence. 'How much deeper into this accursed forest do we have to—'

'Quiet.' Jurgen's command was low, but it carried enough authority to silence Carsten. The trapper knelt, examining something in the mud before rising to his feet. 'Bear shite. Still warm. We're getting close.'

'How close?' Carsten asked. 'A mile? Two?'

'Can't rightly say. Depends if the beast is still on the move or if it's—'

'Can't rightly say,' Carsten replied, barely hiding his contempt. 'I thought you were an expert.'

'When was the last time you hunted bear, Komtur?' Amalric's question carried just enough innocence to avoid being openly disrespectful, though Estienne caught the slight smile playing at the corners of his friend's mouth.

'I'll have you know that I—' Carsten began, but Jurgen cut him off with a sharp gesture.

'Less talk. More vigilance.' The trapper's eyes never left the ground as he moved forward, Clovis at his heel. 'Bear will hear us coming a mile away if we keep chattering like fishwives.'

'Perhaps that's just what we need,' Carsten declared. 'To draw the beast toward us so we might—'

A twig snapped somewhere in the undergrowth ahead. Everyone froze, and Carsten fell silent at last. For a long moment, the only sound was their breathing and the soft whisper of wind through the leaves above. Then Clovis's ears pricked forward, his muscles tensing beneath his black and tan coat. Jurgen immediately nocked an arrow to his bow, his movements deliberate and silent. Following his lead, Estienne hefted his spear, the other knights doing the same.

The forest had gone deathly quiet. No birdsong, no rustle of animals in the undergrowth. Even Carsten seemed to sense the gravity of the moment, his usual bluster forgotten as he stared wide-eyed into the misty shadows between the trees.

Clovis let out a low growl and his hackles rose. Still gripping his bow, Jurgen reached down to rest a steadying hand on the dog's broad shoulders.

'The thicket ahead,' the trapper breathed. 'Something big in there.'

Estienne nodded, tightening his grip on the spear shaft, but the weapon suddenly felt inadequate. If something was concealed in that tangle of vegetation, it was almost certainly aware of their presence.

'Send the dog in?' Amalric suggested. 'Flush it out?'

Jurgen shook his head. 'Be more likely Clovis would only spook the beast to flight. Then we're on the hunt again.'

A deep, rumbling sound cut through the air – not quite a growl, not quite a breath, but something that made the hair on the back of Estienne's neck stand up. Clovis's growl deepened in response, and Jurgen had to tighten his grip on the hound's scruff to keep him from charging forward.

'Mother of God,' Rotger breathed from behind them. 'How big is this thing?'

'Well, we can't very well stand here all day,' Carsten snapped. 'Someone has to—'

He was cut short by the crack of twigs and frantic rustle of undergrowth. The bear erupted from cover with a roar that shook the air, a mountain of muscle and fury that made Estienne's breath catch in his throat. Several broken arrow shafts protruded from its shaggy hide, testament to previous failed attempts to kill it.

Jurgen's bow sang, his arrow taking the beast in the shoulder. The shaft buried itself deep, but the wound only fuelled its rage, and it charged forward with impossible speed for something so massive, covering the ground between them in heartbeats.

'Form up!' Estienne bellowed, trying to bite down his own panic. 'Stick together or—'

The rest of his words were lost in the bear's earthshaking roar. Carsten lunged forward with his spear, more instinct than intent, but the bear swept the weapon aside with one enormous paw. The shaft snapped like kindling, and Carsten stumbled aside with a cry of terror.

Rotger showed more courage, driving his spear deep into the bear's flank. For a moment it seemed the big knight might actually halt the creature's charge, but then his weapon's shaft split with a loud crack. The beast swiped a huge paw at him, and Rotger was sent lurching back to land in the ferns.

'Keep the thing at bay,' Jurgen shouted, loosing another arrow that flew wide of its mark. 'Don't let it—'

The beast spun with terrifying agility, jaws snapping at Amalric as he tried to circle behind it. Estienne stabbed with his own spear, hoping to drive the point into the bear's throat, but lost his footing in the churned earth. The thrust went wide, and he had a moment to feel a sense of primal terror as the beast pounced.

Estienne's spear slipped from his sweat-slicked grip as he dove clear, half expecting the monstrous beast to fall upon him with all its considerable weight. Instead, he rolled to his feet in time to see the bear crash its way through the underbrush with renewed fury.

'It's running!' Amalric shouted, already moving to give chase.

Estienne snatched up his fallen spear and plunged after the bear. Their feet pounded the soft earth as they crashed through the forest in pursuit. Broken branches and torn vegetation marked the beast's path, and they gained ground rapidly – too rapidly, Estienne realised too late. The bear wasn't running from them at all; it was drawing them away from the rest of their group.

The massive creature wheeled suddenly, rising to its full

height. Estienne skidded to a stop, boots sliding through rotten leaves, as he found himself staring up at a wall of muscle and fur. The bear's roar was deafening, hot breath washing over him with the stench of raw meat.

Amalric thrust his spear forward, trying to keep the beast at bay, but the bear's jaws clamped down on the shaft with crushing force. Wood splintered, and Amalric was suddenly holding nothing but a useless stick as the bear reared once more.

Estienne drove his own spear into the creature's belly, feeling it bite deep. The bear's bellow shook the earth at his feet, but instead of fleeing, the wound only intensified the beast's anger.

One massive paw swept out, faster than Estienne could react. Claws raked across his gambeson, shredding the padded armour at his upper arm and opening the flesh beneath. The blow sent him stumbling backward, and his boots caught on an exposed root. He hit the ground hard, the breath driven from his lungs. Above him, the bear loomed, its bulk blotting out the sky. Those killing claws spread wide, ready to end him.

A hiss, before the arrow struck the bear's throat. Its roar turned to a wet gurgle, as it took one stumbling step forward. Then its legs buckled.

Estienne rolled desperately aside as the massive creature crashed to the ground beside him, its last breath rattling out. Jurgen emerged from the trees, already nocking another arrow just in case, but the bear was well and truly dead, its tongue lolling, eyes already glassed over.

For a long moment, the only sound was Estienne's own fevered breathing and the hammer of his heart. Then Amalric's voice broke the silence.

'Well, I suppose that could have gone a little more smoothly.'

'Damn fool thing to do,' Jurgen said, though there was a hint of admiration in his gruff voice. 'Running after it like that. Could have gotten you both killed.'

'Could have,' Estienne agreed, wincing as he pushed himself to his feet. His arm stung where the bear's claws had found him, but at least he'd live. 'But I never doubted you for a minute, old man.' It was then that Clovis padded into the clearing to sit by his master's side. 'Either of you.'

8

Dawn cast long shadows across the plateau. Talshyn's feet crunched on frosty ground as she approached the prisoners, a waterskin clutched in her hands. The leather felt cold against her palms, nearly as cold as the knot that had settled in her stomach since the previous day's bloodshed.

The Christian woman and her companion sat bound with rope, their backs together. Fabrisse's grey robe was now stained with dirt, but she held her head high, refusing to be broken by her circumstances. Talshyn could only admire her for that. Beside her, the young priest wept quietly, his head bowed in prayer or despair. Perhaps both. Neither had slept, that much was clear from the dark shadows beneath their eyes.

Talshyn knelt before them, uncorking the waterskin before raising it to Fabrisse's lips. 'Drink. Please.'

The holy woman's eyes met hers, and Talshyn nearly recoiled from the intensity of that gaze. There was no fear there, only a determination that made Talshyn's chest tighten with shame.

'Why?' Fabrisse asked after she had drunk. 'Why did this happen?'

'The old ways must be preserved,' Talshyn replied.

It was what Moldir had told her so many times. What she had always believed without question.

'The old ways?' Fabrisse's voice carried no judgement, only curiosity. 'You mean the ways of your gods? Gods that would allow the brutal murder of your chief? Your people?'

Before Talshyn could respond, the young priest raised his head.

'Please,' he whispered, 'have mercy. We meant no harm. We only wished to bring God's light—'

'Talshyn.' Moldir's voice cut through the still air. Talshyn jerked to her feet, nearly dropping the waterskin. Her mistress stood only a few feet away. 'Come, girl.'

'Yes, Kam Katun,' Talshyn called back, her voice smaller than she would have liked.

She glanced down at the prisoners one last time. Fabrisse had returned to staring straight ahead, her lips moving in silent prayer, while the little priest had resumed his weeping.

Turning away from the sorry sight, Talshyn followed Moldir through what remained of their camp, trying not to look too closely at the destruction. Burned yurts still smouldered, sending thin tendrils of smoke into the pale morning sky. The ground was churned to mud in places, stained dark with spilled blood. A child's doll lay forgotten in the grass, its sewn face staring accusingly up at her.

They walked until they reached a spinney of wind-bent trees at the camp's edge, far enough from curious ears. Moldir turned to face her, and Talshyn fought the urge to step back. There was something different about her mistress now – something hungry in her eyes that Talshyn had never seen before.

'You have questions,' Moldir said. 'Ask them.'

Valour 71

Talshyn swallowed. 'What happens now? Now that we're not to be converted?'

Moldir's laugh was like ice cracking. 'Now? Now we continue on the true path.'

Talshyn nodded. She had known the answer all along. 'The path of Erlik.'

The god of death. Lord of Tamag – the underworld, where the unworthy were sent to rot for eternity. Moldir had always secretly followed the way of Erlik, not the weak way of Tengri and Eje, gods who demanded nothing but empty prayers and meaningless rituals. The Kam Katun had kept it secret from Tarkhan for years, secret from Shoruk, secret from everyone but Talshyn. Even her title was a lie – she was no Kam Katun, but a Kara Kam – a black shaman.

'And are you still willing to follow me on that path, girl?'

Talshyn knew she had to respond as though her life might depend on it.

'Of course, Kara Kam.'

She imbued that answer with as much conviction as she could, and Moldir's expression bore some satisfaction. But for the first time since she had sworn to follow the path of Erlik, Talshyn felt doubt. The prospect of being converted to the Christian faith had been a tantalising one. The chance to follow a different road than one that only led to darkness.

'He demands blood.' Moldir continued. 'The Christians thought they could turn us from our gods with pretty words and promises. But Erlik's hunger can only be satisfied with sacrifice. Real sacrifice.'

'The prisoners,' Talshyn whispered, understanding dawning. 'You mean to—'

'They will serve a greater purpose.' Moldir's hand shot out, gripping Talshyn's arm with surprising strength. 'You've seen it in your dreams, haven't you? The darkness calling? The power that waits in the depths of Tamag? This is how we will seize it – by spilling the blood of our enemies in Erlik's name.'

Talshyn tried to speak, but her throat had gone dry. She had experienced strange dreams lately – visions of endless black and ancient hunger. But she had dismissed them as nightmares born of too much mare's milk.

'I...' she started, but Moldir's grip tightened.

'You are meant for greater things than being some Christian god's servant. Erlik has chosen you, as he chose me. The dreams are his call. Will you answer?'

A crow's caw split the morning silence, making Talshyn jump. She looked up to see it wheeling overhead, black against the pale sky. When she looked back at Moldir, her mistress was watching her with an intensity that made her skin crawl.

'Yes, Kara Kam,' she whispered.

Moldir's smile revealed her chipped and blackened teeth. 'Good. Now come – there is much to prepare.'

As they walked back toward the camp, Talshyn caught the stench of the dead smouldering on their pyres, smoke rising black against the morning sky. The acrid smell of burning flesh and hair made her stomach roil, but she forced herself to remain still, to show no weakness.

Tarkhan's body lay atop the largest pyre, his rich coat now nothing but fuel for the flames. Shoruk stood before it, his hard face illuminated by the fire. He looked nothing like the loyal warrior who had served their chief for so many years. Power had transformed him into something harder, crueller.

'The gods are watching, Shoruk,' Moldir said, as she stepped closer to him. 'They saw what was done here.'

Shoruk continued staring into the flames. 'What was done was necessary.'

Valour

'Necessary, yes. But blood spilled must be answered for, when it is brother against brother. The gods demand sacrifice – not just these burning bodies, but something more.' She gestured across the camp to where their prisoners were bound. 'Something worthy.'

'The Christian woman?'

'And her companion. Their deaths will please Tengri and appease what was done here last night. But it must be done at the shrine of Kyzaghan.'

Shoruk's brow creased. 'The god of war's shrine lies days to the north.'

'Only there can we properly appease the gods for this bloodshed.'

Shoruk turned from the pyre, his expression darkening. 'By travelling through mountain passes with the threat of coming snows? It is too dangerous. Why not simply kill them here and be done with it?'

Several warriors nodded their agreement, but Moldir stepped forward, her presence somehow growing until she seemed to tower over them all.

'You would deny the gods their due?' She reached out, touching the blood-stained fabric of Shoruk's coat. 'That blood must be answered for, warrior. Answered with the death of those who would turn us from our gods. Or do you think Tengri will simply forget?'

Shoruk's jaw worked as he struggled with the decision. Talshyn could see the doubt in his eyes; his urge to defy Moldir weighed against losing face to his clan. He might have seized his position as their chief, but the old beliefs still held him in their grip.

'The shrine, then,' he finally growled. 'But if we lose warriors to the mountain cold...'

'The strong will survive,' Moldir cut him off. 'As they always have.'

A log collapsed in one of the pyres, sending a shower of sparks into the air. As she watched the embers glow, Talshyn wondered how many more would die before this was done. She knew what was really happening. This wasn't about appeasing Tengri – it was about feeding Erlik's hunger for death. Moldir's way of satisfying her god with yet more sacrifice.

'We should not tarry then,' Shoruk said, turning to his men. 'Uzur, Boril. Gather the clan. I would speak to them before we go. The rest of you, prepare the horses.'

His warriors began to disperse, moving to prepare for the journey ahead. At the call of Uzur and Boril, the clan gathered around Tarkhan's pyre, their breath rising in pale clouds. Talshyn stood to one side, watching faces fall as their new chief told them of the journey ahead. The elderly shifted uneasily, while mothers clutched their children closer.

An old woman stepped forward, her back bent with age but her voice still strong. 'Many of us cannot make such a journey. Not with winter closing in. We will not survive.'

'Those who cannot join us will remain here,' Shoruk declared, his voice carrying across the assembled crowd.

'And what of food? What of horses? How are we to survive without warriors to protect us?'

Shoruk's eyes shifted toward Moldir, then back at the crowd. 'Our gods will watch over you, old woman. Tengri and Eje will protect their children as they always have.'

Protests erupted, voices rising in anger and fear. A young mother holding an infant stepped forward, her face streaked with tears. 'Please, we have children! You cannot—'

Shoruk's hand fell to his sword hilt, and the protests died as quickly as they had begun. Talshyn watched as warriors moved through the crowd, already beginning to gather supplies. They took everything – dried meat, fermented milk, even the heavy blankets that would mean the difference between life and death in the mountain cold.

'You're killing us,' someone whispered, but no one dared speak louder.

Talshyn felt something break inside her as she watched. These were her people – the ones she had grown up with, played with as a child, tended to as a priestess. Now they were being left to die, sacrificed to the very gods who were supposed to keep them safe.

As the warriors began to prepare their mounts, Talshyn's gaze was drawn to Fabrisse. The Christian woman's hands were being secured to a rope, which in turn was bound to a saddle horn. Still, she stood straight-backed, refusing to be broken by her bondage.

Their eyes met, and Talshyn felt something shift in her chest as the holy woman seemed to see right through to Talshyn's soul. There was no hatred in Fabrisse's gaze, no condemnation – only a deep sadness. In that moment, she understood that she had a choice to make. She could continue down this path with Moldir, helping to feed Erlik's endless hunger, or—

'Talshyn.' Moldir's sharp voice cut through her wayward thoughts. 'Come. We ride.'

She turned away from Fabrisse's gaze, but the weight of it remained. As she mounted her horse, she could still hear the soft weeping of those they were leaving behind. The sound followed them as they rode north, a chorus of despair that even the wind couldn't drown out.

9

The great hall rang with laughter and the sound of hands hammering against wooden tables. Flames danced in the twin hearths at either end, their warmth barely reaching the centre where Estienne sat with Amalric and Rotger. Steam rose from a platter of roasted boar, the rich smell of meat permeating the air.

'...and there I was, face-to-face with the colossal beast!' Carsten's voice carried clearly from the high table, where he sat at Marschall Dieter's right hand, gesturing expansively. 'Its eyes blazed with murderous intent, foam dripping from its savage jaws...'

Amalric caught Estienne's eye across the table and made an unsubtle yawning gesture. Estienne had to bite back a laugh. They both knew the truth of that hunt. How Carsten had almost soiled himself when the bear appeared, how his spear shaft had snapped at the first charge, and he had flung himself unceremoniously out of harm's way.

'Notice how the beast grows larger with each telling,' Rotger mumbled around a mouthful of meat. 'Soon it'll be the size of an aurochs.'

Valour

'With balls to match,' Amalric added with a grin.

Estienne tore off a chunk of dark bread, using it to soak up the boar's rich juices. The food was good tonight – better than their usual fare. The kitchen had outdone themselves, perhaps at the behest of Marschall Dieter as reward for the returning heroes. One of whom seemed determined to build his own part up.

'Without hesitation, I met its charge!' Carsten's voice rose triumphantly. 'My spear found its mark, driving deep into the monster's black heart—'

Estienne's knuckles whitened around his cup. It had been Jurgen's arrow that brought the beast down, saving Estienne's life in the process. To hear Carsten claim that victory...

'Brother.' Amalric's quiet voice cut through his rising fury. 'Let him have his moment. We know the truth.'

'And the truth should matter,' Estienne murmured.

Amalric shrugged off the notion. 'All the world sees a braggart for what he is. His lies harm no one but himself.'

'They harm the Order's honour.'

'The Order's honour rests on solid foundations. It cannot be challenged by one man's boasts.' Amalric raised his cup. 'To the real heroes of the hunt – Jurgen and his hound.'

Rotger and Estienne raised their cups in answer. The ale was dark and bitter, locally brewed and strong enough to warm the blood. As Estienne drank, he tried to let his anger subside. Amalric was right; Carsten's lies brought dishonour on no one but himself.

'...and as the mighty beast fell, its death roar shook the—'

Carsten's bragging was cut short by the shrill sound of the warning bell.

It rang out across the fortress, echoing off the stone walls, and for a heartbeat, silence gripped the hall. Then men leaped from benches, reaching for weapons. Tankards clattered to the floor, spilling wine, and the cheerful atmosphere vanished to be replaced by grim faces as everyone flooded from the room.

Estienne followed the surge of knights into the courtyard. The warning bell's toll had given way to shouts from the walls. Through the open gates to the mountain pass, he could see a lone figure stumbling toward them in the gathering dusk.

'By all the saints,' Amalric breathed beside him. 'Is that... one of the friars?'

The figure wore the brown robes of a monk, but they were torn and stained dark with dried blood. Two arrow shafts protruded from his back and thigh, and he swayed with each lurching step, face a mask of exhaustion.

'Brother Rabel?' Estienne pushed through the crowd as the friar staggered through the gates. The man's lips were cracked and bleeding, his eyes wild with delirium.

'Water,' Rabel gasped. 'Please...'

Estienne caught him as his legs gave way. The friar's body was burning with fever, yet trembling as though gripped by winter's chill. Someone pressed a waterskin into Estienne's hands, and he helped Rabel drink. The friar choked on the first swallow, water spilling down his chin.

'Slowly,' Estienne cautioned. 'Where are the others, Rabel? Where is the Lady Fabrisse?'

'I... I don't know.' The words came out as a sob. 'All dead... perhaps. Tarkhan... they killed him. The pagans... they...' Rabel's voice broke.

'Speak clearly, brother.' Marschall Dieter's commanding tone cut through the subdued quiet. 'What happened?'

Rabel's fingers dug into Estienne's arm with surprising strength. 'It was to be a baptism. The whole clan gathered... but then one of the pagans drew his blade. Cut their chieftain's throat

Valour 79

before anyone could move. They began to slay one another. The screaming... there was so much screaming...'

A murmur rippled through the assembled knights. Estienne felt ice form in his gut as he remembered his warnings to Fabrisse. And how she had ignored them.

'The Lady of Avallon?' the Marschall pressed. 'And Brother Galien? Did you see them slain along with the rest?'

'They were... still alive when I... when I left them.' Rabel's voice cracked, his eyes filling with tears. 'I ran... like a coward, I ran. The noise... the slaughter... I couldn't help it. Had to warn you. I left them. God forgive me, I left them to die...'

'You did what you had to,' Estienne said firmly. 'You brought us word.'

But Rabel was beyond hearing as his eyes rolled back and consciousness finally fled, his rigid body going limp in Estienne's arms.

Two serving brothers pushed through the crowd. The older one, Brother Ludger, a man well-versed in the healing arts, knelt beside Rabel's unconscious form, his hands moving with practised efficiency as he examined the wounds.

'The arrows will need to come out quickly,' Brother Ludger muttered, more to himself than anyone else. 'Before infection takes too strong a hold. God willing, we can save him. But only if we're quick about it.'

Estienne helped them lift the fallen friar. Blood had soaked through Rabel's robes where the arrow shafts protruded, the fabric stiff and dark. The serving brothers nodded grimly as they took his weight, one at each shoulder, then guided him toward the infirmary.

'The Lady of Avallon is lost to us,' Marschall Dieter declared, his voice heavy with resignation. 'I can ask no man to venture beyond our walls after her. The pagans will be waiting, and such a mission would be tantamount to suicide.'

Silence fell across the courtyard. Estienne found himself recalling Fabrisse's penetrating gaze in the chapel, as though she could see right through him.

When I look at you, I sense a man running from something, she had said.

Her words had cut deeper than she knew.

Estienne had dismissed her words, but there was truth in what she'd said – he had abandoned more than just his faith in the Holy Land. He had nearly abandoned the code that had made him a knight, the principles that had once guided his every action. To protect the innocent. To stand firm against injustice. To face danger without flinching. These were the tenets he had lived by before disillusionment had taken root.

If he let Fabrisse face her fate alone, whatever remained of the Black Lion would die here and now. He would be just a man without purpose or principle.

'I'll go,' Estienne said, his voice cutting through the silence.

'And I.' Amalric stepped forward to stand beside him. No hesitation, no doubt, just the unwavering loyalty Estienne had come to expect from his friend.

Marschall Dieter turned to Carsten, who shifted uncomfortably, his earlier bravado forgotten. 'What about you, Komtur? We were all taken with your earlier tale of bravery. I would not think to deny you another chance to demonstrate your valour.'

Carsten's face flushed. 'And I am grateful, Marschall. But... perhaps—'

'I'll go too!' Rotger's booming voice drowned out Carsten's stammering. The big knight pushed through the crowd, his usual cheerful expression replaced by grim determination.

'You'll need shield bearers.' The Marschall turned to where

the squires had gathered. Two young lads stepped forward, eagerness writ on their unblemished faces.

'Meister Eggert, Meister Merten? I cannot ask this of you without first—'

'God will guide our path, Marschall,' Eggert said, his young face alight with fervour. 'We will not fail.'

'Yes, Marschall.' Merten was more hesitant, but his voice steadied as he continued. 'We won't let you down.'

'Then time is against us,' Dieter said. 'Gather what supplies you can. You ride at first light. Find the Lady of Avallon and return her to the safety of Rosenau. God go with you. And if you can, bring His judgement to those heathens.'

Estienne felt a familiar tension beginning to build in his gut – a mixture of anticipation and dread. Dark clouds had begun gathering above Rosenau's battlements, the air growing thick with the promise of rain.

'Storm's coming. Big one. It will make tracking nearly impossible.' Carsten's voice dripped with barely concealed relief. 'Perhaps we should wait until—'

'We cannot wait,' Estienne replied. 'Lives may depend on it.'

'But how are we to find their trail in the midst of a rainstorm?'

'I know just the man for that.' Estienne said, as thunder rolled in the distance. 'Assuming he's willing to hunt something more dangerous than bears.'

10

———

Rain hammered down, drenching them all as they rode. Water had long since worked its way through Estienne's thick wool cloak, turning his gambeson into a sodden mass. His destrier plodded forward, hooves breaking through the softening earth with wet sucking sounds, as though the ground itself were desperate to hamper their progress.

Ahead, Jurgen led them through the downpour, the trapper's leather jerkin dark with moisture. His hound Clovis padded beside his horse, nose working the muddy ground despite the cascade of water that threatened to wash away any trace of their quarry. The dog's determination seemed to mirror his master's – where others might have given up the trail, Jurgen pressed on with grim resolve.

They had passed the point where Estienne and the others had handed the missionaries over to their pagan guides. Now Clovis followed the trail Rabel had left while fleeing the massacre at the pagan encampment. Once they reached it, there would hopefully be clues as to where those pagans had taken Fabrisse and Galien,

Valour 83

were they even still alive. If not, their pursuit would end in abrupt failure.

A flash of lightning split the sky, followed almost immediately by a thunderclap that made their mounts flinch nervously. In that brief illumination, Estienne caught sight of the young squires – Eggert and Merten – huddled miserably in their saddles. Even Rotger's usual good humour seemed dampened by the relentless downpour.

'The rain's getting worse,' Amalric said, drawing his horse alongside Estienne's. 'If it continues like this, we'll lose what little trail we have.'

'Then we'd best move faster,' Estienne replied. He raised his voice to carry over the storm. 'Jurgen, can we pick up the pace?'

The trapper shook his head. 'Rain is making it difficult enough as it is. If we end up following the wrong sign it could cost us days.'

'We shouldn't even be here,' Carsten called out. 'We should return to Rosenau and wait for better weather.'

'And what of the Lady Fabrisse?' Estienne snapped, twisting in his saddle to face the Komtur. 'Shall we leave her to the tender mercies of those pagans while we wait for sunshine?'

'Better that than riding to our deaths on this fool's errand.'

'Turn back, if that's what you want, Komtur. But the rest of us will do our duty.'

Carsten's mouth worked as he bit back his retort, but it seemed even he had no answer. Instead, he wrenched his horse's reins and carried on along with the others.

They proceeded with greater caution, as the rain grew even heavier, reducing visibility to mere yards. Estienne found himself watching the surrounding hills with growing unease, all too aware of how vulnerable they were to an ambush in these conditions. But an ambush, it seemed, would be the least of their woes...

The sound reached them before the sight – a deep roar that grew louder as they crested a ridge. Below, what should have been a modest stream had transformed into a churning river, its waters brown with mud and choked with debris torn from its banks. Trees bobbed like twigs in the current, occasionally catching against rocks until the force of the water tore them free.

'God's blood,' Amalric breathed. 'Is this the only way to proceed, Jurgen?'

The trapper nodded grimly. 'Normally you can walk across here without getting your knees wet. But with all this rain...'

Estienne studied the raging waters, trying to gauge their depth and speed. The crossing point was perhaps twenty yards wide. Branches and other debris raced past, weapons that could easily knock a man from his horse or tangle in a mount's legs.

'We'll have to find another way across,' Carsten declared. 'There must be somewhere upstream.'

'The nearest crossing is two days' ride,' Jurgen replied. 'And it's probably as bad as this anyway.'

'Then we travel downstream until we find a better ford.'

'And waste precious time?' Estienne snapped. 'The more we take the more chance Fabrisse and—'

'Better they suffer a few more days than we all drown trying to cross this river,' Carsten shot back. 'I am still Komtur here, and I say we find another way.'

Estienne looked at the rest of the group, watching on expectantly. The squires appeared terrified at the prospect of attempting the crossing, while Rotger's expression was troubled. Only Amalric seemed calm, though Estienne knew his friend well enough to see the tension in his square jaw.

Valour 85

'The water's still rising,' Jurgen observed. 'Another hour of this rain and it'll be all but impassable.'

'Then we make our crossing now,' Estienne said. 'Every moment we delay puts those we're meant to protect in greater danger.'

'They're probably already dead.' Carsten's voice bore a terrified edge. 'You would risk all our lives on the slim chance they're still alive?'

'Even if there's only a small chance they live, we took oaths to protect them.'

'Oaths that won't mean much if we're all drowned in that river.'

Estienne dismounted, his boots sinking into the muddy bank. 'Then stay here if you're afraid, Komtur. The rest of us will find a way across without you.'

Estienne stripped off his gambeson and stowed it on his horse, alongside his mail, sword and shield. His destrier shifted nervously as he checked its girth strap and halter, its flanks trembling at the roar of the water, as though it knew what he intended to do.

'This is suicide,' Carsten declared, but Estienne ignored him.

'If I make it across,' he told Jurgen, gesturing to the length of rope hanging from Eggert's saddle, 'throw me the other end of that. It'll be easier for the rest of you to follow.'

The trapper nodded. 'Try to find a sturdy tree on the far bank. Something that won't tear free when we put our weight on it.'

Estienne gripped his destrier's reins and led it toward the water's edge. The horse balked at first, tossing its head until he spoke softly to it, stroking its neck. Finally, it followed him into the river.

The cold gripped him as he waded in. What had looked deep

from the bank proved deeper still and within two steps he was up to his thighs, the current trying to sweep his legs out from under him. His destrier snorted in alarm as the water rose around its legs, but the well-trained beast trusted him enough to keep moving forward.

Ten feet and he was up to his waist, the freezing water driving the breath from his lungs. Twenty, and the ground dropped away completely. Estienne grabbed his horse's mane, letting it pull him along, as the current caught them immediately, trying to drag them downstream. His destrier's hooves churned the water as it fought against the current, its breathing becoming laboured.

Halfway across, a partially submerged log caught his horse's leg, causing it to lose its rhythm and he his footing. Estienne went under, water filling his nose and mouth as he clung desperately to his mount's mane. Then they surfaced, the horse thrashing in panic as it tried to right itself.

'Easy,' he gasped, spitting out river water. 'Easy, boy.'

His horse steadied enough to resume swimming, but Estienne's arms burned from the effort of holding on, his legs numb from the cold. Each breath was a struggle as spray and rain competed to fill his lungs. But he could see the far bank – almost there.

The destrier's hooves finally found purchase on the river bottom, though the current still tried to tear them both off their feet. Estienne stumbled alongside his mount, and with a final surge of effort, they reached the solid ground. Estienne's legs shook as he helped his horse up the muddy slope, its sides heaving with exhaustion. He took just enough time to ensure the beast was safely clear of the water before turning back to their companions.

'Rope!' he bellowed, his voice barely carrying over the storm.

Rotger's powerful arm sent the coiled rope sailing across the

Valour 87

river, one end held tight in Amalric's grip. Estienne plucked the rope from the air, then secured it to the fallen tree, testing the knot with his numb fingers. Satisfied it would hold, he looked back across the river, seeing Amalric securing it to a similarly sturdy-looking tree.

Estienne nodded for them to proceed. He'd shown it could be done. Now they just had to pray the rope would hold.

Jurgen went first, hefting Clovis onto his horse's saddle before entering the water. The hound whined pitifully but stayed still, as the trapper led his steed with deliberate care, one hand gripping the rope.

'Steady, Jurgen,' Estienne called as a wave threatened to sweep the trapper's feet from under him. 'Take your time.'

Jurgen made no reply, all his concentration focused on each step. Halfway across, Clovis suddenly yelped and tried to scramble higher on the saddle, but the old hunter soothed the hound with a quiet word and moments later they reached the relative safety of the far bank.

The squires went next, accompanied by their horses. Young Eggert led the way, his face pale but determined as he fought his way across. Merten followed, and though he slipped once, sending a collective gasp through the watching group, he managed to maintain his hold on both rope and reins.

Carsten was next, urging his horse into the water with more speed than wisdom, cursing as the current immediately tried to sweep them away. Only his death grip on the rope kept him from being carried downstream, but the mount persevered and they finally reached the far bank.

Rotger's massive frame worked to his advantage as he stood firm against the current. His warhorse followed placidly despite the tempestuous waters, and they made it look almost easy, though Estienne could see the big knight's arms trembling from the effort when he finally reached safety.

That left only Amalric, and Estienne's friend paused on the bank, checking his horse's tack one final time before beginning the crossing. In the time it had taken the others to cross, the rain had grown even heavier, the water level rising noticeably.

'Hurry,' Estienne called. 'Before it gets any worse.'

Amalric nodded and urged his mount forward. They were barely ten feet out when a massive tree trunk came careening downstream, right toward them. The impact knocked Amalric's horse off balance, and in its panic, the beast reared up, wrenching the reins from his grip.

'Amalric!' Estienne's shout was lost to the raging torrent as his friend disappeared beneath the surface, his horse swept away by the current.

For a terrible moment, there was no sign of him, then his head broke water, one hand still miraculously gripping the rope. He tried to pull himself along toward the far bank, but the weight of his sodden clothing and the force of the water made progress almost impossible.

Without hesitation, Estienne grabbed another length of rope from Merten's saddle and tied it around his waist.

'Hold this,' he ordered, throwing the free end to Rotger. Then he was in the water again, fighting his way along the rope line toward his friend.

The current felt stronger than before, trying to tear him away from the rope with every yard he worked his way along it. His muscles screamed in protest as he pulled himself toward Amalric, knowing that if he lost his grip, even Rotger's strength might not be enough to save him.

Amalric's strength looked to be failing, his grip on the rope

Valour 89

weakening as Estienne drew closer. Another piece of debris slammed into him, and he nearly lost his hold completely.

'Hang on!' Estienne reached out, managing to grab Amalric's wrist just as his friend's fingers slipped from the rope.

For a moment, they were both suspended in the current, held fast by the rope around Estienne's waist. Then Rotger and the others began pulling, slowly dragging them back toward the bank. Both men gasped for air as they were dragged through the water, but finally Estienne's feet found solid ground. Together, they hauled Amalric from the river, collapsing in an exhausted heap on the muddy shore.

'I told you this was madness!' Carsten's voice cut through the deluge. 'We've lost a horse and valuable supplies, and for what? To save ourselves a day's travel?'

Estienne dragged himself to his feet, rounding on Carsten so their noses were almost touching. 'We are fine, Komtur. Thank you for your concern.'

Carsten glared back, but gradually the fire in his eyes died when faced with Estienne's fury.

'Peace, brothers.' Amalric put a restraining hand on Estienne's arm. 'We lost a steed, but we all still live. We should be thankful for that, at least.'

Estienne let out a long breath as Carsten turned away, nothing more to say.

Young Eggert stepped forward, leading his mount. 'Brother Amalric, please take my horse. I can ride with Merten.'

Amalric looked like he might refuse, but instead nodded. 'You have my thanks, Meister Eggert. I'll not forget this.'

As they gathered themselves, preparing to press on, Jurgen and Clovis moved to higher ground, studying the path ahead. The rain continued unabated, and thunder still rolled across the hills, as Estienne came to stand beside the trapper.

'Rabel's trail leads north-east,' Jurgen announced, pointing toward a narrow valley between two steep hills. 'I don't think we're far now.'

'Then we'd best not tarry,' Estienne replied, his eyes taking in the trail ahead.

Not far to go. He could only hope it would be in time... and there'd be no more obstacles in their path.

11

——————

The rope bit into Fabrisse's wrists, the hemp having rubbed her skin raw beneath her sodden sleeves. Rain hammered down in silvery sheets, transforming the earth beneath her feet into a treacherous morass, eager to pull her down into its cold embrace. Her dripping-wet hair felt like a lead weight against her skull, strands plastered against her face, and her once-pristine robe clung to her like a shroud, the fabric so thoroughly drenched that water ran freely down her back in icy rivulets.

'*O mi Iesu, dimitte nobis debita nostra, salva nos ab igne inferni...*' Brother Galien's voice quavered beside her, barely audible over the constant drumming of the rain. The young friar's face had gone grey with exhaustion, his tonsured head bowed against the deluge.

A warrior yanked sharply on the rope that bound them, nearly sending them both sprawling into the mud.

'Silence!' he snarled in the Cuman tongue.

Fabrisse gripped Galien's shoulder, offering what comfort she could, feeling him tremble beneath his soaked habit. The line of mounted warriors stretched ahead and behind, their fur-trimmed coats dark with rain. Some sang in their harsh tongue as they rode, songs that sounded more like war chants than anything meant to lift spirits. Steam rose from their horses' flanks despite the cold, and the beasts' breath came out in great white clouds that dissipated quickly in the downpour.

Eventually, Shoruk conferred briefly with two of his men, before sending them ranging ahead. The new chief's authority seemed absolute among his warriors, yet Fabrisse hadn't missed how carefully he positioned himself to avoid direct interaction with Moldir. There was tension there, like a cord pulled taut and ready to snap.

A sudden gust of wind drove the rain sideways, stinging her face like needles. In that moment, she caught Moldir watching her with those dark, fathomless eyes. The priestess's lips curved in what might have been a smile, but there was no warmth in it. Only malice.

Shoruk suddenly raised his fist, calling for his men to stop. The column ground to a halt beside a stream that had swollen with the recent rains, its waters churning brown and angry between its banks. He barked orders to his men, who began leading their mounts toward the water while keeping wary eyes on their prisoners. Two warriors took up positions on either side of Fabrisse and Galien, making it clear that any attempt to flee would end swiftly and violently.

As the warriors led their mounts to drink, Fabrisse sank to her knees in the sodden grass, grateful for even this brief respite. Her legs trembled with exhaustion, and she could feel every heartbeat pounding in her raw wrists.

'Water,' Brother Galien croaked beside her. His eyes had taken on a wild cast, darting between their captors like a trapped animal. 'Please, I beg you...'

One of the younger warriors – barely more than a boy, with

only the first wisps of a beard on his chin – approached with a waterskin. He held it to Fabrisse's lips first, allowing her a few precious swallows. The water was cold and clean, washing away the dryness that had lodged in her throat. Then the boy allowed Galien to drink, but all too briefly. He walked away with the waterskin, causing the friar to moan in dismay.

'*Deus meus, Deus meus, ut quid dereliquisti me*?' Galien's voice cracked on the words. *My God, my God, why have you forsaken me?*

'Brother,' Fabrisse whispered, 'be strong. God has not abandoned us.'

'Hasn't He?' Galien's laugh held an edge of hysteria. 'Where was He when they murdered Tarkhan? Where was He when they loosed their arrows into Rabel? We are alone here, my lady. Alone in this wilderness with devils.'

Around them, the Cumans tended to their mounts and spoke in low voices. Some of the warriors cast suspicious glances toward their prisoners, hands never straying far from their weapons.

'Listen to me,' Fabrisse said, keeping her voice low. 'God is with us always, even in our darkest days. We must have faith.'

'Faith? I had faith when we came here. I believed we could bring God's light to these heathens. But there is only darkness in their souls. Only death. I can see it in their eyes. They mean to kill us, my lady. Slowly. Painfully.'

'Then we shall die with courage in our hearts, as all God's servants should,' Fabrisse replied firmly. 'But I do not believe that is God's plan for us. He will deliver those who trust in Him. We did not see our brother Rabel perish. I do not believe God would allow him to come to such an end. If he reached Rosenau, knights of the Order might even now be on our trail. Salvation is only...'

But Galien had retreated into himself again, rocking slightly as he muttered prayers. Looking at him, Fabrisse felt her heart ache. He was so young, so unprepared for this test of faith. She wished she could reach out to comfort him, but the ropes binding their hands made even that small gesture impossible.

A shadow fell across them, and Fabrisse looked up to see Talshyn standing over them. The young priestess's dark robes were sodden, but she seemed unconcerned by the rain that streamed down her face. She glanced over her shoulder, ensuring the warriors were occupied with their horses, before crouching down beside the prisoners.

'How do you fare?'

'Why do you ask?' Fabrisse replied. 'What do you care?'

'Despite all that has happened, you should know I bear you no ill will,' she said softly.

'Forgive me if that offers little solace.'

'If it is solace you're after, holy woman, then you are in the wrong place. The rains show no sign of abating, and it is still a long way to Kyzaghan's shrine.'

'What is that?' Fabrisse asked, her mouth dry despite the water she had drunk.

Talshyn narrowed her eyes, studying Fabrisse's face. 'A sacred place. Ancient. Powerful. A site we use for sacrifice.'

The word hung between them. 'Is that what you believe we deserve? Death for trying to bring God's love to your people?'

'What I believe matters little.' Talshyn's gaze flickered toward where Moldir sat astride her horse, a dark silhouette against the rain.

'There are better ways,' Fabrisse said. 'Your people need not live in darkness. God's grace—'

'Your god is not here.' Talshyn's voice carried equal measures of pity and certainty. 'These mountains belong to older spirits. Darker ones. Forces you cannot comprehend.'

Despite her resolve, Fabrisse felt a chill that had nothing to do with the elements. She had studied the Cumans' beliefs before embarking on this mission, but clearly there were some aspects she had not discovered.

Still, she lifted her chin. 'God's light shines even in the deepest dark.'

A note of doubt flickered in Talshyn's eyes, but before she could respond, a sharp voice cut through the rain as Moldir called to her apprentice. Talshyn rose quickly, but hesitated for a moment.

'Pray to your god if you must,' she said. 'But do not hope for deliverance. These are the lands of the Qun. Our gods hold sway here.'

Fabrisse watched Talshyn hurry away through the rain. There had been something in her eyes – not just doubt, but perhaps a flicker of compassion. Yet what good was compassion without action? It was clear there would be no help here, and yet she could not allow herself to give in to despair.

Shoruk's voice cut through her thoughts, shouting commands that set his warriors scrambling to mount their horses. The brief rest was over. As rough hands hauled her and Galien to their feet, she was more determined than ever that God would show them a path through this tribulation. Or perhaps... she might find one herself.

As the riders drove them onward through the deluge, the rain finally began to relent, though the clouds remained heavy and threatening overhead. Through gaps in the distant trees, Fabrisse caught glimpses of mountain peaks wreathed in mist. Somewhere ahead lay their destination – Kyzaghan's shrine, where Moldir intended to sacrifice them to her dark god. The thought should have terrified her, but instead it filled her with a cold determination.

The chances of rescue seemed remote. Even if Rabel had survived and found help, who would dare follow them into these wild lands? Yet she remembered the knights of Rosenau, and their warnings about the dangers beyond their walls. Would they come? Could they even find them in this vast wilderness? She had to hope they would at least try.

Brother Galien had retreated deep into himself, barely seeming to notice where they walked. His lips moved constantly in prayer, but no sound emerged. Fabrisse worried for his sanity, but perhaps his obvious distress worked in their favour. The warriors paid little attention to a broken man, and even less to a woman they believed helpless.

Her fingers closed around her rosary beads, counting them by touch. Thirty-nine beads remaining. The cord that held them together had begun to fray, and as they struggled through a particularly deep patch of mud, she snapped it in her fists, then let one bead slip free and fall to the ground along their path.

Faith alone might not be enough.

But God helped those who helped themselves.

12
_____

Before sundown the weather had offered some mercy, the rains abating for the night. Estienne and the others had made camp with a small fire to stave off the cold, but sleep was fleeting. They rose the next morning, and Jurgen led them swiftly along what remained of Rabel's trail. By the time they reached the site of the slaughter Rabel had told them of at high sun, little remained of it.

Blackened circles marked where funeral pyres had burned. Their group moved carefully between abandoned yurts, many now nothing more than collapsing frames of bent wood and torn felt.

'They left in a hurry,' Amalric breathed. 'After burning their dead.'

'No reason for them to take all their dwellings after half the clan was slaughtered,' Estienne replied, looking over the charred bones that remained among the sodden ashes.

Jurgen moved through the camp, checking for sign. The trapper's bearded face betrayed nothing as he knelt to examine marks in the grass.

'Two groups left here,' he announced after some careful study.

'One heading south-east toward the forests. Twenty, maybe thirty people on foot.' He pointed toward the distant tree-line before turning to indicate the opposite direction. 'Larger group went north, toward the mountains. All on horseback.'

'Any prisoners would be with the mounted group,' Amalric said with certainty. 'The clan warriors. Those on foot must be the old and frail left behind.'

'Unless that's exactly what they want us to think,' Carsten cut in. 'This could be nothing more than a clever ruse to lead us astray.'

'They don't know we're following them,' Jurgen replied. 'No reason for any ruse.'

Carsten's sour expression showed his annoyance at being contradicted, but there was no arguing with the trapper's logic.

Estienne moved to where Jurgen crouched, studying the ground himself though he lacked the man's expertise. 'How long ago did they leave?'

'Hard to say with the rain,' Jurgen replied. 'But no more than three days. Ground's still soft where the horses passed.'

'We'd best get on our way, then,' Estienne said. 'North. Toward the mountains.'

To his surprise there were no arguments from Carsten, as they quickly mounted up. Estienne felt a strange kind of relief at leaving the site of the Cuman camp behind. An ungodly slaughter had happened there – brother killing brother – and it left a stain on the earth darker than those pyres.

For the rest of the day they followed the horses' trail. Jurgen's job was made that much easier now they were following a column of mounted men, and the rain-soft earth was churned up so much even Estienne could have discerned the tracks.

As evening drew in, the mountains loomed before them against a darkening sky. Storm clouds began to gather above those peaks, roiling masses of grey and black that promised yet more brutal weather. The wind had picked up, carrying an edge sharp enough to cut through cloth to the flesh beneath.

'We'll need to find shelter soon,' Carsten announced, eyeing the stormfront fearfully.

'There,' Jurgen called out, pointing to a dark opening in the mountainside ahead. 'Cave in the cliffside. We'd do well to camp there.'

No sooner had he spoken than the first heavy drops began to fall. They urged their mounts up the slope, reaching the cave entrance just as thunder cracked overhead like God's own war drum. The opening was larger than it had first appeared, easily wide enough for them to lead their horses inside.

'Steady, boy,' Jurgen urged as his hound stopped at the threshold, hackles raised.

The dog's reluctance did nothing to ease Estienne's growing sense of unease, and he was happy to let the trapper lead the way inside. In the scant light that illuminated the cave he was relieved to see it wasn't home to another bear.

Rotger produced a torch from his saddlebag, and soon flickering light revealed the cave system stretched deeper into the mountain, branching off into smaller tunnels that disappeared into darkness.

'Look here,' Amalric said, holding his own torch closer to the wall. 'There are paintings.'

Estienne moved closer, studying the crude figures rendered in red ochre against the grey stone. Hunters with bows pursuing what might have been deer or elk. Strange spiral patterns that seemed to writhe in the torchlight. And everywhere, the image of a great wolf with its head thrown back in an endless howl.

'Pagan devil-work,' Carsten spat.

'These are old,' Jurgen said, running calloused fingers over the artwork. 'Very old. But these caves are still used. See there?' He indicated what looked like a crude pile of stacked stones. 'An altar to their earth goddess. Raised within the last month, I'd say. These caves aren't just for shelter. They're sacred places of worship to the pagans.'

The young squire Eggert made the sign of the cross, his face pale in the torchlight. 'Do they make sacrifices to their heathen gods here?'

'Maybe,' Jurgen replied grimly.

Lightning flashed outside, briefly illuminating the cave mouth and casting their shadows long against the decorated walls. The thunder that followed seemed to shake the very mountain.

'We'll rest here until the storm passes,' Estienne announced. 'Sacred ground or not, it'll shelter us from that storm.'

He was greeted with some nervous looks, particularly from the squires, but thankfully no arguments. They set about making camp, though none strayed far from the cave mouth. The horses were especially nervous, stamping and snorting in the depths of the cave, and even after they got a fire going, its warm light fought a constant battle against the darkness pressing in around them.

Estienne found himself studying the wolf paintings as night fell. In the flickering light, they seemed almost alive, running endlessly across the stone walls. There was an eeriness to them, and he couldn't shake the feeling that they were being watched – not by anything living, but something far older. Something that had waited in these mountains since before Christ's light first touched these lands.

As the night wore on and the fire burned low, Estienne watched the two squires across the flames – Eggert fidgeted restlessly while Merten sat with his back against the cave wall, knees drawn up to his chest. Neither had spoken much since they'd

Valour 101

made camp, but tension radiated from them like heat from the dying embers.

'They deserve to burn for what they've done,' Eggert said suddenly, his voice echoing in the confines of the cave. 'We should kill them to the last man when we find them. Bring them God's justice.'

'We're here to rescue Lady Fabrisse and Brother Galien,' Merten cut in quietly. 'Not to deliver divine punishment.'

Eggert rounded on his fellow squire. 'Says who? You? All you care about is glory. That's the only reason you came. To prove yourself some kind of knight.'

Colour rose in Merten's cheeks, but his voice remained steady. 'Is it so wrong to want to serve with honour? To protect those who cannot protect themselves? Sometimes it is better to show mercy—'

'Mercy?' Eggert laughed, a harsh sound that made several of their companions stir uneasily. 'These heathens don't understand mercy. And they should be shown none. They must be punished for what they have—'

'And who are you to decide their punishment?' Estienne asked, unable to keep silent any longer. 'God's own appointed executioner?'

'Someone must bring His vengeance to these lands,' Eggert replied, his voice rising. 'Someone must show them the price of defying His will. When we find them, I will—'

'You'll do as you're ordered, boy,' Amalric cut him off sharply. 'Nothing more.'

Eggert's mouth worked silently for a moment before he shot to his feet and stalked deeper into the shadows of the cave. Merten watched him go, concern evident on his young face.

'He wasn't always so... passionate,' the squire said softly. 'When we first came to the Burzenland he was different. Kinder.

We both shared dreams of rising through the ranks of the Order, but Eggert has become more pious over the years. More zealous. I just want to serve. To protect people. Is that so foolish?'

'No,' Amalric replied. 'But this is no game, Merten. And although Eggert might seem zealous to you, there is a real possibility we will have to show no mercy if we are to survive this.'

'I understand that. I do.' Merten's voice grew stronger. 'But surely we should show mercy if we can? We're meant to be better than those we fight against.'

Thunder rolled outside, as Estienne studied Merten's earnest face in the firelight, seeing something of his younger self there. Before reality had stripped away such simple ideals.

'Get some rest,' he told the squire. 'Both of you will need your strength tomorrow.'

'We'll be chasing ghosts,' Carsten's voice cut through the darkness before Merten could react. 'Following tracks that may lead nowhere.'

Estienne's jaw clenched. 'If you have nothing useful to contribute, perhaps silence would serve better.'

'Useful?' Carsten barked a laugh. 'What would be useful is returning to Rosenau before we all join Lady Fabrisse in death. These mountains will be our tomb if we persist in this foolishness.'

Another flash of lightning illuminated the cave entrance. In that stark light, Estienne saw the fear plain on Carsten's face, poorly masked by his show of anger.

'You're welcome to return,' Amalric said. 'Though I'm not sure how you'll justify to the Marschall why you abandoned your command.'

'Abandoned?' Carsten surged to his feet, his voice rising to echo off the walls. 'I am trying to keep us alive, while you all seem intent on getting us killed. This is just—'

Valour

'Master yourself, Carsten,' Estienne cut him off. 'Who would leave a woman of God to suffer at the hands of heathens while he skulks back to safety?'

'She's already dead!' Carsten's shout seemed to shake the cave roof. 'Dead, or worse than dead. And we'll join her if we continue this mad pursuit. She chose to come to this accursed country, and will have to bear the consequences.'

'If you believe that,' Estienne said quietly, 'then you don't deserve to wear that cross.'

Carsten's face mottled with rage. 'You dare... you dare to question my right to—'

'I dare.' Estienne rose to his feet. 'I question your courage. Your honour. Your fitness to lead.'

'Brothers, please.' Rotger's deep voice cut through the tension. 'This serves no one.'

'The big man speaks truth,' Jurgen added from where he sat checking his bow. 'Save your fight for the pagans.'

Carsten threw one last venomous glare at Estienne before sitting himself down once more. It did little to ease the tension.

Estienne forced himself to sit, knowing there was sense in Rotger and Jurgen's words. They would need to be united for what lay ahead. Instead, they were splitting like ice on a thawing lake. They could not let discord take root among their small band. Not if they were to have any hope of succeeding in their mission.

13

The mountain wind cut through Fabrisse's drenched robes like a penitent's lash. Her wrists ached, the binding having worn away her skin to expose raw flesh beneath. Every step required all her concentration as her feet, numbed by cold and fatigue, sought purchase on the treacherous ground.

Shoruk rode at the head of their column, his warriors following him like a pack of wolves. They spoke little as they rode, but occasionally one would laugh at some private jest, the sound carrying no mirth. Fabrisse had no idea how far they were from their goal, but she could only hope it was many days. Despite her discomfort, she knew to endure it was far preferable than the fate that awaited once they reached this shrine to their ancient gods.

Through the matted strands of hair that whipped across her face, she suddenly caught movement along the valley ahead. The sight made her heart sink as she recognised a merchant caravan winding its way south along the narrow mountain trail. Six heavily laden wagons creaked beneath hide covers, the sound carrying clearly in the thin mountain air.

The merchants' guards, eight in all walking alongside the wagons, carried themselves with the wary readiness of men accustomed to danger. Their spears were held at the ready, as though they were well-versed with the perils of the borderlands, yet even that knowledge might not be enough to save them.

Shoruk raised his fist, bringing their column to a halt. His warriors spread out, their bows held ready but not yet drawn. The merchants' guards drew the wagons to a stop and tightened their grips on their weapons, trying to project confidence even as their eyes darted between the mounted figures ahead of them. The tension hung in the air like the moment before a storm breaks.

'Hold steady,' one of the merchants called to his men in Latin, though Fabrisse could not discern the accent. Then he added, 'They're just passing through.'

He raised a hand in greeting toward Shoruk's warriors, the gesture almost pleading in its deliberate slowness.

Brother Galien pressed closer to Fabrisse, his hands trembling despite how tightly they were clasped. She wanted to offer him comfort, but what comfort could she give when her own heart was pounding so fiercely?

One of the merchant's horses whinnied nervously, pawing at the frozen ground. Fabrisse watched as Shoruk turned in his saddle to exchange glances with Moldir. When the priestess gave an almost imperceptible nod, Shoruk's entire demeanour shifted. His casual indifference fell away like a discarded cloak, replaced by the coiled tension of a predator about to spring.

Then he let out a shrill whistle that echoed off the valley wall.

The first arrow took the merchant captain in the throat, the soft, wet thud of impact lost beneath his startled gurgle, and Fabrisse watched in horror as he collapsed to the hard earth. Then Shoruk's blade cleared its scabbard with a singing note that called his warriors to slaughter and they spurred their mounts forward, descending on the caravan like devils loosed from hell.

The air filled with the whisper-thud of arrows, each shaft finding its mark with terrible precision. The guards tried to form a defensive circle around the wagons, shields raised against the deadly assault, but they were hopelessly outmatched.

'Form up! To me!' a grizzled guard shouted, trying to rally his men.

An arrow took him in the eye, the shaft driving deep into his skull. He stood for a moment, weapon still raised, before crumpling like a sack of apples.

'Dear God in heaven, preserve us,' Brother Galien moaned beside her.

He had collapsed to his knees, arms over his head, as if he could shut out the screams. But nothing could block the sounds of slaughter – the impact of arrows, the clash of steel, the terrible crying of panicked horses.

Shoruk's warriors wheeled their mounts in practised formation, firing from the saddle with inhuman accuracy. Their arrows seemed to seek out every gap in armour, every exposed throat and face. One guard managed to raise his crossbow, the snap of its release momentarily cutting through the chaos. The bolt went wide, before a mounted warrior descended on him like a hunting bird. His curved blade rose and fell, rendering the man's face a red ruin. He had no time to scream.

A merchant tried to flee on foot, stumbling back along the trail. 'Mercy!' he cried, 'Please, just take it all.'

Three arrows took him in the back before he'd gone ten paces. He pitched forward, limbs twitching, fingers clawing at nothing as his life bled out in the dirt.

The merchants' horses screamed in terror, rearing in their traces, as some of the wagon drivers sought shelter beneath their

Valour 107

vehicles, while others tried to surrender, throwing down weapons and raising their hands. The pagans gave no quarter – arrows finding cowering men beneath wagons, while blades ended the lives of those who begged for mercy. Fabrisse watched a young merchant boy, no older than sixteen, try to crawl away from the carnage. A mounted warrior rode him down, trampling him beneath his steed's hooves before finishing him with a casual thrust of his spear.

The massacre took mere moments. When it was done, the silence lay heavy as iron, broken only by the soft snorting of horses.

Corpses were scattered across the valley floor, Shoruk's warriors moving among the dead, checking for valuables, gathering scattered weapons, speaking in casual tones. Fabrisse found that most shocking of all – the way they just went about the act of pillage with such disregard for the slaughter they had wrought.

A sudden shout went up, making her flinch.

'Here! We have one!' A warrior dragged a struggling figure from beneath an overturned wagon.

The merchant was young, barely more than a boy, his fine wool tunic now soaked with the blood of his companions. His face was a mask of terror as they forced him to his knees before Shoruk.

'Please,' he babbled in Latin. 'I have family, children! I can pay, I can—'

Shoruk raised a finger to silence the man, then turned and gestured casually to his men – just a flick of his finger to signal the end of a man's life. Fabrisse was frozen in place, paralysed by the horror, but before Shoruk's warriors could carry out the execution, Moldir glided forward through the carnage.

The high priestess moved toward the sole survivor with deliberate reverence, her dark robes rippling in the mountain wind.

When she drew her ceremonial knife, its elaborate blade caught the wan sunlight making it resemble a shard of ancient ice. Runes Fabrisse didn't recognise had been carved into its surface, and the bone handle was stained dark with what could only be blood.

'No!' The word tore from Fabrisse's throat before she could stop it. She lurched forward but strong hands caught her shoulders, Talshyn's grip surprisingly firm as she held Fabrisse in place. 'This is an abomination! You cannot—'

'Do not interfere,' the young priestess whispered. 'It will not end well for you if you try.'

Moldir began to chant in a strange tongue that made Fabrisse's skin crawl. The harsh syllables made her head swim, as though the very words were an offence to God.

The merchant boy's eyes went wide with terror as Moldir pressed the knife to his throat. His lips moved in silent prayer, tears freezing on his cheeks, but he made no other move to defend himself, his fate sealed as it was. The chant reached a crescendo and Moldir drew the blade across in one swift motion. Blood fountained forth, black in the weak sunlight. The boy made a wet choking sound as he tried to breathe through his opened throat, his hands coming up, fingers scrabbling uselessly at the wound, before he toppled sideways.

Moldir knelt, pressing her hand to the still ebbing wound to coat her fingers in blood. Then she stood, turning to where three of the youngest warriors stood watching, their faces masks of anticipation. One by one she anointed them, drawing symbols on their foreheads in crimson script. Each warrior received the mark reverently, as though it were a holy blessing.

'Tengri sees your victory,' Moldir intoned. 'Just as Eje accepts the gift of blood. Both are pleased with this offering.'

The sight of the ritual broke something in Fabrisse. All her teachings about patience and understanding, all her years of

Valour 109

study in how to bring God's light to the darkness, burned away like morning mist in the face of such evil. The rage that replaced them flared bright with its intensity, searing through her exhaustion like holy fire.

'Murderers!' The word tore from her throat, just as she tore her arm from Talshyn's grip. 'God sees your sins! His judgement awaits you all! The fires of Hell burn eternal for those who spill innocent blood! *Vengeance is mine,* sayeth the Lord!'

Her words echoed off the valley walls, carrying across the bloodstained ground. Several warriors shifted uneasily, perhaps recognising the power in the voice of this foreign holy woman. Even Shoruk averted his gaze, unwilling to face her down in her fury.

But Moldir turned toward her, approaching with measured steps, the bloody knife still held in one hand. The high priestess's face was a mask of scorn as she came near, her dark eyes two pools of contempt.

'You dare to invoke your God here, Christian,' Moldir said, her voice carrying with a terrible resonance. 'Those words hold no power in this place. These mountains belong to older gods than yours.'

Fabrisse lifted her chin, meeting that obsidian stare without flinching. 'My God is the one true God, and He sees what you have done here. There will be a reckoning—'

The blow came without warning – an open-handed strike that snapped Fabrisse's head to the side and filled her mouth with the copper taste of blood. For a moment, the world spun, and stars flashed at the edges of her vision.

Rage still burned bright as she forced herself to straighten, to meet Moldir's gaze once more. The priestess's eyes narrowed slightly – perhaps surprised by such a show of defiance, then she turned away, barking orders for the warriors to mount up.

As the pagans began gathering their plunder and prepared to move on, Fabrisse felt the weight of her rosary still clutched in her bound hands. With precise care, she worked another bead free and let it fall. It landed on the bloody ground, almost invisible among the carnage – one more marker of their passage through this godless wilderness.

One more prayer offered up to heaven.

She could only have faith that someone was listening.

14

Estienne's destrier stumbled on the rocky ground, nearly pitching him from the saddle. The beast's sides heaved with exhaustion, foam flecking its dark coat. They'd been pushing hard since dawn, following Jurgen's lead through increasingly difficult terrain as the trapper pursued the tracks of their quarry. The weather had cleared somewhat since their river crossing, though heavy clouds still lurked on the horizon. At least the improved visibility made tracking easier.

'Steady there,' Estienne murmured, patting the horse's neck.

The animal's laboured breathing concerned him, but they couldn't afford to slow their pace. Not with so much ground to make up. Ahead, Jurgen dismounted to study something in the mud. His stern face betrayed nothing as he crouched, running his thick hand over marks in the earth.

'What do you see?' Estienne asked, not wanting to break the trapper's concentration.

Jurgen traced the edge of a hoofprint preserved in a patch of sodden earth. 'We're getting closer. I think they're slowing. Either the prisoners are giving them trouble, or their horses are in need of rest.'

'Theirs aren't the only ones,' Estienne replied, offering his steed another pat of reassurance.

Clovis suddenly gave a low whine, his excitement palpable, muscled shoulders trembling with barely contained energy.

'He's caught something on the air,' Jurgen said, remounting. 'They might not be too far ahead.'

Amalric drew his horse alongside Estienne's. 'God willing, we'll catch them before nightfall.'

'God willing, we'll see them before they see us,' Estienne replied grimly.

They urged their tired horses forward, following Jurgen as he guided them along a winding path between rocky outcrops. The path felt as though it would never end, until they found the merchant caravan just past midday. As they crested a low rise overlooking a shallow valley, the site of the massacre spread before them.

'Lord have mercy,' Eggert gasped.

Estienne's throat tightened at the sight. Six wagons lay scattered across the blood-stained earth, their hide covers torn and flapping in the wind like tattered banners. Spilled cargo lay strewn across the valley floor – bales of fabric, wooden crates, shards of pottery. And amongst it all lay the corpses.

Most of the guards had fallen in a rough circle, as though they'd tried to form a shield wall in their final moments. Their corpses bristled with arrows, the shafts grouped with accuracy around throats, faces and gaps in their scant armour. Other merchants lay where they'd been cut down trying to flee. Clean sword-strokes had opened necks, speaking to the swift efficiency of the killing. These weren't the ragged wounds of a chaotic melee, but the practised work of born killers.

Valour 113

Jurgen led the way as they picked their way down the slope. When they reached the site of the slaughter their horses stepped carefully around the debris.

'Mother of God,' Amalric breathed. 'They stood no chance.'

'But why?' Merten asked from where he sat behind Eggert. 'Why would they just murder them like this?'

'Most likely to leave no word of their passing,' Jurgen replied. 'Let no one tell of who their prisoner was, maybe? Or could be just to plunder these wagons. You can never tell with those pagan bastards.'

Carrion birds had already been at work, leaving eyeless faces staring accusingly at the sky. Signs of methodical looting were everywhere. Broken containers lay scattered about, their contents deemed worthless by the pagans. Even the dead had been stripped of anything worth taking.

The sound of boots hitting earth drew Estienne's attention. Rotger had dismounted and was approaching one of the bodies, his usually cheerful face now a mask of sorrow.

'What are you doing?' Estienne demanded.

'We can't leave them like this.' Rotger knelt beside the nearest corpse. 'They deserve a Christian burial.'

'We don't have time.' Estienne's voice came out harsher than he'd intended. 'Every moment we delay—'

'Every moment we delay will be spent doing God's work,' Eggert cut in, already dismounting to join Rotger. 'Would you have us ride past this horror like soulless pagans?'

'I would have us see to the living before we tend to the dead,' Estienne snapped. 'Or have you forgotten why we're here, boy?'

'We're here because we're God's own knights,' Rotger replied quietly, beginning to drag a merchant's body toward a relatively clear patch of ground. 'That means more than just hunting Christendom's foes. It means offering dignity, even in death.'

Estienne turned to Amalric for support, but his friend's expression was troubled. 'I don't know. It seems wrong just to leave these men for the crows. We owe them that at least.'

'We owe Fabrisse more,' Estienne growled in frustration. 'She still lives – or did when Brother Rabel last saw her. But if we waste time here—'

'Time you've already wasted arguing,' Jurgen interrupted. The trapper had been examining the ground around the wagon while they debated. 'They're barely a day ahead now. Closest we've been since starting this chase. But that advantage won't last if we tarry too long. Your decision.'

Estienne looked to the bodies scattered across the muddy ground – a dozen of them, each requiring proper burial. It would take hours they couldn't spare.

'This is lunacy.' Carsten's voice echoed across the valley as he gestured at the carnage around them. 'It doesn't matter how long we waste. Look at what these animals did here. Look at the slaughter. You think they showed mercy to that woman we've been sent to find? She's dead already – we all know it.'

'You don't know anything,' Estienne bit back. 'Master your fear, Carsten, lest it turn to cowardice.'

Carsten's face twisted with rage. 'How dare you question my—'

'I question everything about you,' Estienne cut him off. 'Your courage. Your judgement. Why the Marschall sought to put you in charge is beyond me. We'd have been better off if—'

'Brothers, please,' Amalric started, but a sharp bark from Clovis interrupted whatever he'd been about to say.

The hound had been sniffing his way around the edge of the wagons, nose to the ground. Now he stood rigid, tail wagging, staring at something in the mud.

Jurgen strode over and knelt beside Clovis, examining what-

Valour

ever had caught the dog's attention. After a moment, he straightened, holding something small between thumb and forefinger.

'Well now,' he said softly. 'What do we have here?'

Jurgen held up a simple wooden bead, polished to a perfect sphere. A rosary bead.

'Could be anyone's,' Carsten said quickly. 'One of the merchants—'

'Clovis says different,' Jurgen replied. 'He's got the lady's scent. This was left deliberate-like, not dropped by accident.'

A spark of hope suddenly ignited in Estienne's gut. Fabrisse lived, and had even left clear sign behind so they could follow her path. He turned to Rotger, who still stood beside the merchant's corpse.

'Brother,' he said quietly. 'I swear to you – once this is done, we'll return. We'll give them all a proper burial. But right now...'

Rotger nodded slowly. 'Right now we have a chance to prevent more Christian souls joining these ones.' He looked down at the merchant one last time, then made the sign of the cross. 'God grant them peace.'

They remounted quickly, Carsten's protests reduced to sullen mutters as he was forced to concede to the group's renewed sense of purpose.

The sun was already past its zenith, beginning its slow descent toward the distant mountains. Despite their new-found determination, Estienne knew time was still running out. Somewhere ahead, Fabrisse was leaving them a trail, gambling her life that they would follow. He intended to make sure that gamble paid off.

15

The forest pressed close around them, offering some shelter from the harsh winds they had been forced to endure. Fabrisse shifted against the rough bark of the ancient pine, trying to find some kind of comfort. Her wrists were still bound, flesh beneath red and weeping, but she refused to give voice to the pain – that would only feed the despair that threatened to overwhelm her.

Their captors had been forced to make camp in this natural depression after one of their warriors had taken a merchant's crossbow bolt in the shoulder. The wound had festered despite Moldir's ministrations, and now the man's fever-wracked groans carried clearly through the still air. Other warriors moved through the camp with restless energy, checking their weapons, tending the horses that stood head-down with exhaustion.

Brother Galien huddled close by, his robes now little more than mud-stained rags. His lips moved constantly in prayer, though no sound emerged. The sight of him – this man who had been sent as her stalwart companion – reduced to such a state made her heart feel as though it were breaking in her chest.

'Be strong, brother,' she whispered. 'Remember how Saint

Sebastian endured his torments with unwavering faith. How Agnes of Rome went to her end singing God's praises—'

'I can't stop thinking about them,' Galien whispered. 'The dead. Those merchants... their lives snuffed out like candle-flame... I can still hear their screams...'

He pressed his bound hands against his ears as though he could shut out the memory, and she could well appreciate his torment. The massacre of the merchant caravan played behind her own eyes whenever she closed them, but she couldn't afford to dwell on it. Not when Galien needed her strength.

'God tests us,' Fabrisse replied, though the words felt hollow even to her. 'His most beloved servants most of all.'

'Perhaps...' Galien's voice dropped to barely a whisper, 'perhaps we were wrong to come here. To think we could bring God's light to such darkness...'

'No.' Fabrisse's tone carried more conviction than she felt. 'These people need His message more than any. Look how they live – trapped in an endless cycle of violence and retribution. Only God's grace can free them from such wretchedness.'

A crow's harsh call split the air, making Galien flinch, before he closed his eyes once more and continued his prayers, louder this time. 'Blessed Virgin, protect us. Holy Mother, shield your servants from evil and the iniquities of those who would see us brought low.'

Approaching footsteps made Fabrisse tense, but it was only Talshyn, carrying two wooden bowls that steamed in the chill air. The young priestess knelt beside them, her hood pushed back, dark eyes regarding them impassively.

'Eat,' she said, holding a bowl of thin soup to Fabrisse's lips. The broth was barely more than hot water with a few threads of meat floating in it, but Fabrisse accepted it gratefully. Even this meagre sustenance was better than nothing.

'The merchants carried dried meat and grain,' Talshyn said as she helped Galien with his portion. 'Most likely they were on their way to trade in the Burzenland.'

'But instead you slaughtered them.' Fabrisse kept her voice gentle, free of accusation. 'Why? What threat did they pose to you?'

'You don't understand our ways. These lands are harsh, and we take what we need to survive. And after what your people have done to us...'

'My people?'

'The Christian warriors who pushed us east. The ones who build their stone castles along the mountains. Who burn our camps and drive us from lands we've held since before memory. They showed no mercy to us. Why should we show mercy to any who follow their god?'

'Because only mercy can break the endless wheel of violence,' Fabrisse replied. 'Because every act of cruelty only feeds the darkness in men's hearts.'

Something flickered in Talshyn's eyes – doubt, perhaps, or recognition of a truth she'd tried to deny. 'Your Christian god... they say he died for the sins of others. That he forgave those who killed him.'

'Yes. And through His sacrifice, all can find redemption.'

'Even those who have done terrible things?' Talshyn's voice had grown so quiet Fabrisse could barely hear it. 'Those who have spilled innocent blood?'

'Especially them.' Fabrisse leaned forward. 'God's grace knows no limits, Talshyn. His forgiveness is infinite. We need only be willing to accept it.'

Talshyn's hands trembled slightly as she gripped the empty bowls. 'Moldir says your god is weak. That only through sacrifice can we honour the old powers. That Erlik demands—'

Valour

She cut herself off, eyes widening as though she'd said too much.

'Erlik?' Fabrisse asked, wondering who this new deity might be, but Talshyn was already rising to her feet.

'I should not speak of such things,' the young priestess said. 'Moldir would—'

'Would what?' The voice cut through the air, sharp and spiteful.

Moldir stepped from the shadows between the trees, her dark robes making her appear more spirit than flesh.

'Nothing, Kam Katun,' Talshyn replied, head bowed. 'I was only—'

'What poison has this woman been pouring in your ear?' Moldir's voice carried the chill of mountain winds. 'What do you think you are doing, letting her corrupt you with lies? Allowing her serpent tongue to make you question our ways?'

Fabrisse fought to keep her expression neutral as Moldir's gaze swept over her. Then the high priestess's attention fixed on the rosary still clutched in Fabrisse's bound hands. With a movement too swift to follow, Moldir snatched the prayer beads away. Her long fingers moved over each one with deliberate precision, until understanding dawned in Moldir's face.

'Clever.' The old woman's lips curved in a smile that held no warmth. 'Very clever. Leaving a trail of crumbs for your would-be rescuers to follow. Though do you really think anyone would come looking for you out here?'

Fabrisse forced herself to meet Moldir's gaze. 'God's will be done.'

'How many times? Your god has no power here, Christian. These lands belong to Tengri. To Eje.'

'And Erlik?' Fabrisse asked.

Moldir's eyes narrowed, and she wondered if she had gone

too far. Then the high priestess reached out suddenly, grabbing Talshyn's wrist with painful force.

'Go. Tell Shoruk what this woman has done. Let him decide how to deal with this... deception.'

Talshyn cast one last frightened glance at Fabrisse before hurrying away. Moldir watched her go, before slowly turning her attention back to Fabrisse.

'Such a tender heart,' the high priestess mused. 'So easily swayed by empty tales of mercy and redemption.'

'They are not empty tales. God's love is—'

'A long way from here.'

Any retort Fabrisse may have planned was lost as someone approached through the brush. Shoruk stepped into the small clearing, his face twisted with fury.

'Talshyn tells me there is something I must see.'

Moldir showed him the incomplete rosary. 'It seems the Christian woman is more devious than I gave her credit for. She has left a trail in our wake for her Christian brothers to follow.'

Shoruk glared down at Fabrisse, his lip twitching in fury before he span on his heel and marched back toward the main camp.

'Artak! Urtak!' he bellowed.

Two warriors approached him from the shadows like hunting wolves, their movements mirror images of each other. They wore matching expressions of cold anticipation as Shoruk gave his commands, though Fabrisse could not hear his words.

She watched as they grabbed their quivers and bows, buckled their sword belts and mounted their small, hardy horses with practised ease. Shoruk spoke to them one final time, gesturing back along the trail they'd followed. Their mission was clear – find any pursuers and deal with them before they could close the distance.

Valour 121

'If anyone is coming for you, they will soon wish they had stayed safe behind their stone walls,' Moldir said, still standing over her like a dark sentinel. 'Now their blood will feed the earth, and their souls will journey to Tamag.'

'There is no darkness that God's light cannot pierce,' Fabrisse replied, but her voice wavered slightly.

Moldir's laugh was like gravel. 'We shall see, Christian. We shall see whose god proves stronger in the end.'

Then she stalked off toward the camp, leaving Fabrisse and Galien alone once more.

In the silence that followed, Fabrisse caught sight of Talshyn, watching from beyond the trees. The girl's face bore none of the same malice her mistress held. She looked almost sorrowful.

Perhaps she had been stirred by promises of what God's light could bring.

Or perhaps that was a hope too far.

16

Branches snagged at Estienne's cloak as they picked their way through the ancient forest. Shafts of wan sunlight pierced the dense canopy at odd angles, creating a confusing play of light and shadow. The air hung thick with the bitter-sweet scent of pine sap and rotting leaves, a heady perfume that reminded him of hunts he and Richard Marshal had embarked on in Normandy, but he tried not to think on those heady days. Not when he was engaged in such grim purpose now.

Jurgen rode slightly ahead, Clovis padding quietly beside his mount's legs. They'd been climbing steadily since dawn through increasingly difficult country, and now they found themselves surrounded by woodland. Estienne wouldn't have admitted it, but it made him nervous. He and the others had said not a word since they'd entered the tree-line, expecting an ambush at any moment.

The trapper's hand suddenly shot up in warning, fingers spread wide. Estienne reined his mount to a halt, the rest of their small party following suit with a jangle of harness and creak of leather. For a long moment, the only sound was the soft snorting of their horses and the whisper of wind through the branches above, a sound that might have been reassuring in other circumstances.

'There,' Jurgen breathed, his chin lifting slightly toward a distant ridge where the trees thinned against the pale sky. 'In the shadow of that tall pine.'

Estienne narrowed his eyes, trying to penetrate the thick undergrowth. His hand unconsciously tightened on his reins as his destrier shifted beneath him, perhaps sensing his tension. At first he saw nothing but branches swaying in the breeze. Then he caught sight of an outline – a horse and rider almost two hundred yards hence, hidden behind the shifting leaves.

'Mounted observer,' Jurgen continued, his voice still barely carrying. 'Been watching us a while, I'd wager.'

'Think he's alone?' Estienne kept his own voice low, though his hand had already strayed to his sword hilt.

'He's the only one that I can see.' Jurgen's expression darkened with concern. 'Though that doesn't mean much. These pagans are shifty.'

'What's the hold-up?' Behind them, Carsten's voice rose in a harsh whisper that carried far too well through the still air.

'Quiet,' Estienne hissed, not taking his eyes off the silhouette through the trees.

'What do you want to do?' Jurgen asked.

Estienne could sense the tension grow more pressing. On the ground, Clovis had sensed it too, a low growl emanating from the hound's throat.

'We can't very well let a scout report back to the clan that we're coming,' Estienne said.

'How should we handle it?'

Estienne didn't reply. He dug his heels into his destrier's flanks, surging forward. The sudden pounding of hooves shattered the forest's silence as his mount crashed through the undergrowth, branches whipping past his face as he rode hard toward the scout. Behind him, he heard Amalric shouting something, but the words were lost to the sound of his horse's charge.

Through the thick woodland he caught sight of the scout wheeling his horse with skill born of a lifetime in the saddle. Though Estienne's destrier ate up the yards, the small steppe pony danced away between the trees before he was even close. As Estienne pushed through a screen of branches that left his face stinging, the pagan was already halfway up the ridge, weaving between the ancient pines with practised ease. The distance between them began to grow despite his larger mount's powerful stride.

Estienne cursed, but the sound died in his throat as movement flashed in his peripheral vision. A second rider burst from behind a massive boulder, curved sword already drawn and catching the sunlight. The ambusher's mount was larger than the typical steppe pony, a beast chosen for power rather than speed, its muscled shoulders bunching as it charged. Estienne had only an instant to register the warrior's snarling face and the deadly flash of steel before he was forced to wrench his reins hard to avoid the killing stroke.

His destrier skidded as they turned, sending a flurry of leaves flying. The sword passed so close he heard the whisper of steel, and the warrior wheeled his mount before Estienne had a chance to draw his own weapon, already coming around for another pass. Estienne fumbled for his own sword, but the awkward angle and his horse's panicked shifting made it difficult to draw cleanly.

The first scout had wheeled his mount on the ridge above, bow already drawn. Estienne heard the thrum of the string as the shaft was loosed, the arrow's flight almost too fast to follow. He lurched backward, desperate to avoid being hit, wrenching back

Valour 125

on the reins as he did so. His destrier reared, and Estienne felt himself lose balance.

The world tilted sickeningly. Estienne felt himself sliding backward, and for a heartbeat the forest span around him. Then he hit the ground hard enough to drive the air from his lungs in an explosive grunt, dead leaves and loose stones offering no cushion. Pure instinct made him roll desperately to avoid his horse's thrashing hooves as the beast stumbled, nearly trampling him beneath its bulk.

His sword had fallen somewhere in the chaos, and his vision swam as he tried to focus. Through watering eyes, he saw the first rider wheeling his mount for another pass, curved blade raised high for a killing stroke. The warrior's face was split by a savage grin, teeth flashing white against his dark beard. Time seemed to slow as Estienne watched him approach, knowing with terrible clarity that he wouldn't be able to move fast enough to avoid the blow.

Rotger's war cry split the air like thunder. The knight crashed through the trees atop his massive destrier, the beast's hooves throwing up clods of earth as it charged right at the horseman. They struck one another, the clash resounding across the clearing, before the horse and rider fell in a mess of noise and thrashing muscle. Rotger somehow kept his seat though his mount stormed onwards, continuing its angry charge.

Estienne scrambled to his feet, spotting his fallen sword glinting among the leaves. He lunged for it just as the second pagan loosed another arrow, and it flitted past to bury itself in a tree trunk. His fingers closed around the sword hilt as the first warrior struggled to his feet, face masked with blood from where he'd struck the ground. The man's mount scrambled to its feet before fleeing into the forest, leaving him to face Estienne on foot.

Their blades met, steel kissing steel, before they both darted back, assessing the other. Then they went again, Estienne gripping his sword with both hands, relying on his power against his lighter opponent. The Cuman was quick, his curved sword darting like a hornet, but Estienne had the advantage of reach with his longer blade. He turned aside a wild slash that would have opened his throat, the edges of their weapons scraping with a sound that set his teeth on edge. Then he stepped inside the warrior's guard, driving his sword up and under the man's ribs with all his strength. Hot blood spilled over his hands, startlingly warm against his cold fingers. The warrior's eyes went wide with surprise, then vacant as death claimed him. He slid from the blade to crumple among the leaves, just as the second pagan barked in alarm.

Estienne looked up to see the archer watching on in horror. Then hate shadowed his features as he plucked another arrow from his quiver. There was nowhere for Estienne to run now. No way he could dodge another arrow at such close quarters.

The sound of more horses approaching gave the Cuman pause, and instead of nocking, he tugged on his reins, wheeling his horse about. Estienne watched him gallop away, just as more destriers burst from the forest.

'The other one's getting away!' Amalric shouted.

Estienne held up his hand as the second scout vanished into the forest at full gallop, his pony's hooves barely seeming to touch the ground as it fled.

'Hold. You won't catch him on a warhorse. And who knows if there are more lying in wait. Let him go.'

Rotger was trotting back into the clearing just as the rest of them arrived.

'Well, that's done it.' Carsten sat atop his horse, glaring in the wake of the escaped rider. 'They'll know we're coming now. Probably already have an ambush laid for us ahead.'

Valour 127

Estienne wiped his blade clean on the dead Cuman's cloak before sheathing it. His hands were steady but his heart still thundered in his chest.

'If they've sent scouts, it means we're close,' he said, studying the corpse at his feet.

'Close to what? A quick death?' Carsten gestured expansively at the fallen warrior, his voice rising with each word. 'These savages wouldn't have sent scouts back along their trail unless they suspected they were being followed. Now they know for sure. They're probably leading us right into a trap even now.'

Jurgen had been examining the ground around the dead Cuman, Clovis sniffing intently at his heel. The hound's hackles were still raised, suggesting more enemies might be nearby. The trapper straightened with a grunt, his leathery face creased with thought.

'You're right about one thing – we're getting close. Their main camp can't be far.'

'So we push on?' Rotger asked, rolling his shoulder with a grimace. 'Even knowing they're waiting for us?'

'We push on,' Estienne said. 'There's no way we can stop now when we're so near to ending this.'

'Madness,' Carsten grumbled. 'Riding into the very teeth of the enemy. God help us.'

As they reformed their column, Estienne cast one last look at the dead Cuman. Without Rotger's timely intervention it was highly likely the pagan would have run him down.

Perhaps God was watching over them.

Perhaps it was too soon to count any blessings.

17

The icy cold waters of the stream bit into Talshyn's legs as she knelt, her fingers raw and numb as she scrubbed at the stains darkening her shawl. It had been her mother's. The delicate embroidery that had once told the story of their clan – the white wolf ascending to the sky with Tengri – was now marred by ugly brown patches that refused to fade no matter how hard she worked the fabric against the smooth river stones.

Bloodstains.

A grim reminder that she could not wipe clean, no matter how hard she tried.

Her hands trembled, not just from the cold but from the memories that plagued her with each movement. The screams still echoed in her mind; the terrible sounds of men she had known since childhood cutting down their own brothers. The way Tarkhan's blood had sprayed across the grass, his eyes wide with betrayal as his life drained away. She had stood frozen, wanting to intervene but stricken by fear and uncertainty, and that moment would haunt her until her dying day.

Valour 129

'Harder,' she whispered to herself, attacking the marred shawl with renewed vigour. 'It has to come out. It has to—'

The temperature dropped yet further as she was bathed in darkness. Talshyn didn't need to turn to know who stood behind her; she could feel Moldir's presence like a shadow falling across her soul.

'You're wasting your time.' The high priestess's voice carried the chill of winter. 'Some things you can never wash clean. Best to abandon them to the past, girl.'

Talshyn's fingers gripped the wet fabric tighter. 'I only wished to preserve what I could, Kara Kam. This shawl was my mother's and—'

'Your mother is dead,' Moldir cut her off. 'Only a memory, and you owe her nothing. It would serve you better to remember the power you do serve. Or have you forgotten your oaths so quickly?'

Talshyn turned to face her mentor. Moldir stood on the bank like a dark monolith, her robes seemingly untouched by the bitter breeze that whipped through the trees.

'I have not forgotten,' Talshyn said, though the words felt hollow.

'Haven't you?' Moldir's eyes seemed to pierce straight through to Talshyn's soul. 'I see the doubt in your heart, girl. The weakness. Erlik will not tolerate such frailty.'

'I am not frail,' Talshyn said through gritted teeth, hoping it conveyed enough conviction to fool this old woman. 'And I will prove it.'

For a moment, nothing. Then Moldir grinned that yellow grin of hers. 'See that you do.'

She turned painfully slowly, before moving away like smoke on the wind. Talshyn remained kneeling in the stream, though she could no longer feel her legs in the numbing water. The shawl hung limp and heavy in her hands, its patterns and the story they told distorted – like the traditions of her people, twisted into something unrecognisable by violence and mistrust.

The Christian woman's words came back to her unbidden: 'God's grace knows no limits. His forgiveness is infinite. We need only be willing to accept it.'

How different those words were from what Moldir had taught her about Erlik's endless hunger. Talshyn had always accepted without question that their god demanded sacrifice, that only through death could they prove their devotion. But now...

She looked down at her hands, red and raw from scrubbing. How much blood had they helped spill in Erlik's name? How many more would die before his thirst was slaked? The thought of Fabrisse's quiet strength in the face of death made something ache in Talshyn's chest. The holy woman hadn't railed against her captors or cursed them – she had instead offered prayers for their souls. Repentance. Forgiveness.

'Forgiveness?' Talshyn whispered to the rushing water. 'If only I—'

A crow's harsh call made her start, for a moment fearing Moldir had returned. But it was just a bird, watching her with gleaming eyes from a nearby branch. Still, she couldn't shake the feeling that Erlik himself was watching her through those beady black eyes, weighing her worth and finding it wanting.

She rose on shaking legs, water streaming from her sodden robes. The shawl was still stained – perhaps irredeemably so – but as she wrung it out, she noticed that the original pattern was still visible. The white wolf still prowled across the embroidery, though its fur was now mottled with blood.

'Mother,' she breathed, pressing the damp fabric to her chest. 'What would you think of what we've become? Of what I've become?'

Her mother had taught her of the gods so many years ago,

before a hard winter had taken both her parents away. Back then she had learned how to honour Tengri, how to thank Eje for the bounty of the earth. Never had those teachings involved the suffering of others.

When had they strayed so far from that path? When had she allowed herself to be led into such...

The sound of thundering hooves tore Talshyn from her thoughts. She turned to see Artak burst into the camp, his horse's sides heaving, foam dripping from its bit. The warrior's face was a mask of rage as he rode toward the centre of camp, where Shoruk stood conferring with his warriors. He had sent two men to scout the path behind and his expression darkened as Artak returned alone.

'Where is your brother?' Shoruk demanded, though from his tone, Talshyn suspected he already knew the answer.

Artak practically fell from his saddle, his legs barely supporting him as he staggered forward.

'Dead,' he spat the word like poison. 'Moldir was right; we are being followed by friends of the holy woman. When we were spotted they chased us down, leaving us no choice but to fight. Those Christian dogs... They showed no mercy.'

Shoruk lashed out with a snarl of rage, kicking over a cooking pot. The hot contents splashed across the frozen ground, steam rising into the cold air. Several warriors stepped back, but Talshyn couldn't look away as their chief raged.

'How close?' he demanded, seizing Artak by the shoulders. 'How close are they?'

'Too close,' Artak replied. 'They follow like wolves on our trail. I counted only six of them, but they are well-armed and armoured, riding their heavy steeds. And they seem determined enough, led by an experienced hunter from what I could see.'

Shoruk released him with a curse, pacing like a caged animal.

The other warriors watched warily, and Talshyn could feel the tension building. Then Shoruk reached for his sword as his gaze swept toward where the prisoners sat bound. Fabrisse remained straight-backed despite her bonds, but the timid monk had curled in on himself like a frightened child. Talshyn saw the intent in Shoruk's eyes before he even drew his blade – he meant to end this chase in blood.

'Then we must give them nothing to hunt,' he growled, stalking toward them.

'Stay your hand.' Moldir's command cut through the tense air as she stepped into the open.

'Why should I?' Shoruk demanded, though his step faltered. 'They follow us for these prisoners. Without them—'

'Without them, we have no sacrifice,' Moldir replied. Her dark eyes fixed on the monk, who tried to shrink further into himself under that terrible gaze, and her lips twisted in a smile that held no warmth. 'And so we must think of another way.'

'The only other way is for us to face them in battle,' Shoruk snarled. 'I am no coward, Moldir, but neither would I see my brothers cut down needlessly.'

Moldir turned to regard him, no shadow of doubt crossed her face, as though she had all the answers. 'This land is ours, Shorukhan. None know it better. And we shall use it to our advantage. With a little help.'

Shoruk's brow creased in confusion as Moldir looked back to the cowering Christian. Talshyn could only assume she had a plan to confound their pursuers. One that would not end well for the little priest.

18

Their horses trod carefully through the woodland. Each of the knights was now garbed in full armour – gambeson, hauberk and helms – but it did little to allay their fears. They'd been moving since first light, pushing hard through difficult country, and the strain was beginning to tell. The encounter with the scouts had left them all on edge, and now every shadow seemed to conceal another ambush, every whisper of wind through the leaves a signal of danger.

Movement somewhere in the gloom, making Estienne's hand tighten on his sword hilt. He held his breath until some woodland animal scurried through the brush.

Ahead, Jurgen moved with the surety of a man who had spent his life in these wild places, though even the experienced tracker's usual confidence seemed diminished. Clovis padded silently at his master's heel, the hound's ears pricked forward, hackles slightly raised. The dog's agitation only mirrored Estienne's own sense of unease.

'We're getting close,' Jurgen murmured, barely loud enough to carry. 'Clovis is never this tense unless—'

'Unless there's prey nearby,' Estienne finished for him. 'Or predators.'

Jurgen nodded his agreement. 'Stay alert. Eyes on the tree-line. They're out there somewhere.'

Amalric and Rotger rode close by, their weapons held at the ready. The big knight's usual cheerful demeanour had given way to grim focus, while Amalric's jaw was set in a hard line beneath his helm. Behind them, the young squires Eggert and Merten brought up the rear, their inexperience showing in the way they flinched at every movement.

Carsten hung back slightly from the main group, his balding head slick with nervous sweat despite the morning chill. The Komtur's eyes darted constantly to the dense undergrowth on either side of their path, his hand white-knuckled on his sword hilt. The man's fear was becoming more obvious with each passing mile.

'We should never have come,' Carsten muttered, not for the first time. 'We should turn back before—'

'Quiet,' Jurgen cut him off, raising a hand in warning.

Clovis had frozen, nose working the air, a low growl building in his chest. They all went still, straining to hear whatever had caught the hound's attention. For a long moment, there was only the sigh of wind through the leaves and the soft jingle of mail. The forest seemed to hold its breath, as though it sensed approaching violence.

A cry split the silence – raw with pain and desperation. The sound echoed through the woodland, making it impossible to pinpoint its source.

'What in God's name—' Carsten was once again silenced as Jurgen raised a hand.

'It's that way,' the trapper said, pointing just off to the east.

As though to confirm his suspicion the cry came again, this time more pitiful than the first.

'Then let's go and see,' Estienne replied.

'Are you out of your mind?' Carsten blurted from the rear. 'It could be a trap.'

'And what if it isn't?' Estienne shot back. 'You just want to leave a man to suffer? We proceed. With caution.'

Jurgen nodded his assent, leading them toward the sound. They picked their way forward with agonising slowness, and sweat began to trickle down Estienne's back despite the morning chill. Another cry reached them, closer now, the sound carrying such raw anguish that young Merten made the sign of the cross.

They emerged onto a ridge overlooking a small valley, and Estienne's gut clenched at what he saw below. One of the friars – Brother Galien, if he remembered the name rightly – had been bound on a crude spit over a wooden stake, positioned with diabolic precision so that any movement drove the sharpened spike into the flesh of his back. He tried to keep himself up, the muscles of his arms straining, but it was obvious he was weakening. The man's brown habit was now stained dark with blood and filth, his face a mask of agony as he struggled weakly.

'Christ's bones,' Amalric growled. 'What kind of devils would do such a thing?'

'The kind that want us to walk right into a trap,' Estienne replied grimly.

His assessment was immediate and stark. The valley was a natural killing ground, with steep cliff faces rising on three sides. A single path wound down from their position, too narrow and treacherous for a horse – the only viable approach to where Galien had been staked out like bait in a pit. The surrounding terrain offered no alternative route.

'We can't just leave him there,' Rotger rumbled, pointing to where several ravens circled overhead. 'For the carrion birds.'

'If we're not careful we might end up staked out right beside him,' Jurgen added, his hound's hackles fully raised, lips drawn back from his teeth in a quiet snarl. 'Clovis knows there's danger down there. Something we can't see.'

Estienne studied ridge that looked down on the valley floor. A perfect hiding places for archers. The path down was wide open and anyone attempting a rescue would be completely exposed for the entire descent.

'They've chosen their ground well,' Amalric said quietly. 'That path is a death trap.'

'There must be another way down,' Eggert insisted, his young face pale beneath his helm. 'Perhaps if we circle around—'

'Those cliffs are too steep to climb,' Jurgen cut him off. 'They've made sure we have only one way in and out.'

Another cry echoed up from below, weaker this time. Galien's head lolled back as he fought to remain conscious. Blood darkened the spike over which he was tied. If he lost consciousness or strength he would be impaled completely. The sight made Estienne's hands clench into fists – this was a deliberate spectacle of cruelty designed to draw them in.

'How long has he been down there?' Merten asked.

'Hard to say,' Jurgen replied. 'But he won't last much longer if we do nothing.'

'What can we do?' Carsten hissed. 'I've never seen a more obvious trap.'

The words hung in the air between them as they all contemplated the terrible choice before them. The ruse was obvious, its jaws wide open, ready to snap shut. Though the pagans were out of sight, it was obvious they couldn't be far. But could they really stand by and watch a brother of the faith die in such agony?

Valour 137

'We have to get down there,' Estienne said, already checking his sword and shield straps.

'You cannot be serious.' Carsten's voice was thick with disbelief. 'They want us to go down there, to die like animals in their snare.'

'Maybe it's a trap.' Estienne turned to face the Komtur, keeping his voice low but fierce. 'Or maybe they have left behind a wounded man to slow us down. Either way, we cannot leave him to die like that. I will not allow it.'

'Better one man than all of us,' Carsten shot back, his face flushed with anger. 'You've seen how these pagans fight. Hiding in the shadows for the most opportune moment. Striking like cowards. If we go down there we'll be slaughtered before we even reach him.'

Amalric stepped forward. 'Brother Carsten, our duty—'

'Duty?' Carsten's laugh held an edge of hysteria. 'Our duty is to survive! To return to Rosenau and warn the Marschall of what we have found. Not to throw our lives away in some foolish rescue attempt.' He gestured wildly at the valley below. 'Look at what they've done to him already. What do you think they'll do to us?'

The young squire Eggert shifted uncomfortably. 'But Komtur, we took oaths—'

'Silence, boy!' Carsten rounded on him. 'You know nothing of this. You have no idea what these savages are capable of. They flay men alive, feed their entrails to dogs while they watch. Is that what you want? To die screaming while they laugh at your agony?'

'Lower your voice,' Jurgen warned. 'Unless you want to announce our presence to the whole valley.'

Carsten turned back to Estienne, desperation creeping into his voice. 'Think, Wace. Use your head instead of your heart for once. We cannot save him. He's already dead, they're just using him to draw us in. Like a wounded deer to lure in wolves.'

'Then let them try,' Rotger rumbled. 'Better to die fighting for a fellow Christian than live as a coward.'

'Easy for you to say,' Carsten sneered. 'You're too simple to understand there's no glory in death. No one will sing a song of your heroics when you're stuck full of arrows in the shit end of nowhere.'

Estienne had heard enough, and he met Carsten's gaze. 'You're right about one thing, Schado. This is a trap. But I would rather die trying to save that man, than live knowing I abandoned him.' Then he looked to the others, seeing the fear on their faces. 'I won't order any of you to follow me. This is a choice each must make for himself.'

Another cry drifted up from below, weaker than before. In the silence that followed, they could hear Brother Galien's laboured breathing echoing off the cliff faces, reminding them that time was running short.

'I stand with you, brother.' Rotger clasped Estienne's arm. 'Whatever comes.'

'And I,' Amalric added without hesitation. 'We face this together, as we have faced all things.'

The squires exchanged glances before Merten said, 'We're with you too.'

Eggert nodded his agreement, though his eyes betrayed his fear at the prospect of walking into a certain trap.

Only Carsten remained apart, his face twisted with barely suppressed terror. 'You're all fools. Dead fools. I won't be party to this suicide.'

'Guard the horses then,' Estienne said, unable to keep the contempt from his voice. 'At least try to make yourself useful.'

Carsten looked as though he might protest, before thinking

Valour 139

better of it and turning on his heel. None of them bothered to watch him go as he skulked off toward the horses. Their attention was fixed on the narrow path that wound down into the valley – a path that might well lead to their deaths.

'My bow is yours, if you'll have it,' Jurgen said. 'And Clovis will give whatever help he can.'

Estienne nodded his thanks, as Brother Galien's weak cries echoed off the cliff face. No more time to spare. Estienne drew his sword, the steel sighing softly as it cleared the scabbard. The familiar weight felt right in his hand, like an old friend. He offered up a silent prayer to Saint Michael, patron of warriors, then gestured for the others to form up.

'Let's go.'

19

Estienne kept his shield raised as he led the way. Even the slightest sound – loose stones shifting beneath his boots, the creak of leather and steel – seemed to resound off the high-sided cliff with unnatural clarity. Brother Galien's laboured breathing carried clearly in the still air, each pained gasp an urgent reminder of their grim purpose.

'Eyes on the ridgeline,' he murmured to Amalric, who followed close behind. 'Any movement, any glint of steel...'

'I see nothing,' his friend replied quietly.

'They could still be up there,' Estienne said as he studied the rocky outcrops above. 'No one goes to this much trouble laying a trap only to abandon it.'

'Then let us pray this was merely to delay us.'

They were halfway down when another cry of pain split the air, the sound raw with agony. Estienne's hand tightened on his sword hilt as he watched Brother Galien struggle weakly. Yet another reminder that time was running out.

'Holy Christ,' young Merten gasped. 'How can men do such things to one another?'

Valour 141

'The pagans have their own gods,' Eggert replied, his young face hard with hatred. 'Demons that feast on suffering.'

'Steady,' Estienne cut them off. 'Keep your eyes on the high ground. And your shields ready.'

The unnatural quiet set his teeth on edge. The pagans had gone to such effort to stage this trap, yet now seemed content to let their victim be rescued. Perhaps Amalric was right – perhaps by leaving a wounded man behind they hoped to delay their pursuers. Estienne could only pray that much was true.

When they finally reached the valley floor, Estienne signalled for the others to form a rough circle while he and Amalric approached the wounded monk. Up close, the extent of Galien's injuries became clear. The stake had pierced his side between two ribs, and what little strength he had left was being spent trying to keep his weight off the point. His face was waxy pale and beaded with sweat.

'Be still, brother,' Estienne said softly. 'We're here to help you.'

'Please,' he gasped. 'Get me out of here.'

'Save your strength,' Amalric told him, drawing his knife. 'We'll be quick about it.'

He began cutting through the ropes that bound the monk to a wooden frame as Estienne bore his weight. Eventually he was freed, and both men lifted the monk as gently as they could to the ground to the sound of pitiful whimpers.

'The bleeding's bad,' Amalric muttered, examining the deep wound. 'We'll need to bind it before we move him.'

'Then let's be quick about it,' Estienne replied.

A pebble clattered down one of the cliff faces, the sound sharp as a thunderclap in the peculiar quiet. Estienne's head snapped up, scanning the ridge, but there was no movement above.

As Amalric set about binding Galien's wound, Estienne's

instincts screamed that this mercy was merely the prelude to something far worse. But what choice did they have? They couldn't leave a brother of the faith to such a cruel fate, even knowing it was almost certainly a trap.

'There, that's the best I can do right now,' Amalric said.

He had done well with what bandages they had, though blood was already soaking through them.

'Rotger,' Estienne said. 'I'll need you to carry Brother Galien to safety.'

The big knight nodded his assent, sheathing his sword, shouldering his shield and kneeling to lift the monk off the ground. Rotger cradled Brother Galien against his broad chest as though the monk weighed no more than a child, but even his careful movements drew fresh whimpers of agony from the wounded man.

Estienne kept his shield raised as they began their careful withdrawal, dividing his attention between their path ahead and the brooding cliffs that hemmed them in. The late afternoon sun had begun its descent behind the western peaks, casting long shadows across the valley floor.

Their footsteps crunched against loose gravel, and even Clovis's padding feet seemed unnaturally loud, though Jurgen's hound moved with the stealth of a born hunter. The trapper himself kept glancing between his dog and the ridgelines, his face creased with concern, arrow nocked to his bow.

'Mother Mary, protect us,' Eggert whispered, his hand straying to the wooden cross dangling about his neck.

'Save your prayers,' Amalric replied quietly. 'Keep your shield up and your sword ready. They'll do you more good if we sight trouble.'

They had covered perhaps half the distance to the valley's mouth when Estienne caught sight of Carsten's distant figure.

The Komtur sat his mount well beyond the narrow pass, positioned safely away from any potential danger, along with the rest of their horses. Even at this distance, Estienne could see how the man shifted nervously in his saddle, no doubt desperate to flee at the first sign of trouble.

Brother Galien moaned softly as they negotiated a particularly rough patch of ground, the sound quickly stifled against Rotger's chest. The friar's face had grown terrifyingly pale, his breathing becoming more laboured with each passing moment.

'Hold on, brother,' Rotger murmured. 'Not much farther now.'

Galien's only response was a quiet whimper as he slipped in and out of consciousness. Mercifully, the mouth of the valley loomed ahead, promising safety. Estienne glanced toward Carsten once more, noting how the Komtur had begun edging his mount even further from the gully entrance.

When they stepped out onto level ground, Estienne almost allowed himself a smile. Almost hailed Carsten in greeting to reassure him all was well. He never got the chance.

The first arrow soared out of nowhere, heralded by a deadly whistle before it struck the ground at Estienne's feet, steel head burying itself in the dirt with a sharp thud. Before he could even shout a warning, the sky erupted.

Shafts rained down from all around, the sound a terrible whisper-hiss, punctuated by the heavy thunk of arrows striking stone.

'Shields!' he bellowed, but the command was barely needed.

His companions had already formed up around Rotger and their wounded charge, creating a wall against the storm of arrows.

'Carsten!' Amalric shouted, his voice carrying above the chaos. 'For God's sake, bring the horses!'

But even as the words left his friend's mouth, Estienne watched their Komtur wheel his mount around. There wasn't even a moment's hesitation – Carsten simply dug his spurs into his horse's flanks and fled, abandoning them to their fate. Their own mounts, left without guidance and panicked by the sudden violence, scattered in all directions.

'Godless bastard!' Rotger's roar of rage echoed off the cliff faces. 'May Hell take your coward's soul!'

An arrow found a gap between shields, thudding into Rotger's shoulder. The big knight didn't even flinch, keeping Brother Galien held protectively against his chest as missiles continued to rain down around them.

Archers had appeared along both ridgelines, silhouettes dark against the dying sun. Estienne counted at least two dozen, with more appearing by the moment. Their bowstrings sang in terrible harmony as they launched volley after volley toward the trapped knights below.

'Stand together!' Estienne commanded as another shaft glanced off his helm. 'Don't let them split us apart!'

No sooner had he spoken the words, than more warriors appeared at the valley's entrance, cutting off any escape route. Others were working their way down the slopes, curved swords drawn.

A particularly heavy volley forced them closer together, shields overlapping as they tried to protect Brother Galien. Jurgen loosed his own arrows as Clovis snarled and barked at his heel, but he could do little against such overwhelming odds.

'We can't stay here,' Merten gasped, blood running down his leg where an arrow had grazed his thigh. 'We have to move!'

'Move where, boy?' Amalric's voice carried an edge of desperation. 'They've got every approach covered!'

An arrow struck Estienne's shield with enough force to punch clean through the wood and emerge mere inches from his face. He snarled his reply, desperate to fight someone, and as if in answer a horn blast echoed across the valley – three sharp notes that carried some meaning to their attackers.

The arrow storm slackened slightly, though not enough to risk lowering their shields. Estienne caught glimpses of more warriors moving into position. They were being surrounded completely, hemmed in like prey in a snare.

'They mean to charge,' he hissed. 'Ready yourselves. But whatever you do, don't break—'

'For the glory of God!'

Eggert's battle cry shattered the air. Before anyone could stop him, the young squire broke from their formation and charged toward the nearest foe. His sword caught the dying sunlight as he raised it high in both hands, shield forgotten in his sudden fervour.

'Eggert, no!'

Estienne's shout came too late.

The first arrow took him in the shoulder, the impact spinning him half around. But still he ran on, his face transformed by Godborne courage. The second shaft struck his thigh, driving through flesh to emerge from the other side. His stride faltered, but his voice never wavered as he screamed defiance at his killers.

The third arrow found his throat.

Eggert stood frozen for a heartbeat, sword still raised, blood seeping from the wound. Then his legs buckled and he collapsed, body rolling limply down the rocky slope, until it came to rest face-down in the dirt.

'No!' Merten's anguished cry broke the silence. 'God in heaven, no!'

As though Merten's grief-stricken cry were a war cry of its own, warriors began to pour down the slopes. Estienne met the charge, snarling his fury, his sword opening a throat with a spray of arterial blood. The warrior's momentum carried him forward, hot blood washing over Estienne's hand as the dying man collapsed against him. He shoved the corpse aside in time to smash another attacker with his shield, feeling bone crunch against the rim.

Beside him, Amalric fought with quiet precision, each stroke aimed for the kill. His blade scythed through leather armour, dealing quick death, but there were too many.

For each warrior they struck down, three more took his place. Rotger had laid down Brother Galien, standing over the wounded priest as he wielded his sword two-handed. A Cuman warrior made the mistake of coming within reach, and Rotger took his arm off at the shoulder, sending him staggering back with a shriek of agony. But even the big knight's great strength couldn't hold back the tide forever.

'Come on then!' he roared, his voice thick with battle rage. 'Come taste holy steel, you pagan dogs!'

But they were already surrounded. Already overwhelmed.

Jurgen's bow sang, his last arrow catching a warrior in the shoulder, but the man barely slowed as he bore the trapper to the ground. Clovis fought to protect his master, the hound's jaws finding Cuman flesh, but it was dragged away snarling by another pagan warrior.

'Estienne!' Amalric's warning came too late.

A warrior had seized Merten from behind, pressing a curved blade against the young squire's throat. Blood already trickled from where the edge had broken skin, and Merten's eyes were wide with terror as he stared at Estienne. All the courage and determination had fled from his young face, leaving only a frightened boy beneath.

Time seemed to stop as Estienne met that desperate gaze.

Valour 147

Every instinct screamed at him to fight on, to die with his sword in his hand as a knight should. But Merten's life hung by a thread, and that thread would snap the moment Estienne raised his blade again. He could not let that boy die, just so he might end his days in glory.

'All right,' he growled, dropping his shield and holding up a placating hand. 'Enough!'

He let his sword fall from nerveless fingers. Beside him, Rotger and Amalric did likewise, though he could see the same bitter resignation in their eyes that he felt in his heart.

Rough hands seized his arms, the warriors binding them behind his back with practised efficiency. He didn't resist – their fate had been sealed the moment Carsten fled, leaving them to die in this godforsaken valley.

The only question that remained was what their captors had planned for them.

20

The prisoners were brought back to camp as the sun began its descent behind the frost-capped mountains. Talshyn watched from the edge of the trees as Shoruk's warriors dragged the captives behind their horses. The tallest among them moved with a proud bearing despite his bonds, a livid scar crossing his left cheek like a stroke of pale lightning. His grey-blue eyes reminded her of winter skies as they scanned the waiting encampment with a predator's gaze. He wore the white tabard like most of these warriors, but instead of the usual black cross it bore a black lion. Even bound and mud-stained, he carried himself as though he were the captor rather than the captured.

Beside him walked another Christian warrior, square-jawed and handsome beneath his dark hair. His shoulders were set with the same quiet defiance, though Talshyn noted how his eyes kept darting to his companion, as if seeking guidance or reassurance, she could tell not which.

The massive warrior who followed them was a bear of a man, his broad chest heaving with exertion as he cradled the wounded

Valour 149

priest in arms thick as tree trunks. Despite his obvious strength, he handled the poor man with surprising tenderness. For his part, the young priest they had staked out as bait had taken on the grey pallor of approaching death, and Talshyn forced herself to look away lest the shame of what they had done to him overwhelm her.

Behind them stumbled the youngest of their captives, barely old enough to grow a proper beard. Though his hands trembled where they were bound before him, he kept his chin raised, meeting the hateful stares of the surrounding warriors with admirable courage.

Finally, an old man brought up the rear of their sorry procession, his face as impassive as stone. Beside him they dragged a hound, the black beast struggling against its leash with fury, jaws snapping at anyone close enough, yellow eyes blazing.

The few warriors who had remained behind emerged from their yurts, gathering in ever-tightening circles to witness this triumph. Some spat curses, while others simply watched with cold satisfaction. Talshyn recognised the hunger in their eyes – these captured men represented everything they had lost, every humiliation they had suffered as the Christians drove them from their ancestral lands. Now they would take whatever revenge was left to them.

'Dogs of the cross,' someone snarled from the crowd. 'Not so mighty now, are you?'

A few warriors laughed, but Talshyn noticed how they fell silent when the scarred knight's storm-grey eyes fell upon them. Even in bonds, there was something about him that demanded respect, as though he were a captured chieftain rather than a lowly warrior.

As Moldir came to greet the triumphant warriors, Talshyn fell into step behind her. She had learned long ago to keep exactly two paces back – close enough to hear, far enough to avoid notice.

'You've done well,' Moldir said, her eyes surveying their captives. 'Though I see fewer prisoners than we might have hoped.'

Shoruk turned in his saddle to view the beaten warriors. 'One escaped. Another died fighting.'

'And the one who fled?' Moldir's voice carried an edge sharp as winter frost. 'You think he will seek out his brethren?'

'He was a coward,' Shoruk spat. 'Abandoned his brothers at the first sign of battle. Rode off like his horse had wings. He will not be back and is not worth the effort of the hunt. We have enough here to appease the gods.'

Something dark and hungry flashed across Moldir's face. 'Indeed. And they shall have their due.'

'Four of my warriors died in the ambush,' Shoruk said quietly, as though attempting to hide his emotion. 'Good men. Brothers. Manyak, who rode with me since we were boys. Konchak, who never failed to find game even in the deepest winter. Their souls cry out for vengeance.'

'And they shall have it,' Moldir repeated. 'Blood answers blood. As it has always been.'

'Let me be the one to end their lives.' Artak's voice broke across the camp as he stepped forward. 'My brother's spirit cannot rest while his killers draw breath. Let me send these Christian dogs to their weak god and let my brother's shade smile down from Tengri's unbroken sky. Let him see his death avenged by my own hand.'

Talshyn watched his fists clench and unclench at his sides, knuckles white with anger. She had known Artak and Urtak since they were children together, had watched them race their shaggy ponies across the summer steppes, sharing the same wild laugh as they galloped. Now Urtak's laugh would never ring out again, and something in Artak's eyes suggested his own mirth had died with his brother.

More warriors stepped forward, their thirst for blood apparent in their eager expressions, and Talshyn saw how Moldir's eyes gleamed with anticipation. But before the high priestess could speak, movement caught Talshyn's attention.

Fabrisse had risen, her hands still bound, her golden hair a beacon of light in the gathering gloom. Blood and dirt streaked her face, but her voice carried clear and strong across the circle.

'If blood must be spilled, then take mine alone,' she said, meeting Artak's rage-filled eyes without flinching. 'Let these men return to their home. I offer myself freely as sacrifice to your gods. Surely one willing soul is worth more than a dozen taken by force?'

At those words something stirred in Talshyn – admiration perhaps, or envy that she would never share the strength of such conviction. Several warriors muttered in answer, some nodding slowly as if considering the fairness of her offer, but Moldir's laugh shattered the moment, the sound setting Talshyn's teeth on edge.

'Your god's mercy has no place here, Christian,' the high priestess said, her voice dripping with contempt.

'My God has a place in the hearts of men everywhere,' Fabrisse countered.

'Silence!' Moldir turned to address the gathered clan, arms raised to the darkening sky. 'Your brothers fell in battle. Their souls can only be honoured by the sacrifice of warriors. Tonight we not only avenge our dead, but earn the favour of Tengri and Eje. Earn the respect of our ancestors. Our brothers so recently fallen.'

Shoruk raised his sword and howled his assent. He was joined by the rest of the clan warriors, their noise like the baying of the wolf pack.

Talshyn saw Fabrisse flinch at the noise, though her chin remained raised in defiance. The holy woman's eyes found hers through the crowd, and they were filled with such profound sorrow that Talshyn had to look away. As Fabrisse and the other prisoners were dragged away and bound to the trunks of trees, Talshyn found herself walking away from the echoing noise of her clan, allowing the surrounding forest to consume her.

Soon, darkness crept across the sky, bringing with it a bone-deep cold that made Talshyn pull her furs tighter around her shoulders. When she eventually returned to the encampment she saw the warriors had begun their preparations – gathering wood for the ritual fires, their low chants mixing with the bitter wind that swept down from the mountains.

She found herself drawn to where Fabrisse sat among the other prisoners. There was something in her quiet dignity that called to Talshyn, like a beacon in the gathering gloom. The Christian woman looked up as she approached, and something in her expression made Talshyn's steps falter. There was no fear in those eyes, no hatred. Only a profound sadness.

'You don't have to be part of this,' Fabrisse said softly as she looked out onto the clan building its great fire. 'There is another path. A better way. One that doesn't demand blood for blood, as your mistress seems so set upon.'

'Be silent.' The words came out harsher than Talshyn intended. 'There is no other way. I have no other path.'

'I feel the doubt in your heart,' Fabrisse continued. 'I see it. Otherwise why would you be here with me and not at the side of your high priestess? You detest the darkness your mistress embraces. And I see the way you tremble when she speaks of

Valour

sacrifice. But God's grace reaches out for all who seek it. Even those who have walked in shadow—'

'Your god is weak,' Talshyn interrupted, echoing Moldir's words. 'These mountains belong to older powers. I belong to—'

'Do you?' Fabrisse's voice was gentle, almost maternal. 'Then why do you tremble when you speak of them? Why do you look fearful at the mention of their names?'

In the distance, Talshyn could hear Moldir beginning her ritual chant – harsh syllables that seemed to make the very air grow colder. The sound sent shivers down her spine, as it always had, though she had never admitted that to anyone.

'I could help you,' Fabrisse whispered, and somehow Talshyn knew it wasn't just empty words. 'All of you. There is still time to turn from this path. To embrace the light instead of the darkness that consumes you.'

For a moment, Talshyn allowed herself to imagine it – walking away from Erlik's endless hunger, from the nightmares that plagued her sleep. She thought of how it might feel to watch the sun rise over the steppes, to feel its warmth on her face, without the weight of that darkness pressing down on her soul. But then she thought of Moldir's rage, of what the Kara Kam would do to anyone who betrayed her.

'No,' she said, stepping back, though every fibre of her being screamed to stay. 'There is no other way. Not for me. Not any more.'

'There is,' Fabrisse pleaded. 'I promise you.'

Talshyn bent close, almost close enough to feel the holy woman's breath. 'Listen to me, Christian. Tonight there will be a ritual. And these men who have come to see you freed will burn. Their souls are bound for Tamag, and there is nothing you or your God can do to save them. Pray while you can.'

She turned and fled before Fabrisse could respond, but she

could almost feel the woman's eyes on her back, full of that same damning pity.

Moldir's chant rose to a crescendo as the wind howled through the camp, agitating torches and carrying with it the promise of violence to come. Talshyn knew that soon the night would be filled with fresh screams, new souls sent to walk Erlik's dark halls.

21

Estienne shifted his weight, trying to find some relief for his aching body. The camp had grown quiet as they built a large wooden frame from the surrounding branches, but that only made the sounds of suffering more pronounced – Brother Galien's occasional whimpers, Merten's mumbled prayers, the pained breathing of his fellow captives.

Fabrisse sat bound close by, and he felt some relief that she yet lived. It did little to dampen the shame of their captivity, though. He had travelled so far to see this woman freed, but now it seemed they were to share a similar fate. Despite their dire circumstances, she maintained that same quiet dignity he'd witnessed at Rosenau, though he could see the toll captivity had taken. Her golden hair, matted with dirt and sweat, her garb torn and filthy.

'They mean to sacrifice us,' she said. 'One by one, to their dark god.'

'What kind of god would demand such sacrifice?' Estienne asked, testing his bonds but finding they were well-secured.

'Erlik. The lord of their underworld. The young priestess, she spoke of him. Their high priestess, Moldir, is no ordinary shaman. She serves darker powers, and has led these people down a path of blood and death.'

'Then we'll send her to meet this dark god of hers,' Estienne growled, though he knew how empty the threat was while he remained bound.

A cruel laugh cut through the darkness, followed by a snarl of fury. Estienne turned to see three warriors circling Clovis, who strained at the end of a rope. The hound's hackles were raised, teeth bared as one of the warriors jabbed at him with a spear. The dog bit back with desperate fury as he snapped at his tormentors.

'Leave him be!' Jurgen shouted, as he struggled against his bonds. 'For God's sake, he's just a dog! What kind of men are you, to torment a helpless animal?'

The warriors ignored him, laughing as they continued their cruel sport. One thrust his spear close enough to nick Clovis's flank, drawing a yelp of pain that made Jurgen cry out again.

'Bastards,' the trapper spat, his voice thick with fury. 'Goddamn heathen bastards! I swear by all that's holy, I'll see you suffer for this!'

'Save your breath,' Fabrisse said quietly. 'They're lost to darkness now. Only God may see them freed of it.'

'It won't be God who sees us freed,' Estienne replied. 'And if we don't do something soon, we'll be beyond help.'

Estienne saw the priestess – Moldir, Fabrisse had called her – emerging from her tent, and the gathered warriors fell silent at her presence. She began to speak to them in her Cuman tongue. Estienne couldn't understand a word, but he could sense she was stirring them into some kind of religious fervour. Their faces came alive, eyes filled with hunger.

Valour 157

'I'm no lamb for the slaughter,' Rotger said suddenly as he shifted against his bonds.

The big knight's muscles bulged beneath his hauberk, veins standing out on his neck as he strained against the hemp, the arrow-wound to his shoulder forgotten.

'Careful, brother,' Estienne whispered, glancing toward the guards who had turned their attention to Moldir. 'Wait for the right moment. If we only get one chance—'

But Rotger was beyond caution. With a growl of effort, he managed to work one massive arm partially free. The rope creaked ominously as he leveraged his tremendous strength against the bindings. For a moment, hope flared in Estienne's chest – if anyone could break free through sheer power, it would be Rotger Havenblast, but that hope died as a shout of warning went up from one of the guards.

The shout stirred something in Rotger, and his throaty growl turned to a primal bellow as he strained against his bonds. The rope tying him to the tree snapped like cracking bone, and he lurched toward the advancing warriors.

There were six of them, all armed. Rotger was hopelessly outnumbered, but it only seemed to stoke his ire. The huge knight bolted at the warriors, catching the first of them with a shoulder charge that lifted the man clean off his feet.

A second warrior tried to grab Rotger from behind, but the knight threw his head back with savage force. The back of his skull met the warrior's nose with a wet crunch that made Estienne wince. Blood sprayed as the warrior staggered away, howling curses in his native tongue.

A spark of hope ignited, but Estienne knew it was only a brief folly. The remaining warriors fell on Rotger like wolves savaging a wounded bear, driving the hafts of their spears into his ribs and back with unfettered brutality. Rotger roared his defiance, the sound echoing off the surrounding trees as he somehow managed to stay on his feet. Blow after blow rained down, the dull thud of wood striking flesh punctuated by grunts of effort and snarls of hate.

One strike caught him behind the knee, buckling his leg with an audible crack. Still Rotger fought on, trying to shield himself as the warriors went for his head and face. Blood ran freely from a split above his eye, painting half his face crimson.

'Stop!' Estienne bellowed. 'In Christ's name, stop!'

His protests only seemed to encourage them, and the sound of wood striking flesh mixed with the impact of boots against Rotger's armoured bulk. When the big man finally fell, they continued to beat him. Rotger had stopped trying to defend himself now, his arms wrapped around his head in a final, futile attempt to stave off their attacks.

Young Merten turned, his eyes tightly shut against the violence, but Estienne couldn't look away. He owed his friend that much at least – to witness his suffering, to remember. Beside him, Amalric was praying, Latin phrases tumbling from his lips in a desperate, angry stream that seemed to have no end.

When the warriors finally stepped back, breathing heavily from their exertions, Rotger lay motionless. Blood ran freely from his nose and split lips, one eye already swelling shut beneath a mass of purple bruising. His chest rose and fell in shallow, pained gasps. One arm lay at an unnatural angle, clearly broken.

'Bastards,' Jurgen spat, but the word held more despair than anger now. 'Godless bastards.'

Like a spectre come to claim the dead, Moldir pushed her way through the surrounding warriors. Bone tokens woven into her hair clicked together like teeth as she glared down at Rotger's prone form. Without speaking, she gestured to her warriors. They moved to obey, dragging Rotger's beaten form toward a wooden frame that had been erected over a carefully constructed pyre.

'Take me instead,' Estienne called out suddenly, forcing steel into his voice despite the fear that clawed at his gut. 'I am a storied warrior who has served king and God alike. I have fought a dozen battles. Surely my soul is worth more to your gods than his?'

Moldir turned and her eyes fixed on him. In their depths Estienne saw only endless cruelty. Then she turned to follow her warriors as they dragged Rotger's bulk toward the frame.

The structure stood like a skeleton against the dark sky, its rough-hewn beams still bearing the marks of hasty axe work. Beneath it, the kindling had been stacked with careful precision.

'Brother,' Estienne called out as they bound Rotger spread-eagled onto the frame, leaving him suspended like a grotesque puppet. 'Have faith. Remember who you are. Remember your honour.'

Rotger managed to lift his head, his ruined face twisting into what might have been a smile, and blood bubbled at the corners of his mouth as he spoke. 'The honour has been mine... brother. Always keep—'

But whatever message he intended was cut short as one of the pagans approached with Rotger's helm. The big knight tried to resist as they forced it over his head, but he was too weak from the beating.

Moldir raised her arms, her sleeves falling back to reveal swirling tattoos that seemed to writhe in the firelight. She began to chant in a language that made Estienne's skin crawl, each word an offence against God himself. The other warriors took up the chant, their voices rising in terrible harmony.

At her gesture, the pagans touched torches to the pyre. The flames caught quickly, hungry tongues of fire licking at the dry wood. Smoke began to curl up around Rotger's legs, and his weak struggle grew more panicked. When the first flames reached him, his scream was made even more terrible by the hollow resonance of his helm – a sound that Estienne knew would haunt him until his dying day.

'Holy mother of God,' Amalric whispered, turning away.

But Estienne forced himself to watch as the flames climbed higher. He owed Rotger that much at least – to witness his end, to remember every detail so that someday, somehow, he could make these savages pay.

The big knight's screams echoed across the camp, the sound distorting inside the steel helm until it barely seemed human. Through it all, Moldir continued her awful chant, her face transformed by ecstatic fervour as she called out to her dark god.

When Rotger finally fell silent, the only sounds were the crackling of flames and the soft chanting of Moldir's prayers. The smell of burning flesh and metal hung thick in the air, an unholy incense that made Estienne's gorge rise. He swallowed hard against the bile in his throat, his hands clenched into useless fists behind his back until his nails cut into his palms.

'Fucking heathen bastards!' he shouted, unable to hold back any longer. 'Is this how you prove your devotion? By burning helpless men? Face me with steel in my hands and we'll see how brave you are.'

The Cumans paid him no mind, going about their business as though nothing out of the ordinary had happened. Some returned to their cooking fires, others to their guard posts. A few passed around a skin of water or wine, laughing and talking in their own tongue. The casual way they resumed their business only fuelled Estienne's rage. He had seen men become hardened to violence – indeed he considered himself one of them – but this was something else entirely.

Valour 161

Beside him, Merten had begun to shake uncontrollably. The young squire's face was chalk-white, his eyes fixed on the burning pyre where Rotger's blackened form still hung.

'Don't look,' Estienne told him quietly. 'Remember him as he was.'

But Merten seemed beyond hearing as his lips moved soundlessly, perhaps in prayer, perhaps simply gibbering his grief. Jurgen sat in grim silence, his face set in lines of hatred as he watched the warriors go about their business.

In the quiet aftermath, Moldir walked among them like death itself. She paused before each prisoner in turn, studying their faces with terrible intensity, as though selecting fruit at market. None of them could hold that gaze until she reached Estienne, who met it with all the hatred he could muster.

'I'll send you screaming to your dark god,' he promised through gritted teeth. 'I swear it by every saint in heaven. When I break free—'

A smile twisted her thin lips, and she issued a phlegmy cackle. When she spoke, the words were harsh like a blade on a whetstone. Without waiting for his response, she moved to stand before Fabrisse, and the two women regarded each other in silence for a long moment. Then Moldir spoke, her words carrying clearly in the still night air.

Fabrisse gave no reply, merely watching with defiance in her eyes, as the priestess turned, bone tokens clacking, and left them alone.

'What did she say?' Estienne asked.

'She said there will be another sacrifice tomorrow.' Fabrisse's voice was steady, despite her obvious horror at what had happened. 'She means to feed you all to her god, one by one.'

'Even you?'

Fabrisse turned to look at him, and he could see no fear there.

'I will be the last. A sacred place has been chosen for my death already.'

He would have offered her some words of reassurance, but hollow promises were worthless now. Estienne tested his bonds once more, but the ropes held fast. Unless something changed, tomorrow would bring another death, and he was powerless to prevent it.

22

Talshyn's stomach roiled as another gust of wind carried the smell of burned flesh across the camp. The stink seemed to cling to her, but she knew no amount of scrubbing would wash away such horror, just as no amount of prayer to Tengri would cleanse her soul of what she had witnessed. The warrior's screams still echoed in her mind, though the camp had grown quiet save for the occasional drunken snore from those who had celebrated the sacrifice with too much wine.

The Christian warrior's blackened corpse remained suspended over the cold ashes, a monument to Moldir's cruelty. His helm caught what little starlight pierced the clouds, the metal warped and twisted by the flames that had consumed it. Where his flesh was visible through gaps in his charred armour, it had turned black as pitch, cracked and splitting like old leather left too long in the sun. Talshyn forced herself to look at what remained of the man. She had stood silent while they bound him, while they forced that helm over his head, while they lit the pyre beneath his feet. Her inaction made her as guilty as those who had brandished the torches. Only that realisation made her turn away.

Moving through the shadows between the yurts, her steps careful and measured despite the trembling in her legs, Talshyn approached the prisoners with a wineskin in hand. Their guard, Uzur, paced a steady circuit around them, his eyes tracking her movement, but he made no move to stop her. After all, she was Moldir's chosen apprentice. What need to stop someone so elevated among the clan?

The night was bitterly cold, and she could see how the prisoners shivered in their inadequate clothing. Fabrisse sat against a tree, her golden hair now hanging in lank strands, yet still she maintained that aura of quiet dignity that had first drawn Talshyn to her. The remaining prisoners huddled close, seeking what little warmth they could find in each other's presence. The young squire had finally succumbed to exhaustion, his head lolling against the shoulder of the scarred knight with the black lion crest.

Talshyn knelt beside the holy woman, pressing the wineskin to her lips. When she had taken a drink, Fabrisse gazed at her without emotion.

'Why have you come?' Fabrisse's words carried no warmth. 'To gloat over what your mistress has wrought?'

'I...' Talshyn's voice caught in her throat as she glanced toward Uzur, but he had turned away. 'I cannot bear this any more. What we've become. This is not the way of our people.'

'What are you saying?' Fabrisse asked, her features softening.

'I need... absolution. I think I must... follow your path. The one you came to guide us upon. Do you still think it possible?'

'There is always light, even in the deepest shadow.' Fabrisse's eyes seemed to pierce straight through to Talshyn's soul, seeing every sin, every moment of weakness. 'God's grace reaches out to all who seek it.'

'Even after what we've done? After what I've allowed to happen? I watched them burn him alive. I did nothing while they—'

'The path to redemption begins with a single step. You need only find the courage to take it.'

Talshyn's hands clenched into fists. 'Moldir will kill anyone who defies her. Erlik's hunger is all consuming, and she has promised him such a feast...'

'I have seen the way she revels in suffering. But no demon's power can match God's love. No darkness can extinguish His light.'

Uzur's footsteps drew closer, and Talshyn fell silent. When he had moved on, she spoke again, her voice trembling.

'If I help you... there can be no going back for me. I will have nothing. No people, no place among the clan. They will hunt me like a wolf hunts the deer.'

'You will have God's love,' Fabrisse replied with absolute conviction. 'And my eternal gratitude. The choice is yours, but it must be made soon. Tomorrow they will burn another, and another, until none are left.'

'Very well.'

Talshyn straightened as Uzur stalked closer once more, and she assumed the imperious bearing expected of a priestess. Inside, her mind raced with consequences. She knew what had to be done, what her conscience demanded. The only question was whether she had the courage to do it, and whether she could live with herself if she didn't.

Her hands moved with practised precision as she took herbs from a pouch at her belt, letting them fall into the wineskin. Henbane gathered under the full moon, chamomile and mayweed dried in the smoke of sacred fires, mushrooms picked from the bole of a dying red oak. Normally these herbs were used to ease the pain of childbirth or help wounded warriors find rest, but in greater quantities they brought the deep sleep of near-death.

Talshyn's heart thundered as she approached Uzur. His face softened slightly at her approach, as it always did. She had known of his fondness for her since they were children, had seen how his eyes followed her, how he always volunteered for duties that brought him near the priestesses' yurts. With luck that devotion would be his undoing tonight.

'The night grows cold,' she said, forcing warmth into her voice. 'I thought you might want something to keep your blood flowing.'

She held out the wineskin, and Uzur's face cracked into a rare smile.

'You're too kind, Talshyn.' His fingers brushed hers as he took the wine, and she fought not to recoil from the contact. 'Though Shoruk would have my hide if he caught me indulging on watch.'

'Surely one small drink won't dull your senses?' She touched his arm lightly, hating herself for using his affection this way. 'And why would he mind? You have always been the most trusted of all Shoruk's men.'

Uzur's chest swelled slightly at the praise, and he glanced around furtively before raising the skin to his lips. Talshyn counted his swallows – one, two, three – before he lowered it again. In the darkness, she could see a drop of wine glistening on his chin.

'Strong stuff,' he said, blinking rapidly as the herbs began their work. 'Where did you...'

His words slurred into nothing as the potent mixture rapidly took hold. His eyes grew unfocused until they rolled back,

Valour 167

showing only whites before closing entirely. Then he slumped to the cold earth. Perhaps the concoction had been stronger than she thought.

Talshyn knelt beside Uzur's prone body, laying a hand to his chest. Thankfully he still lived. The moment stretched as she waited, hardly daring to breathe, until she was certain the sound of him collapsing hadn't alerted anyone. Only then did she allow herself to move, fingers trembling as she retrieved his knife from its sheath.

She hurried to where the prisoners sat bound, the knife clutched so tightly that her knuckles throbbed. The scarred knight tensed as she approached, muscles bunching as though he might try to break free, but Fabrisse whispered something in their western tongue that made him relax slightly, though suspicion still burned in his grey eyes.

The hemp parted easily beneath the sharp blade as she sawed through their bonds. Freeing them all seemed to take an eternity, and every rustle of movement made her heart leap into her throat.

'We must go now,' Talshyn said to Fabrisse. 'No time to waste.'

Fabrisse nodded in agreement, but the old man in his hunting leathers spoke urgently to her.

'The trapper's hound,' Fabrisse said, her voice barely above a breath. 'He won't leave without it.'

The knight with the lion tunic also spoke. Hatred burned in his eyes as he looked toward where the burned warrior's body still hung, then at Talshyn.

'He means to kill me?' Talshyn breathed.

'No,' Fabrisse replied. 'But he sees the sense in collecting their weapons before we flee. If we are caught by the clan as we run there will be no way to defend ourselves if we don't.'

Talshyn glanced toward where the clan's warriors slept off

their celebration, their snores carrying clearly in the still air. 'The weapons are stored in Shoruk's tent. The hound is tied near the horse lines. But we must hurry.'

'Very well,' Fabrisse replied. 'Lead them.'

Talshyn nodded, beckoning them after her. Thankfully the scarred warrior's footsteps were unnaturally silent for one so large. The old man followed with all the guile she would have expected from someone who spent his life on the hunt.

The camp felt like a beast holding its breath as she led them between the yurts, avoiding the dying fires where a few men still slumbered. The hound lay curled beneath a wooden frame where shields and saddles hung. Its tail began to thump softly against the hard earth as they approached, and the hunter dropped to his knees beside it. His hands were gentle as he checked its wounds, fingers probing carefully through matted fur. Talshyn saw tears glinting in the old man's eyes as he whispered to the animal in his own tongue, and worked quickly to free it. When he lifted the beast in his arms, it didn't make a sound, as though it understood the need for silence as well as any man.

Talshyn didn't wait, leading them on through the gloom. Shoruk's tent lay just ahead and Talshyn's breath caught as she saw a single guard, Boril, dozing beside the entrance, chin resting on his chest. His spear lay across his lap, and a half-empty cup of wine had tipped beside him, its contents frozen into a dark stain on the ground.

She was suddenly numbed by panic, but the knight was still moving, stalking through the shadows until he was behind the sleeping man. One arm wrapped around Boril's throat, cutting off any sound he might have made, and he thrashed briefly, boots scrabbling against the cold earth, before going limp. The knight lowered him carefully to the ground and turned toward the tent.

Talshyn and the hunter waited as he disappeared inside. Each

Valour 169

consecutive heartbeat setting her teeth further on edge. What if Shoruk wasn't as drunk as she'd hoped? What if he woke to find an armed Christian in his tent?

When the knight emerged, he carried an armful of weapons – swords, knives, even the hunter's bow with its quiver of arrows. Talshyn allowed herself to finally breathe, before she led them back the way they had come, each step painfully slow now that they were encumbered with steel and the wounded hound.

Eventually they reached the edge of the camp, where the others waited in the shelter of a huge pine. The scarred knight handed out the weapons, though Talshyn noticed how his eyes kept darting between her and the camp. Then he spat something in his harsh tongue, and the other warrior, the handsome one, replied in just as harsh tones. It took Fabrisse's calming words to curb their ire, but Talshyn could still see the suspicion in their eyes.

'What do they say?' she asked Fabrisse, hating how her voice trembled.

'They fear you will betray us. But they also know that you cannot be left behind.'

Talshyn turned to look at the camp. The fires still burned low, smoke rising straight and true toward Tengri's infinite sky. She could see the yurt where she had spent countless hours learning Moldir's ways, studying the old magic. Everything she had ever known lay within that camp – her people, her past, her very soul.

'They are right,' she replied. 'I can never go back.'

'Then come with us,' Fabrisse replied, reaching out to touch her arm. 'God will light your path.'

In that moment Talshyn felt as though a heavy burden had suddenly been lifted from her shoulders. 'Very well. I will come.'

When Fabrisse smiled it held such warmth it could have staved off the winter cold. She turned, telling the others what had been decided. The scarred knight began to protest, but Fabrisse silenced him with a look that could have frozen fire. After a moment's hesitation, he gave a curt nod and gestured for them to move out.

As they melted into the darkness, Talshyn cast one final glance at the life she was leaving behind. The camp looked peaceful now, as it had in her childhood before Moldir had led them down darker paths. Before Erlik's hunger had consumed her.

Then she turned away and followed her new companions, where only God's grace awaited.

23

A shout tore Shoruk from his dream, its echo cutting through the dawn. His heart thundered as more cries joined the first – urgent calls that carried clear warning. He lurched upright, hand closing instinctively around the hilt of his sword before his bare feet had even touched the ground. As he burst through the yurt's heavy hide flap into grey morning light, the shouts seemed unnaturally loud, competing with the pounding of blood in his ears.

He blinked hard against the sudden brightness. All around him, warriors emerged from their own dwellings, weapons half-drawn, faces twisted with confusion that mirrored his own.

'Shorukhan!' The cry came from near the centre of camp. 'Come quickly!'

Through the press of bodies, Shoruk saw Boril being supported between two warriors. The man's head lolled forward, and his eyes, when they managed to focus, were glazed and distant.

'What's wrong with him?' demanded Shoruk, moving closer.

'I do not know,' Darman replied. 'We found him like this.'

Shoruk's gaze snapped to where the prisoners had been

bound. The ropes that had tied them still hung from the trees, but the Christian woman and her rescuers were gone.

'What happened?' he demanded, pushing past his warriors. 'Where are they? Who was on watch?'

Close by, Uzur looked to be rising from a slumber. His eyes were rimmed with shadow and bloodshot.

'Talshyn...' His voice was slurred, as though he spoke through a mouthful of honey. 'She brought me wine during the night watch. It must have been...'

'Poisoned,' Shoruk spat. 'The treacherous bitch poisoned you.'

His hand tightened on his sword. Of course. The young priestess had seemed too interested in the Christian woman, too eager to speak with her. He should have seen it coming, should have recognised the signs of her betrayal. But then, how would he? She had been part of the clan, a friend since childhood and priestess in waiting. There was no way he could have foreseen such duplicity.

'How long?' Shoruk asked. 'How long have they been gone?'

Uzur shook his head as he swayed on his feet. 'Can't be sure... Was still dark when she... when they...'

'Which way?' Shoruk demanded, seizing the front of Uzur's coat. 'Which way did they go?'

'I don't...' Uzur shook his head, fear in his red-rimmed eyes. 'I don't know.'

'They fled north.' Artak's voice cut through the still air as he checked the ground nearby. 'Toward the mountains. The tracks are clear enough.'

Shoruk let go of Uzur, who staggered backward. He moved toward where Artak knelt and studied those distant peaks, their snow-capped summits lost in the gathering clouds.

Valour 173

'How far ahead?' he asked, though he already dreaded the answer.

'Hours,' Artak replied grimly. 'They must have a few miles' head start by now. Shall we saddle our horses?'

Shoruk gazed up uncertainly at those mountains beyond the canopy of leaves. The terrain there was treacherous at the best of times – narrow passes that wound between sheer cliffs, loose scree that could send a man tumbling to his death with one misplaced step. And now, with winter's grip tightening, those peaks would be even more deadly.

'The horses will struggle up there,' Darman said, moving to stand beside them. 'The paths are too narrow, too steep. We'd have to dismount and lead them, and even then...'

Shoruk saw sense in those words, but the thought of letting the prisoners escape, of allowing such an insult to go unpunished...

'The Christians know nothing of how to survive in those mountains,' offered Artak. 'They'll freeze or starve or fall to their deaths soon enough.'

'Perhaps. Perhaps not.' Shoruk replied. 'Talshyn knows these lands well enough. And the old hunter they travel with managed to follow our trail. He may just as easily find a way through those peaks.'

'How much have we risked already?' Darman asked quietly. 'All to sacrifice one Christian woman to the gods. Now you would have us hunt armed men in the mountains? Would you have us throw our lives away in those cursed peaks?'

The words struck home. Shoruk was responsible for his clansmen, and each life was more precious now than ever. Especially after all they had sacrificed to wrest control from Tarkhan.

'The Christian woman and her companions will die up there anyway,' Artak said. 'The cold will take them, or hunger. Why waste more lives hunting them down when the mountains will do our work for us?'

A murmur of agreement rippled through the gathered warriors. Shoruk could sense their weariness, their desire to cut their losses and move on. Perhaps they were right, but there was still an urge for a reckoning in Shoruk he could not suppress.

'And what of the traitor?' he asked. 'What of Talshyn? Are we to let her betrayal go unpunished?'

'She made her choice,' Darman said. 'Let the mountains have her too. Let the spirits judge her faithlessness.'

'And who would judge yours?'

The ice in that voice almost froze them in place. Shoruk turned to see Moldir standing there like a spirit of vengeance, her dark robes encasing her in darkness.

Darman's eyes grew wider in fear. 'I was... only...'

'You would let them go?' Moldir's words stabbed out like shards of ice. 'You would allow such betrayal to pass unavenged?'

Shoruk forced himself to stand his ground, though every instinct screamed at him to retreat. 'The mountains are too—'

'The mountains?' Moldir laughed and it was as dry as ashes from a pyre. 'You fear frozen peaks more than the wrath of Tengri? More than Eje's fury? Our gods demand blood for this insult. And you would deny them their due?'

Warriors shifted uneasily, their eyes darting between Shoruk and their high priestess. The air crackled with tension thick enough to choke on.

'The clan has already lost too many,' Shoruk said, fighting to keep his voice steady even as fear gnawed at his resolve. 'It grows weaker with each new warrior we sacrifice to this venture. Would you have us throw more lives away in those treacherous peaks?'

'Weaker?' Moldir's black eyes fixed on him with terrible intensity. 'We grow weaker in the eyes of our gods because you lack the

Valour   175

courage to do what must be done. Because you would let a Christian witch corrupt one of our own, steal her away, and simply shrug as though it means nothing.'

Shoruk felt the weight of the gathered warriors' stares, saw the doubt beginning to creep into their eyes. His leadership had been brought into question, and he could not allow it to pass. He had led these men in battle, had proven himself worthy to replace Tarkhan, but Moldir still spoke with the authority of the gods themselves. Each word seemed to carry a power that resonated with something deep in their souls.

'You twist my words, woman.' He stepped forward. 'Do not seek to question my—'

'That serpent-tongued Christian has poisoned Talshyn's mind with lies,' Moldir shrieked, her voice rising like the howl of a winter storm. 'Led her away from the true path, just as she would lead all of us away from our gods if given the chance. And now you stand here, making excuses about mountains and weather, while their trail grows cold?'

Shoruk suddenly felt control slipping through his fingers. 'I make no excuses. But I have to—'

'Perhaps I was wrong about you.' Moldir's voice dropped to a whisper that somehow carried to every ear. 'Perhaps you have grown too soft, too willing to bend before the winds of change rather than standing firm against them. Too much like Tarkhan.'

'I am nothing like Tarkhan.'

'Then prove it,' she replied. 'Make a sacrifice, here and now. Show the gods you are still faithful.'

'I will,' Shoruk barked, hefting his sword as though he might fight any man or beast to prove it. 'I will sacrifice whatever you deem fitting.'

Moldir's movement was so swift that even battle-hardened warriors had no time to react. Her ceremonial dagger appeared in her hand from nowhere, its curved blade catching the grey light as she seized Uzur by his hair. The young warrior was still too disoriented from the poisoned drink to defend himself as she drew the blade across his throat in one fluid motion, opening him from ear to ear.

Blood fountained forth, spattering across the muddy ground, an offering to hungry gods. Uzur made a wet choking sound as he collapsed, his hands clutching uselessly at the mortal wound, fingers slick with his own lifeblood as it poured between them. His eyes were wide with confusion and terror as he tried to understand what was happening to him.

'Thus die all who fail in their duty.' Moldir's voice carried across the sudden silence. 'Such weakness allowed the Christian witch's poison to spread through our clan like a disease, turning even our own priestess from the true path. But we *shall* hunt her down. The mountains *will not* shield her from Tengri's divine wrath. His gaze reaches beyond the highest peak. Eje's hunger delves deeper than the lowest valley. They will find no shelter. No peace.'

Shoruk's hand tightened on his sword as Uzur's death throes ceased, but he quelled his impulse to avenge him. To challenge Moldir now, before all these warriors whose faith in the gods ran deeper than their loyalty to any mortal chief, would be suicide. Not just for him, but for any hope of holding his clan together.

Even now, a low murmur ran through the gathered warriors. Shoruk saw the fear in their eyes, the way they shifted uneasily as Moldir's words struck at their holy fervour. These were men who would face any enemy without fear, without doubt, but the threat of their gods' wrath touched something more primal. Something that lived in the marrow of their bones, in the stories they'd been taught since childhood.

Valour 177

'Prepare for the hunt,' he heard himself say. 'We ride as soon as our horses are saddled.'

Warriors scrambled to obey. As they dispersed to gather weapons and supplies, Shoruk caught Moldir's smile. She had won here, had forced his hand through fear of their gods. And as he watched Uzur's blood seep into the thawing earth, he wondered how many more of his warriors would die before this madness reached its end.

24

Wind howled through the pass with an inhuman voice, one that threatened to tear them from the mountainside. Their path wound ever upward, barely wider than a man's shoulders in places, at times opening out to reveal a dizzying drop that fell away into shadow – an abyss so deep that the valley floor below was lost in swirling mists.

Estienne pressed himself against the cliff face, gripping the rough stone. Each step required careful consideration, the path treacherous with loose scree, and he tested his footing before committing his weight, watching as stones skittered over the edge to be swallowed by the void below.

A glance upwards and he could see the clouds roiling overhead, dark and heavy with the promise of more foul weather. They seemed almost close enough to touch, as though he might reach up and pluck some kind of heavenly salvation from them. But salvation, he knew, was still far beyond their grasp.

'Careful,' he called back to the others, his voice fighting against the constant drone of the wind. 'One at a time. Keep to the wall and watch your footing.'

Valour 179

Behind him, Merten struggled to support Brother Galien's weight. The monk's face was grey with pain and exhaustion, blood seeping through the crude bandages where the stake had pierced him, his every lurching step drawing a soft whimper.

'Just... just let me rest,' Galien gasped. 'I can't...'

'You can and you will,' Merten replied. 'We didn't come this far to give up now.'

'The boy speaks true,' Amalric added, raising his voice above the wind. 'Rest is for the dead, and you're not dead yet, brother.'

Behind him, Jurgen cradled Clovis in his arms, the hound's black coat matted with dried blood where the Cumans had worked their cruelty. Despite his injuries, the dog's yellow eyes remained alert, scanning the path ahead as though he could still guide his master.

'How far until we reach safety?' Fabrisse asked from the rear of their group.

She helped Talshyn navigate a particularly narrow section, the young priestess's dark robes whipping about her in the cutting wind.

'Impossible to say,' Estienne replied. 'All I know is, we cannot stop.'

He still wasn't sure what to make of Talshyn's sudden change of allegiance. She had freed them, true enough, but trust was harder won than that. Especially after what they had witnessed. After Rotger...

The memory of his friend's screams threatened to unman him, but he forced it down like bile. There would be time for vengeance later. Time to make the pagans pay for what they had done. For now, they had to survive.

'Riders!'

Amalric's shout shattered the wind's howl. Estienne turned, bracing himself against the rock face as he squinted along the path below. Dark shapes moved in their wake – mounted warriors picking their way along the trail they had ascended. Even at this distance, he could make out the distinctive fur-trimmed coats of the pagans, their curved bows at their saddles, and the sight made his blood run cold.

'How many?' he called back, though part of him dreaded the answer.

'Too many,' Amalric replied grimly. 'I count at least two dozen. They'll have to dismount to follow, but...'

He didn't need to finish the thought. The path was too narrow, too treacherous for Estienne to lead them any faster. Brother Galien could barely walk, and Jurgen wouldn't abandon his hound. At their current pace, they would never reach safety before the warriors caught them.

Estienne allowed the rest of them to pass him, urging them on, as he came to stand beside Amalric. He could see what his friend meant now. The horses had almost reached the narrow pass. It would not take them long to catch up, which meant there was only one option left.

'One of us must remain,' Amalric said, as though reading Estienne's thoughts. 'Someone needs to stay behind, delay them.'

'I'll do it.' The words left Estienne's mouth without hesitation.

'No.' Amalric's voice carried an edge he had never heard before. 'We both know you're the better sword. The stronger back. And God knows you're much luckier than I. Without you, they'll never make it through these mountains.'

'I won't leave you here to die.' Estienne took a step toward his friend, but Amalric raised a hand.

'Brother.' Amalric stepped closer, a sad smile playing at the corners of his mouth. 'For once in your life, don't argue. You know I'm right.'

'There has to be another way,' Estienne insisted.

'There isn't.' Amalric clasped his shoulder, his grip firm and familiar. 'We both know it.'

And he did, but Estienne simply could not allow Amalric to sacrifice himself. Vows had been made when he was but a boy, a code learned from one of the greatest knights of his age, and the Black Lion could never abandon his friend to certain death.

'I will not let you do this, Amalric. You know I can't. I am sorry, but it must be me. You have to understand that.'

'I *do* understand that,' Amalric replied, as a tear spilled from his eye.

Before Estienne could respond, before he could voice any of the thousand things that needed to be said, Amalric's fist drove into his stomach. It punched the air from Estienne's lungs, and he stumbled backward against the cliff face, knees giving way beneath him as he struggled for breath.

'Forgive me,' Amalric said softly, as he drew his blade. 'And know that it has been my honour to serve beside you. To call you brother.'

Then he turned and charged back down the path toward their pursuers.

'No,' Estienne gasped as he crawled forward, still floundering from Amalric's blow.

All he could do was watch as his friend, the man who had saved his life more than once, ran back along the mountain path toward the teeth of the enemy. Still he crawled, dragging himself to his feet. The breath had been knocked from his lungs, but gradually he began to suck in the chill air. He could not let Amalric die like this, alone atop this accursed mountain. He had to join him in one final fight.

Estienne grasped his sword, ready to wrench it free and charge after his brother when a hand caught his arm.

'There's nothing you can do,' Fabrisse said quietly, her grip surprisingly strong. 'He has chosen this path, and God bless him for it. There is no need for you both to perish.'

'He's bought us time with his blood,' Jurgen added. 'We need to use it, or it means nothing.'

Estienne wanted to tear free and charge down after his friend, but these people needed him – needed his strength, his guidance. With a snarl he slammed his half-drawn sword back into its scabbard and turned to lead them higher.

The path widened slightly as it curved around an outcropping, offering a clear view of the path below. There Estienne paused, looking down to see Amalric had positioned himself at a natural bottleneck where the path narrowed between two rock faces. Already the pagans were advancing toward his position.

The first to reach him was young and eager, charging in with his sword raised high. Amalric's blade met him with brutal swiftness, opening his throat, and dropping him like a stone.

The second warrior showed more caution, testing Amalric's guard. Steel rang against steel, the sound sharp and clean in the thin mountain air. When the warrior overextended, Amalric's savage backhand took his head from his shoulders. The body stood for a moment, a fountain of blood spurting from the neck, before toppling into the abyss.

More warriors approached warily now, having seen the fate of their companions. Arrows whispered through the air, most glancing off the cliff face or falling short, but one found its mark in Amalric's shoulder. He grunted in pain, staggering slightly, but held his ground with sword raised in challenge.

'Come on then, you pagan dogs!' His voice carried up through the pass. 'Come see what it means to die by the hand of a Christian knight.'

Two warriors charged together, trying to overwhelm him, but the narrow path worked against them. Amalric took another arrow in the thigh as he met their charge, but his blade still moved with desperate precision. The first attacker's chest opened like a ripe fruit, before the second lost his sword arm at the elbow, the limb still gripping his weapon as he toppled screaming into the void.

'We have to keep moving,' Jurgen bellowed above the wind.

Estienne dragged his eyes away, fighting the urge to race back down the mountain. He led them on, pulling his way upward, helping those who struggled, until they reached another plateau. From its edge he risked another look back down the mountain track, to see a sight that filled him with equal pride and horror.

Blood ran freely down Amalric's surcoat now, turning the white vestment red, but there were now four corpses at his feet. Another arrow struck him high in the chest, the impact driving him back a step, but he barely seemed to notice.

'God's blood,' Merten breathed beside him, his young face pale with awe and horror. 'I've never seen anything like it.'

'Nor will you again,' Estienne replied quietly.

The remaining pagan warriors stood back, too fearful to approach the deadly Teuton, but they suddenly made way for a broader figure who approached with deadly purpose.

'Shoruk,' Fabrisse whispered. 'Their clan chief.'

The warrior approached with all the confidence of a mountain lion as Amalric stood waiting, his sword pointed toward the ground. Blood dripped steadily from its point, marking time like a water clock counting down his final moments.

'For God and Saint Mary,' Amalric roared, his voice echoing through the mountains.

Shoruk's charge was like lightning – swift and terrible. Amalric managed to catch the first blow on his sword, but the impact drove him back a step, feet slipping on the scree. The Cuman's second strike came low, a vicious cut aimed at the legs, and though Amalric tried to pivot away, his wounded thigh betrayed him. He stumbled, and the curved blade bit deep into his side, parting mail links and slicing through his padded gambeson.

His sword fell from nerveless fingers, before tumbling into the abyss. Shoruk drew his blade free from Amalric's side slowly. A lingering cruelty that only lit more fire in Estienne's heart. Then Amalric collapsed to the mountain path.

As he watched his friend fall, a roar of pure rage tore from his throat and he started back down the path, heedless of the danger. In that moment he wanted nothing more than to reach Shoruk, to crush the man's throat with his bare hands.

'Estienne, please,' Fabrisse's voice cut through his fury. 'He died to save us. Would you have that mean nothing?'

The truth of her words stopped Estienne in his tracks. Amalric had known exactly what he was doing, had chosen this end to give them a chance. To waste that gift would be the gravest betrayal of all.

'They're coming,' Merten gasped, eyes wide as he watched the pagans begin to proceed up the path unhindered. 'He has bought us time, but not enough.'

And the boy was right. Though Amalric had sacrificed himself to delay the enemy he had only bought them scant time. And there was nowhere for them to hide atop this mountain.

'That boulder,' Jurgen said suddenly, gesturing to where a massive stone perched precariously near the path's edge. 'If we can shift it—'

'Come, then,' Estienne commanded as understanding dawned.

Estienne and Merten joined the trapper, pressing their shoulders against the rock. Together they strained against its weight,

Valour

and for a moment nothing happened – the boulder was as immovable as the mountain itself.

Then, with a grinding sound, it began to shift. Small stones cascaded down as the massive rock wobbled on its precarious perch.

'Heave, damn you!' Estienne growled through gritted teeth.

The boulder teetered for a moment, then toppled, sending the three of them staggering. It rolled down the path, before wedging itself between either side of the rocky trail. The gap it left could be climbed over eventually, but it would slow their pursuers significantly. Perhaps even enough to make the difference between capture and escape.

As they turned to continue their ascent, Estienne cast one last look at where his friend had fallen. 'Rest well, brother.'

Then he took the lead once more, the memory of Amalric's slaughter burning like a coal that might never grow cold.

Not until the debt was paid.

PART TWO: FLIGHT FROM THE DARK

CARPATHIAN MOUNTAINS – 1223AD

25

Rain lashed against Estienne's face as he led their ragged group higher into the mountains. His armour hung like a leaden weight, his exhausted legs threatening to buckle with each laboured step, but he forced himself onward. Rivulets of water coursed down the mountainside, turning the narrow path into a watercourse that only made their footing more treacherous.

Behind him he could just hear Jurgen's quiet litany of reassurances to his wounded hound. Clovis whimpered softly as the trapper carried him, the hound's black coat matted with rain. Behind them, Merten struggled to support Brother Galien, whose prayers had devolved into incoherent mumbling, his face grey with exhaustion and fever. Fabrisse and Talshyn struggled in their wake, but neither offered a word of complaint, despite the conditions. Estienne could only wonder how long he would be able to push them on for.

But he knew there was no other choice.

Water streamed down his spine in an icy river as he led them across a patch of exposed ground, making him suppress a violent shiver. And yet the physical discomfort was nothing compared to the hollow ache that had taken root in his chest since watching Amalric charge back down that mountain path. The image was burned into him – his friend's bravery, his strength. His sacrifice.

Amalric's end was one every knight should aspire to, and still that fact gave Estienne no comfort. He should have been the one to stay behind. Should have been the one to...

'Estienne,' Fabrisse's quiet voice cut through his dark thoughts as she drew alongside him. 'We must rest. Brother Galien can barely stand.'

He glanced back at the friar. Galien's face had taken on an alarming grey pallor, his lips moving in constant prayer as Merten practically dragged him forward. The young squire's own face was a mask of grim determination, though Estienne could see how his arms trembled with the effort of supporting the wounded man.

'Just keep going,' he replied. 'We need to put more distance between us and the pagans. You know what they'll do to us if they catch us.'

The memory of Rotger's screams came to Estienne like a flash of lightning, and Fabrisse's slight nod showed she understood all too well. Despite the hardship, they pressed on through the driving rain, following a narrow defile that wound between massive boulders worn smooth by centuries of wind and water.

They eventually found shelter beneath an overhanging rock where two massive boulders had fallen together, creating a space barely large enough to protect them from the worst of the rain. Estienne stood at the edge of the overhang, studying the terrain ahead while the others caught their breath. The path split before them – one route descending toward what might have been a valley, though it was lost in the sheets of rain that turned the world beyond into a grey blur. The other climbed higher into the

Valour 191

mist-shrouded peaks, disappearing into clouds that writhed around the mountaintops.

'The lower path leads west,' he said, squinting against the rain that drove into his face. 'Back toward the Burzenland. That looks to be the best route to take.'

Jurgen squinted along the track that fell away. 'If you say so. I've never been out this far before, so your guess is as good as mine.'

Talshyn suddenly spoke rapidly in her native tongue. Fabrisse replied to her, and the two seemed in disagreement about something.

'What's wrong?' Estienne asked.

'She says we cannot take that route. The rains will have flooded the passes below. We would be trapped between the rising waters and those who hunt us.'

The prospect of putting their lives in the hands of this girl, who had until recently served their enemies, made Estienne wary. But they had little choice – none of them knew these mountains as she did. Even Jurgen, for all his experience, was a stranger here.

'And how do we know we can trust her?'

'She risked everything to help us escape,' Fabrisse replied. 'Why betray us now, when she could have simply left us to die in that camp?'

'Because her people are hunting us? Maybe by leading us right to them she'll be offered forgiveness?'

'She would not do that,' Fabrisse said, for the first time displaying some anger in her voice. 'I know her. I trust her.'

'Know her? Trust her? Like you did those Cumans, right before they slaughtered their own people and took you prisoner?'

'If I may,' Jurgen said in his gruff voice. 'The girl most likely speaks truth – these rains can turn a dry gulley into a death trap faster than you can blink. Remember how bad that river crossing was? That was after just a day of bad weather. And besides, if she meant us harm, she could have left us to burn like poor Rotger.'

The old hunter's words carried weight, and his instincts had kept them alive this far. Still, Estienne hesitated, studying Talshyn's face for any sign of deception. The young priestess met his gaze, though he could see fear in her dark eyes. Whether it was fear of their pursuers or fear of him, he couldn't tell.

'Very well,' Estienne said finally. 'We take the higher path. But if this is some trick to deliver us to her dark gods, I'll send her to meet them myself.'

With that, he led them upward, the steep path growing narrower as it wound ever higher into the mountains. The rain began to slacken as afternoon wore on, no longer the punishing deluge of before but a steady drizzle that left everything slick and treacherous. Through breaks in the clouds, Estienne caught glimpses of the valley far below, the world beyond reduced to a patchwork of grey and green.

As the sun began to set, he saw a dark opening in the cliff face, the promise of shelter from the bitter mountain wind proving too tempting to resist. Inside, the cave was little more than a crack in the mountainside, its rough walls pressing in close enough to brush their shoulders. Water dripped from the low ceiling in a constant patter, forming small pools on the uneven floor. The entrance was barely wide enough for two men to stand abreast, though that would make it easier to defend if the worst happened.

Their small group clustered inside, doing what they could to dry clothes and find some warmth against the elements. Somehow, Jurgen managed to build a small fire with what fuel they could find in the cave, the damp wood producing more smoke

Valour 193

than flame, but before long they were huddled around it looking only a little less miserable.

Estienne sat watch as the sun set, scanning the gloom for any sign of their pursuers. Behind him, Fabrisse tended to Brother Galien by the fire. The friar's laboured breathing and occasional whimpers of pain echoed off the narrow walls, each intake of air seeming to cost him more effort than the last.

'The wound festers,' Fabrisse said quietly as she examined the injury where the stake had pierced him. 'Without proper care, without herbs and clean bandages...'

She didn't need to finish the thought. They all knew what infection could do to a man, how it could eat him alive from the inside while they watched helplessly.

'He should never have been here,' Estienne said, more to himself than to her. 'None of you should. I warned you these lands were dangerous.'

'And yet here we are,' Fabrisse replied, her tone gentle but firm as she cleaned the wound with water from a pool in the cave. 'Just as we were meant to be.'

'Meant to be?' He couldn't keep the bitterness from his voice. 'Was Rotger meant to burn in their pagan rite? Was Amalric meant to die on that mountain path? Is that what your God intended when he led you out here beyond the walls of Christendom?'

'Amalric saved us all,' she said, looking up at him. 'His sacrifice had meaning.'

'Meaning? Is that what it had? And was I meant to run like a coward as my brother died?'

'Is that what you think you did?' She reached out to touch his arm. 'Ran like a coward?'

'I abandoned him. Left him to die alone. After everything we had gone through together...'

'He chose his path,' she said softly. 'As we all must choose.'

Estienne wanted to rage at her, to tell her she couldn't understand. She hadn't known Amalric – hadn't fought beside him, hadn't shared his bread and wine, hadn't seen the quiet strength that lay beneath his easy smile.

'I should have been the one,' he said finally. 'It should have been me holding that path. I'm the stronger sword. It should have been me.'

'And then he would be standing here, carrying the same burden you carry now.' Fabrisse's voice held no judgement, only compassion. 'The living must honour the dead by continuing their work, not by following them to the grave.'

The truth of her words cut deep. Amalric had died so they might live, and every breath they drew was a testament to his sacrifice. To spurn that gift would be the gravest betrayal of all.

A soft whine cut through the drum of rain as Clovis padded past, the hound's claws clicking against stone with each careful step. Despite its injuries, the dog moved with growing confidence, as though each step helped shed the memory of its torment at Cuman hands. It settled beside Jurgen, who sat cross-legged near the cave's mouth, his fingers gently stroking the hound's head.

'Amazing how resilient they are,' the old hunter said quietly, scratching behind Clovis's ears. 'Beat them, starve them, treat them worse than dirt, and still they find it in their hearts to trust again.'

'Some might call that a gift,' Fabrisse answered. 'To forget their pain so easily.'

'Aye, they might.' Jurgen's bearded face creased in a slight smile. 'Shame we're not all blessed with it.'

Estienne could well appreciate the words. There were things he would rather have locked away, never to think on again. All he had lost in England, for one. His friendships with the Marshals. Even the dream he had allowed himself of a future with...

'There is something you would rather forget?' Fabrisse pressed. 'Or perhaps forgive?'

Jurgen gazed out at the night, as though lost in some distant memory. 'I wasn't always a hunter living alone with nothing but a hound for company. Had a proper life once – wife, children, a place in the world.'

'But you lost it?' she asked, not even trying to hide her sadness.

'No. It was taken. Raiders came one spring. Not pagans, just common brigands. The sort that prey on isolated homesteads. I was away hunting, when I returned...'

'It must have been hard, my friend,' Estienne said. 'That kind of loss could break a man.'

'Wanted to die myself, those first few months,' Jurgen said, his calloused fingers moving in slow circles through the hound's fur. 'Seemed the easier path. Every new sunrise I saw felt like a betrayal of those I'd failed to protect. But eventually I realised living isn't just about drawing breath. It's about finding purpose again. Doing something worthwhile with the time we're given.'

Estienne cast his eyes over the group – Fabrisse curled protectively near Brother Galien, Merten's young face finally peaceful in slumber, Talshyn wrapped in her dark robes. They were his burden now, his responsibility to protect, but he could not yet envision it making Amalric and Rotger's sacrifice worthwhile.

'And has it helped?'

'The pain never really leaves,' Jurgen said. 'But it changes. Becomes something you can carry, instead of something that carries you.'

Estienne couldn't imagine his pain changing. Right now it

was like a chip of ice within him. A shard of hate he wanted to bury in Shoruk's eye and in the heart of that witch he served. Only time would tell if that changed. For now, he could only spare enough thought for their survival.

26

They had set out from their cramped shelter as dawn crept across the mountains. The rains had finally ceased, and Fabrisse watched Estienne pick their path through the treacherous terrain with grim determination, despite his obvious exhaustion. The knight led them higher into the peaks until Talshyn called out, her dark eyes fixed on a shadow in the mountainside.

'There,' she said. 'It is a way through the heart of the mountain itself. It contains a shrine my people have used since before memory.'

As Fabrisse relayed Talshyn's words, she could see how it pained Estienne to cede leadership to someone he still viewed with suspicion, but after a moment's hesitation, he nodded for her to take the lead. They had little choice now but to trust in the young priestess's knowledge of these secret paths, though Fabrisse noticed how the knight's eyes never strayed from her as they approached the cave's gaping maw.

'We'll need torches,' Estienne said, as they paused at the entrance.

'Here,' Jurgen replied, stepping over the dark threshold and dropping to one knee. He held up a crude-looking torch that had been left at the entrance. 'Looks like someone thought ahead. These caves have seen use before.'

He began the painful process of lighting them in the damp of the cave, and before long they had three torches to penetrate the dark. Estienne, Merten and Jurgen raised one apiece, before leading the way inside.

Veins of quartz on the walls caught their torchlight and winked like lightning in the gathering gloom. Fabrisse shivered, as the wind that gusted from the cave depths carried whispers that might have been voices, might have been her imagination.

Beside her, Talshyn walked with her dark eyes fixed on that waiting blackness. 'Our ancestors first tamed these peaks and discovered these secret ways. Now the clan fears to follow them. They believe spirits guard these depths, protecting their secrets from the living.'

'And do you share their fear?' Fabrisse asked. 'Of these spirits they speak of?'

Talshyn shrugged her slight shoulders. 'I have walked these paths before, when Moldir... When I was learning our ways. The spirits here are old, yes, but they cannot harm us. Not like men can. Not like...'

'What is she saying?' Estienne cut in, eyeing Talshyn with suspicion.

'She only talks of the ancient spirits that live in this place,' Fabrisse replied.

'The only spirit that matters is the Holy Spirit,' Brother Galien muttered. Though his wound still ailed him, he had regained some colour in his face. 'And He will protect us from any pagan devils that lurk in these depths.'

'It's not just pagans we should be wary of,' Jurgen said, his voice harsh in the echoing confines. 'Anything could be lurking in here. Clovis doesn't like it, but then, he's had his fill of dark places. Haven't you, boy?'

The hound whined softly in response, pressing closer to his master's leg.

'None of us are strangers to darkness,' Fabrisse said, remembering what they had all suffered in their own ways. 'But these caves offer sanctuary rather than peril. The Lord works in many ways, after all.'

'The Lord has nothing to do with this place,' Estienne replied grimly. 'I doubt He even knows it exists.'

They proceeded in single file, Estienne leading the way. The passage descended at a shallow angle, its walls smooth, and Fabrisse could make out crude symbols carved into the rock. Spiralling patterns seemed to writhe in the flickering light, and everywhere the image of the great wolf that was the clan's totem. Some of the carvings were so old they had almost vanished, while others looked fresher, their edges still sharp against the ancient stone.

The passage opened abruptly into a vast chamber that devoured their torchlight. The darkness felt alive, pressing against their small circle of fire as though they were keeping wolves at bay. As they moved further in, details emerged from the gloom with terrible clarity, like corpses surfacing in still water.

Crude altars of stacked stone rose from the uneven floor, their surfaces stained with the accumulated gore of countless sacrifices. The blood had soaked so deeply into the rocks that they looked black as pitch, somehow still glistening after all these years.

Their torchlight revealed offerings placed in small niches carved into the walls: copper trinkets green with age, strings of bone beads that might have been human or animal, fragments of painted pottery arranged into strange patterns. Each item seemed invested with malevolent purpose, as though centuries of worship had given them a kind of terrible life.

'Holy Mother of God protect us,' Brother Galien breathed, his face chalk white. 'This is an unholy place. We should not be here. The very air reeks of damnation.'

'Control yourself, Brother Galien,' Estienne growled. 'There is nothing to fear from the dead.'

Movement caught Fabrisse's eye, and she saw Talshyn had drifted toward one of the altars. Her fingers hovered over its blood-darkened surface, her face a study in conflicting emotions: reverence, fear, shame.

'Moldir made offerings here,' Talshyn said softly, her voice carrying strange echoes in the vast space. 'To Erlik, lord of the underworld. The Dark One who hungers eternally. She taught me that only blood could satisfy his appetite. That sacrifice was the purest form of worship.'

Fabrisse felt her stomach turn at the implications of those words. Had Talshyn borne witness to such horrors? Had she been a part of them? The thought of that almost made Fabrisse shudder but she forced herself to maintain composure. This girl needed understanding now, not condemnation.

Jurgen's torch swept higher, illuminating the chamber's vaulted ceiling. The light revealed rows of crude stone shelves carved into the living rock, and arranged upon them were skulls. Dozens of them, some bearing the marks of violent death.

'Christ's bones,' Jurgen muttered. 'What kind of devils are these people? What dark god demands such offerings?'

'He thinks us evil?' Talshyn asked, looking at the horror on Jurgen's face. 'Thinks me wicked?'

Fabrisse shook her head, keen to deny it. 'No, he just—'

'We are not monsters,' Talshyn said, but her voice held more sorrow than anger. 'We were led astray. Moldir spoke of ancient

Valour

powers, of gods that demanded blood. But I think now she spoke only to satisfy her own hunger. Her own darkness. This place is—'

'What is she saying?' Estienne demanded again, rounding on Talshyn. 'That she was a part of this?' He advanced on the young priestess, but she stood her ground. 'Answer me! Did you help murder these people? Did you watch while they died screaming, like you watched them burn Rotger?'

Talshyn raised her chin slightly, and though fear showed plain in her dark eyes, there was something else there too – a quiet dignity as though she might accept her punishment if that was what Estienne decreed.

'Stop!' Fabrisse moved to place herself between them. She pressed one hand against Estienne's chest, though the raw fury in his eyes made her want to step back. 'This is not the way. This is not what He would want.'

'Stand aside,' he growled. 'This doesn't concern you.'

'No. I will not let you punish this girl for the crimes of others. She has more than repented. She risked everything to help us escape. Would you repay that debt with brutality? Would you make yourself no better than those we flee?'

'Debt?' Estienne's voice echoed harshly off the chamber walls. 'The only debt I owe is to my brothers who died because of her people's savagery. To Rotger. To Amalric...'

His voice caught, and Fabrisse saw the grief beneath his rage. For a moment, he looked terribly young despite his scars and battle-weary bearing.

'And will more death ease their passing?' she asked quietly. 'Will another soul sent into darkness bring them peace? Or will it only add to the weight of sin that already hangs heavy in this place? Mercy is the only righteous path here. The only path to God.'

The chamber fell silent save for the steady drip of water. Fabrisse held Estienne's gaze, willing him to see past his pain to the truth of it. After what felt like an eternity, he took a step backward.

'You speak of mercy?' he said, his voice thick with emotion. 'Of God's path? I have seen too much evil done in God's name to believe mercy alone can heal this land's wounds. Sometimes steel is the only answer to darkness. Sometimes violence is the only language men understand.'

'Then you know nothing of true faith,' Fabrisse replied, not unkindly as she reached up to touch his scarred cheek, feeling him flinch at the contact. 'Christ died not for the righteous, but for sinners. His sacrifice was made precisely so that we might rise. So that mercy could triumph over vengeance. So that even the darkest soul might find its way to light.'

'Pious words,' Estienne replied. 'But piety won't help anyone if she decides to betray us.'

'She won't,' Fabrisse replied. 'I know she won't.'

Estienne leaned in closer. 'Pray she doesn't. For all our sakes.'

Jurgen cleared his throat softly. 'We should move on. This is no place to linger.'

Beside him, Clovis whined in agreement, his yellow eyes fixed on the shadows beyond their circle of light.

They raised their torches and proceeded deeper into the mountain's heart, leaving the chamber behind. As they walked, Fabrisse found herself praying not just for their survival, but for Estienne's soul. The knight's rage was understandable, even righteous in its way, but if he could not find it in his heart to forgive, then darkness had already won a victory greater than any pagan god could claim.

27

The cave mouth gaped. A wound in the mountain's flesh, ancient and foreboding. Shoruk stood at its threshold, surrounded by his warriors, their torches guttering in the bitter wind. Their exhaustion showed in every movement after clearing the boulder that had blocked their path, but he could not allow them rest. Not while those Christian dogs eluded them.

Still, Shoruk hesitated at the cave mouth. They had left their horses behind, watched over by two of the clan's warriors, and he felt naked without his steed. Now he was to delve into the depths of a mountain on foot, trespass on the territory of their gods. It would have been enough to give any man pause.

'We waste time,' Moldir hissed, her voice carrying over the moan of the wind. 'The gods grow restless, and we have tarried too long already.'

Shoruk took a deep breath. Since the death of Tarkhan, the priestess had grown bolder, more demanding.

'This place is sacred. The men are—'

'The men are rightfully mindful of the gods,' she snapped. 'As you should be, Shorukhan. But there is little to fear from this place.'

Shoruk wasn't so sure. The torchlight threw strange shadows across the carved symbols that flanked the entrance – spiralling patterns that seemed to writhe in the uncertain light, and everywhere howled the great wolf that was their clan's totem. But these were old carvings, worn by centuries of wind and rain until they were barely more than suggestions of their original forms. Perhaps whatever power they once held had long since faded. As he looked to his warriors though, it was clear they still feared the place. None would meet his eyes directly. They knew what this shrine was, what ancient rites had been performed in its lightless depths.

'Forward,' he commanded, despising the tremor that threatened to creep into his voice. 'We have prey to run to ground.'

They reluctantly crossed the threshold. Shoruk could hear their words clearly; murmured prayers to Tengri, hurried gestures to ward off evil. Even hardened veterans now moved like spooked mares, their eyes darting between shadows that seemed to shift of their own accord.

'This is Erlik's shrine,' Artak breathed. 'My father told tales of this place. Of those who entered uninvited and were never seen again.'

'Your father was a drunken fool,' Shoruk replied. 'There is nothing to fear here.'

But he struggled to even convince himself. He had heard those same tales as a child – stories of warriors who had sought shelter here during winter storms, only to be found weeks later frozen in death without a mark upon them.

Dismissing the thought, they delved further, their torches struggling against the darkness. The passage wound deeper into the mountain's heart, the rough walls pressing in close enough that Shoruk could feel the ancient stone brush against his shoulders.

'The spirits here are hungry for blood,' one of the younger warriors muttered. 'I can feel it.'

'Then we shall feed them,' Moldir's voice cut through their whispers. 'The Christians have defiled this sacred shrine. Their deaths will appease the old powers.'

Shoruk watched his men exchange uneasy glances. They had followed him into battle without hesitation, had spilled blood for the clan countless times, but he had never seen them so fearful. This was a place of ancient power, where the barrier between worlds grew thin. Even the bravest warrior knew better than to trespass in the realm of gods.

The deeper they pressed, the more the place seemed to pulse with malevolent purpose, and Shoruk found himself yearning for open skies and the endless plains. This cramped space felt wrong, an affront to everything he held sacred.

'Perhaps we should seek another way,' Darman suggested, his usual confidence notably absent as he voiced what they were all thinking. 'The mountain passes—'

'Enough.' Moldir's command cut through the darkness as she glided forward, and Shoruk's warriors parted before her like leaves in a gale. 'You fear these shadows? You who are descended from warriors of an ancient line? Men who have conquered the plains? I am your Kam Katun, and through me, Tengri's power flows. Through me, the spirits are appeased. Or do you doubt the gods? Perhaps you would prefer to kneel before the Christian cross? To abandon your ancestors to darkness while you pray to their weak god?'

The accusation hung in the air as her eyes fixed on each warrior in turn. Shoruk watched his men shift uncomfortably, caught between their fear of the spirits and their fear of being thought cowards. He knew he should speak, should assert his authority as chief, but the words stuck in his throat.

'The Christians mock our ways even now,' Moldir pressed. 'They have brought their false faith into these sacred depths, thinking to hide from Tengri's justice. Will you let such sacrilege go unpunished?'

'No,' several warriors muttered, their earlier fear transforming to anger at her words.

She was playing them like a bone flute, and Shoruk could only watch as their resolve hardened.

'Forward then,' she commanded, and this time none hesitated.

They surged past Shoruk into the darkness, their earlier caution forgotten in their eagerness to prove their courage. He should have been proud of their newfound resolve, but all he felt was his authority crumbling. He was chief in name only now. It was Moldir who truly led them, who bent their will to her purpose. A realisation that sat ill in his gut like spoiled meat. One that he would have to redress, as soon as he was able.

28

Sudden brightness stabbed at Estienne's eyes as they emerged from the cave into daylight. He raised a hand, waiting for his vision to adjust after so many hours in darkness, as around him the others did the same.

The forest spread before them; a vast sea of green, stretching away toward distant peaks still wreathed in morning mist. Ancient pines towered overhead, their massive trunks wider than a man's embrace, branches weaving a canopy that filtered the evening light into dappled patterns.

'I know this place,' Jurgen muttered as he studied their surroundings. 'We're still a good ten miles from the Burzenland. Maybe more. And the terrain gets worse before it gets better. But we're almost there.'

Estienne felt frustration gnaw at him on hearing those words. Ten miles might as well have been a hundred with their group in this state. His own legs felt like lead, and the weight of his mail shirt seemed to increase with every passing moment. Brother Galien sagged against Merten's shoulder, the monk's face grey as old ash, his breathing coming in heavy gasps. The wound where he'd been impaled had begun to weep again, and it would be a miracle if it wasn't infected.

'I... I need to stop,' the friar wheezed, as though confirming Estienne's worst thoughts. 'Please... I can't...'

'No stopping,' Estienne replied. 'Not until we reach safe ground. Can you hold on that long, brother?'

Galien managed a weak nod, though his eyes were glazed with pain.

Merten adjusted his grip on the monk. 'I've got him. We won't fall behind.'

Estienne felt a sudden touch of pride at the young squire's determination. He had seen his friend Eggert cut down by the pagans, watched a knight burned alive and another die with utmost courage, and yet here he was showing bravery all his own. When they got back to Rosenau, Estienne would make sure the Order learned of this boy's valour.

'Let's not tarry, then,' he said, nodding to Fabrisse who offered a nod of her own.

She and the pagan priestess had no words to say as the group pressed on through the undergrowth.

The going was difficult, the ground slick and treacherous. Their progress was sluggish, and even Jurgen's faithful hound seemed to be struggling, padding silently beside his master, head low.

'How's he holding up?' Estienne asked quietly as Jurgen walked beside him.

'Tough old boy,' the trapper replied, patting Clovis with affection. 'Takes more than a few pagan bastards to break his spirit. Don't it, lad?'

At the mention of their pursuers, Estienne glanced toward the priestess. Talshyn's eyes darted constantly between the trees, and there was something in her bearing that set Estienne's teeth on edge. She had helped them escape, saved their lives even, but he couldn't shake the feeling that she would betray them at the first sign of danger, just as Carsten had when he'd fled at the first sign of an ambush. Only time would tell if his suspicions were right.

On he led them, keeping a steady pace through the trees as the ground rose steadily and dusk quickly turned to night. It wasn't until they had travelled a mile or more from the cave that Clovis stopped. The hound's hackles rose, its ears drawn back as it turned back to glare along the path they had forged.

'What is it, boy?' Jurgen whispered.

Estienne squinted back along their route, scanning the moonlit treetops. The first torch appeared through the canopy – a single point of flame dancing in the gloom. Then another joined it, and another, until there were a dozen lights dotting the darkness they'd left behind. Each new flame made Estienne's heart sink further.

'God in heaven,' Merten breathed. 'They've followed us through the caves.'

Estienne resisted the urge to point out his talent for the obvious, as Talshyn burst into rapid speech, her fingers twisted in her dark robes as she spoke, eyes wide with fright. Fabrisse listened intently before translating.

'She says this is impossible – no Cuman warrior would dare trespass upon those caves. They would rather face death than the wrath of their ancestors. Shoruk must be desperate indeed to risk such sacrilege.'

'Sacrilege or not, they are on our trail,' Estienne replied grimly.

His mind raced as he weighed their dwindling options. Brother Galien stumbled again, nearly dragging Merten down with him. They couldn't hope to outpace those warriors, not with their wounded slowing them. Splitting up might give some of them a chance to escape, but that would mean leaving the weakest to certain death.

'We could try to lose them in the deeper woods,' Jurgen suggested, though his tone held little hope.

'And how far would we get?' Estienne asked. 'Galien can barely walk, and the rest of us are almost dead on our feet.'

'Then what choice do we have?'

No choice at all it seemed, and the realisation of that only fuelled more fire in Estienne's belly.

'Then we run,' he said, through gritted teeth. 'And we pray we find shelter before they find us.'

Every instinct screamed at him to stand and fight, to meet his enemies with steel in hand, but he knew that would only get them all killed. Instead, he turned and urged them onward, hoping they would find enough strength to carry on into the night and somehow lose their pursuers in the dark.

Even as they ran, the forest seemed determined to betray them. Every branch snagged at their clothes like grasping fingers, every root conspired to trip their weary feet. But on they stumbled, a gaggle of exhausted souls pushing themselves beyond endurance.

Fabrisse maintained her composure, though Estienne caught the way her eyes kept darting backward, measuring the distance between them and their pursuers. She helped Talshyn over a fallen log, the two women supporting each other despite their differences. The young priestess's face was a study in terror, though she above all knew what fate awaited if they were caught.

Merten half-carried Brother Galien, his face set in lines of pure stubbornness as he refused to let the wounded monk fall behind.

'Just a little further,' he kept repeating, though whether to Galien or himself, Estienne couldn't tell. 'Just a little further.'

'Leave me,' Galien mumbled back, his voice barely audible. 'I'm only slowing you down...'

'No one gets left behind,' Merten replied fiercely. 'We will not lose another soul to those bastards.'

A branch whipped across Estienne's face, drawing blood, but he barely felt the sting. In the distance, the sounds of pursuit had begun to carry on the wind. The pagans were gaining, and the folly of it all struck Estienne then. They were like children playing a game they could never win, believing they could outrun these seasoned warriors.

The bitter memory of Amalric struck Estienne – his friend standing alone on that mountain path, sword raised in defiance. The image was so vivid he could almost hear the ring of steel. How many more sacrifices would this cursed land demand? What final price had to be paid to see these people delivered from strife?

He knew the answer.

It was but one life.

Estienne halted in his tracks, the others coming to a stumbling stop behind him, too out of breath to ask why. Drawing Jurgen aside, Estienne spoke in low, urgent tones as he stripped off his surcoat and began to unbuckle his mail hauberk.

'You have to keep them moving. Don't stop, no matter how much they struggle. I'll drive the pagans away as best I can.'

The old hunter's face darkened with understanding. 'No. We're not leaving another man behind. Not after...'

'You'll do as I command,' Estienne replied, iron entering his voice though he hardly felt the conviction. 'Get them to the safety of the Burzenland, then make for Rosenau with all speed.'

'I know how to hunt in this terrain. Let me—' Jurgen started, but Estienne shook his head.

'You're the only one who knows the forests. Without you, they'll never find their way back.'

With difficulty, Estienne shrugged the mail armour over his head as Jurgen turned, squinting into the darkening forest. 'Very well. If my guess is right, there's a river a few miles hence, with a mountain pass beyond. I'll aim for that. We'll need to rest before we can make the rest of the journey. I'll wait for you to find us there.'

Estienne nodded as he discarded his armour to the ground, grateful for the thought. 'Don't wait long. A day at most. If I'm not back by then, I'm not coming.'

'As you say,' Jurgen agreed. 'But make sure—'

'Estienne...' Fabrisse had drawn closer, her eyes narrowed. 'You can't mean to—'

'I am afraid I do, milady.' He cut her off. 'Someone must draw them away from our trail. Buy the rest of you time. There's no other way.'

'No. I will not allow it. You have to stay with us.'

'The decision has been made, Fabrisse. There is no changing it.'

The look of defiance left her eyes, to be replaced by one of sorrow. 'Then God will go with you, Estienne Wace.'

'He hasn't been with us so far. So I suggest you follow Jurgen and do as he says. That's your only chance. God clearly has other matters to attend.'

'We'll wait for you as Jurgen says,' Merten said suddenly, his young face fierce despite his obvious fear. 'At the river. We'll wait.'

Estienne couldn't bring himself to answer that. To tell him that most likely he would never make it. Instead, he turned and plunged into the forest, angling away from their path. The pagan dogs were on their scent. It was time someone made them the prey.

29

Ancient trees loomed overhead as Shoruk's men picked their way carefully between their massive trunks. Ahead, Artak moved like a hunting wolf, his eyes fixed on signs only a seasoned tracker could read. Grief had hollowed his cheeks and hardened his gaze since losing his brother, and that loss had bred a hunger that could only be satisfied with Christian blood.

'Here,' the scout called softly, dropping to one knee beside a fallen log thick with moss. 'They passed this way not long ago.'

'How far ahead, do you think?' Shoruk asked, studying the disturbed earth.

'No more than a mile at most. The mud hasn't had time to dry.'

'Then we're gaining on them.' Shoruk turned to address his warriors, but the words died in his throat as Moldir stepped forward.

'And we must hurry,' she said, her voice carrying an edge that made even Shoruk's hardened warriors shift uneasily. 'The gods will show their displeasure if these unbelievers are allowed to escape.'

'The gods will have their due,' he replied, conscious of the weight of watching eyes. 'But first we must run down our quarry.'

'Then let's not waste time with talk,' Artak growled. 'Every moment we delay, they put more distance between us.'

'Mind your mouth,' Shoruk snapped back at Artak's petulance. 'I am still chief here.'

Artak's eyes stared defiantly, but he mastered himself with visible effort. 'As you say, Shorukhan.'

There was silence then, broken only by the sound of young Batu's bow creaking as he drew it nervously, spooked by shadows. His eyes darted between the ancient red oaks that loomed overhead.

'Steady, boy,' Shoruk growled, 'unless you want to put an arrow in one of your brothers.'

'S-sorry, Shorukhan.' Batu lowered the bow, his face flushing with shame. 'It's just... the forest feels like the trees themselves have eyes.'

'There is nothing to be wary of but the enemy we seek,' Shoruk replied. 'And there is only one warrior among them. The rest are women, boys and an old man and his hound. Now come. The clan will have blood.'

They pressed deeper into the forest, fanning out as they strode through the thick ferns, the shadows growing more oppressive with every step. Even the most hardened warriors among them grew quiet, brandishing their weapons as though feeling unseen eyes upon them. Artak ranged ahead, dropping down every now and then to scan for sign, which grew increasingly difficult to discern in the light of their dimming torches. Just as Shoruk began to wonder if their quarry had escaped, he heard a sharp noise from the far flank, as though an axe had struck a tree.

'What was that?' he demanded.

Valour 215

'I... I don't know,' someone replied through the shadow.

'Where is Darman?' another said immediately. 'He was just here.'

By the gods, was he cursed to be surrounded by idiots?

'Darman,' Shoruk called out, his voice sounding unnaturally loud in the stillness. 'Where are you?'

The silence that answered seemed to mock him.

'Darman!' he shouted again, louder this time. 'Where are you, you son of a whore?'

'He was just here,' Boril whispered. 'Not ten feet from me.'

'Spread out,' Shoruk ordered. 'Find him. But stay within sight of each other.'

Immediately his men obeyed. Shoruk scanned the brush, desperate for any sign of his lost clansman. All the while he could feel Moldir's malevolent presence as she watched him, judging his every move.

They hadn't gone far when Batu's terrified cry split the night. 'Chief! By all the gods... Chief, come quickly!'

The raw fear in the boy's voice made Shoruk's blood run cold. He crashed through the undergrowth toward the sound, before coming to a staggering stop. Batu stood frozen, staring at something propped against a massive oak tree. At first, Shoruk thought it was some kind of wooden idol, until his eyes adjusted to the gloom. Until he saw what the Christians had done to his warrior.

Darman sat with his back against the trunk, head bowed. His weapons, twin blades of burnished steel, had been impaled into his chest in the shape of that accursed Christian cross.

'Father of the sky,' Artak breathed, making the sign against evil. 'What kind of beasts are we hunting?'

'They are not beasts,' Shoruk snarled. 'This is the work of one man. And he cannot be far away.'

'We should not have trespassed on the shrine to Erlik,' Boril muttered, his face pale in the darkness. 'These woods belong to him. Can't you feel it? Can't you smell the death in the air?'

'Silence!' Shoruk rounded on him, fury warring with his own growing dread. 'This is just a man. And he bleeds like any other.'

'Men don't move like shadow,' another warrior said, his voice trembling. 'Men don't kill without sound or trace. This is a creature sent to punish us for our—'

'Enough!' Moldir's voice cut through the darkness. 'You disgrace yourselves with such cowardice. Even now the spirits of your ancestors watch, and all you would do is shame them.'

But even her words seemed to carry less weight here, in this dread forest. Shoruk saw the fear in his warriors' eyes, saw how they huddled closer together like sheep seeking safety in numbers. They were coming apart, their discipline crumbling in the face of this unseen enemy that struck without warning.

'Where's Tamaz?' someone whispered. 'He was just here...'

'I saw him just over—'

'Quiet!' Shoruk hissed. 'You will draw whoever is watching to our—'

But it was too late. Panic had taken root, spreading through his remaining warriors like poison through the blood.

'Tamaz? Brother, answer me!'

'Gods above, what is hunting us?'

Their voices grew louder, more desperate, each call betraying their position to whatever lurked in the darkness. Shoruk wanted to roar them into silence, but he knew it would do no good. Fear had broken them more thoroughly than any blade.

Young Batu's nerve was the first to snap completely. The boy's face had gone white, his eyes wide as a spooked horse's. His bow clattered to the ground as he backed away from the others.

'No. We have insulted the gods,' he murmured. 'They mean to have their due.'

Valour 217

'Stay where you are,' Shoruk commanded, seeing the boy's intention written in every trembling muscle. 'We have to stay together.'

But Batu was beyond hearing, and with a strangled cry, he turned and fled into the darkness. His feet pounded the soft earth as he disappeared into the night, each footfall echoing through the trees until the sound ended in a wet crack followed by an agonised scream.

'Damn it,' Shoruk snarled, as Batu cried for help like a lost child. 'Come, we cannot leave him.'

He followed Batu's trail, flanked by his men. In the light of their torches they found him lying in a hollow, his leg bent at an impossible angle where a sword stroke had shattered it. Blood black as ink in the darkness pumped from the wound, and Batu's screams had faded to whimpers.

'We have to get him to a healer,' Artak said, moving to help the wounded youth.

'No.' Moldir's command froze Artak in place. 'The weak must be left behind. The hunt is all that matters now.'

Shoruk rounded on her, frustration finally boiling over. 'These are my warriors, witch. I will not abandon them to die in this cursed place.'

'Then you are as weak as this boy.' Moldir's eyes seemed to swallow what little light remained. 'And Tengri despises weakness, Shorukhan. Or have you forgotten that along with your courage? Have you forgotten why we came here in the first place?'

'Tengri holds no sway here,' Shoruk spat. 'Can't you feel it? These woods belong to Erlik. The doors to Tamag lay wide open all about us.'

He regretted the words as soon as they left his mouth, as Moldir's face twisted with such fury that several warriors took involuntary steps backward.

'You dare question the wisdom of our gods?' she hissed. 'You think you know better than I? Perhaps I was wrong about you, Shorukhan. Perhaps you are no better than Tarkhan after all.'

Before Shoruk could respond, a shout rang out through the darkness – clear and deliberate, like a challenge. Every head snapped toward the sound as a torch flared to life on distant hillside. The flame illuminated a lone figure that stood like a sentinel against the night sky. Even at this distance, Shoruk could make out the hulking silhouette of the Christian warrior, the last of their number that yet lived.

'After him!' Artak snarled, already moving forward, but Moldir grabbed his arm.

'No. This is a distraction.' Her eyes fixed on Shoruk. 'The holy woman is the true prize. The one who would have turned us from our gods. The one who turned Talshyn from us. While we chase this warrior, she slips further from our grasp.'

'Let her run,' Shoruk growled, watching as the knight turned and walked deliberately into the darkness beyond the hilltop. 'This one has killed our brothers. Made sport of us in these woods. He deserves our attention more.'

'Fool!' Moldir stepped closer. 'The gods demand the woman's blood. Her death will please Tengri far more than some common warrior's.'

Shoruk rounded on her, his patience finally snapping. 'I care nothing for your desires, witch. Look at what this knight has done to us. To my brothers. He has earned my blade, and I will have blood.'

'You would defy me?' Moldir's voice dropped to a dangerous whisper. 'After everything I have given you?'

'You gave me nothing.' Shoruk's hand tightened on his sword. 'I took what was mine by right. And now I choose this fight, not because your gods demand it, but because my heart does.'

The air was still between them, and for a moment, Shoruk thought she might strike him down with whatever dark powers she commanded. Then she offered a cruel smile.

'Very well, Shorukhan. Chase your worthy opponent. But when he leads you to your doom, remember that I warned you.'

Shoruk ignored her portent, already striding toward the hillside as he addressed his men. 'Follow me. This bastard will die before the dawn.'

They began to move with haste, leaving Moldir to follow them through the darkness. What did Shoruk care for warnings, anyway? The gods would have what the gods demanded no matter what he did. Only one thing was certain now – Shoruk would have this warrior's head, or he would die in the taking of it.

30

Dawn brought with it some relief from the stifling cold of night, but Fabrisse barely noticed it through her exhaustion. Her legs trembled with fatigue, as behind her, Brother Galien's shallow breathing seemed to grow more strained with each passing mile.

Jurgen led them onward, his face a determined mask as he picked their path through the dense undergrowth. The old trapper moved with practised efficiency, pausing occasionally to study the position of the sun or where they were in relation to the distant mountain peaks. His faithful hound Clovis padded silently beside him, and the sight of man and beast supporting each other filled Fabrisse with some hope. But that hope did nothing to stave off the nagging shame.

She could not shake the weight of guilt that pressed down upon her, heavier than any stone. Rotger's screams still haunted her, the memory of his last moments making her stomach twist. The thought of Amalric's sacrifice at the mountain pass plagued her every step – two brave souls lost because of her foolish mission. And now Estienne had chosen to remain behind, likely racing to his death to buy them time. All that blood spilled because she had believed she could bring God's light to these savage lands.

'The river's close,' Jurgen announced, his gruff voice barely carrying over the sound of wind in the branches. 'Can you hear it?'

Fabrisse strained her senses and caught the distant murmur of rushing water. The sound grew stronger as they pushed forward through a tangle of thorny brush that snagged at their already ragged clothing. When they finally emerged onto a rocky bank, the sight of the fast-flowing river sparked another flicker of hope.

'We're almost within the Burzenland's borders,' Jurgen said over the rushing noise. 'Still many miles from safety, but this is the final stretch. Just over those mountains and we're back in Christendom.'

Young Merten helped Brother Galien sink down onto a fallen log, the monk's face grey with exhaustion. Talshyn hovered nearby, her eyes constantly scanning the forest behind them. The young priestess had proven herself since their escape, but Fabrisse could see how the others still watched her with suspicion, but she knew all too well that trust, like faith, had to be earned through actions rather than words alone.

'Do we rest here?' Merten asked, his face streaked with dirt and worry. He looked so terribly young in the stark light of morning, reminding Fabrisse that he was little more than a boy thrust into circumstances far beyond his years.

'No, we need to keep moving,' Jurgen replied. 'But once we've forded this river I'll keep an eye out for a likely place to make camp. Now, drink your fill and we'll make our way across. There's no telling when we'll find a better source of water.'

They took turns drinking from the rushing river, the icy water reviving their spirits even as it numbed their hands.

Fabrisse helped Brother Galien drink, supporting his trembling form.

'Have faith, brother,' she said. 'God has not abandoned us yet.'

But as she spoke the words, she wondered if perhaps He had. What divine purpose could there be in all this suffering? What lesson in watching good men die while she lived on?

When they had drunk their fill, Jurgen forged ahead into the river. He tested the depth with a long branch, probing carefully before committing to each step and the others followed in his wake, forming a human chain with Merten bringing up the rear. The icy current tugged at their legs, threatening to sweep them off their feet, but together they stood firm against it.

Brother Galien's crossing proved the most challenging, as he could barely support his own weight, but Fabrisse and Talshyn flanked him, their combined strength enough to keep him upright as they guided him between the slippery stones.

When they finally reached the opposite shore, they were soaked from the waist down, but Jurgen was of no mind to build a fire. Instead, they wrung out what water they could from their garments and forced themselves to keep moving. The terrain grew steadily more challenging as they pushed onward, the gentle slopes giving way to steeper inclines that tested their already depleted strength. More than once someone slipped, only to be caught and steadied by their companions as they moved as one, each supporting the others.

Eventually they reached a thicket ahead, that looked impenetrable at first glance, but Jurgen found a narrow trail that wound between the worst of the brambles, leading them deeper into the gloom between ancient pines and a solid cliff face. Fabrisse squinted through the sudden dark and caught sight of something leaning against the cliffside that slowly resolved itself into the angular shape of a cabin. The structure hunched against a rocky outcropping, its log walls weathered, the roof covered in a thick blanket of pine needles that had accumulated over what must have been years of neglect.

'Hold here,' Jurgen murmured, raising his hand. 'Let me check it first.'

They watched as the trapper approached the cabin with caution. He pushed open the door, Clovis close to his knee, before he entered. It only took him a moment to discern it was safe, before he appeared again, this time with a smile on his face.

'Trapper's cabin,' he explained with some relief. 'Hunters use them as temporary shelters during the hard seasons. This one's been empty a while by the look of it, but the walls look solid enough.'

'So we'll be safe here?' Fabrisse asked, thinking of Brother Galien who seemed ready to drop.

'Safe as any place in these woods,' Jurgen replied. 'It's our best chance to rest and tend to the wounded.'

Fabrisse helped Merten guide Brother Galien toward the cabin while Jurgen led them into the interior. Stale air washed over them as they entered, carrying the musty scent of decay. The cabin's single room was spare but dry, a crude hearth dominating one wall, while rough-hewn benches lined the others. Dried herbs still hung from the rafters, though they had long since become desiccated.

'Wait,' Jurgen said sharply as Merten moved to lay Brother Galien on one of the benches. The trapper knelt beside the hearth, running his fingers through the ashes. 'These are still warm.'

Fabrisse felt her chest tighten as she realised the implications. Someone had used this cabin recently, but who? And would they offer help, or present another obstacle to their journey?

'Should we move on?' Merten asked, his voice betrayed how much he dreaded the prospect of further travel.

Jurgen shook his head. 'No choice now. Brother Galien won't last much longer without rest and proper care. We'll have to risk it. But first we need wood for the fire. The nights are still bitter cold up here.'

'I'll see to it,' Merten replied, turning back for the door.

While the young squire ventured out to gather firewood, Fabrisse helped Brother Galien onto one of the benches, trying to make him as comfortable as possible. His skin burned beneath her touch, and the wound where he had been impaled showed angry red streaks spreading outward – clear signs of infection.

'Here,' Talshyn said softly, kneeling beside them. 'Let me see.'

The young priestess examined the wound with gentle fingers, her dark eyes narrowed in concentration.

'Do you think you can do something for him?' Fabrisse asked.

'There are herbs in these forests that will help. Yarrow for the bleeding, goldenseal for infection. I can gather them now.'

'I would be grateful, but be careful, and don't stray far.'

As Talshyn slipped out into the surrounding forest, Jurgen worked to clear the ash from the hearth. Clovis lay near the open door, eyes fixed on the forest beyond.

'We're almost back to Christendom,' Jurgen said quietly as he worked. 'Another couple of days' travel, maybe three if we have to move slow. Then it's just a matter of finding a village willing to shelter us until we can get word to Rosenau.'

'That's... good news,' she replied, gripping Galien's clammy hand.

'You don't sound too glad about it,' Jurgen said, without turning around.

Fabrisse let out a despondent breath. 'So many dead because

of my foolish notions. I thought I could bring God's light to these lands, but I've only brought suffering.'

Jurgen paused in his work, regarding her with those keen eyes. 'You wanted to change the world for the better. The hope that those pagans might embrace God's light was a genuine one. You shouldn't be regretful of that. It wasn't your notions that got those men killed, foolish or not. It was the evil that still hunts us.'

Before Fabrisse could respond, Clovis's head snapped up, ears pricked back. A low growl rumbled in the hound's chest as heavy footsteps approached the cabin. Jurgen reached for his bow, but the string was still in the pouch at his belt. No time to string it before...

A figure stood silhouetted in the doorway, arms full of firewood. For a moment, Fabrisse and Jurgen knelt frozen as recognition slowly dawned.

Carsten Schado stood staring at them, forehead gleaming with sweat despite the cold, his white surcoat stained and torn. The firewood clattered to the floor as his face became a mask of shock.

'You,' Jurgen growled, the single word managing to convey his unbridled contempt.

'Jurgen, my friend, I—' Carsten began, but stopped as Jurgen rose to his feet.

'Friend?' The trapper's face twisted with disgust. 'You lost the right to call any of us friend when you fled and left us to die. Good men have paid a dear price for your cowardice!'

Carsten drew himself up, trying to summon some remnant of his former authority. 'You don't understand. I had no choice. The situation was hopeless and someone had to get help from Rosenau—'

'Get help?' Jurgen's voice dropped dangerously low. 'And come to our rescue? How fast did you think that would happen? Fast enough to see Eggert spared? Or Rotger? Or Amalric?'

'They're all...'

'Dead. Yes. Because you were too craven to bring the horses and give us a fighting chance.'

'No,' Carsten protested, though his voice had lost its strength. 'It was hopeless. We would all have died if—'

'If what?' Jurgen snarled. 'If you hadn't abandoned your brothers to save yourself? If you hadn't broken every oath you swore as a knight of your Order?'

'Is this true?' Fabrisse asked, seeing the guilt writ in Carsten's eyes. 'You left them to die?'

'My lady, please. God forgive me if I—'

'God may forgive you,' Jurgen spat. 'But I wonder if your brothers at Rosenau will be so quick to show it.'

Carsten's defiance crumbled, his shoulders slumping at the prospect of his cowardice being exposed. 'I... I never meant... I was on my way back to warn them, I swear. But... I got lost. Found this cabin. I've been starving for days. I just thought...'

'You thought only of yourself,' Jurgen finished for him. 'And when we return to Rosenau everyone will know it. I doubt your Marschall suffers cowards among his ranks.'

The colour drained from Carsten's face at the mention of Marschall Dieter. Fabrisse saw his hand stray toward his sword hilt, whether some reflex or for a darker purpose she couldn't tell. The gesture did not go unnoticed by Jurgen, whose fingers tightened around his useless bow.

The sound of footsteps outside broke the sudden tension. Merten walked through the door with an armload of wood, Talshyn close behind him with her gathered herbs. Both froze at the sight before them.

'Schado,' Merten breathed, his young face twisting in fury as he recognised the man who had abandoned them. The firewood clattered to the floor. 'You left us to die!'

'Easy now, boy,' Carsten warned. 'You forget your place—'

'My place?' Merten's bark held a bitter edge. 'My place was beside my brothers when the pagans attacked. Where was yours, Komtur? Running like a cur with your tail between your legs?'

'Merten, don't—' Fabrisse started, all too late.

The young squire hurled himself at Carsten with a snarl of rage. His attack caught the older knight off guard, fist catching his jaw and driving him back against the cabin wall. Carsten's greater size and experience told quickly as he seized Merten's arm and twisted, using the boy's own momentum to throw him to the floor.

Merten hit hard, the impact driving the breath from his lungs. Before he could recover, Carsten's boot pressed against his chest, pinning him down. The knight's sword rasped free of its scabbard, the steel catching what little light penetrated the cabin's gloom.

'Stop!' Fabrisse's command echoed in the confines as she stepped between them, heedless of the naked blade. 'Have we not seen enough death? Enough lives needlessly wasted? We survive together or we die alone – those are our only choices now.'

Carsten's sword hovered over the prone squire for a moment. Then he stood back and returned the blade to its scabbard. Merten pushed himself to his feet, his expression suggesting that this confrontation was far from over.

'The lady speaks wisdom,' Jurgen said carefully, though his eyes never left Carsten. 'We've got wounded to tend and miles yet to travel. Those miles will be easier if we're of the same purpose.'

'Agreed,' Carsten said.

'Agreed,' Merten added, though with less conviction.

Carsten turned, as though noticing Talshyn for the first time. 'Does someone want to tell me who this is?'

'We need to explain nothing to you,' Fabrisse replied. 'All you need to know is we're staying here until Estienne returns.'

'Wace still lives?' Carsten asked.

Fabrisse couldn't tell whether he was relieved by the prospect. 'God willing.'

Carsten nodded, before turning to slump down upon a bench.

Fabrisse kept her eye on him, refusing to trust him, especially now that Talshyn had returned. She could only hope that Estienne would manage to find them. And soon.

31

Estienne's boots slipped on loose shale as he forced himself up the steep incline, each step threatening to send him sprawling. His lungs burned, limbs trembling from a night of ceaseless flight as the forest had given way to narrow rocky passes. But he couldn't afford to rest. Not with the hunters drawing closer with each passing moment.

'Keep moving,' he growled through gritted teeth. 'Keep moving or you're a dead man, Wace.'

The sun had reached its zenith as he climbed higher, working his way across boulders and treacherous scree. Each step threatened disaster as rocks shifted beneath his feet, the sound of sliding stones echoing off the cliff face, all too loud. They would be sure to hear him. Hunt him down like the wolves they were.

Let them fucking come. Let them follow. Every step they took pursuing him was another step away from his companions. At least this way they had a fighting chance.

The memory of Amalric's final words cut through his exhaustion: 'For once in your life, don't argue.' The words burned worse than his aching limbs, worse than the bitter cold that had settled into his bones. He should have been the one to stay behind. Should have been the one to hold that mountain pass while the others escaped. But Amalric had denied him even that, choosing instead to make the ultimate sacrifice himself.

'Damn you for a stubborn fool,' Estienne muttered.

But at least he hadn't died for nothing. He had given them precious time to escape. Estienne would be sure to do the same.

A rock clattered somewhere below, the sound sharp as snapping bone in the crisp morning air. Estienne pressed himself against the cliff face, chest heaving as he tried to quiet his rasping breath. Voices carried on the wind – harsh Cuman words urging one another on. The hunters were gaining ground, and it was enough to shake Estienne from his musing. No time to lament. Only time to run.

His legs felt leaden, each step a battle against his body's desperate plea for rest. But Estienne had not survived war in England, had not endured the horrors of Outremer's deserts, by giving in to weakness. He was the Black Lion, trained by William Marshal himself – and he would not allow these pagan dogs to run him to ground like common prey.

Drawing on his last reserves of strength, Estienne forced himself onward. His teeth ground together as he pushed through the wall of fatigue by sheer force of will.

An arrow whipped past his head, striking the rock face and clattering its way along the mountain path. Estienne threw himself sideways as a second shaft followed, but this one found its mark. White-hot pain lanced through his shoulder as the arrow tore through his gambeson, drawing blood. The shaft opened a furrow across his flesh rather than burying itself in muscle, which was a small enough mercy.

A shout echoed from behind in the Cuman tongue, close enough to instil yet more urgency into Estienne's flight, as if those

Valour 231

arrows weren't enough. He scrambled upward, no longer trying to move quietly. Speed was all that mattered now as his boots kicked loose a cascade of stones that clattered down the slope. He didn't dare look back as the sound of pursuit grew closer, the hunters moving with haste, their eager voices filling the air.

A ravine opened before him, its walls dropping away to nothing as Estienne skidded to a halt. His mind raced as he considered his options. The gap was too wide to jump – even fresh and rested he couldn't have made that leap. No way back unless he wanted to face a procession of angry pagans armed to the teeth and baying for his blood. And a rock wall rose to his left, almost sheer. His only way out of this.

Estienne's fingers probed for purchase as he pulled himself up the rock face. His feet scrabbled against the uneven surface, and he found an outcrop with which to propel himself upwards. Each moment he thought the Cumans might race out onto the ledge to find him climbing, sticking him with arrows while he was in such a vulnerable spot. It was with relief that he finally grasped the ledge above, and strained to pull himself up.

He rolled onto his back, then his belly, gasping for air as he peered over the edge in time to see the first of them arrive. Below, an archer crept carefully along a narrow ledge, bow half-drawn as he searched for his quarry. The man's attention was focused straight ahead, expecting his prey to appear from around the corner at any moment, not realising he was already above him.

Estienne's hand closed around a rock almost as big as his head. He hefted it and paused for a heartbeat. The throw would have to be perfect. One chance, no more.

He drew in a breath, then whistled sharply. The archer's head snapped up, eyes widening as he spotted Estienne. Shock flashed across his face as he tried to bring his bow to bear, but it was already too late. Estienne hurled the rock with all his strength, every ounce of fury fuelling the throw. The stone caught the Cuman square in the face with a wet crack that echoed off the ravine. His head snapped back, bow falling from his fingers as he toppled backward into space, arms windmilling uselessly. His scream cut off abruptly as he struck the ravine floor far below.

Estienne was already pushing himself back to his feet. Then he was running again, legs burning, eyes searching for any means of escape. But it seemed there would be no way out.

The path ended abruptly at another sheer drop that fell away into nothing. Estienne's boots scattered pebbles over the edge, the tiny stones toppling into the churning waters of a river far below. It was a beastly serpent of white water, swollen by the recent rains, its roar drowning out everything but the pounding of blood in his ears, the sound promising death to any fool who dared test its fury.

Shouts echoed behind him, the harsh Cuman tongue carrying clearly above the torrent. Estienne had run out of time. Run out of mountain. The drop was easily sixty feet to the water – enough to kill a man if he struck a rock beneath the surface. But then, a swift death might be preferable to what awaited him at pagan hands.

An arrow soared overhead, telling him his choices were few. A glance back, and he saw them fifty feet further down the slope. They had spotted him now, there was nowhere left to flee. Fight or jump... and he knew to fight was to die.

His sword would be worse than useless in the water, and he drew the blade, casting it aside. It felt like a sacrilege as it clattered against stone, but better to lose steel than life.

His gambeson followed, his boots next. The icy air bit at his exposed flesh, but that discomfort would soon be the least of his concerns.

Another arrow flew past him. Shoruk's voice rang out above

the sound of the river, the words incomprehensible but their meaning clear. Another look back to see the clan chief's face twisted with hatred as he urged his archers forward. A half-dozen bowstrings creaked as arrows were drawn.

Enough tarrying, Wace.

He took three quick steps and hurled himself out into empty air just as arrows filled the space where he had stood. For a moment he was suspended between earth and sky, the wind taunting him, the river reaching up to embrace him with foaming arms as his stomach lurched.

Then the waters took him.

The impact drove the air from his lungs, his body breaking through the surface like a spear. Cold struck, stealing what little breath remained before the current seized him instantly, dragging him under with irresistible force. Water filled his nose, his mouth, as the river tried to claim him for its own. The shock of it nearly made him gasp, nearly made him draw water into his lungs.

His head broke surface just long enough to snatch a desperate breath before the rapids gripped him. The world became a chaos of foam and spray and sharp rocks, each impact threatening to shatter bone. A floating log struck his ribs with crushing force, sending numbing pain through his chest. Each breath was a battle now, won in the brief moments his face cleared the surface.

Keep fighting, he thought as the river raged about him. *Do not give in. This is not your end.*

Estienne was locked in battle now, more vicious than any he had faced before. He fought to keep his head above water, legs kicking against the river's pull. The cold began to seep into his bones, replacing the burn of exhaustion with a deeper, more insidious pain. His fingers had gone numb, yet still he clawed at passing debris, searching for anything that might slow his headlong rush downstream. A branch scraped across his face but he couldn't feel the pain through the numbing cold.

The current slammed him against another rock, spots dancing across his vision as his head struck stone. The river dragged him under once more, spinning him through darkness until he no longer knew which way was up. His lungs screamed for air. The cold pressed in, promising peace if he would only stop fighting. Just let go, it seemed to whisper. Let the current take you. Let the darkness win...

'For God and Saint Mary,' Amalric's voice came to him through the darkness.

His friend's final words sparked something in his fading consciousness. An ember of defiance that refused to be quenched.

Estienne kicked hard, driving himself toward what he hoped was the surface. His head broke through into air and he sucked in a desperate breath. Through water-blurred vision, he caught sight of a fallen tree extending out over the river, its branches dipping into the rushing water.

With the last reserves of his strength, Estienne kicked hard, angling himself toward the outstretched limbs. His fingers, nerveless with cold, scraped across bark as the current tried to tear him away, but somehow he managed to grasp a wayward branch, feeling his shoulder wrench in its socket as the river's fury tried to take him.

Hand over hand, he dragged himself through the churning water toward the bank, his muscles screaming in protest as he fought against the current's relentless pull. Twice his grip nearly failed, his frozen fingers threatening to betray him, but still he maintained his hold.

Eventually his feet found purchase on the muddy bank, and he heaved himself from the river's grasp, crawling on hands and knees until he collapsed on solid ground. River water gushed from his mouth as his body tried to expel what he'd swallowed, each racking cough sending a spasm of pain through his chest. But he was alive.

Dark spots danced at the edges of his vision as exhaustion finally claimed its due and his battered body gave in. The last thing he saw was the river rushing by, as though angry it had failed to kill him, before consciousness fled and the world faded to black.

32

Sunlight crept through the crude shutters of the trapper's cabin while dried bundles of plants that Fabrisse couldn't name swayed gently from the rafters. The fire crackled, Merten, Jurgen and Clovis huddling close to it. Where Carsten was Fabrisse had no idea, and she wasn't of a mind to enquire.

Brother Galien lay still on his pallet, his breathing steadier than it had been through the long night. Fabrisse pressed her palm to his forehead, feeling blessed relief as she found his skin cooler, the raging fever finally breaking. The angry red streaks that had spread from his wound were receding, though the flesh around it remained tender and swollen.

'Thanks be to God,' she said. 'And to your knowledge of these herbs.'

Talshyn knelt beside her, fresh bandages torn from strips of cloth laid out with careful precision beside her. 'The medicine within those plants is strong. Though even I am surprised at how well they have worked. Perhaps your God is also watching over his servant.'

'I hope he is watching over all of us,' Fabrisse replied, while

Valour   237

the young priestess ministered to Galien so carefully he barely
stirred. 'But it is your work that has helped him the most. You
seem well-versed in the healing arts. I assume that was part of
your duties among the clan?'

'It was,' she replied, running a damp rag across Galien's brow.

'How does one become a priestess among your people?'

Talshyn's hands stilled briefly, her eyes becoming distant with
memory. 'I was barely able to speak when Moldir chose me. She
said the spirits had marked me, and took me from my family,
taught me the sacred ways – how to read the signs in nature, how
to speak with spirits, how to heal... and how to harm. She taught
me of Tengri in the sky and Eje in the earth, but eventually I was
inducted in the secret ways of Erlik, who is more powerful than
both.'

The last words were heavy with regret. Fabrisse reached out,
letting her hand rest lightly on Talshyn's arm. 'And now? What do
you believe?'

'I don't know any more. Everything I was taught feels...
tainted. Corrupted. Like looking into clear water and seeing
serpents writhe beneath the surface. As though every sacred
place and shrine I have ever known is now somehow stained with
blood. Or perhaps... they always were.' She looked up suddenly,
her eyes intense. 'Tell me about your holy places. What is it like
where you learned your faith?'

Fabrisse smiled, remembering the provincial quaintness of
Avallon. 'Imagine a place built for contemplation and learning.
Walled grounds where sisters walk in quiet reflection, halls filled
with ancient texts that are copied with loving care. Gardens
where we grow herbs for healing, not unlike these you use,
though we pray to saints rather than spirits.'

'And there is no sacrifice?' Talshyn asked, wonder creeping
into her voice. 'No loss, so that your god may be appeased?'

'Not in the way that you might understand it. But there are other kinds of struggle – with faith, with obedience, with one's own doubts. But no, no violence. The only blood shed is Christ's, so that we may be saved.'

'It sounds... peaceful,' Talshyn replied. 'When I was young, before Moldir took me, I used to dream of such peace. But then she taught me that power comes only through suffering. That Erlik's hunger could never be satisfied with mere prayers.'

'There is another way,' Fabrisse said softly.

'I want to believe,' Talshyn answered, so quietly Fabrisse barely caught the words. 'But I've seen too much darkness. Done too much...'

'Some of the greatest saints were once the greatest sinners. God's forgiveness knows no bounds. We need only be willing to accept Him into our lives.'

Talshyn said nothing more, while together they finished tending to Galien in companionable silence as morning light slowly filled the cabin. Their peace was shattered as the door banged open, letting in a blast of bitter mountain air. Carsten stood framed in the doorway, his fingers drumming restlessly against his sword hilt as he surveyed the room.

'This has gone on long enough,' he declared, his voice carrying a forced authority that rang hollow in the close confines of the cabin. 'The friar improves, and we waste precious time playing nursemaid while our enemies could be closing in. Jurgen knows these lands well enough. We should make for the Burzenland now, while we still can.'

The fire popped and hissed in the sudden silence that followed his words. Fabrisse watched as Jurgen slowly straightened from where he'd been sat, his face hardening. Beside him, Clovis rose from his place by the hearth, and a low growl rumbled in his chest as he sensed his master's unease.

Valour 239

'I gave my word to wait,' Jurgen said, his quiet voice carrying more authority than all of Carsten's blustering. 'One day at most, we agreed. Or perhaps such promises mean nothing to you?'

'Promises?' Carsten barked a laugh that held more than a touch of hysteria. 'What good are promises to dead men? Every moment we delay gives those savages more chance to find us. Estienne Wace is not coming. Now, I am as grief stricken as anyone at the loss of my brothers. God knows Rotger and Amalric—'

'Don't speak their names,' Merten cut in, his tone sharp. 'You lost that right when you fled and left them to die.'

Clovis's growl deepened, hackles rising at the young lad's anger. The hound's eyes fixed on Carsten with predatory intent.

'How dare you?' Carsten's hand tightened on his sword hilt, though Fabrisse noted he kept his distance from the grumbling hound. 'I am still a knight of the Order! My authority—'

'Your authority means nothing here,' Jurgen interrupted, not even raising his voice. 'You threw away your authority along with your honour when you abandoned your brothers. If you're so eager to run, then run. It seems to be what you do best. But we're going to wait.'

Colour flushed Carsten's face. 'You peasant dog! I should—'

'Please,' Fabrisse interjected, rising from beside Galien's pallet. 'This quarrelling serves no one. We must remain united if we're to survive this—'

The door crashed open so hard it slammed against the cabin wall, making them all jump. Cold air rushed in as someone stumbled across the threshold, and Fabrisse's heart leaped as she recognised Estienne, though he looked little like the strapping knight who had led them through the mountains.

His shirt and trews were soaked through, hanging heavy from his powerful frame which shook violently. His face was pale as parchment, lips tinged blue with cold, but his eyes burned with terrible intensity as they fixed on Carsten. He took an unsteady step forward. Then another.

The cabin seemed suddenly so small as Estienne advanced on Carsten, each stumbling step driven more by fury than strength. His hands shook – from cold or rage, Fabrisse couldn't tell – but she saw how they curled into white-knuckled fists at his sides.

'Wace, please,' Carsten began, his earlier bluster now gone as he backed away until he reached the wall. 'I only thought to save... to warn...'

'To save yourself?' Estienne's voice was hoarse. 'While Rotger burned? While Amalric died fighting for us on a mountain path? While those pagans hunted us like animals?'

He took another lurching step forward, and Carsten raised his hands as though he might ward off Estienne's reckoning.

'I had no choice!' Carsten's legs gave way and he slid down the wall, landing hard on the wooden floor. 'You don't understand. None of you understand what I've seen. What I've endured.'

His hands came up to cover his face, but not before Fabrisse saw the tears starting to flow. She moved closer as something in Carsten's voice called to her. This was a man in need of saving. A man deserving of mercy if anyone was.

'Tell us then, Brother Carsten,' she said softly, raising her hand to halt Estienne's advance. 'Help us understand.'

Carsten's hands fell away from his face, revealing the tears that had run in a stream down his face. 'Five years I have been on this accursed frontier. And when I first came it was worse than ever. We were meant to keep the Burzenland safe, but in those early days our numbers were few and we could not save everyone. I was posted to a village at the very edge of the mountains. Raiders came, but in larger numbers than we could have antici-pated. They cut down my entire command. Hacked them apart while I... while I hid among the dead. Covered myself in their blood to survive. I can still hear the screams. Every time I close my eyes I see their faces. That's why when we came under attack I couldn't help. I—'

'So you ran?' Estienne growled. 'Left your brothers to die.'

'It's true,' Carsten sobbed. 'I am a coward.'

'And you deserve to die for it.' Estienne advanced as Carsten covered his face with his hands once more.

'We need every man,' Jurgen said from where he stood by the fire. 'Even a coward's blade might make the difference if those pagans catch us again.'

Fabrisse watched the struggle play across Estienne's face – rage warring with exhaustion, hatred with pragmatism. The muscle in his jaw worked as he stared down at Carsten's huddled form. Finally, he stepped back, swaying slightly with fatigue.

'You'll answer to the Order when we return,' he said, his voice heavy with disgust. 'But for now, you'll do your duty. God help us all.'

He turned away, shoulders slumping. It spurred them all to sudden purpose, and they worked swiftly to warm him. Jurgen built up the fire until flames roared up the chimney, driving back the chill. Fabrisse helped Estienne take off his sodden clothes as Talshyn went about preparing a broth from the herbs and mushrooms she had foraged. Even Clovis appeared determined to help, pressing his warm bulk against Estienne's leg and whining softly when the knight's violent shivering didn't cease.

'Here,' Merten said, unwrapping his own cloak from his shoulders and draping it carefully across Estienne's back.

'Keep it,' Estienne tried to protest through chattering teeth. 'You'll need—'

'Please,' Merten insisted quietly, settling beside him in front of the fire. 'It's the least I can do, after what you did for us.'

Estienne nodded gratefully, pulling the cloak tighter about him. 'Thank you.'

'How did you find us?'

'Managed to stay ahead of the pagans till daybreak,' Estienne replied between careful sips of the hot broth. 'Had to jump in the river to escape them. The current carried me a long way downstream and when I finally dragged myself out, I headed west, as best I could discern. Saw smoke from your fire and followed it here. Though if I could follow it...'

'So could they,' Jurgen finished grimly.

Silence fell as they all considered what that meant. Fabrisse studied their faces in the firelight, seeing the fear there. The helplessness.

'We should rest while we can,' she said finally. 'Then be gone in the morning when Estienne and Galien are well enough to make the rest of the journey. And I suggest we all pray. God knows what trials await us on the path home.'

No one argued. They had survived this far through courage, will and God's grace. She could only pray there was enough spare to see them safely home.

33

Fabrisse helped Brother Galien sit up from his pallet as dawn light crept into the cabin. His face was still pale as chalk, but the herbs Talshyn had gathered had worked their healing wonders and his wound's infection had begun to fade. The others were preparing themselves to leave, not wishing to waste any daylight on the journey back home.

'Unless I've missed my guess, the pass lies just a few miles east,' Jurgen said as he laced up his leather tunic. 'Through a narrow valley between the peaks. If we push hard, we might reach it by sundown. From there it's a clear run to the Burzenland and Rosenau.'

Estienne nodded in agreement. 'Then push hard we will.'

Fabrisse steadied Galien as he tried to stand, noting how his legs trembled with the effort. 'Can you manage the journey? There's no shame in admitting if you need more rest.'

He managed a weak nod, though pain tightened the corners of his mouth. 'God's grace has seen me resurrected, my lady. And His strength flows through me still. I'll make the journey if I have to do it on my knees like a penitent.'

'We'll put him on Carsten's horse,' Estienne said. 'There'll be no need to crawl, Brother Galien. Don't fear.'

'Then let's be away,' Jurgen added, giving Clovis a fuss as the hound whined softly at his touch. 'Every moment we delay gives them time to pick up our trail.'

Merten nodded his assent, while Carsten said nothing. The Komtur had been silent all the night, clearly in no mood to provoke anyone's ire. In turn, no one had so much as looked at him, and Fabrisse could sense the shame and disdain that permeated the small cabin.

She smoothed her tattered robe that was now little better than a beggar's garment, stained with blood and mud. 'I'll fetch fresh water for the journey. There's a stream nearby, yes?'

'Aye, just past those pines,' Jurgen replied, gesturing to the east. 'But take Clovis with you. We're not safe here.'

She nodded, taking up a waterskin left by whoever the cabin's previous occupant had been. The leather was cracked with age but still watertight. Jurgen gestured with his hand, and the hound padded after her. As she stepped out into the crisp morning air, the dog remained by her side, and there was something oddly comforting in having him there.

The morning dew had left the grass slick as she picked her way toward the stream. In the daylight she could see more of the hound's black and tan coat that still bore the cruel marks left by the pagan warriors. It brought back a now painfully familiar sense of guilt. This beast had suffered, along with others, because she had set out on her mission of conversion. Because she had been so determined to bring the light of God.

Fabrisse shook her head clear of those thoughts as she neared the stream. It would do her no good now to dwell on it. There would be time aplenty to repent for that loss when they made it back to Christendom.

Carsten's destrier stood tethered nearby, a magnificent bay stallion that seemed ill-suited to its craven master. The horse stamped nervously at their approach, steam rising from its flanks in the chill morning air. Its ears flicked back and forth as though sensing some hidden danger, and it pulled against its lead rope with barely contained panic.

'Easy there,' Fabrisse murmured, giving the beast a wide berth, as she uncorked the waterskin.

The stream gurgled softly as she knelt beside it, clear water tumbling over moss-covered stones. She dipped the waterskin beneath the surface, watching it fill and feeling the numbing cold bite into her fingers. The morning was eerily still; even the birds seemed reluctant to break the silence that hung over the forest. Only the stream's quiet song and the occasional stamp of the horse disturbed the unnatural peace.

A sudden change in Clovis drew her attention. The hound had gone rigid, his muscles bunching beneath his coat as he stared at something beneath a nearby pine. His lips pulled back from yellowed teeth as a low growl rumbled in his chest. Fabrisse's heart began to race as she watched him pad forward, powerful shoulders bunching as he began to paw at what appeared to be a windblown pile of leaves and earth.

'Clovis?' she whispered, rising slowly from the stream's edge. 'What is it, boy?'

The hound's digging grew more frantic, scattering the thin covering of debris. Beneath it, something pale caught the morning light, and Fabrisse stifled a gasp as she recognised the unmistakable curve of a human hand, waxy and grey in death.

Fighting down her rising gorge, she approached carefully. The smell hit her first – that sweet-rotten scent she knew from ministering to the sick. Clovis had revealed enough now that she could make out more of the corpse, face-down in the disturbed earth. He wore the rough garb of a woodsman, the fabric soaked dark with blood, an unmistakeable puncture mark in the centre of his back.

The body couldn't have lain here long. The autumn cold had preserved it somewhat, but decay had barely begun its work. As she stared at the scene with growing horror, her mind raced. The cabin's previous occupant, perhaps? But who had killed him, and why attempt to hide the body so poorly? Unless...

The horse stamped nervously, diverting her attention, and she realised she and Clovis were no longer alone.

'Our four-legged friend has made quite a discovery there.'

Carsten's voice made her start. He stood a few paces away, the weak sunlight catching the black cross on his white surcoat, the symbol of faith he had betrayed so thoroughly. She hadn't heard him approach – had he been watching her all along, waiting to see what she might find?

'Indeed,' she replied carefully, noting how his hand rested on his sword hilt, fingers flexing against the worn leather grip. 'And only recently buried, I would guess. Care to explain it, Komtur?'

'Are you accusing me—'

He stopped as Clovis growled, a deep resonant noise from deep in the hound's chest.

'No games this time, Carsten. It's plain to anyone with eyes what has happened here.'

'He attacked me.' The words tumbled out too quickly, his voice pitched higher than usual. 'When I first reached the cabin. He came at me with a knife, raving like a madman. I had no choice but to defend myself.'

Clovis's growl deepened as Carsten took a step closer, dead leaves scrunching beneath his boots. The hound positioned himself between them, muscles tensed, which only emboldened Fabrisse further.

Valour   247

'Such a wound would be in his chest,' she said quietly, keeping her voice level despite how wary she was. 'Not his back.'

She could see Carsten bristle at the obvious suggestion, his pale skin turning an ugly shade of crimson. 'You weren't there. You don't understand what happened. He... he tried to steal my horse. Turned to run after I disarmed him. I was just defending myself. Don't you see?'

'By stabbing an unarmed man in the back? By hiding his body like a common murderer?'

'I did what I had to!' Spittle flew from his lips as his voice rose to a shout that echoed through the trees. 'What do you know of it, woman? Nothing. You weren't even here.'

He advanced another step, and Clovis bared his teeth with a snarl. Carsten's eyes darted between them, calculation replacing his rage as he weighed his options. One hand still gripped his sword hilt while the other clenched and unclenched at his side.

'What now, Carsten?' Fabrisse asked, fighting to keep her voice steady even as her heart hammered. 'Am I next? How many more will die for you to keep this crime hidden? All I need to do is—'

'Scream?' The edge in his voice made her blood run cold as his sword cleared the scabbard. 'Do you think you'll have time before I—'

'Before you what?'

Estienne's question cut through the tension. He stood at the edge of the clearing, unarmed, but still the more imposing of the two knights. His scarred face was terrible in its fury, blue-grey eyes promising nothing but violence.

Carsten visibly shrank as Estienne approached, all his earlier menace evaporating like morning mist. Behind him came Jurgen and Merten, but they faltered at the sight of the exposed corpse, understanding dawning in their eyes.

'It's not what you think,' Carsten stammered, backing away until he stumbled over a fallen branch. 'He was dangerous. Mad. These forests breed wild men, you know the truth of that. I had to protect myself. I had no choice.'

'Like you had no choice but to abandon us to the pagans?' Estienne's voice carried the coldness of a killer that made Fabrisse suddenly fearful of him.

'I was going to get help!' Carsten's protests grew increasingly shrill, as sweat ran freely down his face now despite the cold. 'I would have returned with more men from Rosenau. Would have brought the whole Order to save you all! You don't understand, someone had to survive to warn them. To tell them what happened—'

'Lies upon lies.' Estienne snatched the sword from Carsten's limp grip. 'You're not fit to wear that cross. Not fit to call yourself a knight.'

Carsten fell to his knees in the mud, hands raised in supplication. 'Please, brother. Show mercy.'

'You dare speak of mercy?' Estienne took another step forward, blade rising. 'After what you've done—'

'Wait.' Fabrisse stepped forward, placing herself between them. 'This isn't the way.'

'Stand aside,' Estienne growled. 'He deserves death for his cowardice. For this murder. For betraying everything the Order stands for.'

'Perhaps he does.' She met Estienne's rage-filled eyes without flinching. 'But that judgement belongs to God and to the Order he's betrayed. Not to us. Not here. Not now.'

For a moment she thought he might push past her and exact his own justice, but gradually the fury in his eyes dimmed, replaced by a coldness that somehow felt much worse.

'Strip off that surcoat,' he commanded as he lowered the

Valour 249

blade. 'And your sword belt. You're not fit to wear either. I will take care of this weapon until we get back to Rosenau. Maybe there we'll find someone worthy enough to wield it.'

Carsten's trembling fingers fumbled with the buckle as he removed his sword belt, then pulled the white surcoat over his head. Without the trappings of his station, he looked smaller somehow, pathetic and diminished.

'We should bind him,' Merten suggested, his young face hard with contempt for his former superior. 'Ensure he can't cause more harm.'

'He'll cause no more trouble,' Jurgen cut in. 'Will you, Schado? Otherwise Clovis will have your balls for breakfast. Besides, dawn's getting old and we've miles yet to cover. Let him walk as he is – a coward stripped of honour.'

Fabrisse watched as Merten dragged Carsten to his feet and shoved him back toward the cabin. The boy then picked up the discarded surcoat and stuffed it into a pannier at the destrier's saddle. Estienne untethered the horse, and together they left the glade and its corpse behind.

When they returned to the cabin, Talshyn was waiting with Galien, and with some effort they helped him up onto their horse, before Jurgen led them westward toward salvation.

Carsten trudged behind, head bowed. Fabrisse glanced back, past the disgraced Komtur toward the glade with its half-buried corpse. She offered a silent prayer, not just for the soul of the man Carsten had killed, but for Carsten himself. Even the darkest heart might find redemption through God's grace, even a murderer, and she would be sure to plead for mercy once they reached Rosenau. It was doubtful Carsten would be spared because of it, but at least his soul might find some redemption.

34

The path wound between ancient oaks and towering pines, scant sunlight falling on the loamy earth at their feet. The trail climbed steadily upward, bordered by thick brambles and stands of young birch. Though the trek was taxing, it was nothing compared to the treacherous mountain paths they'd left behind. Here at least a man could walk without constant fear of plummeting to his death. Still, Estienne kept his guard up, scanning the woods ahead for any sign of movement.

He kept one hand on the lead rope of Carsten's destrier, where Brother Galien swayed gently in the saddle. The monk's colour had improved somewhat since they'd got him mounted, but his breathing was still laboured. The others looked to be doing well, and Merten and Jurgen he had little concern for, since they had both proven themselves more than resilient. Talshyn and Fabrisse were also in good spirits considering what they had been through, sharing a few words now and again in the Cuman language – Estienne could only assume to offer one another encouragement.

Behind them, Carsten tramped along stripped of arms and

Valour 251

dignity alike. Part of Estienne hoped the disgraced knight would make a break for it – run off into the wilderness to die alone, as he deserved. It would save them all a lot of trouble once they reached Rosenau.

'What will happen to him?' Fabrisse asked, her voice quiet so only Estienne might hear. 'To Carsten, I mean. When we return?'

Estienne glanced back to where the Komtur trudged at the rear of their group. 'Justice demands his head. For abandoning his sworn brothers to die. For murdering an innocent man in cold blood...'

'And yet?' Fabrisse prompted.

'And yet his family holds considerable influence.' Estienne spat. 'They are merchants from Lubeck. Though it is seldom spoken of, their contributions to the Order's coffers saw Carsten elevated to his position as Komtur. Despite his vows, he is still part of a powerful dynasty, and such men rarely face true justice for their crimes.'

They walked in silence for a moment as Estienne tried to quell his anger at the unfairness of it. He should have killed Carsten when he had the chance – that would have been the surest way to see justice done – but he knew he had to stay his hand. Even though Amalric and Rotger had been his friends, it was only the Order who had the right to exact justice on one of their own.

'Perhaps mercy would serve better than vengeance,' Fabrisse said finally, her words measured and careful. 'Even the greatest sinners can find redemption through God's grace, if they truly seek it.'

Estienne barked a harsh laugh that held no mirth. 'You still believe that? After everything you've witnessed? After all this killing?'

'I must. If I abandon hope in man's capacity for good, then

what was any of this for? Why risk bringing God's light to these lands at all?'

'Some men are beyond redemption. Some sins cannot be forgiven. Not by God, not by man.'

'That is not for you or I to decide.' She touched his arm lightly, the gesture somehow conveying both compassion and reproach. 'Vengeance belongs to God alone. We are but His instruments, and we must trust in His justice.'

'Well, if you ask me His justice is slow in coming,' Estienne muttered, unable to quell his impatience for a reckoning.

'The Greek philosophers say: the mills of the gods grind late, but they grind fine.'

'Do they?' Estienne replied, his hand falling to his sword hilt. 'Well, I prefer my justice more immediate. And applied with steel rather than scripture.'

Jurgen's sharp whistle cut through their conversation. Estienne turned to see the old hunter had frozen mid-step, one hand raised in warning, his face suddenly taut with alarm. Even Clovis had gone rigid beside him, the hound's hackles rising as he stared back along the path they'd just climbed, sniffing at the wind.

'Hide yourselves,' Jurgen hissed, already dashing toward the undergrowth. 'Now!'

They scattered for cover like mice before a hawk. Estienne pulled Carsten's horse into the woodland, muttering soothing words. Merten was at his side in an instant, and he gestured for the boy to take Galien deeper into the wood before turning back to the path. He crouched, concealing himself behind the hawthorn as he watched for what had so spooked Jurgen.

The first rider materialised from beyond the treeline with a nocked bow, his small horse picking its way carefully along the trail. The warrior's dark eyes scanned the thick foliage to either side as his horse plodded onward.

Valour 253

More followed in his wake, moving with the easy confidence of men born to the saddle. Then Estienne saw him – Shoruk, the man who had killed Amalric, who had driven them to this desperate flight through the mountains. Moldir rode at Shoruk's side, hunched like a dark raven over her saddle. Even at this distance, there was something that made Estienne's skin crawl with revulsion just at the sight of her.

His hand moved to his sword hilt, fingers curling around the familiar grip. The steel whispered against leather as he began to ease the blade free. One swift rush, one charge, and he could end this here and now...

Fabrisse's hand clamped down on his wrist, her grip surprisingly strong. Her eyes met his in a silent plea for restraint.

'Don't,' she breathed.

Estienne trembled with the effort of quelling his need to attack. His blood was up, but warred with his good sense. He might kill Shoruk, and Moldir into the bargain, but it would surely cost him his life. All the while the Cumans conversed in their harsh tongue as they rode past, their words carrying clearly in the thin mountain air. A score in all – too many to fight, even if they were caught completely by surprise.

It felt like an eternity before the last rider disappeared around the next bend. Only then did Estienne breathe normally again, his hand unclenching from his sword hilt as his heart thundered.

'That was too close,' Jurgen muttered once they'd regrouped.

'Much too close,' Estienne agreed. 'After I lost them in the river they must have doubled back through the mountain to collect their horses, and guessed our only path back to the Burzenland was this one.'

'And now they've cut us off,' Jurgen said grimly. 'We'll never make it to Rosenau without going through them.'

'Could we wait them out?' Merten asked, his young face

pinched with worry as he held on to the reins of Galien's horse. 'Surely they can't block the pass forever. They'll have to come back along it sooner or later.'

'We don't have the supplies for a waiting game,' Jurgen replied. 'Two days of foraged food at most, and precious little else. By the time we've waited them out, we'll have starved.'

'What about going around?' Estienne suggested. 'Surely there must be another way home. Some path we haven't considered.'

'Aye, there might be,' Jurgen said slowly, his face creased in thought as his eyes fixed on something above them, hidden in the swirling clouds that crowned the nearby peaks. 'Though you won't like it. None of you will. There's an old goat track that leads over the high passes. Few know of it, fewer still would dare to use it.'

'Sounds like we have no choice?' Estienne said.

'No choice at all.' Jurgen's voice was grim. 'With women and wounded it might be better to take our chances against the pagans. Narrow ledges barely wide enough for a man to edge along sideways. Places where the wind howls so fierce it'll pluck you off the mountain like a hawk snatching a rabbit. And that's in good weather.'

'You can't be serious,' Carsten spoke up, his voice shrill with fear. 'We'll all die up there! The cold will probably kill us, let alone the climb itself.'

'You can take any route you wish, Schado,' Estienne snapped back.

'Maybe I will,' Carsten said, drawing himself up with a pathetic attempt at dignity. 'But I have a right to defend myself. I demand the return of my sword, at least. I have the right to—'

Estienne rounded on him. 'You lost any rights when you abandoned us to die. When you murdered a man to save your own worthless hide.'

Valour

'Be reasonable, Wace. You can't—'

'I can and I will. Push me on this. Give me an excuse to finish what I should have done the moment we found you cowering in that cabin.'

The naked threat in his voice made Carsten shrink back, whatever courage he'd mustered evaporating. Estienne turned to Jurgen.

'How long would it take? To cross over the high passes?'

The old hunter squinted up at the cloud-wreathed peaks, measuring the challenge with experienced eyes. 'Two days, if we're lucky. If the weather holds.'

That was a big 'if', but Estienne knew they had no choice. He looked to Brother Galien, who nodded weakly, then to Fabrisse. The determination in her eyes matched his own.

'Then we go,' he announced.

Above them, the clouds grew darker, promising weather that would make their desperate climb even more treacherous. But there was no choice now.

The only way home was up, into the teeth of the mountain's fury.

35

Jurgen had not been lying about their route. The mountain path hugged the cliff face, the drop stretching away to their left. Each time the wind gusted along the narrow passage it threatened to tear them all from their precarious perch.

'Hold steady,' Jurgen called back, his voice nearly lost to the constant keening of the wind. 'Ground's treacherous as a storm at sea here. One wrong step and you'll be feeding the crows at the bottom of the mountain.'

'Comforting thought,' Merten muttered, his young face twisted with strain as he guided their lone horse along the treacherous route.

Brother Galien swayed in the saddle, his face grey as the stone. Fabrisse and the young priestess flanked the horse, ready to steady the monk if he started to slip.

'Easy now,' Fabrisse murmured as the horse shied from a sudden gust, its hooves scraping dangerously close to the edge. 'God's hand guides us. Trust in His protection.'

Estienne was starting to wish he shared her faith, but the

higher they climbed into this treacherous environment the further from God they seemed to be.

'This is madness,' Carsten's voice drifted back from somewhere in the middle of their line, brittle with barely contained panic. 'We should have found another way. Any other way. We're all going to die up here, I know it.'

'Save your breath for walking,' Estienne snapped. 'We've all heard more than enough. If these women can make the journey without complaint, I'm damn sure you can.'

But there was some truth to Carsten's bluster. The path grew narrower with each bend, and it was becoming increasingly difficult to guide their single horse along the track. Estienne began to think that the next misstep would be their end, but as though in answer to a prayer, a plateau opened before him, the path widening into a roughly circular space perhaps thirty feet across. Solid ground had never felt so welcome beneath Estienne's feet as he watched the others follow from the narrow passage, each face etched with the strain of their precarious journey.

'We rest here,' he announced, despite every instinct screaming at him to keep moving. 'We all need to catch our breath.'

'Thank Christ,' Merten breathed, as he led the horse to within the lee of the cliff face, his hands trembling as he checked its hooves.

Brother Galien almost fell from the saddle as Fabrisse and Talshyn helped ease him down. The pagan priestess checked his wound before speaking in her language.

'The bleeding has started again,' Fabrisse translated, as the pagan woman produced a handful of dried leaves from a pouch at her belt. 'Her herbs will help with the pain, though it may make him sleep.'

'Better sleep than suffering,' Merten replied, helping the

monk settle against a boulder. 'God knows he's endured enough already.'

As the women tended to Galien, Estienne prowled the edges of the plateau. It offered them some protection from the wind, with the cliff rising sheer on one side. The path they'd traversed was the only obvious approach, and narrow enough to defend if they had to. For the first time in days he felt as though the pagans were no longer a threat. Now all they had to contend with were the elements.

'Estienne!' Jurgen's call drew him to where the hunter stood beside a boulder, half-buried in scree at the plateau's edge. 'Look here.'

Carved into the ancient stone were Latin letters, their edges softened by centuries of wind and rain. Estienne traced them with his fingers, remembering the Latin he'd learned in his youth.

'*Legio II Adiutrix*,' he read aloud.

'What does that mean?' Jurgen asked as he squinted at the letters.

'Second Legion, the Rescuers. There are dates here too – *Anno Domini 104*. They must have used this pass during their campaigns against the Dacians. These mountains have known soldiers before us, it seems.'

'Romans?' Merten asked, drawn by the discovery. 'All the way up here?'

'They went everywhere,' Estienne replied, a strange comfort coming from touching these ancient signs. 'Built roads, fortresses. Carved civilisation out of the wilderness. Though even their empire couldn't tame these peaks.'

'What devils might we encounter up here that the Romans couldn't tame?' Carsten demanded, his voice pitched higher than usual as he hovered at the edge of their group. 'What spirits

Valour 259

haunt these godless mountains?'

'The only devils we need fear are the ones pursuing us,' Estienne replied, though he couldn't entirely dismiss Carsten's fears. There was something about these heights that made a man feel small, insignificant against the vast scale of stone and sky.

'We should move on,' Jurgen said, Clovis pressing close against his leg as though sensing his master's unease. 'These mountains have eyes, and I'd rather not linger where the ghosts of old warriors might take notice of us.'

Estienne nodded his agreement. 'Very well. Let's get Brother Galien mounted and be on our way. The sooner we're over this range, the better.'

They resumed their precarious journey, the wind growing stronger as they climbed higher. The path narrowed again, forcing them to proceed with agonising slowness as the horse's nervous snorts echoed off the cliff face.

Eventually the path twisted around a jutting shoulder of rock, offering their first clear view of the path still to come. Clouds wreathed the distant peaks, and Estienne felt the weight of responsibility settle deeper onto his shoulders. Soon they would be forced to abandon the horse, and getting Brother Galien across those narrow trails might prove—

Merten's startled gasp echoed from behind him. Estienne turned to see Carsten with his fist bunched in the squire's hair, the blade of a knife held across Merten's throat. Where he had got it from was anyone's guess, and Estienne cursed himself for not taking more care to search the man for weapons. The blade trembled slightly, betraying the fear behind Carsten's desperate move.

'Stand back,' Carsten snarled, his eyes bearing the wild look of a cornered animal. 'I'll not let you drag me back to Rosenau a prisoner. Not to face the Marschall's justice.'

'Think about what you're doing,' Estienne said, keeping his

voice steady despite his rage building. 'There's nowhere for you to go, Carsten. The pagans are blocking the path to the only other way home. This will only end in your death.'

'Better to die free than in a cage at Rosenau.' Carsten's laugh held an edge of hysteria, as he let go of Merten's hair, still pressing the knife to his throat, grasped Galien's ragged hassock and dragged him from the saddle. 'You think I don't know what awaits me? The shame? The punishment? I'll not hang just for trying to survive.'

'The path you're on leads only to damnation, Carsten,' Fabrisse called out, as Galien slumped against the rock wall. 'But there's still time to choose another way.'

'Spare me your sermons, woman. I'm done listening to righteous prating.'

Estienne stepped forward, his hands held out on a placatory gesture. 'Carsten, we can be reasonable—'

'Fuck you, Wace. That time is passed.'

He shoved Merten aside with enough force to send the boy stumbling toward the precipice. Jurgen lunged forward, catching him before he could fall, pulling him back from the edge as Carsten vaulted onto the horse's back. The animal whinnied in protest, hooves scraping against stone as its new rider wheeled it around.

'Carsten!'

Estienne's roar echoed off the cliff face, but Carsten paid him no heed, spurring the horse back the way they'd come. The animal's iron-shod hooves clacked off the stone as it picked up speed, each impact sending loose scree cascading into the void. There was nothing any of them could do but watch as horse and rider disappeared around the bend, the sound of their flight fading under the constant moan of the wind.

'Traitorous bastard,' Merten gasped, rubbing at his throat where Carsten had almost opened him up.

'Are you all right?' Estienne asked.

'I'll live,' the squire replied. 'But what about him?'

Brother Galien sagged against the rock where he'd fallen, his face even greyer than before. Without the horse, he would have to make the rest of the journey on foot. The thought of how that would slow their progress made Estienne's fists bunch with renewed frustration.

'Damn that bastard,' Estienne snarled through gritted teeth. 'I should have killed him when I had the chance. I knew this would happen.'

'He won't last long out there alone,' Jurgen said. 'Either the pagans will find him, or the wilds will claim him. These mountains don't suffer cowards.'

'We can't spare thought for his fate,' Estienne replied, forcing his anger down. 'We need to move. Now.'

Brother Galien tried to push himself upright, but his legs buckled beneath him. Estienne moved closer, grabbing his arm to help him to his feet.

'Leave me,' the monk whispered, his face twisted with pain. 'I'll only slow you down.'

'No.' Estienne's voice brooked no argument as he dragged the monk upright. 'I'll not abandon another brother to these mountains.'

'None of us will,' Merten said firmly, taking up position on Galien's other side. 'We go together, or not at all.'

'Merten is right,' Fabrisse said, laying a hand on Galien's cheek. 'God's grace has brought us this far. It will see us the rest of the way.'

Estienne wasn't so sure about God's grace – he'd seen too much suffering to put much faith in divine protection. But as he looked at the determination in the faces around him, he felt a rare pride kindle in his chest. They might be wounded, exhausted and half-frozen, but they weren't broken. Not yet.

They formed up once more, and as they resumed their journey, the wind howled around them like the souls of the dead. Ahead, the path disappeared into wreaths of cloud, offering no glimpse of what hardship awaited. But it was too late for them to yield now.

36

Shoruk reined his horse to a halt, the bitter wind blowing along the pass and cutting through his furs. There in the distance, squatting between the peaks like some great grey toad, the fortress of the Christians reached toward the sky like an insult carved in stone, a monument to everything his people had lost.

The sight of those walls took him back to childhood, to nights spent huddled around the fire as his grandfather's tales painted pictures of glory in the dancing flames. He could still hear the old man's voice, rough as bark but warm with pride, describing how these lands had belonged to their people since the first horse was tamed. Those stories would pour from him like water from a spring – tales of vast herds that thundered across these slopes, of how their people had followed the seasonal migrations as free as the wind itself. In those days, the only boundaries had been the distant horizon, where Tengri's realm touched the earth where Eje dwelt.

'In my youth,' his grandfather would say, gnarled fingers gesturing at the stars, 'a man could ride for ten days in any direction and never see sign of man's passing. The land belonged to those strong enough to claim it, as it should be.' Then his voice would grow thick with anger as he spoke of the Christians and their creeping advance, of how their steel-clad warriors brought their accursed god and their unyielding might.

Now those same slopes lay bare and empty, what little grazing remained claimed by Christian settlers who grew crops instead of hunting game. The mighty herds were gone. Each year brought fresh insults as more fortresses rose from the earth, pushing them further east.

Shoruk spat his frustration, but the gesture felt empty, a child's defiance against the tide that threatened to wash away all that his people had ever been. His grandfather's tales seemed to mock him now – stories of glory that had crumbled to dust.

'We've lost them.' Artak's voice carried an edge of defeat as he drew his mount alongside Shoruk's, his face lined with exhaustion, dark circles beneath his eyes from the relentless pursuit. 'If they are ahead of us, they will have reached the safety of the fortress by now.'

Shoruk grunted acknowledgment. They had pushed their mounts mercilessly through the night, but the light of day had revealed no tracks. Now they could see along the pass all the way to the borders of the Christian territories and there was no sign of their quarry. It seemed it had all been for nothing.

'So what do we do now, Shorukhan?' Artak asked. 'Should we turn back? Try to find what remains of the clan?'

'What remains of the clan?' Shoruk answered. It seemed so long since he had even considered them.

'Yes, the clan. If they still live, they face winter with scant supplies. If we find them we can—'

'We took most of the food,' Shoruk said. 'The best horses, the strongest warriors...'

He left the rest unsaid, but the implications hung heavy in the chill air.

'So we abandon them?'

'We begin again,' Shoruk replied. 'We build the Clan of the White Wolf anew as our ancestors have done time and again. It is just a matter of where.'

'There might be better hunting grounds to the east,' Artak suggested carefully, his eyes fixed on the horizon. 'Fresh pastures, new territories.'

'To the east?' Shoruk laughed. 'Did you not hear Boril's tale those days ago? Of the army that sweeps west like a grass fire, devouring everything in its path? They crushed the princes of the Rus. Buried them alive beneath their victory feast, as the conquerors danced and drank above them. To ride toward that army means death.'

'Then what should we do?' Artak demanded, his patience finally fraying. 'We cannot stay here, skulking in the shadow of those stone walls. Our horses grow thin, our warriors restless. Winter comes, and with it—'

'You think I don't know that?' Shoruk rounded on him, teeth bared in a snarl. 'You think I don't feel the weight of every life that depends on my choices? That I don't see how far we've fallen?'

Artak fell silent, chastened, but Shoruk could see the doubt in his eyes. The same doubt Shoruk felt gnawing at his own heart with every decision, every compromise, every retreat. They were trapped between the Christians' steel and the eastern horde's fury, with winter's dread fingers already reaching for their throats. Whatever choice he made now would likely end in death, and the only question was how.

The sound of distant hooves drew their attention back along the pass. A lone rider approached, his mount's sides heaving with exhaustion, but it was enough to set his warriors on edge. Shoruk raised his hand as his men plucked arrows from their quivers, ready to loose death at his command.

As the stranger drew closer Shoruk saw he was bright red about his round face, and it was obvious he was no rider by the way he sat his horse like a man unused to long hours in the saddle. His eyes darted between the arranged warriors like a rabbit sizing up a pack of wolves, throat bobbing as he swallowed his fear.

'Save your arrows,' Shoruk commanded, studying the stranger as he reined in before them. 'No use wasting them on this one, he is no threat.'

Despite that, Shoruk kept a wary eye on the man as he began to babble in his Christian tongue. His hands shook as he gestured, making placating motions that only served to emphasise how pathetic he was.

'Kill him and be done with it,' Ozil suggested. 'One less Christian dog to plague us.'

'Patience.' Shoruk raised his hand for silence. 'Let's see what he wants so badly that he would risk riding right into our arms.'

The stranger seemed to gather what dregs of courage remained to him as his trembling hands moved to his saddlebags, the motion deliberate and slow. He withdrew a bundle of white fabric, holding it out like a peace offering. As it unfurled in the wind, Shoruk recognised the black cross of the Christian warriors. The man gestured to the cross, then pointed south, toward a high mountain. Shoruk knew it well, and what it hid – an ancient pass through the peaks that led to the safety of Christian lands. His meaning was clear enough, even without sharing a common tongue. Their quarry had chosen the treacherous route, hoping to avoid Shoruk's position.

'This man is a coward bearing gifts,' Artak mused, a note of

Valour 267

dark amusement in his voice. 'One of their own, turned traitor, perhaps? See how his hands shake? He reeks of fear and deceit.'

'Like a dog kicked too many times by its master,' Shoruk agreed, lip curling in contempt.

Among their enemies, it seemed there were those who would betray their brothers to save their own worthless hides. The thought was oddly satisfying – proof that the Christians were not as righteous as they pretended to be.

With a dismissive gesture, Shoruk waved the stranger away. It would not do to sully their weapons on this cur. There was nothing to gain from it.

The man needed no further encouragement, wheeling his horse around so quickly he nearly lost his seat. Then he spurred it into a gallop, as though demons themselves were at his heels.

'You should have killed him,' Artak said, hand falling to his bow.

'Let him run,' Shoruk replied, watching the rider gallop away. 'His death holds no value to us. I have had my fill of—'

'The gods have shown us the way.' Moldir's voice cut him off as she guided her horse forward. 'Tengri himself shows us the path to our prey.'

Shoruk studied the mountain the stranger had indicated. The high route was deadly even in good weather, its narrow paths and treacherous drops claiming the unwary. Recent storms would have made it worse, coating the rocks with ice. Only desperation would drive anyone to attempt such a crossing.

'The gods show us nothing but our own doom. That pass is death, waiting to swallow anyone mad enough to attempt it.'

'You would abandon the hunt?' Moldir's lip curled in contempt. 'After they have defiled our sacred places, stolen one of our own, made mockery of us. The gods still cry out for vengeance.'

'Look at those clouds,' Shoruk said, fighting to keep his voice steady as he pointed to the darkness gathering above them. 'The weather itself warns us away. Any fool can see what's coming. We would have to abandon our horses again. And for what? To chase ghosts?'

'The gods demand it,' Moldir countered. 'Or have you forgotten the price of defying their will? Have you grown so weak, so fearful, that you would let these Christians escape judgement?'

The accusation struck deep and Shoruk felt his warriors shifting uneasily behind him. Every moment of hesitation, every sign of weakness, eroded the authority he had bought with Tarkhan's blood. He was aware now more than ever that power seized through violence could be lost in just the same way.

'I think of our survival,' he said through gritted teeth. 'The pass will claim the Christians without our help. Let nature exact whatever vengeance the gods demand.'

'Nature?' Moldir's laugh was sharp as ice. 'You speak to me of nature? Do you even remember who I am? I have forgotten more of nature, the gods, the old ways, than you will ever know.' She urged her horse closer, until he could smell the stink of her breath. 'Do not think to challenge me on any of it, like you have challenged me on so much else. I thought you were one of the faithful, Shorukhan, but perhaps I was wrong. Perhaps you never truly believed at all. Perhaps you are as false as Tarkhan was.'

The warriors' murmuring grew louder. Shoruk could see their faces in the gathering gloom, how they glanced between him and the priestess with growing uncertainty. Some nodded at Moldir's words, while others shifted uncomfortably in their saddles, looking to their chief for guidance. The strength of Shoruk's leadership that had held them together since Tarkhan's death was cracking like river ice in spring.

'Do you doubt me now?' he said reluctantly, but he had to

Valour

know where their loyalties truly lay. 'Speak your minds. Let us hear what wisdom the clan's warriors would offer their chief.'

'The Kam Katun speaks truth, Shorukhan,' Boril offered. 'We cannot let them escape. The gods watch us even now. Their eyes are upon us, always.'

'The gods will watch us freeze to death and do nothing, more like,' Ozil countered, his horse stamping nervously beneath him. 'That pass has claimed souls beyond the counting, in better weather than this.'

Discontent spread through their ranks as warrior turned against warrior, brother against brother, their harsh voices a jumble of anger and fear. Some called for pursuit, others for retreat to safer ground. The bonds of clan and kinship that had held them together began to fray beneath the weight of doubt and hopelessness.

'Listen to them squabble like dogs over a bone.' Moldir's voice dripped with scorn, cutting through the clamour as she glared at Shoruk. 'Is this what the mighty Clan of the White Wolf has become? A pack of curs, crying about cold hands and empty bellies? Tarkhan at least had the courage of his convictions, even if they led him astray. But you... you are nothing but an imposter, wearing the mantle of leadership. A child playing at being chief.'

Shoruk dragged his gaze away from her, seeing the dread written plain on every face. The shame of his hesitation, the sting of Moldir's accusations, the memory of his grandfather's tales of glory twisted into a ball of fury in his chest.

His roar of rage echoed along the pass, silencing every voice as he wheeled his horse around so violently that the beast reared.

'To the pass!' The words tore from him in a flood. 'Let any man who fears the mountains remain behind for the gods to judge. The rest of you, follow me.'

He spurred his mount back toward those peaks, not knowing

if his warriors would follow or abandon him. The immediate thunder of hooves in his wake told him they had chosen to ride with their chief, at least for now.

Behind them all, Moldir's laughter rang out, high and terrible.

37

A sheer wall of weathered granite rose endlessly to Estienne's right, while to his left, empty air promised a swift journey to the ground far below. The bitter wind knifed through him, numbing his limbs and stealing his breath. Still he pushed them on, but there was no other way than forward now. They were committed to this journey for good or ill.

'I don't like the look of those clouds,' Jurgen said from up ahead, gesturing to where dark masses roiled above the peaks. 'Another storm's brewing. We need to find shelter before it hits, or we'll all freeze.'

Behind the trapper, Merten struggled to support Brother Galien's weight. The young squire's face was etched with strain as he guided the wounded friar's faltering steps.

'Just lean on me, brother,' Merten murmured. 'One foot in front of the other. Like walking to chapel.'

Galien managed a weak laugh. 'Chapel never... seemed so far away.'

'Save your strength,' Fabrisse said, close to the friar's other side. 'God's grace will see us through.'

'Can we at least rest soon?' Galien wheezed. 'Please... just a moment's rest.'

'No rest,' Estienne said. 'Not yet. Keep moving.'

He hated pushing them so hard, but the alternative was too dire to countenance. He would not lose another companion to these damned peaks, and the only way he could ensure that was to push them all beyond their limits until they reached safety.

The path ahead narrowed to little more than a strip of stone, barely clinging to the mountain's face. Ancient wooden supports jutted from the rock wall at irregular intervals, creating a walkway where the mountain path had fallen away. The timbers were grey and rotted with age, each beam looking ready to crumble at a touch, like the bones of long-dead men.

Jurgen held up a hand, bringing their exhausted group to a halt. 'This section's seen better days. Built by older folk than us, these supports. Maybe the Romans, maybe someone even more ancient. But they're well past holding any real weight now.'

A sudden gust of wind sent splinters of ancient wood spinning into the void. Clovis whined softly, pressing closer to his master's leg, his yellow eyes fixed on the treacherous path ahead.

'We'll have to cross one at a time,' Jurgen continued, his voice grave. 'Any more weight than that and the whole thing might go.'

'There must be another way,' Merten said, his young face pale as he looked out over the precipice. 'Brother Galien can barely walk as it is.'

'There is no other way,' Fabrisse replied softly. 'This path or none at all.'

'I'll go first with Clovis,' Jurgen said, as he scratched behind the hound's ears. 'Stay close, boy. Nice and steady now.'

Estienne watched as man and beast began their careful traverse. Jurgen moved with deliberate care, testing each step before committing his weight. Loose stones clattered into the abyss, as Clovis followed in his master's footsteps, tail low, muscles bunched with tension beneath his dark coat. Their crossing seemed to take an eternity, before they reached the far side.

Jurgen turned back, his face lined with concern. 'Right then. Brother Galien next. And remember to tread careful, like. These old timbers will betray you worse than that bastard Carsten.'

Merten helped Brother Galien to the edge of the bridge. The monk's face had gone white, his breathing shallow and rapid. Sweat beaded on his brow despite the bitter cold, and his hands trembled where they gripped Merten's arm.

'I cannot,' Galien mumbled, eyes squeezed shut as he swayed on his feet. 'God forgive me, but I cannot.'

'You can and you will,' Fabrisse said firmly, laying a steadying hand on his shoulder. 'God's grace will see you across. Think only of each step. The path is treacherous, yes. Just as Christ's path is treacherous, yet leads us to salvation.'

Fabrisse's words seemed to steady the monk. With Merten's support, Galien began his halting progress along the narrow ledge.

'Small steps, brother,' Merten encouraged. 'That's it. Don't look down. Eyes on the far side.'

Each foot of progress seemed to take an age, punctuated by Galien's laboured breathing and the constant moan of the wind. When he finally reached the far side, the friar collapsed to his knees, prayer spilling from his lips in a breathless stream.

Talshyn went next, moving with sure-footed confidence. She kept one hand trailing along the cliff face, her dark robes billowing in the constant wind. Unlike the others, she seemed almost at ease on the precarious ledge, as though the mountains themselves recognised her as one of their own.

Fabrisse's crossing was slower, more cautious, but she maintained her composure even as fragments of the path crumbled beneath her feet. Merten followed, the wood creaking beneath his heavier tread but still holding. Estienne found himself holding his breath until the squire reached safety, and then only he remained on the near side of the gap. As he set his boot on the wood, a deep groan emanated from the rotted supports. The sound sent ice through his veins.

'Quickly now,' Jurgen called. 'Those beams won't hold much longer.'

Estienne forced himself not to panic despite the urgency building in his chest. The ledge felt impossibly narrow, barely wide enough for him to pass. One misstep, one moment of carelessness, and he would be consumed by the hungry void.

He was barely halfway across when the first support gave way with a sharp crack like breaking bone. The bridge beneath his feet began to tilt with a grinding shriek of wood against stone.

'Jump!' someone shouted.

Estienne lunged forward as the path collapsed behind him. His fingers scrabbled at bare rock as the ground fell away. For one heart-stopping moment he hung suspended on the ledge, then strong fingers seized his arms – Jurgen and Merten dragging him to safety as the last of the wooden supports tore free in a thunderous cascade of splintering wood and tumbling rock.

The sound of falling debris seemed to go on forever, fading slowly until only the moan of the wind remained. Where the path had been, was now only a narrow ledge.

'Well,' Jurgen said grimly as he helped Estienne to his feet, 'looks like we won't be going back that way.'

The last echoes of the collapse had barely faded when another sound reached them. Distant shouts carried on the bitter wind, and Estienne recognised the harsh tongue as he peered back along their route.

'They've found our trail,' he said grimly, still unable to see the pagans dogging their path.

Jurgen cocked his head, face creased in concentration as he listened. 'Not too far behind, from what I can tell. That collapsed footway won't slow them down for long either.'

'How far to safety?' Fabrisse asked.

'Too far,' Jurgen replied. 'But we must keep going. There's no other way.'

'No, there isn't,' Estienne agreed. 'So let's keep moving. There's no telling what salvation we might find. All we have to do is stay ahead of them.'

They pressed on, each step a battle against exhaustion and the treacherous ground. The path wound ever upward, the air growing thinner at every turn. Their breathing came in short gasps, lungs burning from the effort. Brother Galien's condition had deteriorated rapidly and he could barely stay upright now, even with Merten's support. Each step drew a soft whimper of pain, his face twisted in discomfort.

'Rest,' he gasped, legs buckling. 'Please... I need to rest. Just... just a moment.'

'No rest,' Estienne said. 'They'll be on us if we stop.'

He glanced back the way they'd come, expecting to see dark figures appearing through the swirling mist at any moment. As he did, loose scree shifted under his boot and Estienne's foot shot out from under him. Empty air took him as he began to fall, his heart lurching into his throat. Then a hand seized his arm, arresting his slide toward oblivion.

Talshyn's grip was surprisingly strong as she helped steady him. Their eyes met and Estienne saw something there beyond the exhaustion. A woman he could trust, perhaps? He suddenly felt some guilt for the way he had regarded her until now. Before she had been his enemy, despite all she had done to free them, to tend Galien. Now she had all but saved his life. It was clear she had no more to prove.

'My thanks,' he said, knowing she couldn't understand but feeling compelled to speak it anyway.

She smiled back, speaking words in her own language. Before Estienne could respond, more shouts echoed off the cliff face, closer now. Too close.

'They're gaining on us,' Merten said, as he struggled to keep Brother Galien upright. 'If we could just find somewhere defensible...'

The friar sagged in Merten's grip, nearly dragging them both down. 'Can't... can't go on. Leave me. Save yourselves. I only slow you down.'

'We leave no one behind,' Estienne growled, the memory of Amalric's sacrifice suddenly niggling him like a raw wound. 'Not this time.'

He moved to Brother Galien's side, and in one smooth motion hoisted the monk onto his shoulders. The added weight made his legs tremble, but he locked his knees, refusing to buckle.

'What are you doing?' Merten asked. 'You can't carry him the rest of the way.'

'I can damn well try,' Estienne replied through gritted teeth. 'Now move.'

They pressed on, Galien's weight pressing against his aching shoulders, each step sending jolts of agony through his exhausted frame. Sweat ran freely down his back despite the bitter cold, the weight seeming to increase with each passing moment.

He glanced back, seeing figures moving along the trail below them. There were too many to count, but numbers were of little concern right now. Five or twenty, it wouldn't matter either way if they were caught.

They pushed on through the gathering gloom, each step a

victory against exhaustion and despair as more shouts echoed from below and the pagans riled themselves up for the pursuit ahead.

Let them. The climb would be as difficult for those warriors as it was for their tiny band. And when he got the chance, when there was nowhere left to run, Estienne would make it more difficult still.

38

'Keep moving,' Shoruk snarled over his shoulder, not breaking stride to see if his warriors followed.

The narrow ledge barely accommodated a man's width, with the mountain's sheer face pressing in on one side and empty air yawning on the other. The path twisted upward, revealing glimpses of dizzying heights that made even Shoruk's stomach lurch.

'We shouldn't be here,' Artak muttered, his voice barely audible over the wind. 'These mountains belong to the dead.'

'Silence,' Shoruk snapped, though the same thought had been gnawing at his gut. 'Would you have us turn back now? Let those Christian dogs escape after what they've done?'

'They've already escaped,' Artak said, his face haggard with grief for his fallen brother. 'They're too far ahead, and we lose more men with every mile of our pursuit. The mountains favour them, not us.'

Shoruk rounded on the warrior, seizing him by the front of his furs. 'You forget yourself, Artak. I am still chief here. Would you have us bathe the clan in shame? Tell our women and children that we abandoned the hunt because the path grew difficult?'

Artak's eyes hardened, but he looked away first. 'No, Shorukhan. I would not.'

'Then keep your doubts to yourself.' Shoruk released him with a shove. 'We are the Clan of the White Wolf. We do not abandon our prey.'

The words rang hollow even to his own ears, but he turned and continued the climb. Behind him, he heard the soft chuckle of Moldir. Her amusement stoked his rage like a bellows to flame. She had been pushing him from the start; whispering about Tarkhan's weakness, about the glory that awaited a warrior bold enough to seize power. Now she pushed him still, though to what end he could no longer say.

A gust of wind nearly tore him from the path, and Shoruk grasped a jutting stone to steady himself. Below, the world was lost in a void that promised only death. Above, the mountain's peak was shrouded in cloud, offering no glimpse of how much farther they must climb. They were caught between earth and sky, neither realm welcoming them.

'We are close,' Moldir called, her voice carrying an unnatural clarity through the howling gale. 'I can feel them. Their fear calls to me like blood to a wolf.'

Shoruk clenched his jaw at her words. Let her rant to the gods. All that mattered was catching those who had fled – the Christian woman who had turned his people against each other, and that treacherous bitch Talshyn who had freed them.

'With me,' he ordered once more.

His warriors had no choice but to follow, just as he had no choice but to lead. The hunt had taken on a life of its own, with a purpose greater than any of them. A beast that could only be sated with blood.

The path ended abruptly before them, halting the column of warriors, and Shoruk approached the edge with careful steps. A section of ancient bridge had collapsed entirely, taking with it the rotted wooden supports that had once braced it against the mountainside. Empty space now separated them from where the path continued on the far side.

Behind him, the warriors shifted uneasily, exchanging glances that spoke volumes. They had followed him loyally through blood and hardship, but this... this was beyond what even the bravest warrior could be asked to face.

'What do we do, Shorukhan?' Ozil asked, his voice thin with barely disguised terror. 'We cannot cross this.'

Shoruk stared at the gap, mind racing. They could turn back, try to find another route, but that would put them even farther behind, if such a path even existed. By then, their quarry would be long gone, safe behind their borders.

Moldir pushed through the gathered warriors, her dark eyes fixed on the gap. 'Will you let this obstacle thwart the will of the gods? After we have come so far?'

Shoruk felt his temper rise. 'What would you have me do, woman? Grow wings and fly across? The gap is too wide to jump, the edges too weak for ropes.'

'The gods would provide a way if you had faith enough to beseech them!' Her voice rose to match the howling wind. 'But you have always been weak in your devotion, Shorukhan. Perhaps Tarkhan's faltering faith was not his alone.'

A murmur ran through the warriors at this accusation. Shoruk felt their eyes upon him, questioning, judging. His hand moved to his weapon, fingers tightening around the grip. One stroke would silence her. Yet he stayed his hand, for her words had struck deeper than she knew.

Was this truly the will of Tengri? Or had they been following

Valour 281

a path of blood laid out by Moldir's hunger and his own pride? Tarkhan had believed the future of the clan lay in peace with the Christians. Shoruk had killed him for that belief, convinced it was weakness. But now, standing on this barren mountainside with half his warriors dead or lost, he wondered if the old chief had seen something he had not.

'Perhaps,' he said slowly, 'this is a sign. The mountain itself bars our way. Maybe Tengri does not wish us to continue this pursuit.'

'Of course he does. He tests our devotion. And we will demonstrate that devotion with blood and sacrifice as we always have.'

'We have sacrificed enough,' Shoruk said, gesturing to the diminished band. 'Uzur, Darman, Tamaz... good men all, who have followed me faithfully, as have my other warriors. I will not throw any more lives away chasing ghosts through these cursed peaks.'

Moldir stepped closer, her face inches from his. 'What kind of chief are you, Shoruk? What kind of leader abandons the hunt when the prey is within reach?'

'I am the kind of chief who serves his clan. Not the kind who serves the whims of a mad priestess.'

Moldir's eyes widened at the challenge, her thin lips drawing back from yellowed teeth.

'Choose your next words with care. Every chief can be replaced.'

'Replaced?' Shoruk's voice dropped to a dangerous growl. 'Is that a threat, Moldir?'

Her lips broke into a smile that never reached her eyes. 'Merely an observation. Erlik does not favour the weak.'

The name hung in the air gusting between them. Erlik, the dark god of death, lord of Tamag. Not a deity to be invoked

282   RICHARD CULLEN

lightly, especially not by one who claimed to follow Tengri of the endless blue sky.

'So it is Erlik you serve now,' Shoruk said flatly. 'Not Tengri. Not the clan.'

A heavy silence had fallen over the gathered warriors. Some made warding signs, fingers tracing symbols of protection against evil. Eyes darted between their chief and the priestess as the tension escalated.

'I serve those with power,' Moldir hissed, abandoning all pretence. 'Tengri is distant, watching while our people are driven like sheep from their lands. But Erlik... Erlik hungers. Erlik acts. Erlik rewards those who worship him.'

'And you expect us to accept that?'

'I do not expect, Shorukhan. I demand, as your Kam Katun. And so do the gods. One of you must offer yourself. Step forward into the embrace of Tamag, and your brothers will be granted safe passage. Your name will be remembered in song for genera-tions. Your spirit will ride forever at Erlik's side, mighty among the dead.'

Artak spat on the ground. 'Madness. You speak madness, woman.'

'Madness?' Moldir rounded on him, eyes flashing. 'Your brother was killed by these Christian dogs. Would you dishonour his memory by turning back now, when our enemies are so close? Give me one warrior's life, and I will give you your vengeance. We will span this gap and slake the thirst of the gods in Christian blood...'

As he watched, memories cascaded through Shoruk's mind. Moldir stoking his ambition, urging him to take what was not yet his. Moldir standing silent as he drew his blade across Tarkhan's throat, her eyes gleaming with satisfaction as the old chief's blood soaked into the earth. Moldir presiding over the torture and

Valour   283

execution of the Christians, demanding sacrifices to appease a god whose name she had never before invoked.

How had he been so blind?

She had never served the clan or its people. She had been feeding on their suffering, growing stronger as they grew weaker, pushing them toward extinction to satisfy her dark god's hunger.

'Enough,' he said, the word cutting through her fevered speech.

Moldir turned to him, her face contorted with rage. 'You dare interrupt me? You, who owe everything to my guidance? Where would you be without me, Shorukhan? Still licking Tarkhan's boots, watching him lead our people into servitude to the Christians and their weak god.'

'Where would I be?' Shoruk echoed, his voice forcibly calm. 'My people would be alive. We would be preparing for winter, not dying on this godsforsaken mountain chasing your vengeance.'

'Not my vengeance,' she snarled. 'Erlik's right. He demands blood for the insult done to him. He demands sacrifice.'

'Then let him have it.'

Shoruk's blade cleared its sheath with a soft sigh of steel against leather. Moldir's eyes widened in disbelief as the curved blade found its mark, sinking deep into her chest. Her mouth opened in a silent scream, dark blood welling between her thin lips, as her bony fingers scrabbled at his wrist.

'For Tarkhan,' Shoruk whispered, twisting the blade deeper. 'For the clan you would have sacrificed to your god.'

With her last strength, Moldir leaned close, her blood-slicked lips brushing his ear. 'Erlik waits for you in Tamag.'

Shoruk wrenched his blade free and Moldir staggered backward, clutching at the gaping wound in her chest, dark robes growing darker still as they soaked with blood. Her heel found the edge of the precipice, loose stone crumbling beneath her weight. Then she fell in silence, consumed by the void below.

No one moved as the wind howled. Shoruk wiped his blade clean on his sleeve and sheathed it with deliberate slowness, his eyes never leaving the warriors who stood before him. In their faces, he saw a storm of conflict – relief warring with fear, approval with uncertainty.

Artak was the first to break the silence. 'You killed the Kam Katun. Her spirit will haunt us. The gods will abandon us.'

'The gods abandoned us long ago,' Shoruk replied, his voice carrying across the windswept ledge. 'Or have you forgotten how we came to be here, driven from our lands like frightened deer, forced to survive on the edges of other men's territory?'

'So what now, Shorukhan?' Ozil asked. 'Do we turn back?'

Shoruk studied the gap thoughtfully. Fifteen feet of empty space separated them from the continuation of the path. A daunting leap, but perhaps not an impossible one for a man with nothing left to lose.

'No,' he decided. 'We do what we have always done. We hunt.'

Artak shook his head. 'Moldir is gone. We need not follow her mad quest any longer.'

'This is not about Moldir or her gods,' Shoruk said sharply. 'This is about us. About who we are. The Clan of the White Wolf. When we hunt, we do not abandon our prey until it is brought down. When we fight, we do not yield until victory is ours or we are dead. That is our way. That has always been our way.' He pointed across the gap. 'They lie along that path. So that is the way we go.'

Artak frowned, studying the gap. 'How? The leap is too far for any man.'

Shoruk did not wait. Instead, he took a deep breath, focusing on the narrow ledge on the far side of the gap. Fifteen feet of empty air. A distance that might be crossed in a single bound, if a man had strength enough, courage enough, and perhaps a touch of madness.

He sprinted forward, his feet pounding against the stone path. His final step hit the crumbling edge, and he launched himself into the air.

The wind tore at his clothes, his hair whipping about his face as he flew across the gap.

Then his chest slammed into the far edge, knocking the wind from his lungs in an explosive grunt. His fingers scrabbled desperately for purchase as his lower body dangled in empty space. For a terrifying instant, he felt himself sliding backward toward the abyss, loose rock crumbling beneath his grasping hands.

With a roar of defiance, Shoruk heaved himself upward, muscles straining as he fought. His boot found a tiny outcropping, giving him just enough leverage to haul his body up onto solid ground. He lay there for a moment, chest heaving, heart thundering against his ribs.

Rising to his feet, Shoruk turned to face his warriors across the gap. Their faces were masks of astonishment, jaws slack with disbelief.

'Well?' he called. 'Are you wolves or sheep? Will you join me in the hunt?'

A taunting question, but one he knew they would answer.

For the warriors of Shorukhan's clan were no sheep.

39

Estienne's muscles trembled with the effort of carrying Brother Galien, his body pushed beyond endurance by the treacherous climb. But he did not relent. He would sooner collapse and die than abandon the wounded man to the mercy of these accursed heights. And their accursed pursuers.

'Almost there,' he grunted, though in truth he had no idea how much farther they might need to go before reaching safety. If safety even existed in these desolate peaks.

Ahead of him, Merten stumbled, the young squire only just managing to catch himself before tumbling back down the slope. Fabrisse walked beside Talshyn, the holy woman and the pagan priestess leaning on each other for support. Behind, Jurgen kept the rear, bow in hand, faithful Clovis next to him as always.

The summit opened before them suddenly, and Estienne nearly dropped to his knees with relief. The trail levelled out into a small plateau nestled against the mountainside, but it was what lay at its centre that made his breath catch.

'Christ in heaven,' he gasped.

Stone walls rose up before them, weathered by centuries of

Valour 287

wind and rain but still standing defiant. An abandoned fort, built into the rock of the mountainside as though it had grown from the stone itself. The structure had been built with unmistakable precision, with its clean lines and perfect symmetry, though time had done its work to soften those edges.

'Roman?' Jurgen asked, coming to stand beside him. 'Looks like they weren't just passing through.'

'No,' Estienne replied as he studied the structure more carefully. 'Looks like they guarded this pass.'

A wooden gate hung askew from rusted hinges, the timber grey with age and rot. The walls stood approximately twelve feet high, not nearly the height of a proper fortress, but all the way up here it was doubtful they'd have to be. The eastern section had collapsed entirely, leaving a jagged breach that gaped like an open wound.

'Can we shelter here?' Merten asked, voice thin with exhaustion but tinged with desperate hope.

'We can at least take a look,' Estienne said, already moving toward the fort's entrance, Brother Galien's weight seeming suddenly less burdensome at the prospect of safety, no matter how meagre.

They approached the gate with measured steps, eyes scanning for any sign of movement or recent occupation. Clovis trotted by Jurgen's side, tail wagging slightly, which Estienne took as a good sign. If there was any immediate threat, the hound would have surely alerted them.

The rotted gate groaned as Jurgen pushed it open, and Estienne peered through. The sight that greeted them was one of desolation and decay, yet it stirred something akin to hope in Estienne's breast. They had found shelter... of a sort. And after everything they had endured, that seemed miracle enough.

Estienne ducked beneath the low arch of the entranceway,

Brother Galien's weight forcing him to stoop even lower. His eyes caught something carved into the stone above – a crude insignia weathered by centuries of mountain winds, but still the unmistakable shape of a winged horse.

'What does that mean?' Merten asked, coming to stand beside him.

'It means brave men stood here before us,' Estienne replied. 'Soldiers of Rome who held this pass against all comers.'

'Fat lot of good it did them in the end,' Jurgen grunted, casting his gaze around the desolate interior. 'This place is falling to pieces.'

He had to admit, Jurgen had a point. The courtyard was a testament to the slow decay of that once magnificent empire. Fallen stones from the crumbling walls lay scattered across the uneven ground. Rotted timbers jutted from the earth, as weeds pushed stubbornly through cracks in the paved ground, nature silently reclaiming all these men had built.

'We need to find him some shelter,' Fabrisse said, already moving toward what appeared to be the remains of a covered area against the far wall. 'Brother Galien cannot endure much more of this cold.'

Estienne nodded and followed her. With as much gentleness as his exhausted muscles could manage, he laid Brother Galien on the driest patch of ground beneath the partial roof.

Merten had wandered toward the eastern wall – or rather, where the eastern wall had once stood. Now there was only a jagged gap, opening directly onto a sheer drop down the mountainside. The squire's initial relief at finding the fort had turned to dismay as he surveyed their surroundings.

'This place is barely defensible,' he said, kicking at a loose stone. 'That entire section is exposed. And the walls that still stand are too low to offer proper protection.'

Valour   289

'The boy has the right of it,' Jurgen confirmed with a grim nod. 'When those pagans catch up to us, this place won't hold them for long.'

Estienne cast his gaze around the abandoned fort, taking in its crumbling walls. Merten and Jurgen were right – it offered little in the way of true protection. But it was all they had. He looked from face to face, seeing the fatigue, the determination despite what they had endured and what they still faced. They had followed him this far, trusting him to lead them to safety. Now they had reached the end of their desperate flight.

'This is where we make our stand,' he said. 'We've run far enough. Let the pagans come. I'd rather die facing them than running like a frightened hare.'

No one spoke for a long moment, the only sound the keening of the wind through the broken walls. Then Jurgen nodded, a grim smile tugging at the corner of his mouth.

'Well then, if we're to die here, we'd best make it costly for them.'

Every muscle in Estienne's body pleaded for rest, but his mind raced as he took in their surroundings. The fort's weaknesses were many – the collapsed eastern wall, the rotted gate, the low height of the remaining defences. But they had no choice but to fight here. This weathered remnant of Rome's glory would be their battlefield.

'We need to prepare,' he announced, pointing to the remains of a watchtower in the north-western corner. 'Jurgen – you'll take up position in that building. Find what masonry you can to conceal yourself.'

Jurgen nodded, hefting his bow before making his way toward the crumbling stairs. Clovis followed at his heel.

'Merten,' Estienne continued, turning to the young squire. 'Gather those fallen stones. We can't rebuild the eastern wall, but we can slow them down if they try to come at us from that direction.'

'It won't stop them for long,' Merten said, but he was already moving to comply.

'It doesn't need to stop them,' Estienne replied. 'It just needs to look solid enough, so it funnels them toward where I want them to be.'

He turned to the women next. 'You will help me shore up the gate.'

Fabrisse and Talshyn followed him as he strode across the courtyard to where several rotted timbers lay. He seized one, muscles straining as he dragged it toward the entrance, where the ancient gate hung askew. With the help of the women, he wedged one end against the ground, then braced the other against the gate, creating a crude support.

Another half dozen times they dragged timbers across the courtyard and jammed the splintered wood into place. It was not perfect by any stretch, but it might at least slow any attempt to force the gate.

Across the fort, Merten worked with equal determination, his young face streaked with sweat as stone by stone he created a shoulder-high barrier across the eastern breach. It was no proper wall – barely more than a pile of rubble – but it would force attackers to slow and climb, and that might be all Estienne needed to give them at least a fighting chance.

Dusk descended rapidly, and stars began to emerge in the darkening sky. When there was nothing more to be done, the rest of them huddled beneath the shelter where they had lain Galien. Estienne stood alone on the western wall, where a narrow walkway remained intact enough to bear his weight. Somewhere out there, in that vast darkness, their hunters approached.

The soft tread of footsteps made him start. He turned to see not only Fabrisse but Talshyn approaching. The pagan priestess stood slightly behind the holy woman, her dark eyes downcast, her slender form seeming to draw in upon itself as though trying to become less visible.

'Estienne,' Fabrisse said in greeting.

'You should be resting,' he replied, addressing Fabrisse but deliberately ignoring Talshyn.

The sight of the young priestess stirred something within him – despite what she had done for him on the path to the summit, he could not bring himself to look her in the eye.

'We need to speak with you,' Fabrisse replied, moving closer. 'Or rather, Talshyn does.'

'I have nothing to say to her,' he replied.

'Perhaps not. But she has much to say to you. Things that need to be heard, especially now.'

'Now?' Estienne almost laughed. 'When we are all most likely about to die? What could possibly matter now?'

'Understanding,' Fabrisse replied simply. 'Truth. Things that always matter, no matter how close we are to the end.'

Estienne fell silent, his mistrust of the priestess warring with his respect for Fabrisse. The holy woman had shown strength beyond measure throughout their desperate flight. If she believed this conversation necessary, perhaps he owed it to her to listen.

'Very well,' he conceded. 'Speak.'

Fabrisse turned to Talshyn, who nodded her reply, signalling that she should speak freely on her behalf.

'She says she expects no forgiveness for what her people did to your friends. She does not ask for absolution. But she wants you to understand that she mourns them as you do. She weeps for their souls. For all of them.'

'Tears change nothing,' Estienne replied coldly.

'She knows. But you must understand how she was deceived.

She was taught to honour Tengri, the sky god, and Eje, the earth mother. But as the years passed, her mistress began to speak more of Erlik, a different god. A god of death. It wasn't until it was too late that she realised what that truly meant. That she had to escape or face damnation.'

'So she freed us to save herself,' Estienne concluded bitterly.

Fabrisse relayed Estienne's words solemnly. Talshyn shook her head and spoke, her voice dropping to almost a whisper.

'She says that staying would have been safer,' Fabrisse replied. 'If she had simply played her part she would not now be fleeing for her life, branded a traitor to her people. She freed us because she could no longer watch innocent blood spilled in the name of a god who feasts on suffering.'

Estienne studied Talshyn's face in the moonlight. The priestess met his gaze, her dark eyes seeming haunted by memories. In that moment, he saw not the servant of evil, but a young woman caught in circumstances beyond her control, who had finally found the courage to break free. In that moment he felt the hard knot of rage within him begin to unravel, but he could still not bring himself to offer forgiveness.

'Tell her... Tell her I understand what it cost her to help us. And that whatever else happens, her choice was not in vain. She showed courage. Our God will see that, even if her own gods do not.'

Fabrisse translated, and Talshyn nodded. It seemed to be enough for the girl. Since Estienne had no more to offer, it would have to be.

They left him then, to the sound of the wind and the darkness. To his memories of friends lost. To look out in anticipation of the enemy that was stalking closer with every passing moment. To the final chance they would bring him... a chance at vengeance.

40

This old fortress held memories in its ancient flagstones, of battles long forgotten, of blood spilled in the name of gods both old and new. Talshyn could feel it beneath her fingers as she ground the herbs against the cold stone, working in the weak light of the waning fire. Her movements were precise, each gesture an echo of countless mornings spent preparing herbs under Moldir's watchful eye. The thought of her former mistress sent a shiver down her spine. How many times had she gathered these same plants, ground them in the same way, all in service to her wicked schemes? At least now this was for a nobler purpose. Perhaps there might be some redemption to be found in that.

The yarrow released its sharp scent as she crushed the dried flowers, but it was alraune root that was the more potent ingredient. That was where the magic lay in this concoction. The mixture took on a sickly greenish tint as she worked, the colour of corruption. Only fitting.

Across the fort's interior, she could feel the others watching her. Their murmured conversations in their strange tongue washed over her, meaningless yet still ominous. Talshyn could not blame them for their suspicion, despite all she had done for them. Even now her people were coming to descend upon this place and leave none alive. Only Fabrisse's gentle voice carried any warmth when she spoke, though Talshyn understood little of what was said between the holy woman and her companions.

Glancing up she could see Estienne's grey eyes burned into her, his face set in a grimace of perpetual suspicion. Even after she had helped them escape, even after she had snatched him from the edge of the precipice and pulled him to safety, he regarded her as a snake in their midst. Perhaps he was right to do so. After all, had she not been raised in darkness? Taught to worship powers that thirsted only for death?

A soft moan drew her attention to where Brother Galien lay, the monk's sleeping face twisted in discomfort. The sight pulled at something deep in her chest – a yearning to help rather than harm, to heal rather than destroy. But even had she wanted to, now was not the time. This salve she worked with stone and sweat was not to restore the poor priest. It had a much more dire purpose.

'What are you making?' Fabrisse's question came in Talshyn's own tongue.

The holy woman sat nearby, her golden hair catching the fire-light like a halo, though exhaustion had carved deep lines around her eyes.

'Medicine,' Talshyn replied, the lie tasting sour as she carefully wrapped the finished powder in a strip torn from her robe.

Better they did not know its true purpose. Better they remained ignorant of the old magic she wove, learned in darker times beneath different stars.

Fabrisse's eyes held a knowing look that made Talshyn's skin prickle. The holy woman spoke again, this time in her own language, presumably translating for the others. Estienne's

Valour 295

response was sharp and suspicious, though Talshyn could only guess at his words.

She found herself studying Fabrisse's face, seeing weariness but also hope. It seemed this Christian woman would not be bowed, no matter the hardship she faced. Her God must have been truly powerful to bestow such a gift, but Talshyn could still not fully accept she would be offered the redemption promised. Fabrisse had told her the Christian god offered forgiveness to all who sought it, but when she saw the barely quelled hate in Estienne's eyes she found that hard to believe. If even his most devoted followers could not find mercy in their hearts, what hope remained for one such as her? What salvation could there be for a servant of Erlik?

Jurgen's shout shattered the quiet, the old hunter's voice carrying sharp and urgent from his position in the crumbling watchtower. He spoke in a blur of foreign words, but his meaning was clear enough as he gestured urgently toward the mountain path.

They had found them. Just as she had known they would. Just as she had feared they must.

The fort erupted into motion around her. Estienne picked up his makeshift torch and strode toward the gate, his sword singing free of its scabbard. Merten helped Brother Galien to his feet, the monk's pained gasps cutting through the clamour. Fabrisse stood, smoothing the folds of her torn gown as though preparing to preach some sermon, and not face the killers who had stalked them night and day.

Talshyn tucked the powder carefully into the folds of her robe as she followed the others up onto the walkway above the main gate. The ancient stones felt treacherous beneath her feet, slick with moisture and crumbling at the edges. Her heart thundered against her ribs as silhouettes emerged along the mountain path that led up to the gate.

The warriors of the White Wolf Clan gazed up at the walls before them, their curved bows strung and ready, arrows nocked but not yet drawn. She recognised them all: Artak with his perpetual scowl, Chilbuk gripping tight to his bow, Ozil standing proud despite the obvious exhaustion in his stance. But one among their number was conspicuously absent. The one she had dreaded seeing the most.

'Where is the Kam Katun?' The words escaped her before she could stop them, her voice carrying above the droning wind.

Shoruk stepped forward, the lead wolf separating from its pack. Talshyn's breath caught at the sight of him. Blood had dried on his sword arm in a dark glove that spoke of recent violence. His fur-trimmed coat was torn and fresh scratches marked his narrow face. But it was his eyes that held her, harder than she remembered, yet somehow clearer. Gone was the fevered gleam that had haunted them since Moldir began buzzing in his ear, what seemed so long ago now.

'The witch will trouble us no longer.' He spat on the ground, as though to cleanse his mouth of some foul taste. 'She has gone to walk the endless night, as all servants of Erlik must.'

Talshyn's fingers dug into the ancient stone. She had been in thrall to that woman since she was a child. Had served her. Feared her. Loved her, in a way. Now she was dead it was hard to comprehend, as though she had lost and gained something all at once. Been robbed but also given the most precious gift.

Estienne stepped forward on the wall and spoke, before Fabrisse translated his words into the Cuman tongue: 'Turn back. There need be no more death. We have all lost too many. Go home, and tend to your people. Let this end here.'

Valour 297

She was answered by a harsh laugh that rippled through the gathered warriors like wind through winter-bare branches.

Shoruk's face twisted in a sneer. 'Oh, it will end here, Christian, for our hunt is almost over. Your god of mercy will not save you from the Clan of the White Wolf.'

Fabrisse relayed the words to Estienne. Talshyn could see his face darken as he registered the fate Shoruk had decided for them.

'Then let us end this,' Estienne snarled as Fabrisse spoke his words in Cuman. 'Single combat. You and I. Let us settle this with honour and spare the lives of your men and my people.'

Talshyn saw darkness descend over Shoruk's face. His eyes found her among the defenders, and hatred blazed in their depths with such intensity that she nearly stepped back from the force of it.

'Your warrior speaks of honour?' Shoruk growled, his gaze never leaving Talshyn. 'While that faithless bitch stands among you? She betrayed her people, her gods, everything she was sworn to protect. Swallowed down your Christian lies like a calf on its mother's tit. I will not fight you alone. The clan fights as one. There will be no mercy, and we will have all your heads before the dawn comes.'

'You have already lost too many men to this pursuit,' Fabrisse called out in Cuman. 'Think of those who yet live. Think of those who depend upon you.'

'They are gone now,' Shoruk bellowed. 'Lost to Tarkhan's weakness. To Moldir's lies. To this whore's betrayal.'

He raised his blood-soaked hand and pointed accusingly at her. This time though, she did not shrink back. This time his accusation burned within her like a fire.

'The clan betrayed itself,' Talshyn called out, her voice stronger than she felt as she stepped forward on the wall. 'When you murdered Tarkhan. When you chose darkness over light. When you let Moldir poison your heart with her whispers.'

'Darkness?' Shoruk's laugh was bitter as winter. 'What do you know of darkness, little priestess? You who would kneel to the Christian's nailed god? You who would abandon the ways of your ancestors for empty promises?' He gestured to the blood on his sword arm. 'The Kam Katun's blood stains my flesh, but soon it will be cleansed with your blood and the blood of these Christians.'

'Shoruk, please. You must listen—'

But Shoruk had already turned to his warriors, voice rising like a war horn. 'See how she hides behind stone walls, like a rabbit in its burrow. But there is nowhere left to run. No hole deep enough to escape what must come. Today we reclaim our honour. Today we feast on Christian flesh!'

He drew his curved sword with a flourish. In response, his warriors raised their own weapons, a howl rising from their throats. Then, with a gesture from their chief, they began to disperse, melting away into the shadows like spirits until only he remained, his contemptuous gaze fixed on the fort.

Shoruk smiled up at her. 'You should have kept running. These walls will not protect you. This I swear by Tengri of the endless sky.'

Then he too was gone, vanishing into the dark as completely as if the earth had swallowed him whole. The momentary silence hung heavy, broken only by the whistle of wind through ancient stone.

Estienne spoke in his tongue, ordering the others with quick, sharp words. But Talshyn needed no translation. The fight was about to begin. And for good or ill, she had picked her side.

41

Estienne stood atop the crumbling parapet, gripping his sword tight. Morning was coming, but the night chill still clung to the battlements, and he drew it deep into his lungs, savouring what might be his last taste of pre-dawn air.

Glancing back to the courtyard behind, he could see their meagre defences stood ready – piled stones across the breached eastern wall, the gate held shut with a few timbers. Now to see if they would hold.

In the remnants of the watchtower, Jurgen sat with bow in hand, the loyal Clovis at his side. The old hunter's face betrayed nothing as he tested the draw of his bowstring. He caught Estienne's eye and nodded once – a silent acknowledgement of what was to come.

Looking back out, Estienne saw a flicker of movement at the base of the wall. Then another. And another. Dark shapes moving with the practised stealth of men born to the hunt.

'Ready yourselves!' he called, voice steady despite the hammer of his heart.

The warning had barely left his lips when the first arrows came whistling through the air. Estienne ducked behind the battlement as one shaft splintered against stone inches from his head, sending fragments flying. When he braved another look, the pagans were already scaling the walls.

He stood back, hefting his blade, resisting the urge to say a brief prayer. No time to beg God's help now as the first warrior crested the wall twenty paces away, dark eyes gleaming with hatred as he swung a leg over the battlement.

Estienne charged. His sword nearly took the Cuman's head from his shoulders, steel parting flesh and bone with terrible efficiency. Hot blood spattered across stone as the body tumbled back into the dark.

A second warrior appeared where the first had fallen, curved blade already slashing toward Estienne's face. He caught the strike on his cross-guard, steel echoing all too loud as the Cuman snarled, spittle flecking his dark beard, as they strained against each other.

Estienne felt the warrior commit his weight forward and stepped aside, letting his opponent's momentum carry him stumbling onto the battlements. Before the man could recover his balance, Estienne's blade took him in the back, punching through leather and muscle to pierce his heart.

The thrill of victory quickened him. But more were coming.

As he wrenched his sword free from the corpse, Estienne cast a swift glance across the fort. At the eastern breach, Merten crouched behind his barrier, sword held ready. In the watchtower, Jurgen's bow was pulled taut, waiting for a target.

Could they even hope to survive this? Or was all that mattered the manner in which they died?

Estienne dismissed the thought as another warrior hurled himself over the wall, this one wielding a wicked-looking dagger.

He raised his sword to meet the attack, blade gleaming in the new dawn light.

* * *

Merten's hands trembled as he crouched behind the haphazard wall of stones and rubble, fingers slick with sweat around the grip of his sword. The eastern breach yawned before him, darkness slowly giving way to the grey light of dawn. From his position, he could see Estienne atop the battlements – a whirlwind of steel and fury as he cut down the first attackers.

I'm not ready for this.

The thought came unbidden, a fear that made shame burn in his belly. He pushed it away, remembering the countless drills in Rosenau's dusty courtyard, the hours spent memorising forms and counters under the stern gaze of his betters.

'Keep your shield up,' Amalric had always told him. 'A lowered guard is like an invitation.'

But he had no shield now. Only a sword and the pitiful pile of stones that would hold for mere moments once the assault began in earnest.

Movement at the breach focused his attention and almost stopped his heart. A figure crouched at the gap, bow already drawn. Merten ducked as the arrow whistled overhead, burying itself in the wooden support behind him with a solid thunk. Heart hammering against his ribs, he rose again, sword held ready.

The pagan was already climbing through the breach, nocking another arrow as he went. Merten swallowed the knot of fear in his throat and lunged forward. Steel met wood as his blade slammed into the Cuman's bow. The impact sent a tremor up Merten's arm, but the bow split beneath the force of his strike.

The warrior cast aside the useless fragments, lips peeling back from yellowed teeth in a snarl of rage, as he drew a curved blade from his belt.

They met in a clash of bodies, the Cuman's greater weight driving Merten back a step. The curved dagger slashed at his face, missing by a hairsbreadth as he twisted away. His own return stroke went wide, his stance hampered by the uneven footing.

The warrior's knee drove into Merten's stomach, forcing the air from his lungs in an explosive gasp. He staggered, but some instinct made him raise his sword in a desperate parry as the dagger came flashing down again. Their weapons scraped together, steel shrieking against steel. Merten felt his arms tremble with the strain of holding back the warrior's greater strength. Then a twist, a moment's opening, and searing pain as the dagger found a gap at his side, sliding into his guts with terrible ease.

Hot wetness spread across his tunic as the pagan warrior wrenched the blade free. Merten staggered back, one hand pressed to the wound, fingers coming away red and slick. The world seemed to blur, sounds growing distant, yet somehow his grip on his sword remained firm.

'Come on then,' he gasped, raising the blade once more despite the fire in his side. 'Come and finish it.'

The pagan's lips curled in contempt as he advanced, dagger held low and ready, confident in his prey's weakness. Behind him, two more figures appeared at the breach, climbing through with predatory grace.

Too many. Too many.

The first warrior lunged, dagger aiming for Merten's heart. Time seemed to slow as he raised his sword in a desperate, wild swing. The blade caught the pagan across the shoulder, opening a

Valour 303

gash that fountained blood, but the momentum left Merten wide open.

He saw the dagger coming, knew with certainty that he could not avoid it. Then the warrior jerked, eyes going wide with shock. An arrow's shaft protruded from his throat, dark blood pumping from the wound. Then he toppled sideways.

Merten cast a grateful glance toward the watchtower where Jurgen was already nocking another arrow. The remaining warriors hesitated at the sight of their fallen comrade, exchanging swift words in their harsh tongue.

The brief respite allowed Merten to retreat a few steps, each movement sending fresh agony through his wounded side. Blood soaked his tunic now, dripping between his fingers, yet still he raised his sword, gritting his teeth as the Cumans advanced once more.

In that moment, he was no longer Merten the squire. He was a knight of the Order, defender of the innocent, a sword of Christendom.

'For God and Saint Mary,' he whispered as he prepared to meet the enemy.

* * *

Jurgen sent another arrow humming at the pagans, giving Merten a chance to retreat to better ground. From his perch in the crumbling watchtower, Jurgen had a hunter's view of the battlefield, the wind carrying the harsh cries of men fighting for their lives.

None of it disturbed his calm. His breath remained steady, his gnarled hands sure as he nocked another arrow. Beside him, Clovis stood alert, hackles raised, a constant low growl rumbling in his chest like distant thunder.

'Easy, boy,' Jurgen murmured, his eyes never leaving the chaos below.

He tracked a warrior climbing the western wall near where Estienne fought. The distance was perhaps thirty paces – a challenging shot, but Jurgen had been putting arrows through the hearts of running deer at twice that range since he was a boy. He drew the bowstring to his cheek, the familiar pressure against his fingers comforting in its constancy. A breath in. A breath out. The arrow flew.

The warrior jerked as the shaft took him high in the back. His hands clawed at empty air for a heartbeat before he fell backwards, tumbling from the wall to land in the courtyard with a sickening crunch that Jurgen felt more than heard.

Without pause, he reached for another arrow, his fingers closing around another shaft when instinct made the hairs on his neck rise. He spun, dropping his bow even as he reached for the knife at his belt.

Too slow.

The pagan had already crossed the tower, his curved blade slashing down in a wicked arc. Jurgen twisted aside, feeling the sword bite into the wooden support where his head had been a heartbeat before. He drew his knife in a fluid motion, ducking beneath a second strike that would have opened his throat.

The tight confines worked in Jurgen's favour, restricting the longer reach of the warrior's sword. He slipped inside the man's guard, driving the blade toward his belly. The warrior sidestepped, his own weapon awkwardly positioned in the tight space, and they grappled, each seeking leverage.

Jurgen felt the sharp bite of steel between his ribs – not the sword, but the blade of a knife he hadn't seen, driven upward with brutal efficiency. Hot pain bloomed through his side, and he staggered back, one hand pressing against the wound.

'Shit,' he grunted.

The warrior pressed his advantage, advancing with a weapon in each hand.

Then Clovis launched himself across the space, a blur of fangs and fury. The hound's powerful jaws clamped around the warrior's sword arm, tearing through fabric and flesh with equal ease. The pagan screamed, dropping his weapon as he slashed at the dog with his dagger. The momentary distraction gave Jurgen the opening he needed, and he drove forward, burying his knife to the hilt in the warrior's neck.

He saw the man's eyes go wide with shock, mouth opening and closing like a fish on land. Blood bubbled between his lips as he slid to the floor, Clovis still growling and shaking the captured arm with savage determination.

'Enough, boy,' Jurgen gasped, slumping against the tower wall. 'He's done.'

The hound released his grip, returning to his master's side, dark muzzle stained with crimson. Jurgen sank to his knees, one hand pressed to the wound in his side. The blood flowed freely between his fingers, hot and vital. He'd seen enough in his time to know what this meant.

Below, the battle continued to rage. Nothing he could do to help now.

Jurgen reached out with his free hand, stroking Clovis's head. The hound whined softly, pressing against his master's side.

'Good boy,' Jurgen sighed. 'You've been a good boy.'

* * *

'*Pater noster, qui es in caelis, sanctificetur nomen tuum...*'

Fabrisse's voice remained steady as she knelt on the cold stone floor, the familiar Latin prayer a shield against the chaos that raged beyond. Beside her, Brother Galien clutched his simple wooden crucifix, his pallid face twisted with fear.

'*Adveniat regnum tuum. Fiat voluntas tua, sicut in caelo et in terra...*'

The sounds of violence filtered through the stones of the small chamber, once perhaps a storehouse, now serving as their final sanctuary. Through a narrow gap in the masonry, she watched Estienne atop the western wall, his sword rising and falling with brutal efficiency, each blow delivered with the cold precision of a butcher, yet even from this distance she could see the toll it was taking on him. His movements, while still deadly, had begun to slow as he jumped down from the wall, staggering back across the courtyard as he was surrounded.

Elsewhere, young Merten limped away from the eastern breach, one hand pressed to his bloodied side. Fabrisse's heart clenched at the sight of him – so young, so determined, and so clearly outmatched by the seasoned warriors he faced.

'*Panem nostrum quotidianum da nobis hodie...*'

Brother Galien's voice joined hers, wavering but resolute. His eyes were closed, features suddenly relaxed in the serenity of prayer despite the death that approached their door. Fabrisse found an unexpected strength in his faith, in the quiet courage of this man who had endured so much.

'*Et ne nos inducas in tentationem, sed libera nos a malo. Amen.*'

The prayer ended, but Fabrisse began it again immediately, the ancient words a bulwark against fear. Against despair. She had come to these mountains to bring God's light to those who dwelled in darkness, to offer salvation to souls in need of grace. How bitter the irony that her mission should end like this, her words unheard, her purpose unfulfilled.

A shadow fell across the entrance to their shelter, and the prayer died on her lips. A warrior stood silhouetted against the encroaching light, curved blade held low at his side. His dark eyes held no malice, merely the dispassionate regard of a hunter who had cornered his prey.

There was nowhere to flee, no weapon to raise in defence, and so Fabrisse moved without thought, placing herself between the warrior and Brother Galien. If death must come, let it find her first. She would not abandon her charge in these final moments.

The warrior raised his blade, muscles tensing for the strike. Fabrisse did not close her eyes. She would meet death with the same courage she had tried to bring to life.

A flicker of movement behind the warrior caught her attention – a small figure moving with uncanny silence. Talshyn's face was set in grim determination, her dark eyes focused on the task at hand as she raised her cupped palms. Before the warrior could turn, she blew a cloud of greenish powder directly into his face.

The effect was immediate and horrifying.

The man dropped his weapon with a strangled cry, hands flying to his eyes as though trying to claw away visions only he could see. His screams were unlike anything Fabrisse had ever heard – not the cries of agony but the howl of a soul confronted with terrors beyond comprehension. He staggered backward, crashing into the wall before sliding to his knees, hands still pressed to his face as he babbled in his native tongue.

Fabrisse crossed herself, murmuring a swift prayer against evil, as the warrior crawled blindly past them and out of the entrance. His screams faded as he disappeared into the chaos of the battle.

'What did you do to him?' she asked Talshyn, unable to keep the tremor from her voice.

'What was necessary.'

Before Fabrisse could respond, another clash of steel rang out from the courtyard, followed by a chorus of shouts. The battle was reaching its end, and with it, their fate would be decided.

'Stay here,' Talshyn commanded, already moving toward the entrance. 'I may yet have a part to play in what comes.'

As she slipped away, Fabrisse found herself once again at prayer, though whether for victory, for mercy, or for understanding of God's ways, she could not have said.

* * *

Shoruk's warriors had flooded into the ancient fort like a tide. Still the knight stood at the centre of the courtyard, blade bloodied, chest heaving with exertion. Warriors lay dead at his feet – good men who had followed Shoruk into these cursed mountains – and from the look on the knight's face, he was not done yet.

This had to end.

Shoruk raised his hand, signalling his remaining men to stand back. This kill would be his alone, a matter of honour... and perhaps of redemption. Since Moldir's death, each step of this hunt had felt more hollow than the last, as though he were following a trail that would only lead to his own ensnarement. But this, at least, would be clean. A warrior's death for the enemy who had caused them such grief. Or one for himself.

He approached with measured steps and the knight watched him come, blue-grey eyes cold as stormy skies above his scarred cheek. Blood streaked his face, but his stance betrayed no weakness.

'Your gods have abandoned you, Christian,' Shoruk said, knowing the words would not be understood but needing to speak them, nonetheless. 'As mine have abandoned me. Now there is only the truth of steel.'

No response from the knight save a slight narrowing of those cold eyes. But what had he expected? Nothing left now but battle.

Shoruk feinted left, testing his opponent's reflexes, then attacked with a lightning-fast slash from the right – a move that had opened the throats of more than one enemy in the past.

The knight parried with a speed and strength that almost numbed Shoruk's arm. Before he could recover, the Christian countered with a thrust that forced Shoruk to dance backward, the point of the sword missing his belly by a finger's breadth.

He is so much faster than he looks.

The realisation sent a cold thrill down Shoruk's spine – not fear, not yet, but a seed of doubt. He attacked again, a flurry of strikes meant to overwhelm through sheer aggression. The knight met each blow, his blade a blur of motion as he turned aside cut after cut.

Shoruk felt a flicker of genuine concern now. This was not going as expected. The Christian should have been exhausted, weakened by days of pursuit and fighting his clan brothers. Instead, he fought with cold precision. Seasoned and in control, yet brutal and wild all at once.

They exchanged another series of blows, steel ringing against steel in the ancient courtyard. Shoruk's confidence wavered further as the knight matched him move for move, anticipating strikes before they were fully formed. Then a moment's hesitation cost him, the knight's blade slipping past his guard, opening a deep cut across his sword arm. Pain lanced through him, hot and immediate, and he felt the strength drain from his fingers. His weapon was suddenly unwieldy, too heavy to lift.

But pride would not let him retreat. There was no yield left in him. He was the Shorukhan of the White Wolf. He would win or he would die.

Switching his weapon to his left hand, he raised it once more, though the movement felt awkward. 'Come, Christian. Finish what you began.'

Shoruk attempted a desperate swing that went wide, leaving him exposed. The Christian's blade thrust forward, punching through leather and flesh to bury itself in Shoruk's chest.

The first sensation was not pain but a spreading chill that radiated outward from the wound. Shoruk felt his legs give way, knees striking stone as his sword clattered to the ground. The knight stepped back, pulling his blade free with a motion that almost drew the last breath from his lungs.

He tried to speak – to curse his killer or perhaps offer some final defiance – but blood filled his throat, choking the words before they could form. His vision began to darken at the edges, the world receding.

Grandfather, I am coming...

* * *

Talshyn watched from the shadows of a crumbling archway as Shoruk's body crumpled to the ground, blood spreading in a dark pool beneath him. Estienne stepped back, blade still dripping, eyes betraying nothing as he watched his enemy's life ebb away.

Around the courtyard, the remaining warriors faltered, their zeal broken by the sight of their leader fallen. Some already looked to the fort's entrance, weighing the merits of retreat against the shame of abandoning their chief's body. Others gripped their weapons more tightly, rage overcoming reason as they prepared to throw themselves at the knight in vengeance.

Talshyn saw her chance, and stepped forward into the court-yard, raising her arms, letting her dark robes billow in the morning breeze. All eyes turned to her.

'Hear me, warriors of the White Wolf!' she called out. 'The

Valour 311

gods have laid out their judgement. Shoruk has fallen, as Moldir has fallen. Their thirst for blood has led only to their deaths.'

She moved among the warriors with feigned authority, drawing on the memory of her former mistress. She had watched Moldir perform a hundred times, and now it seemed so easy to mimic her. In turn she saw these men she had grown up with suddenly view her with different eyes.

'The signs are clear for those who wish to see,' she continued, turning slowly to meet the gaze of each warrior in turn. 'Tengri himself has shown his displeasure. Those who led us here – first Tarkhan, then Moldir, and finally Shoruk – all have been struck down.'

The warriors lowered their weapons, uncertainty written across their tired faces. They had followed Shoruk out of loyalty and tradition, but with him gone, the purpose of their deadly pursuit seemed suddenly empty.

'I am Kam Katun now,' Talshyn proclaimed, standing straighter, infusing her voice with the same confidence Moldir had wielded so effectively. 'Tengri has granted me visions of our future. There is no victory here, only more death. The spirits of our ancestors speak through me, and they demand we end this bloodshed.'

She watched her words take effect, saw the shift in the warriors' eyes from battle-fury to uncertainty, then to acceptance. It was a transformation she had witnessed many times when Moldir worked her influence. The warriors looked to one another, then back to her, waiting for leadership. They were men born to follow, trained from birth to respect the authority of chief and priestess. With Shoruk dead and Moldir gone before him, Talshyn stood as the clan's sole remaining voice.

'Bring Shoruk's body,' she commanded, gesturing to the fallen chief. 'We will bear him back to the grasslands with honour, where his spirit may ride the endless skies with his ancestors. His name will be remembered in the songs of our people.'

Two warriors moved immediately to obey, lifting Shoruk's bloody corpse with surprising gentleness. His face, in death, had lost the hardness that had defined him in life. He looked almost peaceful now.

'The rest of you, gather our dead,' Talshyn continued. 'We return to the plains. Our hunt ends here.'

As the warriors began to withdraw, gathering their fallen with solemn efficiency, Talshyn caught sight of Fabrisse watching from the entrance to the shelter. The Christian woman offered the slightest shake of her head, as though she knew what Talshyn was abandoning by going back to her people, to her gods. For a moment, Talshyn remembered the quiet conversations they had shared during their flight through the mountains. Fabrisse's words about forgiveness, about a god who offered redemption to even the darkest souls. About a different path that Talshyn might have walked.

A path she would walk no longer.

'May your god protect you,' she said softly, words meant for Fabrisse alone. 'As mine will protect me.'

Then Talshyn turned and led the remaining warriors out of the ancient fort.

She did not look back again.

* * *

Estienne stood motionless in the centre of the courtyard, sword hanging heavy in his hand. The battle fury that had sustained him ebbed away, leaving only exhaustion in its wake. He watched in numb silence as Talshyn led the remaining warriors from the fort, Shoruk's body borne between them with surprising dignity.

Valour 313

Their retreat seemed like a vision glimpsed through a fever haze. He had been prepared to fight to the last, to sell his life as dearly as possible, but the sudden end to it all left him feeling adrift.

A soft whining drew Estienne's attention toward the watch-tower. On seeing no sign of Jurgen up in his perch, Estienne rushed to find the trapper. At the top of the stone stairs, Clovis sat nudging Jurgen's still form with his muzzle. The hound looked up as Estienne approached, blood matting the dog's dark coat – some his own, some belonging to the enemy he had savaged in defence of his master.

'Jurgen...' The trapper's name came out as little more than a whisper as Estienne knelt beside him.

The old hunter lay still, his face composed. A stain darkened the front of his leather jerkin where a blade had found its mark. Even in death, he held his hunting knife in a white-knuckled grip, his final enemy lay sprawled nearby, arm torn to shreds by Clovis's fangs.

Estienne placed a hand on the hunter's cold shoulder, feeling the sudden, sharp sting of grief. He had known Jurgen only briefly, yet the man's quiet competence and unsentimental courage had earned his respect. Without him, they would never have made it this far.

Clovis whined again, laying his head on his master's chest as if still hoping for the familiar touch of Jurgen's hand.

'I'm sorry, boy,' Estienne murmured, reaching out tentatively to stroke the hound's blood-matted fur.

He rose to his feet, muscles protesting every movement as he made his way back down to the courtyard. Merten leaned against the ancient wall, offering a grim nod. He had given a good account of himself, and Estienne would be sure to mention it when they reached Rosenau.

Through a gap in the fort's crumbling wall, he could see the mountain path winding westward toward the Burzenland. Their road home lay open before them at last, the path to safety no longer barred by those who had hunted them so relentlessly. They had survived, if only barely.

'Estienne?' Fabrisse's voice came softly from behind him. She stood with Brother Galien leaning heavily on her arm, his face grey with exhaustion but his eyes clear. 'What now?'

'Now we bury our dead,' he said simply. 'And then we go home.'

42

Estienne's back ached as he laid the final stone atop the cairn they'd built for Jurgen's body. They had done their best with what little they had – wrapping him in his own weathered cloak, face covered with a square of linen torn from Fabrisse's underskirt. It would have to be enough. Estienne doubted the old man would have cared anyway.

They'd managed to dig a shallow depression in the cold earth just outside the fort's walls, but the rocky soil had defeated their improvised tools. Instead of a grave, they'd laid the old hunter to rest beneath stones gathered from the fortress ruins – a monument that would hopefully weather the passing seasons long after they were gone.

Clovis sat at the head of the mound, his nose resting on his paws, eyes fixed on the pile of stones. Occasionally, the hound released a long, mournful whine, the sound cutting Estienne to the quick.

'*Requiem aeternam dona ei, Domine,*' Fabrisse finished, making the sign of the cross over Jurgen's resting place. '*Et lux perpetua luceat ei. Requiescat in pace.* Amen.'

'Amen,' murmured Brother Galien, his voice barely audible even in the stillness.

The friar leaned heavily on a makeshift staff, his face grey with exhaustion. Some yards away, Merten was standing within the shadow of the fort's crumbling walls. The young squire's face was pale, his gaze fixed on Jurgen's cairn. He seemed lost in his own thoughts, removed from their small ceremony, and Estienne felt suddenly concerned by the young man's apparent detachment.

Clovis whined again, his devotion absolute, undiminished by death. The others had begun to drift back toward the fort, but Estienne lingered, unwilling to leave Jurgen alone just yet, though he knew such sentiments were foolish.

'We need to move, boy,' he said finally, kneeling down beside the hound. 'There's still a long road ahead.'

The dog's ears twitched, but still he remained beside his master's grave, eyes meeting Estienne's with a sorrow that seemed almost human. Something tugged at Estienne's heart, and he reached out, laying a gentle hand on the hound's head. Up close, he could see the wounds that marked Clovis's dark coat, some still crusted with dried blood. Wounds earned in defence of them all.

'I know,' he said softly. 'I know what it is to lose those you care for. But he wouldn't want you to die here, boy. You need to come with us.'

Estienne stood, and for a long moment, Clovis remained motionless. Then, with apparent reluctance, he rose and cast one last look at the cairn before padding after Estienne. Together they walked back toward the fort, where Fabrisse waited with Brother Galien in the gateway. The holy woman's eyes shone with unshed tears as she watched their approach, but her voice did not crack when she spoke.

'God sees his faithful servant home,' she said. 'May his soul find peace.'

Estienne had no reply. What peace had Jurgen found in his final moments, a blade buried in his guts? What comfort had faith offered as he was killed in this forgotten outpost? But the time for such arguments had passed. The dead were beyond care now. It was the living who concerned him, and their journey home.

'We should—' he began, but the words died in his throat as he saw Merten stagger suddenly, one hand grasping at the crumbling wall for support.

The young squire's legs gave way beneath him, and he sank to his knees, then pitched forward onto the rocky ground.

'Merten!' Estienne bolted forward, reaching the squire's side in a few desperate strides and dropping to his knees.

His hands trembled slightly as he turned the young man over, cradling him against the cold ground. Merten's tunic and trews were soaked through with blood, the fabric sticking to a jagged wound in his side. Damn the boy for a fool. How long had he hidden this?

'Merten,' Estienne murmured, tapping the squire's pale cheek. 'Merten, can you hear me?'

The boy's eyes fluttered open, and recognition dawned in them as he focused on Estienne's face. 'I'm sorry.'

'Don't speak,' Estienne commanded, tearing open the blood-soaked tunic to better assess the wound. 'Save your strength.'

But it was too late. The wound was beyond healing – a deep slash that had laid open flesh and muscle down to the bone. Blood still seeped from it, though sluggishly now, as if the young squire had little left to give. Fabrisse knelt beside them, and touched a hand to Merten's forehead. A simple shake of her head spoke more than any words.

'Why did you not speak of this?' Estienne demanded, a surge of anger cutting through his grief. 'Why keep silent when we could have helped?'

A ghost of a smile touched Merten's lips. 'What... help could you have given? We are... too far from... Rosenau. There was no help to give. Better to die on my feet... than lie helpless while... you tended me.'

'Fool boy,' Estienne growled, but there was no real heat in it.

'I can... fetch water,' Galien offered, hovering uncertainly nearby. 'Perhaps if we clean the wound—'

Fabrisse silenced him with a look. Then she met Estienne's gaze, understanding passing between them. They could do nothing now but ease the boy's journey to the next world.

Merten's pale lips worked silently for a moment before he managed to speak. 'It was my honour to journey by your side. To... fight. My one regret is... I will die a squire. Never to know the honour of knighthood. Too late...'

Estienne's hand went to the hilt of his sword. It was not too late.

'I was knighted by William Marshal himself,' he said. 'The greatest knight who ever lived. By his authority, passed to me, I have the right to bestow that honour upon another.'

Estienne rose, drawing his sword with ceremonial slowness. He held it before him, point downward, as he had seen the Marshal do those years ago at the docks of Sandwich.

'In the name of God, Saint Michael, and Saint George,' he intoned. 'I, Ser Estienne Wace, do make thee, Merten of the Burzenland, a knight in turn.' He placed the flat of his blade against Merten's right shoulder, then his left. 'Thou art now and forever a Knight of the Order of Saint Mary. Take thy place among our brotherhood.'

As the blade lifted from Merten's shoulder, a smile of joy

spread across his face, so untainted by pain or fear, that it transformed his features. Then his eyes drifted closed, the smile still fixed upon his lips. One final breath escaped him, soft as a sigh, and he slumped into Fabrisse's arms.

'*Requiescat in pace*,' she murmured.

'He was a good lad,' Galien said quietly as he leaned on his staff. 'Brave beyond his years.'

Estienne grunted in agreement, not trusting himself to speak. Slowly he sheathed his sword, hands curling into fists at his sides.

'You did him a great honour,' Galien continued. 'Knighting him at the end. It must have meant everything to him.'

'Cold comfort to the dead,' Estienne replied.

'Perhaps. But comfort, nonetheless. We all seek meaning in our lives. Merten found his in striving toward knighthood. You gave him that gift. Do not discount its value.'

Estienne turned, regarding the frail monk with narrowed eyes. 'And what meaning would you assign to this? What divine purpose required the sacrifice of a boy not yet sixteen summers?'

Galien shrank in the face of Estienne's anger. 'I cannot claim to know God's mind, but I know that Merten's sacrifice was not in vain. He died that others might live.'

'God's mind? You think He is watching? You think He had anything to do with this? Those pagans were right; our God is not here. What manner of deity allows such suffering? What divine plan requires the deaths of good men while vermin like Carsten Schado live on?'

The thought of Carsten sent fresh rage coursing through him. That craven dog who had abandoned them to die. He might be waiting at Rosenau even now, spinning tales of his own bravery, explaining how he alone had survived the terror of the pagans.

But not for long. Estienne would see to that. Justice would be served, even if he had to deliver it with his own hands.

Galien took a hobbling step away, his sermon about God's intent clearly at an end. Estienne stooped to gather Merten's body, to lay one more of his brothers in the earth.

'Let me help,' Fabrisse offered, as he took Merten in his arms. 'You needn't bear this burden alone.'

'No,' he replied, lifting up the boy's corpse. 'This is my duty.'

When he turned from her there was but one thought now festering in his mind – whatever happened he would settle accounts with Carsten Schado. The thought burned in him like a fever, driving back the chill of the mountain. There would be a reckoning. By his sword, there would be justice.

But first, there was this final duty to perform.

This last respect to be paid to a fallen knight.

43

Every step was agony.

Estienne guided Brother Galien down the treacherous goat track that wound its serpentine path down the mountainside. The monk's arm was draped across Estienne's shoulders, dead weight that threatened to pull them both to the ground with each uncertain step.

'Just one more mile,' Estienne lied.

They both knew it was far more than a mile. The peaks still loomed above them, wreathed in mist, while Rosenau lay what felt like a thousand leagues of broken stone and narrow ledges away. A journey that would test even a hale man, let alone one half-dead and another battered by days of fighting and flight.

He suddenly slipped, his legs betraying him as he tightened his grip on the monk's arm, steadying them both.

'Watch your step,' came Fabrisse's voice from behind.

The holy woman followed close with quiet determination, occasionally reaching out to steady Galien when the path grew especially narrow. Her golden hair hung lank about a face wracked with exhaustion, but her eyes remained clear and hopeful.

Ahead of them, Clovis picked his way down a trail that had narrowed to little more than a goat's notion of a path. It was a painfully slow descent. Time blurred, marked only by the gradual shift of shadows as the sun crawled across the pale autumn sky.

In the distance, Estienne thought he could make out the faint silhouette of woodland – the first sign that they were leaving the desolate heights behind. The sight gave him a fresh surge of determination. They were still alive, still moving, still clinging to the brittle edge of survival when by all rights they should be cold corpses left to feed the crows.

Rotger, Eggert, Amalric, Merten, Jurgen – their ghosts seemed to hover at the edges of his vision, watching his struggle with hollow eyes. Had their sacrifice been worth it? Would dragging the broken remnants of this doomed mission back to Rosenau give their deaths meaning?

Estienne had no answers. All he knew was the next step, the next breath, the next heartbeat. Survival its own notion of vengeance.

It wasn't until the pale sun reached its zenith that the narrow track finally began to level somewhat, giving way to a more gradual descent that wound between jagged outcroppings. Estienne felt a flicker of relief. Perhaps the worst of the mountain was behind them. The thought had barely formed when Brother Galien's legs buckled beneath him.

'Easy, man.' Estienne tightened his grip, but the monk was beyond hearing, his slight weight suddenly a dead weight.

They crashed to their knees together on the stony ground, Galien slumping forward. Estienne caught him before his face struck the rocks, cradling the monk's head as Fabrisse hurried to their side. Her gentle hands examined Galien's pallid face, lifting his eyelids, pressing fingers to his throat to feel the flutter of blood in his veins.

'I cannot...' Galien's cracked lips barely moved, his voice a hollow sound that the wind nearly stole away. 'Cannot go on.'

Estienne exchanged a glance with Fabrisse. The holy woman's face was grave, but he saw no surrender there, only weary determination.

'Brother Galien,' Estienne said, and when there was no response, he gripped Galien's shoulders, giving them a gentle shake. 'Look at me.'

The friar's eyes fluttered open, unfocused at first, then gradually steadying on Estienne's face.

'Listen well, for I'll say this but once. Good men have died to get us here, to this place. Their sacrifice has purchased your life, Galien. To surrender now would render their deaths meaningless.'

Galien's eyes filled with tears, but something flickered there – a spark rekindling where only despair had been. Fabrisse leaned closer, her voice gentle where Estienne's had been harsh, but no less firm for it.

'God has preserved us through these trials for a purpose, brother. We are His instruments still. Our suffering is not without meaning, nor is our survival without purpose. The road seems endless now, but dawn always follows the longest night. Trust in His grace, and find strength for just a few more steps.'

Galien drew a shuddering breath, then another. 'Forgive my weakness. You speak truth, both of you. I will try.'

Together they helped Galien to his feet. The monk swayed but remained upright, leaning heavily on Estienne once more. They resumed their journey, each step still an ordeal but taken with renewed purpose. Clovis had waited patiently during their pause, and now the hound led the way once more, picking out their route as though guided by some instinct to reach home.

When they finally rounded the shoulder of the mountain, the landscape opened before them. Rolling foothills gave way to patches of pine forest, dark against the brown and gold of autumn fields. A silver thread of river wound through the valley far below, and beyond it, just visible on the horizon where earth met sky, stood a familiar silhouette.

Rosenau.

Its grey walls rose from the distant landscape, a stone sentinel guarding the mountain pass. From this distance, the fortress looked like a miniature carved from soapstone, yet the sight of it struck Estienne like a fist.

'Look,' he said, gesturing with his free hand.

Fabrisse squinted against the pale sunlight, her breath catching as she spotted the distant fortress. Even Galien lifted his head, a sound escaping him that might have been a laugh or a sob.

On they pushed with renewed vigour. The terrain gradually grew more forgiving as they descended further, the narrow mountain track widening into something that resembled an actual path. Though each step remained an effort, at least now they were within reach of journey's end.

Galien was barely conscious now, stumbling more often as his strength ebbed. Fabrisse trudged behind them, her own exhaustion evident in the drag of her feet and the stoop of her shoulders, though she offered no complaint.

'There's a stream ahead,' Estienne said, spotting a silver thread winding through the rocks below. 'We'll rest there and—'

He stopped, suddenly alert as he caught sight of movement on the road ahead. Riders approaching from the direction of Rosenau, moving at speed.

Valour 325

'Stay here,' he commanded, easing Galien to the ground as gently as he could. He gripped the sword at his side, steel rasping softly as he drew it a few inches from the scabbard.

Friend or foe? His eyes narrowed against the glare as he tried to make out details. Was this yet more pagan hunters come to plague them just as the end was in sight? Or were these allies, come to their aid?

Clovis growled low in his throat, hackles rising as he sensed the growing tension. Estienne rested a calming hand on the hound's head, fingers threading through the coarse fur.

'Easy, boy,' he murmured. 'Surely we deserve a bit of luck...'

The riders drew closer, four in number, and Estienne felt the knot in his gut ease as he recognised the distinctive black crosses on white surcoats that marked knights of the Order of Saint Mary. The lead rider pulled up sharply as he caught sight of them, his hand raised to signal the others. For a moment they seemed frozen in shock, as though confronted by ghosts. Then the leader removed his helm, revealing the grizzled face of Otto von Augsburg, a veteran of the Order who Estienne had known since arriving in the Burzenland.

'By all the saints,' Otto breathed, crossing himself. 'Estienne Wace?'

The knight dismounted with surprising agility for a man nearing his fiftieth year. His companions followed suit, their expressions shifting from wariness to astonishment as they took in the battered, bloodied figures before them.

'Brother Otto,' Estienne replied. 'Are you a sight for sore eyes.'

Otto approached cautiously, as though he couldn't quite believe what he was seeing. 'We thought you dead, man. All of you.'

'We are the only survivors,' Estienne confirmed, the words bitter as gall. 'The others...'

He trailed off, unable to speak of it. Otto seemed to understand. He barked orders to his companions, who immediately began rummaging through their saddlebags, producing waterskins.

Estienne accepted with hands that shook slightly from exhaustion. The water was warm and tasted of leather, but it flowed sweet as wine down his parched throat. He forced himself to drink slowly, knowing too much too quickly would only make him sick. The other knights tended to Fabrisse and Galien, who now sat on the ground, having finally succumbed to fatigue.

'How did you survive the ambush?' Otto asked when Estienne had drunk his fill. 'Carsten said—'

'Carsten?' Estienne snapped. 'Carsten Schado is at Rosenau?'

Otto's brow creased at the harshness of the words. 'Aye, he returned two days past. Said you were all lost. Killed by the pagans. That he alone escaped to bring word.'

'Did he, now? I imagine he spun quite the tale of his heroics.'

'He said he tried to save as many as he could, but was overwhelmed. Had to flee to bring word back to Rosenau.' Otto hesitated, studying Estienne's face. 'That's not how it was, is it?'

'No,' Estienne said softly. 'That is not how it was at all.'

One of the other knights, a broad-shouldered man with a shock of red hair, looked up from where he knelt beside Brother Galien. 'This one's half-dead. He needs a physician, and quickly.'

Otto nodded. 'We'll take them all back to Rosenau immediately. Petrus, your horse for the monk. Reinhard, yours for the holy woman.'

The knights obeyed without question, helping Brother Galien to his feet. The monk was barely conscious, his head lolling as they lifted him into the saddle. He seemed incapable of holding the reins, so Petrus mounted behind him, securing him with a strong arm around his waist. Fabrisse accepted assistance with

Valour 327

dignity, though Estienne noticed how her hands trembled as she gripped the saddle, her strength failing after maintaining such composure throughout their ordeal.

Otto turned to Estienne, offering the reins of his own destrier. 'Take my mount. You look ready to drop.'

Estienne shook his head. 'I'll walk.'

'Don't be a fool, man. You can barely stand.'

'I will walk,' Estienne replied, his voice firm. 'And see this journey ended on my own terms.'

'As you wish.' Otto gestured to the fourth knight. 'Conrad, ride ahead and alert the fort to prepare for wounded. We'll follow at whatever pace Wace can manage.'

Conrad nodded, wheeling his horse around and spurring it down the path at a gallop. Petrus followed with Brother Galien secured before him, while Reinhard escorted Fabrisse.

Otto mounted, and they continued toward Rosenau with Estienne maintaining a steady, determined pace despite his battered body. Clovis padded faithfully by his side as each step brought him closer to the reckoning that had sustained him through the long nightmare of their flight.

Dusk painted the sky a deep purple by the time Estienne approached the gates of Rosenau. The massive wooden doors stood open to receive him, and torches had been lit along the walls to guide his way. Clovis whined softly at his side as they neared the threshold.

'Almost there, boy,' he murmured.

The portcullis was raised, and Estienne passed beneath its iron teeth. Within, the courtyard was filled with knights and serving brothers who had gathered to witness the return of the man they had thought dead. Word of his approach had clearly spread quickly. Faces turned toward him as he entered, conversations dying mid-sentence as he limped through the gate. Some crossed themselves, as though confronted with a spirit of the dead. Others simply stared, unable to reconcile the bloodied vagabond before them with the proud knight who had ridden out so many days ago.

His eyes scanned the faces in the gathering crowd, searching for one in particular, when a commotion near the keep drew his attention. A figure pushed through the press of bodies, his monk's robes flapping as he approached.

'Estienne!' Brother Rabel's voice was thick with emotion. 'Praise God! Praise His infinite mercy!'

The friar's face was alight with joy and disbelief, and he looked much improved from when he had staggered through these same gates riddled with arrow shafts.

'God has performed a miracle this day!' the friar continued. 'You have returned the Lady of Avallon and my brother Galien to us. Praise be to—'

'Where is Carsten?' Estienne demanded.

An immediate hush fell over the gathered crowd.

'He is here,' the monk confirmed. 'He arrived two days past, bringing word of... of tragedy. But I know not where he—'

'What did he say happened?' Estienne pressed.

Rabel frowned. 'He said you were all dead. Killed by pagan warriors. He spoke of... of his anguish at having to abandon his brothers. The Marschall was greatly grieved by the news.'

'And where is the Marschall now?' Estienne's voice had grown dangerously soft.

'He rode out yesterday to meet with the Hochmeister at Kronstadt. Some urgent matter regarding the king of Hungary.'

Estienne felt a flicker of disappointment. He had hoped to bring his case directly to Marschall Dieter, to see justice carried out by proper authority. But perhaps this was better.

Valour 329

'Carsten!' he bellowed, his voice echoing off the stone walls of the courtyard. 'Come out and face me, you craven bastard!'

The courtyard fell utterly silent, but there was no response, no sound of approaching footsteps. Estienne turned to a nearby squire.

'Find Carsten Schado. Tell him Estienne Wace has returned from the dead and would speak with him. Tell him I await him outside.'

The boy nodded, eyes wide, before darting off toward the keep. Estienne watched him go, then with the last of his strength, lowered himself onto a barrel in the centre of the courtyard. He drew his sword, resting the blade between his knees, and waited.

44

The torches burned low along the walls, their dancing light barely reaching the centre of the courtyard where Estienne waited upon that empty barrel. The chill seeped through his tattered clothes, into his bones already aching from days of hard travel and harder fighting, but still he was warmed by rage. He wore it like armour now, since he had none of his own. No mail to protect him, no shield, only a sword. His fingers brushed the hilt, feeling the worn leather beneath his calloused touch. He had taken this sword from Carsten after his own was lost. Only right that he deliver it back to the bastard.

Amalric had carried such a sword. So had Rotger. Neither would wield steel again. They had been killed by pagans in a godless land, but Estienne had played his part to avenge them. Now that part was almost at an end.

The crowd was still gathered in the courtyard, knights and serving brothers alike forming a loose circle around him, their breath pluming in the night air. All attention was on Estienne, but every one of them turned when a figure emerged from the keep.

Carsten Schado stepped into the torchlight arrayed for battle, hauberk gleaming beneath his surcoat, the black cross stark against white. A sword hung at his hip, his helm tucked beneath one arm, his shield gripped in his other hand. His face was a mask of righteous indignation as he surveyed the gathering. When his gaze finally settled on Estienne, those pale eyes narrowed.

Estienne rose from the barrel, ignoring the protest of his battered body. One more fight. That was all he needed. One more battle to settle accounts.

'Carsten,' he called. 'I have returned from the dead to name you traitor and murderer. You left us to die. You stabbed a man in the back. And then you rode back to Rosenau with tales of our deaths, claiming false glory while better men than you died in the mountains.'

A murmur rippled across the courtyard, knights exchanging glances, serving brothers shifting uneasily. Carsten's face flushed in the flickering light, but he straightened his posture, mustering what dignity he could.

'These are ravings. The delusions of a man driven mad by exposure. I did everything in my power to save our brothers. It was only when all hope was lost that I fled to bring word back to Rosenau.'

The courtyard had gone deathly quiet now, every eye fixed on the two men.

'If you speak truth, if you have nothing to hide, then why come to face me dressed for war?'

Carsten shifted his weight, the mail beneath his surcoat clinking softly, fingers tightening around his helm. 'I am a Knight of the Order, and a Komtur besides. I will not be questioned by some half-brother who has not even spoken his vows.'

'And yet, here we are.'

Movement at the edge of the crowd caught Estienne's eye as Fabrisse pushed her way through the gathering of men. Her face was marred by concern as their eyes met across the courtyard. Carsten saw her too, and Estienne recognised the sudden panic on his face. She would be able to confirm the truth to Estienne's words, and no one would doubt the Lady of Avallon.

'Look at him,' Carsten gestured suddenly with a theatrical sweep of his arm. 'Raving about betrayals and murder without a shred of proof. Clearly the ordeal has addled your wits, Wace. You are all but dead on your feet.'

'It should be easy for you to kill me, then,' Estienne replied, his voice deadly calm in the stillness.

The blunt statement sent another ripple through the onlookers. They could sense impending violence, and Estienne was determined not to disappoint.

'Enough of this!' A gruff voice as Otto von Augsburg pushed through the circle. 'Brothers of the Order do not raise steel against each other. It would undermine everything we stand for.'

'Well spoken, Brother Otto,' Carsten said. 'Such a thing would go against every statute of the Order. Our oaths must be upheld.'

'Oaths?' Estienne's voice was as dry as autumn leaves. 'What oaths did you uphold when you left your brothers to die? When you abandoned us to the pagans? When you stabbed a man in the back to save your own skin?'

Otto's face darkened, his eyes flicking between Estienne and Carsten as he weighed the accusation. 'These are serious charges. They should be brought before the Marschall, or even the Hochmeister himself, not settled with blood in the courtyard.'

Carsten nodded vigorously. 'Yes, yes. Let the Marschall judge when he returns from Kronstadt. Let proper—'

'The dead will not wait,' Estienne cut in, voice like iron. 'Rotger, Amalric, Eggert, Merten, Jurgen—'

Valour

'You are not even a true Knight of the Order,' Carsten's voice rose, panic clear in his tone. 'You have no right to accuse me.'

'And yet I do. And so will the Lady Fabrisse. And so will Brother Galien.'

That was enough to silence him. Carsten knew his lies could no longer deceive. Estienne had left him no option but one.

'Very well, Wace. If it is a fight you want, it is a fight you shall have.'

Otto raised a gnarled hand. 'He is your sworn brother, Carsten. You cannot do this.'

Carsten's eyes narrowed with familiar disdain. 'He is no brother of mine.'

With deliberate slowness, Carsten donned his helm. Estienne gripped his sword in both hands, advancing to meet his enemy as Otto, realising there was no more to be said, stepped from his path.

Knights and serving brothers backed away, widening the circle. Some looked concerned, others eager to witness what was to come, but all accepted the inevitability of what was about to unfold.

Estienne stopped in the centre of the courtyard, allowing Carsten to advance. On any other night this would have been nothing but a formality, but not this night. His foe was no seasoned warrior, but he was fully armoured, where Estienne was dressed in rags. Well-rested where Estienne teetered on the edge of exhaustion. Still, he liked his odds.

Carsten's sword arced through the air, aimed at Estienne's unprotected head, the blade whistling as it cut through empty space.

Estienne was no longer there.

Despite the fatigue that weighted his limbs, despite the wounds that pulled and burned with every movement, Estienne stepped aside with ease. The sword passed a hair's breadth from his face, leaving his opponent open, but he did not counter immediately. Instead, he circled Carsten with measured steps, forcing him to track Estienne's movement. Carsten's breathing came in sharp, panicked gasps, his chest rising and falling beneath the weight of his hauberk.

'I will punish you for your lies,' Carsten snarled, his voice muffled by his helm.

Estienne said nothing. Words were no longer needed. Only steel spoke truth now.

Carsten attacked again, this time with more control, his series of thrusts and slashes driving Estienne back toward the edge of the circle. Each blow that Estienne parried jarred his already aching shoulders, but the pain was distant, unable to breach the wall of his hate.

'Fight back, damn you!' Carsten growled, frustration edging his voice.

Estienne's only response was to slide past another wild swing, his movements economical, every step and turn calculated to conserve his dwindling strength. Carsten's attacks grew more desperate, more reckless, the sound of his breath rasping within his helm, growing more laboured with each passing moment. The armour that had seemed such an advantage now betrayed its wearer, becoming burdensome and making his movements clumsy.

Still Estienne circled, patient as death.

Carsten overextended on a thrust, the momentum carrying him forward a half-step further than intended. It was the opening Estienne had been waiting for and he moved with sudden violence, his sword an instrument of retribution. The blade cracked against Carsten's sword hand, breaking the fingers beneath his mail mitten. Carsten yelped, sword dropping from

Valour

his broken hand to clatter against the courtyard stones, as a gasp went up from the crowd.

'Pick it up,' Estienne said.

Carsten hesitated, his eyes visible through the narrow slit of his helm, darting between his fallen sword and Estienne's implacable face.

'Pick. It. Up.'

Slowly, Carsten bent to retrieve his weapon, holding it gingerly in his damaged hand. As he straightened, Estienne was already moving again.

He battered against Carsten's shield, each blow struck with precision. Every impact splintered wood and fatigued the arm that bore it.

Crack. The edge of the shield split, a fissure running through the painted cross.

Crack. That fissure widened.

Crack. A chunk of shield broke free, falling to the stones at Carsten's feet.

The Komtur retreated, desperately trying to defend himself against Estienne's relentless assault, his arm trembling from the effort of holding the damaged shield.

'Wait,' Carsten yelled, 'wait, I yield—'

But Estienne was beyond hearing. This was not for him alone. This was for the dead. They deserved justice. They deserved vengeance.

His sword came down in a brutal arc. The blade struck Carsten's helm with a sound like hammer on anvil, the shock of it travelling down Estienne's arms to rattle his gritted teeth.

It drove Carsten to his knees, his damaged shield slipping from his grasp, sword abandoned as he raised his broken hand in surrender.

The courtyard was silent, the only sound the harsh rasp of

Carsten's breathing within his dented helm. Estienne stood over him, sword still raised. The rage that had driven him this far had not abated; if anything, it burned hotter now.

With trembling hands, Carsten fumbled at the buckle that secured his helm. After several clumsy attempts, he succeeded in pulling it free, revealing a face transformed by terror. Blood ran from his nose, his eyes wide with the fearful comprehension of a man facing his own end.

'Please,' Carsten whimpered, 'mercy. I... I beg you.'

'Like you showed mercy to that trapper when you stuck a knife in his back?' Estienne asked, his voice so low that only Carsten could hear the words. 'Did you think of mercy when you rode away and left us all to die?'

'I was afraid,' Carsten whimpered, tears cutting clean tracks through the blood on his face. 'I am a coward, I know it, not suited to my position. But I don't deserve this. Please...'

For a fleeting moment, something like pity flickered in Estienne's heart, but it was there and gone in the same instant. He adjusted his grip on the sword, raising it for the killing stroke.

'Stop this at once!'

The command broke the silence of the courtyard. Estienne froze, sword still poised, as Marschall Dieter strode into the circle, his travel-stained cloak billowing behind him. His face was flushed with fury, hand already on the hilt of his own sword.

'What madness is this?' Dieter demanded, his gaze sweeping from Estienne to the kneeling Carsten and back again. 'Have we fallen so far that brothers of the Order now settle disputes by spilling each other's blood on the stones of our own fortress?'

Carsten's eyes widened, a desperate hope kindling in them. 'Oh, thank the Lord.'

Something broke inside Estienne at those words. A fragile

Valour

thread of restraint, the last vestige of the code that had once governed his life, snapped like an over-taut bowstring.

His blade came down with precision, striking Carsten just above the ear, sheering through his mail coif and splitting the skull beneath. Blood sprayed across the stones as Carsten collapsed, his body twitching once, twice, then lying still.

'Damn you, Wace!' Dieter's roar echoed off the walls, his face contorted with rage. 'Seize him! Seize him now!'

Estienne didn't resist as men surrounded him. His sword clattered to the ground, and he swayed on his feet, held up only by the two men grasping his arms. Dieter came to stand before him, close enough that Estienne could see the anger burning in his eyes.

'You have committed murder here today. Murder of a brother of the Order, in defiance of my direct command. Take him to a cell. Let him contemplate what he has done until I decide how to address this... stain on our honour.'

As they began to drag him toward the keep, Estienne's eyes sought out Fabrisse in the crowd. She stood where he had last seen her, face strangely impassive. No grief, no horror, as though she had already been hardened to the violence of what she had just witnessed.

Then the knights hauled Estienne into the keep, and she was lost to his sight.

45

The pale square of light that passed through the window cast little warmth into the cramped cell. Estienne sat with his back against the damp stone wall, legs stretched out before him on the thin straw-covered pallet. His shoulders ached from the stone's chill, but he made no effort to move. Pain had become a companion of sorts these past days. What was a little more to add to the tally?

A bowl of fresh bread and salted meat sat half-eaten beside him, along with a cup of clean water. Such simple fare, yet after everything he'd endured in the mountains, it might as well have been a king's banquet.

Considering he was a prisoner, he couldn't grumble about the accommodation. There were no moans of fellow captives, no scurrying rats, just the stifled silence interspersed by the moaning of wind. A mercy, perhaps. He'd heard enough screams to last several lifetimes.

Rotger's face came to him, the big knight's resonant cries of agony muffled by his helm as flames licked at his legs. Then

Amalric, his steady gaze in that final moment before he turned back to face the pagans alone, buying them all the time they needed with his blood.

'For God and Saint Mary,' Estienne murmured, the words breaking the silence of his cell.

That final memory was a fresher wound than any that marked his body. The gashes had started to heal, the bruises fading, but the mark on his soul remained raw and weeping. Amalric had been with him through the crucible of the Holy Land. Had offered him something to believe in when all else was lost. He had been Estienne's brother in all but blood, and now he was gone. And with him, the last dregs of Estienne's faith.

He leaned his head back against the wall and closed his eyes. The one deed that brought him no regret was splitting Carsten's treacherous skull. The moment his blade had bitten through mail and bone, a savage joy had flooded him. Not the righteous satisfaction of justice served, but something darker, something set free that had been imprisoned within him since he'd watched his brothers die one by one.

The Marschall would likely have him hanged for it. Or beheaded, if he was feeling merciful. Estienne found he couldn't summon the will to care. He'd faced death too many times to fear it now. Let them string him up from the gibbet. He had done what needed doing, and there was no taking it back now.

The quiet creak of the door's hinges brought him back to himself, but he didn't bother opening his eyes.

'Come to tell me when I'll swing?' he asked.

'I had thought you a man of greater faith, Estienne Wace.'

The voice was not Marschall Dieter's. Estienne's eyes snapped open to find himself faced with the imposing figure of Hermann von Salza, Hochmeister of the Order of Saint Mary. Even in the dimness of the cell, his presence seemed to fill the small space. Von Salza was not a big man, but he carried himself with the calm assurance of one accustomed to command.

The Hochmeister settled himself on the wooden stool across from Estienne, his movements deliberate and unhurried. Estienne pushed himself straighter, wincing at the protest of his muscles.

'A man's faith is often tested by what he endures, Hochmeister.'

Von Salza nodded slowly, studying Estienne with unnerving intensity. 'Indeed. And you have endured much, I am told. The loss of good men. Brothers.'

'Brothers,' Estienne echoed. The word tasted sour. 'Rotger Havenblast. Amalric von Regensburg. Jurgen. Young Merten and Eggert. All of them good men, whose deaths diminish the Order.'

'And Carsten Schado?' von Salza asked mildly.

'Carsten Schado should never have been allowed to call himself a Knight of Saint Mary. His cowardice cost those lives. He abandoned us to die. Fled while his brothers faced slaughter.'

'So I have been told. By Lady Fabrisse, among others.' Von Salza's expression softened slightly. 'She has endured much, that holy woman. Yet her faith remains unshaken. And she has displayed remarkable courage.'

'She has,' Estienne conceded. 'Though her mission brought nothing but death.'

'And you, in turn, brought death to my fortress.' Von Salza leaned forward, hands folded before him. 'I regret the suffering you and your companions endured, Wace. I regret that the Order did not recognise Carsten's true nature before lives were lost. But I cannot overlook what you have done.'

Estienne met the Hochmeister's gaze unflinchingly. Here it was, then. The sentence.

Valour 341

'You killed a brother knight in full view of the entire garrison,' von Salza continued, his voice level. 'Whatever his crimes, whatever your justification, this cannot be permitted. The Order maintains its place in these wild lands through discipline and unity. If knights may execute their brothers at will, what separates us from the savages we are sworn to fight?'

'Justice,' Estienne said flatly. 'Truth. Honour. All the things Carsten pissed away when he left us to die.'

Von Salza's expression remained impassive. 'Be that as it may, my decision is made. You are to be expelled from Rosenau immediately. Forbidden to return to any territory controlled by the Order of Saint Mary.'

Estienne studied the Hochmeister, trying to discern the thoughts behind that weathered face. 'I've killed one of your knights. Why not my head?'

'Because it would be a damned waste,' von Salza said, rising from the stool. 'Because we are all but finished in these lands and leaving one more corpse behind us would serve no good purpose. Despite what you have done.'

'What does that mean?'

'The winds are shifting, Wace. King András grows increasingly resentful of our presence in the Burzenland. His barons whisper in his ear, jealous of the Order's growing power.'

'You're saying the Order will be expelled from Hungary?'

'I'm saying that a new beginning may soon be forced upon us all.' Von Salza moved toward the cell door. 'Travel far from these lands, Estienne Wace. Find a new purpose for your particular talents. Preferably one that doesn't involve killing those who deserve mercy as well as those who don't.'

With that, he pulled open the heavy door. Framed in the threshold stood Otto von Augsburg, his bearded face unreadable.

'Otto will see you out,' von Salza said. 'May God guide your path, Wace. I suspect it may prove longer and harder than either of us can imagine.'

The Hochmeister disappeared down the corridor, leaving Estienne alone with Otto. The older knight jerked his head toward the passageway.

'Come on, then,' he said. 'No sense dwelling in the dark while the day beckons.'

Estienne rose gingerly, following Otto's imposing form up from the depths of Rosenau. He squinted against the golden light of late afternoon as he emerged into the courtyard. The brightness was almost painful, forcing him to shade his eyes with one hand as he took in the familiar scene. Nothing had changed in the few days of his imprisonment, yet everything seemed somehow different.

The same guards stood at their posts along the walls, the same servants hurried to and fro on their errands. A pair of squires led horses from the stables, their chatter drifting across the yard. The forge rang with the steady rhythm of a hammer on steel, the smith's apprentice working the bellows with sweat-slicked arms.

But Estienne noticed how the brothers and servants gave him a wide berth as he crossed the yard, some out of respect, others out of fear. He caught whispers trailing in his wake, felt eyes following him as he moved. The spot where Carsten had fallen had been scrubbed clean of blood, but in his mind's eye, he could still see the dark stain spreading across the cobbles.

No regrets. Not for that.

'Estienne.'

He turned to see Fabrisse of Avallon near the stables, her slender figure now clothed in fresh garments befitting her station. The simple grey robe and white wimple were pristine, a far cry from the rags she'd worn during their desperate flight through the mountains.

'Lady Fabrisse,' he acknowledged, inclining his head slightly.

She approached, her hands folded before her. 'I had hoped to speak with you before you departed.'

'You've heard, then.'

'The Hochmeister informed me of his decision regarding your fate.'

'And did you have any influence on that decision?'

'I merely offered an accounting of what happened, to the best of my recollection.'

'Then you have my thanks, milady.'

She regarded him with a look so intense he almost couldn't hold her gaze. 'It is not you who owes the thanks, Estienne.'

'What will you do now?' he said quickly, keen to change the subject.

'Return to Avallon, in time.' She glanced toward the eastern horizon, where the mountains loomed dark against the sky. 'I had hoped to bring God's light to the people beyond those peaks. But perhaps the time is not yet right.'

'I think we've both learned the time is most definitely not right. If indeed it ever will be.'

'I have to believe it will. I have to believe what we did was for a purpose.'

'Believe what you must, if it helps you...'

He stopped himself before he uttered anything cruel. He knew what had happened was not her fault. She had only wanted to shed the light of God in dark lands. How could she have known the true darkness that awaited?

'I am sorry for the suffering my mission brought,' she said after a moment. 'But I am not sorry to have known you, Estienne Wace. To have witnessed your courage.'

'And I yours,' he replied sincerely.

Whatever doubts he harboured about her God, about the wisdom of her mission, he could not question her bravery in the face of death.

Fabrisse stepped closer, reaching up to place her hand against his scarred cheek. Her touch was cool and gentle, feeling like a benediction of sorts.

'May God watch over you, Estienne,' she said softly. 'Wherever your path may lead.'

Before he could respond, she turned away, her grey robe whisking about her ankles as she moved toward the keep. Estienne watched her go, the ghost of her touch lingering on his cheek, as he wondered if they would ever cross paths again.

'We have a horse ready for you,' Otto said impatiently.

Estienne turned to see him gesturing towards the western gate of the fortress. He followed Otto across the courtyard where his few belongings had been packed and tied behind the saddle of a sturdy skewbald gelding. Not a destrier, but a serviceable mount nonetheless, well-muscled and clear-eyed.

He checked the supplies with practised efficiency: a wineskin, hard bread, smoked meat that would last several days. A sword hung from the saddle, but there was nothing in the way of armour. He had to be grateful for the weapon, at least. In one of the saddlebags, he found a small leather pouch containing a handful of silver marks. Enough to see him accommodated for a couple of weeks.

As he rifled through those meagre possessions, his fingers closed around something small and smooth tucked into a fold of cloth. He drew it out, turning it over in his palm. A small stone, worn smooth by desert sands, with the pattern of a flower running through it. The gift given to him by that little girl what seemed so long ago now.

Valour

Estienne stared at it, running his thumb over its polished surface. His good luck charm, that had seen him survive his ordeal in the Holy Land. Had he kept it with him on his journey to rescue Fabrisse, might things have turned out differently? Would those who had died still draw breath?

No. What happened in those mountains wasn't happenstance or the will of gods. It was the deeds of men. Fate hadn't killed his brothers; steel and fire and malice had done that.

He slipped the stone back into its hiding place as footsteps approached.

'Estienne.'

Brother Galien stood behind him, leaning heavily on a walking staff. The monk's face was still pale and drawn, but there was a vitality to him that had been absent during their desperate flight through the mountains. Beside him stood Brother Rabel, his expression solemn.

'Brothers.' Estienne acknowledged them both with a nod. 'I see you're recovering well, Galien.'

'Thanks to you,' the friar replied. 'A debt I cannot repay, though I will remember you in my prayers.'

'As will I,' Rabel added. 'For as long as I draw breath.'

'Save your prayers for those who need them more,' Estienne said. 'I've little use for them where I'm bound.'

'And where is that?' Galien asked.

Estienne shrugged. 'Away from here. Beyond that...' He let the thought hang unfinished between them.

Galien stepped forward, pressing something into Estienne's hand. A simple wooden crucifix, crudely carved but smooth with handling.

'Take it,' the friar said. 'Not for your sake, but for ours. That you might remember us as we will remember you.'

Estienne closed his fingers around the cross, knowing a

refusal would only pain the man who owed him his life. 'I'll keep it safe.'

'There's something else,' Rabel added, gesturing toward the edge of the courtyard. 'Something that perhaps belongs with you now.'

Estienne followed his gaze to see Clovis sitting by the wall, the black and tan hound's eyes fixed unwaveringly on him.

'He's been there since they took you to your cell,' Rabel explained. 'Hasn't moved except to take food and water when offered. It seems he's waiting for you.'

'Clovis?' Estienne called softly, doubtful Rabel was right in his assumption.

The hound's ears pricked forward at the sound of his name. He rose in one fluid motion and trotted across the yard, tail wagging as he approached.

Estienne knelt, ruffled the dog's ears, as Clovis leaned in, a satisfied whine escaping his throat.

'I suppose you're coming with me, then,' Estienne murmured.

With nothing left to say, Estienne nodded his goodbye to the friars and mounted his horse. He took one last look at Rosenau, the fortress that had been, however briefly, his home. Within its walls, he had found purpose, brotherhood, a sense of belonging. Now all that was closed to him.

'Clovis,' he called, and the hound's head snapped up, eyes bright with attention. 'Come.'

Together they passed through the gates. Estienne didn't look back.

There was no point in dwelling on what was lost.

The only way was forward.

MORE FROM RICHARD CULLEN

Another book from Richard Cullen, *Crusade*, is available to order now here:

https://mybook.to/CrusadeRCBackAd

ACKNOWLEDGMENTS

And so, the *Chronicles of the Black Lion* trilogy comes to an end, and Estienne Wace rides off into the sunset... for now.

These first three novels have been a labour of love for me, and once again I'd be remiss if I didn't thank Caroline Ridding and all the team at Boldwood for helping me get them out there. Special mention to Gary Jukes and Candida Bradford for copyediting/proofreading duties respectively, and Claire Fenby for handling all that marketing witchcraft. Thanks also to David Nicolle, whose historical work on the Teutonic Knights was invaluable for the writing of *Valour*.

And, as ever, thanks to you for reading.

Best,

Richard Cullen

ABOUT THE AUTHOR

Richard Cullen is a writer of historical adventure and epic fantasy. His historical adventure series *Chronicles of the Black Lion* is set in thirteenth-century England.

Sign up to Richard Cullen's mailing list for news, competitions and updates on future books.

Visit Richard's website: wordhog.co.uk

Follow Richard on social media here:

 x.com/rich4ord

 instagram.com/thewordhog

 bookbub.com/authors/richard-cullen

ALSO BY RICHARD CULLEN

The Chronicles of the Black Lion

Rebellion

Crusade

Valour

The Wolf of Kings

Oath Bound

Shield Breaker

Winter Warrior

War of the Archons (as R S Ford)

A Demon in Silver

Hangman's Gate

Spear of Malice

The Age of Uprising (as R S Ford)

Engines of Empire

Engines of Chaos

Engines of War

WARRIOR CHRONICLES

WELCOME TO THE CLAN ✕

THE HOME OF
BESTSELLING HISTORICAL
ADVENTURE FICTION!

WARNING:
MAY CONTAIN VIKINGS!

SIGN UP TO OUR
NEWSLETTER

BIT.LY/WARRIORCHRONICLES

Boldwood

Boldwood Books is an award-winning fiction publishing company seeking out the best stories from around the world.

Find out more at www.boldwoodbooks.com

Join our reader community for brilliant books, competitions and offers!

Follow us
@BoldwoodBooks
@TheBoldBookClub

Sign up to our weekly deals newsletter

https://bit.ly/BoldwoodBNewsletter

Printed in Dunstable, United Kingdom